Love and War in British Palestine

Love and War in British Palestine

Gad Shimron

Translated from Hebrew by Uri Themal

ISBN-13: 978-1517691448
ISBN-10: 1517691443

Jerusalem, Summer 1942

"This scorcher can drive you completely bonkers," muttered Tamar as she was slowly sipping the cool water that the attentive and experienced waiter had served her in a hazy moist glass along with a cup of steaming coffee.

Her eyes skimmed superficially over the banner headlines in the *Palestine Post* that a short, pudgy man in his thirties was reading at the next table. He was sweating slightly in his elegant summer coat with a bright shirt and colorful tie. "**Rommel at El Alamein, a hundred kilometers from Alexandria,**" screamed the headline.

"In the south of the Russian front, soldiers of an alpine unit of Nazi Germany's Wehrmacht hoisted the swastika flag on the summit of Mt. Elbrus, the highest mountain in the Caucasus, whilst preparing for the conquest of Grozny. The Allied High Command is concerned about a potential pincer movement by the German army in the direction of Palestine."

"They want to come even here? When will this Nazi nightmare finally end?" Tamar's thoughts drifted back to the weather, the blue sky, and the bright sun. "In Vienna we called this 'imperial weather', but there each heatwave was followed by a refreshing downpour," her stream of memories and reflections flowed on. "Here in Jerusalem, in the middle of summer, one can only dream of a refreshing rain shower."

A sweet smile spread across her face that surprised her friend Alisa. "Tamar, come on. Why are you beaming like the Mona Lisa?" Alisa remarked with the skill of an experienced gossip. "You radiate like a pious virgin from *Mea She'arim*[1] who has captured the randy looks of a handsome young man."

Alisa suspected that Tamar's smile was in response to the whistles of the soldiers who were sitting on the back of a truck that, at that moment, drove past the cafe. She looked especially at one of them who sat on the far right, a young man with a round face, the roundest that she had ever seen, who craned his neck as if he wanted to gain an extra second to catch another quick glance. She did not know that Tamar's smile had a completely different purpose.

From the first day of her immigration to Palestine four years ago, Tamar wanted to be like a *Sabra*[2]. Now she was suddenly aware that her daydream about the Vienna weather was expressed in Hebrew.

"There are three things that are always, but always, done in one's mother tongue throughout one's entire life," Grandpa Siegfried had explained to her once. "Doing sums, cursing spontaneously and dreaming." It was the dream, in Hebrew, of a Vienna rain shower in the Jerusalem midsummer that now brushed the outline of her face with a smile.

"Excellent Heinz. The taste of real coffee, no bitter chicory replacement, which causes heartburn," she replied to the waiter who hovered around her table and asked her with professional courtesy if she would like something else.

---

[1]An ultra-orthodox neighborhood in Jerusalem

[2]The Jewish Palestinian native-born who are compared to the fruit of the cactus – externally prickly, but sweet inside.

"It is obvious that you come from a good home," he told her by way of flattery.

The waiter had it on the tip of his tongue to let rip with a comprehensive description as to how the police had nabbed Yom Tov Habashush, one of the biggest coffee traders in the country, who had wanted to smuggle 2.5 tons of coffee to make a pretty penny on the black market, but who got slapped with a £75 fine or 30 days in prison for his failed attempt.

Tamar was unaware that Heinz – Heinz Kramer – had worked for some of the most important newspapers in Germany before his immigration to Palestine. Among journalists and readers, he was known as a 'hit', one who had brought at least three scoops every week. But his talent for tracking down information and synchronization of sources was inversely proportional to his ability to grasp Hebrew.

And so he was forced to retrain, like many of his fellow immigrants who had fled from Nazi Germany and its expanding empire. The successful journalist from Berlin became a hardworking waiter in a kind of European-style cafe in the heart of Jerusalem. But, even in remote Palestine, Heinz Kramer kept the irresistible tendency to tell the customers about the events of the day, often at the expense of his work efficiency.

"We were able to organize a serious amount, thanks to our boss's good connections," continued Heinz in his coverage of the event, but in a nutshell. He also noted with satisfaction that the cafe's kitchen had received a respectable quantity of American milk powder so that he hoped to be able to serve quality ice-cream today, "Quite unlike the tasteless rubbish you buy at the kiosk for 5 *Mils*[3] with a glass of soda water."

---

[3]Currency unit under the British Mandate in Palestine; 1000 Mils=1 Palestine Pound

Heinz Kramer would have liked to continue offering the customer a newspaper in live broadcast, but his eye caught the waving hand of the customer at another table, whom he recognized as the wife of a wealthy lawyer. She had long been appreciated by him because of her particularly generous tips.

"Tell me, what's so bad about our lives?" Alisa opened her monolog, which she had held back during Heinz's report. As usual, her first words gave no indication where she was heading and what issues would flow from the verbiage of her mouth. "The coffee is excellent and reminiscent of peace times. And you think it's hot? You call that hot? Tel Aviv has a humidity of 80 percent right now and people keel over. You told me yourself that your parents have written from the prison camp in Mauritius that the average temperature there is almost 35 degrees Celsius all year long and that they have higher humidity there than in Tel Aviv."

Alisa paused for a moment, took a deep breath, and continued enthusiastically, "and that's nothing. Henry, the smart soldier who keeps on trying to flirt with me, yes, the leg-amputee from the surgery ward, told me that in the Egyptian desert the average temperature is now 45 degrees Celsius in the shade. And do you know what? There is no shade."

Tamar followed her friend's detailed account with amusement.

"By the way, it is said that a man is a creature with two legs and eight hands, but now that he has only one leg, his eight hands have gotten a few more, all of which he sends continuously towards the cleavages and backsides of the nurses" laughed Alisa. "By the way, do you know who has four legs and a hand? A happy Rottweiler."

Her roaring laughter caused a few heads to turn around towards their table.

"Anyway," Alisa went on, totally ignoring the looks. "Henry told me that as soon as the sun goes down, swarms of mosquitoes and all sorts of insects replace the flies that bother them all day. 'It is all this bastard Noah's fault', he says in his cute New Zealand accent and then complains about Noah and his sons, who had released a pair of mosquitos and a pair of flies from the ark after the flood. 'Just a little slap or an almost invisible squeeze by Noah or his sons on Mr. or Mrs. Mosquito and the world would have been different', said Henry, but stressed that the insect plague is nothing compared to the incessant shelling from Rommel's *Afrika Korps*."

❄ ❄ ❄

Alisa's voice was pleasant, if somewhat unusual, stronger than normal so that it drowned out the noise of the bustle on the terrace of the Cafe "Vienna." Her long monolog, which began as a response to Tamar and wandered into new, undefined directions, penetrated well into the ears of the two men who looked like insurance agents or bank employees.

The two sat at a table nearby and occasionally exchanged short sentences as they read their newspapers intensively. From the body language, the respect, and attention that the younger man devoted to the words of the pudgy one, it was easy to determine who the ranking senior of the two was.

In contrast to the large headline on the front page of the *Palestine Post* about the progress of the Nazi troops, the last page dealt with local issues, such as rationing of meat, threats of a teachers' strike in the Jewish population area because they had not been paid for months and the distribution of fuel vouchers for car owners, bus and taxi companies.

As an observer from the side, but one that had a perfect view, the chubby man could not help but notice the generous bosom of the girl with the powerful voice. "She has a Polish accent, but only a slight one," he remarked to himself.

She wore a floral, airy dress, suitable for the hot summer days, with a plunging neckline that allowed impressive freedom of movement to the soft, round mounds that automatically attracted his eye. On her feet she wore elegant shoes with low heels, and during the conversation with her friend, she also aired her conviction that "if high heels were a really good idea, men would wear shoes with ten-inch heels."

However, he was especially interested in the second woman: tall, slender, black hair, full and shiny, with a complicated hairstyle that was inspired by some movie, shapely figure and legs that even a Hollywood star like Esther Williams would have been proud to parade.

This sight more or less fit the description that he had received in the early morning hours at a briefing from his commander, Captain Haig, in the headquarters of the Criminal Investigation Department.

The assignment was: discrete observation of a young Jewish woman.

"And Roberts, I want you to get to know Jim Lennon, a newcomer to our department who arrived from Ireland this week," Captain Haig said by way of introducing the young man, who was already in the room.

"Observe her. Stay close to her and try to listen to whom and about whom she speaks," ordered Captain Haig. "From interrogations of *Stern Gang*[4] prisoners we accumulated material, which indicates a possible affair with Aaron Levi."

"Who is this Levi? I've never heard of him," interjected the veteran detective with a kind of remark that showed

---

[4]An extreme Zionist underground movement, founded 1940 in British Mandate Palestine. Its aim was to liberate the country from the British Mandate and its members were considered outlaws.

interest and sometimes brought employees who wanted to be promoted to the attention of the boss.

"He is almost unknown to us," Haig continued with the briefing. He paced back and forth in the small room as he hit his open hand with a small leather whip, which was a symbol of position and authority for British officers.

He stated all he knew about Levi: a student of history at the Hebrew University; considered a brilliant student; his teachers predict a great future for him. "But in contrast to the image of the young, introverted student who is deeply engrossed in his studies and is removed from reality, it seems as if we are speaking of a rising star at the top of the *Stern Gang*. We believed that we had destroyed the organization. Morton, our Tel Aviv colleague, had eliminated their leader, Yair Stern, half a year ago. But they continue to work at reduced capacity. We, unfortunately, have only an unconfirmed photo of Levi. Look at it carefully and memorize it." He handed a blurry photo across the table.

The photo, which he took from the officer showed a blurred face with the inscription: "Aaron Levi." Apparently, this photograph was made of him when he was still in high school.

"Excuse me, sir, does this shadowing have something to do with the flurry of activity in the yard?" interrupted Lennon.

"No, not at all," Haig responded somewhat impatiently. "The day before yesterday we received a confusing report that German paratroopers were seen in the area of Jericho. I admit that we initially responded to this news as we always do with reports that we get incessantly from civilians who have watched too many spy movies. For example, the landing of an Italian sabotage unit on the beach of *Netanya*, which turned out to be a couple that was looking for a little romance; or the false alarm by a Bedouin who had smoked a little too much weed and claimed that he had seen German motorcyclists patrolling in the desert near Beersheba. However, since yesterday, due to new reports, there is a growing consensus that an unknown number of German paratroopers, probably five or six, has really landed in *Wadi Kelt*, either with a spying or sabotage mission. Large military and police forces were urgently dispatched to Jericho and its environs."

"As I said, your job has nothing to do with this matter, though, you never know; in this crazy country, everything is possible."

Captain Haig sighed, although it was not clear what he wanted to express with that, went back to his briefing and stressed the need to keep a distance from the target.

"Don't do anything. Only surveillance and reporting. No nonsense and no shit, understood? God apparently loves fools, for he has actually created many of them." A tiny smile hinted that he liked the joke he had invented, "and most of them he has deployed in the military police."

"In short, be alert and don't fuck-up. Here is the file of your target; read, memorize, internalize."

From a superficial examination of the thin cardboard file with the name "Tamar Henrietta Landwehr", Roberts learned that his target, Tamar Landwehr, was 22 years old, born in Vienna, had landed in Palestine with valid documents in 1938 and was a graduate of the Hadassah School of Nursing on Mount Scopus.

Her parents were among the illegal immigrants who had been exiled to the remote island of Mauritius at the end of November 1940, following a decision of his Majesty's Government to avoid upsetting the Arabs in the country. Arab loyalty was important for the UK because of the war, which had already reached the gates of the country.

The file contained a few copies of long letters, full of longing, written in neat German handwriting, which she had sent her interned parents on the remote island in the Indian Ocean.

Roberts looked again at the picture of Levi, the commander of the underground movement. Something about the facial features of "Aaron Levi", the actual target of the operation was familiar.

Roberts tried to concentrate. But unlike the animated films he had loved so much as a child, where all the mosaic pieces instantly formed a whole picture accompanied by funny musical sounds, Levi's features were left without special impact in his memory. Throughout the entire journey in the police van to the city center, he could not get rid of the vague feeling that there was something familiar about this Aaron Levi. He secretly cursed Captain Haig, who had lumbered him with the rookie detective now sitting on the narrow seat between him and the driver and trying to engage him in idle chitchat.

❄ ❄ ❄

From eavesdropping on the conversation of the two young women, Roberts learned that they had been friends since their training and had worked alternately at Hadassah and the Augusta-Victoria Military Hospital, and that they had decided to take a day off to come down from Mount Scopus and enjoy a few hours in the centre of Jerusalem.

The girl named Alisa was eager to enjoy the evening at Cafe "Raviv" in *Beit Hakerem*[5]. "Look what's in the paper! The best music in the country in the most beautiful garden in Palestine–Joe Nadel with his orchestra; and bus number 1 runs until midnight." She also mentioned a popular entertainment venue in *Talpiot*.

"Just not *Talpiot*," Tamar responded with a burst of aggression, which was inexplicable. She suggested something

[5]At the time a new, upmarket suburb south-west of Jerusalem

more cultural, for example, the Palestine Philharmonic in the Edison Auditorium with Penina Salzman as a soloist featuring works by Handel, Chopin, and Beethoven.

The two did not succeed in finding a common denominator and they left the matter while getting immersed in a trivial conversation.

But suddenly Tamar tuned out of the conversation. She did not hear Alisa's last sentences. She also did not note the critical looks from the man at the next table.

Her eyes were focused on a figure on the sidewalk on the other side of Jaffa Road, under a promotional poster for the film *Waterloo Bridge* with Vivien Leigh and Robert Taylor kissing, in garish colors, whilst leaning on a railing that the poster-painter imagined as the Waterloo Bridge. The figure – a big, burly man with short blond hair in tattered and dusty plain clothes – caused Tamar to squirm in her seat.

He walked slowly, trying to hide a slight limp. For some reason, maybe because of the limp, her eyes were drawn to his shoes: high, heavy, military style, completely inappropriate for the Jerusalem heat.

Six or seven cheerful Australian soldiers, most of them with large beer bottles, were staggering along from the opposite direction towards the limping man, forcing him to slow his pace even more.

From her seat on the Cafe "Vienna's" terrace, Tamar could see only part of his profile before he reached the corner of Sollel Street and disappeared. But she did not need more than that. "Wolfgang? I must be dreaming," galloped the thoughts in her head. "He resembles my Wolfgang like two peas in a pod. Wolfgang Schwarte? The Templer from the German colony? He's been out of the country for three or four years. Anyway, he's in Germany and is probably doing his military service in the Wehrmacht like all young men. And what would Wolfgang, a German soldier be doing here now, in the middle of the war in the center of Jerusalem? That's impossible, but yet, it is Wolfgang."

She felt dizzy.

She heard the shrill screech of a nervous crow that was just circling above them, her heart pounding wildly in her chest like tom-tom drums. "Tamar, what is the matter with you? Call an ambulance, she has fainted," Tamar only just heard how Alisa was giving instructions with professional competence. Before she lost consciousness, she murmured in a confused hotchpotch of Hebrew and German "*Wolfgang sheli, mein Wolfgang.*"

Funeral in Jerusalem, 1995

A sharp westerly wind drove the first black winter clouds along, drowning out almost all her words except: "It's amazing how God sometimes makes carbon copies."

Jonathan had already noticed her earlier during the long funeral procession; how she was lagging behind with her narrow back, straight as an arrow, bearing her long years proudly.

After the cantor had finished his part and said, "Wreaths can be laid now," in an almost neutral tone intended to express a hint of doubt about the "flower ritual" practiced by the secular majority, which had been adopted from the Christian tradition despised by the cantor; only then did she move towards the small pile of earth and the grieving family.

She walked with the typical gait of those who suffer from back pain. Knowing that in the middle of the bending motion, a sharp pain would pierce her spine, she gently laid down a small bouquet of cultured cyclamen, which had been cultivated in some greenhouse even in autumn. They were pink and purple, wrapped in cellophane printed with decorative squiggles, such as can be found in colorful plastic buckets at any supermarket entrance.

Then, again in slow motion, she drew herself up, looked at the pile of earth, and approached Jonathan, stretched out her hand and murmured some usual condolences.

"Sorry, but you had said something about copies," asked Jonathan while ignoring the corpulent Aunt Hedvah, who made her presence felt by pushing forward from the side. "Copy of whom? Of what?"

"Too bad we meet under such circumstances. My name is Alisa. I'm a friend of your grandmother's from days of yore in the nursing school on Mount Scopus. And yes, you are a perfect copy of your grandfather," she said quietly, almost in a whisper. She examined him closely, with her clear eyes, like a photographer at work.

She wanted to continue saying something, but had to clear the space on the small piece of ground between the graves for Aunt Hedvah and a group of "Mossad" veterans, his father's friends from that era of the "actions", who insisted on demonstrating presence at various family events. Finally, she disappeared among the hundreds of mourners who had come to pay final homage to his Grandmother Tamar.

❄ ❄ ❄

The browsing in old photo albums, an integral part of any *shive*[6], was accompanied by polite tut-tutting as an expression of grief about the beauty and charm of those whose life's journey had ended, mixed with suppressed joyous exclamations at the discovery of old familiar faces. Statements such as "that's me at the *Tu Bishvat*[7] - celebration in Sarah's garden, on the edge of that hill over there, where a new neighborhood is being built right now," alternated and were replaced by "the guy with the balaclava on the right, that's my grandfather during the war of liberation, after the conquest of *Katamon*."

---

[6]Seven days of strict mourning (shiv'ah in Hebrew, Shive in Yiddish and among German Jews).
[7]A religious festival, also known as the 'New Year of Trees'.

Jonathan couldn't suppress a smile when he heard the term "war of liberation", which placed the speaker immediately in a certain age group, for who else still called it "war of liberation?"[8] He looked curiously at the photo in the album, the existence of which had almost been forgotten and was taken out of a dusty drawer only in honor of the bereavement.

A man of average height, with a round, well chiseled face, light hair – the receding of which towards the middle of the forehead could not be covered up entirely, looked out from the small, black-and-white photo. The wavy edge was cut with scissors in the style of yesteryear. When Jonathan delved further into the photo, he could still hear Alisa's remark at the funeral a few hours earlier ringing in his ear. "What copy? How does she get copy into her head? What similarities and what nonsense? I do not resemble grandpa, and father did not look like grandpa either. Where does she get that? And she had even stressed that it was an amazing resemblance? Ah well, that's the memory of the old. There is nothing you can do about that."

In the middle of the drawing room, where he and his family were receiving the mourners, was a set of framed photos on a heavy chest of drawers, in the center of which the images of his father and mother, Ronen and Nizza, were highlighted, each one alone and both together.

Jonathan used to hear about his father Ronen with annoying regularity and how he was his exact "copy." This usually happened during commemorations.

Jonathan was born in August 1967, two months after his father had fallen as a tank commander in the reserve service during one of the last battles of the Six Day War in the Golan

---

[8]The 1948 war is generally referred to as the "War of Independence" nowadays.

Heights. The reserve battalion's outdated Sherman tank went up in flames after being hit by a bazooka on its right side, so that the entire crew was killed. Not by chance did the Sherman get the nickname "Ronson" during WWII after the famous lighter, due to its tendency to catch fire easily.

This story flickered around in his head while scrutinizing the physical similarity between his father and grandfather. "Father, yes. I resemble him. But grandpa? Never."

To be honest, he could never stand Grandpa Asher, although he had showered him with love and warmth, when, due to the demand of circumstances, he had to replace his role of grandfather with that of father. Together with his wife, they sought to raise their grandson who did not know his father and had lost his mother before he was registered in kindergarten.

Jonathan's mother, Nizza, was killed in a car accident when her little Austin A-40 crashed into a large tree, on the old road to Jerusalem, between Kibbutz *Nachshon* and the junction at *Beit Shemesh*. The car was totally destroyed and the woman in it was killed immediately.

Years later, Jonathan ran into a policeman who baffled him with a detailed description of the accident that had ended his mother's life: "Do you know why I remember this accident so well," asked the policeman, whose name Jonathan had forgotten in the meantime. "A few months earlier, I was, in fact, the first police officer who reached the accident site where Margalit Sharon, the first wife of Arik Sharon, had lost her life. She drove a blue Austin A-40 and was killed by a collision with a tree on the way to Jerusalem, only a few kilometers from the scene of your mother's accident. Just how many cars of this type existed back then in that small country of the sixties? Two of them were involved in an almost identical accident. You must admit that this is amazing, is it not?"

Why was this anecdote buzzing around in his head right now, beginning like the "*Geva* Newsreel", which in his childhood was shown before each movie? He had no answer.

Finally, the story was pigeonholed on the edge of his memory, replaced by the thought of the amount of work involved in sorting through all his grandmother's objects and cleaning out her closets. He will still have much to do at the end of the *Schive*.

❄ ❄ ❄

Two days.

Two days was all it took, to his surprise, to clean Grandmother Tamar's old apartment and remove all her belongings. During this time, he had effectively and without much effort erased the many long years of her existence in this corner of the planet.

Jonathan immersed himself in this cleaning task immediately after the *Schive.* He toiled like a possessed man.

These two days were very tiring and not just because of the physical effort, but also due to sneezing fits caused by his dust-mite allergy that always seemed to attack him at critical times. Those microscopic creatures that love dust and moisture and promise the producers of anti-allergenic drugs adequate income had enjoyed a long period of debauchery and luxury in Grandmother Tamar's cabinets.

With the help of a van that he had borrowed from the fleet manager at his workplace, he brought boxes of used clothing and old-fashioned utensils that he had found on the shabby kitchen shelves to the local *WIZO*[9] Chapter. Of

---

[9]Women's International Zionist Welfare Organisation with branches in many countries and locations

all the pots, pans, and crockery, he kept only an elegant Rosenthal service, hoping to sell it through an internet site that he had recently heard about from a colleague. A set of white teacups with matching saucers was also rescued from *WIZO*, because of his love of history. What caused him to notice it was the rather unusual stamp with which the bottom of the dishes had been marked immediately after the end of World War II when the Japanese Empire was conquered by the US Army:

MADE IN OCCUPIED JAPAN

He sold the furniture for a thousand *shekels* to a peddler from *Taybeh*[10], who drove around the neighborhood in a clapped-out Volkswagen-Kombi, equipped with a hoarse loudspeaker and a squeaky recording: "*Alte Sachen*[11]; buy everything, furniture, beds, fridges, washing machines, sewing machines; old stuff, *aaalte saaachen!*"

Five large boxes of books were left for a few coins at a second-hand bookstore on King George Street in Tel Aviv. "Do you know how many copies of Churchill's Memoirs were sold in the Israel of the sixties? Those were the days when people actually read books!" the owner said angrily as if contempt for the book was meant as a personal insult to him in contemporary Israeli Society. "More than 120,000 copies of Churchill's Memoirs were sold in the then small country, but, believe me, for years no one has come to my store to buy this book. Only my love of books prevents me from selling them by weight to the paper mill in *Hadera* for shredding."

[10]An Arabic village in the centre of Israel, making the dealer an Arab, but his touting Yiddish.

[11]Yiddish: Old stuff, the usual cry of house-to-house traders in Israel's earlier years.

One book, **The Forty Days of Musa Dagh** by the writer Franz Werfel in German, was suddenly pulled with a decisive grip from a particular batch meant for sale, because of the dedication on the first page, in faded blue ink. Jonathan tried to decipher what was written but failed, with the exception of the year '1934'.

❄ ❄ ❄

Like in a Hollywood movie, there was a surprise in store for him at the end of the arduous sorting of grandma's belongings. A kind of *Afikoman*[12], unexpected, with a mysterious fragrance. On her closet's top shelf were boxes of various sizes, most of them tagged with labels of companies that had been flourishing before the Second World War in Vienna and Prague. "Looks like Ali Baba's cave," he muttered to himself when he saw the contents of the boxes: a jumbled, mixed assortment of old gifts, some still in their original packaging, which were crumbling by now, but which Grandma had still kept.

"These are beautiful things. Pity to throw them away," she had explained to him years ago when she had engaged him – despite his protests over his sensitivity to dust – to help with her periodic venting of her cabinets. "For example, a beautiful Murano-glass fruit plate from Venice. What, is it not worthwhile to keep it and make someone happy with an original gift?" Meanwhile, the Murano plate was still in the exact same spot in the cabinet, patiently waiting to become "an original gift" in order "to make someone happy."

Soon he was exhausted from the task of sorting and was satisfied with a superficial glance at the contents of each box

---

[12]The last piece of *matza* (unleavened bread) eaten at the end of the Passover meal. It is hidden and 'found' by children. A 'surprise' that has to be 'redeemed'.

before placing it next to the pile of boxes labeled "give away" or "distribute."

He had almost ignored that surprise package, a long, flat carton tucked at the side of a crate, full of fabric rolls and closed packets of small kitchen towels among other things, so it could easily be overlooked.

For a moment he considered the possibility of dispensing without opening the package, but something about the faded photo – depicting an elegant woman dressed in the fashion of the thirties, her hands, or rather gloves, highlighted with the inscription, in Gothic letters – BATA Made in Czechoslovakia – caught his attention.

The opening flap of the carton had long lost its strength and remained in his hands as he pulled on it. With rapid shaking, he poured the contents of the glove box on the table.

First, old receipts from Zimmermann's Day Care and Orphanage in *Talpiot*[13] fell out, held together by a rusty paperclip that had left brown stripes on the paper.

"Paid for six months," was written on all of them, with ascending dates beginning with January 1940, except for one from August 1944 where it said "paid for two months and account closed."

Another shaking and from the depths of the package fell about twenty wavy-edged photos, all black and white, some already in various shades of brown. Jonathan sorted the pictures. Six photos, different landscapes, a beautiful young woman, whom he immediately recognized as his Grandmother Tamar in her youth. Ten group photos in which he again saw his grandmother with other unknown people. The largest picture immortalized a group of people in festive clothing, displaying different positions in and

---

[13]At the time, a new suburb on the southern outskirts of Jerusalem

around an old Ford with an open canvas roof. On the back of the photograph was written in faint pencil with round female characters: “Christmas outing December 1938.” Other photographs showed the smiling figure of his grandmother next to another young woman of her age, and two nice tall men – one dark-haired, the other blond. “This is Alisa. Undoubtedly, the second young woman is Alisa, the old lady from the funeral,” he mumbled to himself.

Although these images were tiny, making it difficult to identify specific details such as facial features or eye wrinkles, the depicted persons projected a sense of joy and deep friendship.

Two photos of Grandma Tamar, in which she appears young and happy, show her lying in the arms of the young blond man. “Trip with Wolfgang to Jericho,” was the caption on the back in the same, hard to read handwriting. Jonathan examined the images carefully while becoming aware of the raging pulse and cold sweat that was spreading over his temples, in view of the striking similarity between the cuddling blond guy and his own appearance as a young man.

A small white envelope had also dropped from the old glove box. Inside Jonathan found a folded piece of paper, in fact, the lower half of a larger page, which had been cut off, bearing a faded stamp in English, Hebrew and Arabic. It was dated the August 9, 1944. It bore the following entry in a nib-scribbled handwriting by an official whose name he could not read: “After reviewing all documentation and with the approval of all relevant authorities, I hereby declare that the child, Ronen Landwehr, born on the December 25, 1939, is legally adopted, and, with the authority vested in me by his Majesty’s Government and the High Commissioner for Palestine, his name is changed and entered in the Birth and Population Register accordingly.”

❄ ❄ ❄

He had found Alisa's address quickly, thanks to the kind help of the staff at the Hadassah School of Nursing and the exemplary accuracy of the entries in the office of this central medical institution.

"In the Year 1941, in which your grandmother studied here – at that time she was called Tamar Landwehr – we found one Alisa and two Alices," replied cheerfully an employee called Anat, who helped him with enthusiasm. "One Alice has been living in New York for decades and the second has died. And how do I know this? Because, four years ago, the old girls organized a party to celebrate the fiftieth anniversary of their graduation and we helped them at the time to locate the graduates. The driving force behind this historical event was Alisa Schneider. She lives in a nursing home in *Bat-Yam*, something with 'Mediterranean', but I've actually got her phone number."

The determination to find Alisa, that had driven his actions up to this moment, disappeared in the instance he wrote down her phone number. "What does it matter to you why she had hidden receipts from an orphanage," argued the voices in his head from the nightmares of his short nights. "You are stirring up a hornet's nest here. Why do you need it? What are you looking for anyway? What is this family nostalgia that inspires you to seek answers from a stranger, an old woman who might perhaps even be confused about this?"

Finally, he picked up the phone. He dialed the number with a speed as if he was pursued by a demon armed with an ax, threatening to cut off his fingers.

The receiver on the other end was picked up after the second ring.

"Oh, Jonathan, I knew that you'd call," Alisa answered in a loud, clear voice. "Yes, tomorrow afternoon at five suits me. Tell the doorman, to let you park in my space, which is free, after I stopped driving when my illness, which is killing me, broke out. Well, I have a lot to tell you. My former girlfriend, Tamar, whom I loved very much and with whom I have not spoken for more than fifty years because of a foolish quarrel, was always a character full of contrasts. I just hope that at the end of our conversation, you will say 'I already knew that,' because if not ..." She did not finish the sentence.

Jonathan wanted to ask now, on the phone, what the significance was of the adoption certificate from the British Mandate period and who the mysterious Wolfgang in the photo was. But he did not make it, or rather, he was afraid to ask and was left dumbfounded and with the sound of the disconnected line in his handset.

Tel Aviv, Summer 1942

The improvised task force consisted of two British soldiers and three burly fellows from the free Polish army, all in advanced stages of drunkenness. They dragged Yitzchak Cohen physically from the open terrace of Cafe "San Remo" directly onto the narrow sidewalk of Hayarkon Street.

"You can thank your lucky stars that we are in a good mood and not really mad at you;" the British Sergeant Major with a red face and a huge mustache, which extended beyond both sides of his face, gave him a friendly pat on the back while delivering a long explanatory speech, driven by pints of cheap beer. "Tell your commander for Civil Defense, or Regional Protection, or whatever you call it, tell him that you were kicked out of your combat zone by Sergeant Major Adams, a veteran of the campaigns in Norway, France, Crete, and the Western Desert, because he was not ready to be disturbed by anyone during his first serious furlough this year." Adams looked around for approval from his drunken mates and continued to ramble: "Tell him that Sergeant Major Adams decided to throw you off the porch after he had come to the conclusion, based on his diverse combat experience, that the Italian pilot has not yet been born, who would manage to target Tel Aviv, even with the help of the dim table lamps of Cafe 'San Remo', which apparently exceed the maximum blackout rules. In short, tell him that he should stop screwing up our leave and that he can kiss my arse."

When he had finished speaking, he let out a deep, loud breath, belched leaving a strong smell of beer residue and cheap tobacco, which an experienced smoker would have identified as a brand of cigarettes called Latif. Roaring with laughter, staggering, satisfied with the successful removal of a Civil Defense inspector, who had tried to end their short furlough because of the stupid blackout provisions, the soldiers returned to the terrace of the greatest entertainment establishment in Tel Aviv, hugging and happy about their alcohol-fueled friendship.

Cohen, during the day a senior official of the Tel Aviv Municipality's Water department and in the evening a volunteer Civil Defense inspector, did not understand exactly what had inspired the soldiers to throw him onto the street. He had wanted to do nothing more than his duty.

Despite the tense security situation and the occasional appearance of Italian planes coming from Rhodes and dropping bomb loads on various targets in the country, a significant slowdown in compliance with the blackout provisions was noticeable. "A Sodom and Gomorrah attitude – entertainment at all costs under the motto 'eat and drink for tomorrow you die,'" concluded Cohen to himself. He shook the dust from his clothes and congratulated himself on his luck that the incident ended with a soft landing on the pavement and had not come to blows. "At least this time the blood-alcohol level did not lead to an outbreak of violence," he comforted himself. He was wondering, whether his son, who served as a gunner in an RAF bomber squadron and, who until his recruitment had drunk nothing stronger than lemonade at the newsstand on the corner of Allenby Road and Rothschild Boulevard, also spent his holidays drinking himself into oblivion. "Actually, why do I blame them," he thought, as he left the scene of the conflict with measured steps. "The Sergeant Major has no doubt experienced countless cruel, bloody encounters and, who knows if he will survive the next battle. And my Hayim, how does he cope with the reality of having breakfast with members of the squadron in the morning and a few hours later, in the evening, their names are already deleted from the crew ledger? I hope he just returns from the war safe and sound. Why did I let him enlist at all? So many young people ignore the calls to volunteer for the British Army. They stay at home, study, work, enjoy the economic boom, earn good money and only Hayim had to go and save the world?! Well, maybe I did not quite fail in the education of my own scoundrel." A satisfied smile spread across his face.

❄ ❄ ❄

The Kings Quartet, whose members boasted that, before the war, they used to play in Europe's leading symphony orchestras or famous classical quartets in Germany, Austria, and Czechoslovakia, even continued playing through the minor disturbance on the spacious terrace of the "San Remo" caused by the unexpected appearance of Inspector Cohen. Dozens of satisfied customers were floating in varying degrees of elegance on the dance floor to the beautiful sounds of the excellent quartet, enjoying the sea breeze, which was bringing relief from the oppressive heat and sticky humidity. Others sat around in groups, relishing the romantic atmosphere created by the dim light of the small lamps, which were placed in the middle of each of dozens of round tables, which had so annoyed Inspector Cohen.

They were talking, joking, and forgetting about the war and its consequences.

"Sam, I am glad to see that you have a very successful evening today," remarked the gentleman with the big paunch; he was well dressed and sat on a stool at the end of the bar. He spoke to the bartender, whose ability to listen to customers as well as initiate conversations belonged to the basic skills of his profession.

"We can't complain, Mr. Krueger. It's really good. The beer tap never stops flowing and the barrels are emptied at an incredible speed."

"Do you have an explanation for the sudden prosperity here?"

"They say that due to the situation at the various fronts, the British are pumping an enormous amount of subsidies into the country," the bartender informed him while giving a glass the last finishing touches with his towel. "In recent weeks, more and more new faces from around the world appear in the city. Of course, these are mostly British and Australians, but also free Greeks, Poles, Indian soldiers, as well as Sudanese working on the extension of the railway network across the Middle East. I happened to overhear a conversation between two RAF soldiers who were exchanging their impressions of the chaos in radio communications with air-traffic control and the many 'near-misses' due to lack of coordination between the different procedures operated by the various air forces flying here."

"But why should this happen?" Krueger wondered with a purely naive question.

Sam laughed. "You are not well informed, my friend. There's a squadron of free Poles here, at least one transport squadron of the Royal Greek Air Force and a squadron of the Free French; they are actually stationed in Lebanon and Syria but train here with the British. And God knows who else is flitting around here. But, in any case, there are many Americans. I've heard that, for fear of bombardments by the German *Luftwaffe*[14], they have stationed dozens

---

[14]German Air force.

of radar-guided anti-aircraft batteries around the Haifa refineries; they are manned by British teams with extensive experience gained during the London 'Blitz'. The gunners are accustomed to the highest alert levels from London and are, therefore, trigger happy, but this mess in the airspace here drives them nuts. I've heard that a squadron of four Polish Spitfires on a training flight was only by a miracle not shot down over the Bay because they had forgotten to coordinate their activities with all authorities. However, you are right when you say that there are many Australians and New Zealanders, but for us, Americans are the best."

"Yanks? Interesting. Why?"

"From my cousin who works at *Lod* airport, I heard that hundreds, perhaps thousands of American pilots and flight crews have recently arrived there, where they have their temporary headquarters. From there, they are stationed in different areas all over the country. In addition, hundreds of officers and soldiers are involved in the construction of a large US Air Force field hospital, not far from Tel Aviv, at a place called *Tel Latwinsky*. These Americans, from simple soldiers to pilots, are rolling in money."

"The Americans are spending money like water. They come for a bit of furlough to Tel Aviv, hire the most elegant rooms in hotels on Hayarkon Street, eat in good restaurants, and pour out buckets of dollars for a steak on the black market."

Sam refilled Mr. Krueger's whiskey glass.

"There are so many Americans that even the exchange rate on the black market fell last month. But the girls are crazy about the Yanks. It seems as if President Roosevelt stocks up every soldier he sends to this side of the Atlantic with luxuries."

"Right. I've heard that they have an endless supply of cigarettes and chocolate," Krueger added.

"Forget the cigarettes. Their kitbags are full of nylon stockings, for which the girls are willing to do almost anything to get them," summed up the bartender.

He had taken a liking to the corpulent client from the first time they met. That was just six weeks ago. When the stout fellow had first entered the room, he immediately headed for the bar, perched himself on a stool at its far end and has appeared there almost every night since.

The new customer had introduced himself immediately: "Pleased to meet you – I'm Hendrik Krueger – a businessman from Johannesburg. I work with the Acquisitions Branch of the South African Defense Department, and I love whiskey."

He drank at least two glasses of whiskey almost every night, "Black & White"; and on the first night he jokingly explained that it was unacceptable for white and black to be together in his own country, so he requested that his whiskey be served "in two separate glasses."

Krueger was never drunk. He always paid cash and made sure to leave a good tip for Sam, the bartender, before returning to his room at the nearby Hayarkon Hotel.

Proportionate to the degree of their increasing familiarity, the bartender extended the range of services he provided to Kruger. For example, he gave him a recommendation to the exclusive brothel that operated on the second floor of the new building at the top of Ben Yehuda Street, not far from Mughrabi Square.

"You can get a quickie for a few coins from a street hooker in a wet yard, but then you run the risk of getting a dose of the clap. By the way, there is a similar service in *Jaffa* for half the price. But that's not for you. I'll send you to Madame Lasker, who runs a special establishment for officers and gentlemen," the barman informed Krueger, "clean, elegant rooms with ceiling fans; there are even large mirrors on the walls and the ceiling, so they say."

Sam told Krueger that this facility was informally monitored by the Royal Medical Corps, with the connivance of the British high command, who understood the need of men in uniform to sometimes let off steam – best done between well-shaped female breasts. According to rumors circulating in the city, the military doctors were served free of charge in return for their regular examination of the prostitutes. "And these ladies? They're all great: young, pretty, European, Jewish, and educated." However, the prices are accordingly.

Sam, whose real name was Shmuel – called Sammy by his friends; only Krueger called him Sam – got a small commission from Lasker for these referrals.

One reason for Lasker's commercial success was her ability to secure a steady supply of clients, thanks to the implementation of an unwritten agreement with various functionaries of the Tel Aviv entertainment industry – hotel-porters, taxi drivers, barkeepers – whom she gave a nice gratuity for each client she got through them. She also rewarded several senior police officers in cash and services – British, Arabs, and Jews – a kind of informal insurance premium, which granted her industrial peace. In contrast, for example, the owner of the establishment in 31 Ahad Ha'am Street, who wanted to be smart, did not pay the right people and was raided by a police officer with a foreclosure-warrant accompanied by a photojournalist. Madame Lasker assumed that the efficient 'San Remo' bartender had similar agreements with other institutions in the sex industry.

She wasn't wrong.

In fact, the bartender referred clients to two other brothels, but also served as a paid informant of the CID. Sammy-Sam fulfilled this task with full knowledge of his real employer, *Shai*, the intelligence service of the *Haganah*[15]. He was a

---

[15]The militant Jewish underground movement in Palestine prior to the creation of the State of Israel, later to become its official army.

regular *Shai* operative and his work as a barman offered a good cover story, occasionally yielding useful information.

But this bartender had a different relationship with Krueger, maybe a little closer than usual. In contrast to the typical superficiality with which personal relationships were usually established on both sides of the bar, he really liked Krueger. The usually generous tip, which he received from the oversized South African, undoubtedly had an impact on their good relationship, at least initially. But Sam discovered that Kruger was a pleasant interlocutor, educated, with a good sense of humor.

He spread the first joke he had heard from Krueger among all his friends. "Listen to this joke that makes the rounds in South Africa" began Krueger. "A boy asked his father, 'Dad, what actually is politics?' The father frowned, thought for a moment, and replied, 'Let me give you an example from home. I finance the family, so I am the administration; your mother spends the money, so she is the Government; our maid is the proletariat, so she is the working class; you represent the people, and your little brother is the future. Do you understand?' The boy looked at him confused. 'Not exactly,' he answered, 'but I'll think about it tonight.' Sometime during the night, the boy wakes up to the screams of his little brother who is full of shit and no one changes his nappies. The boy goes to his mother, but he sees that she doesn't care and keeps on sleeping. So he goes to the maid and sees how she and his father are having sex. Having no choice, he takes care of his young brother himself. 'Now I understand what politics is,' he says to his father in the morning. "The government does not care for the people, the administration screws the working class, and the future is full of shit.' "

Sam also noticed that his regular client was really curious and was not ashamed to ask seemingly stupid questions. He said with undisguised pride that he was writing down his experiences and sending them in the form of articles to the monthly magazine of the South African Farmers Federation. It was due to this close relationship that the bartender gladly and willingly answered the many questions posed by the curious Krueger on a variety of topics.

"Contrary to what is written in the newspapers, there is no shortage of any goods except sugar and coffee," he replied at length to the question about the economic situation. "Officers who come here from Britain say that the situation in Palestine cannot be compared with the rationing there. According to their stories, strict rationing is enforced in London, and a genuine shortage exists, while here, there is rationing too, but the allocations are more generous. The main thing is that the black market is flourishing. The borders are more or less porous and smuggling from Lebanon, Syria, and Transjordan, even from Egypt, ensures that prices don't rise sky high and the population has money. A lot of money. The economy in Palestine is thriving because of the war."

One evening, Sam explained to Krueger that the unpleasant fight, which had broken out on the street only a few meters from the 'San Remo' entrance, was caused by a group of young men and women who belonged to a Jewish organization supporting voluntary service in the British Army and fighting those they considered slackers. The fight ended with injuries and police intervention.

"The protesters harangue the young couples who come here to enjoy themselves with insults. They demand them to serve voluntarily in the British army, especially now that the German army is so close, or at least, to join a group of pioneers founding new Jewish settlements. Sometimes this results in violent clashes."

Sam also explained to Krueger the difference between the young people who are for recruitment and Orthodox Jews, who often gather on Hayarkon Street.

"They belong to the 'chastity squad' swinging posters that require Jewish women to be modest and resist the temptation to enjoy themselves with the 'uncircumcised'." He briefly explained the concept of 'uncircumcised'.

"I do not like the religious and certainly abhor religion," admitted Krueger. "Even when I was little and was dragged to church, I learned that a successful sermon must have a good beginning and a good ending. Preferably, they should be as close together as possible."

❄ ❄ ❄

About an hour after the incident with the diligent blackout-inspector, Krueger returned to the Hayarkon Hotel and hung the "*please do not disturb*" sign on the outside of door number 34, which had been his temporary home for the last few weeks. On a table in the corner stood a large, state-of-the-art radio made by Philips. This smart electronic device was the only personal item in the room. All the other items belonged to the standard furnishings list of a hotel room in Tel Aviv.

"I really appreciate your willingness to equip the room with a radio from the hotel's inventory, but I prefer to use my own. It is an ideal device to receive broadcasts from the other side of the world and with its help; I can receive programs from my beloved South Africa during the night hours." That was the convincing explanation he gave the Deputy General Manager, who visited the new guest and was wondering why this client insisted on putting a private radio in his room instead of getting one from the hotel.

The radio, which was now standing on the corner table in room 34, actually had an excellent reception capability. Despite displaying the Philips company trademark on its front, the internal parts of the device had never left the assembly line of the Dutch factory in Eindhoven. They had been commissioned by the German military intelligence service, the *Abwehr*[16], and were manufactured by electronics experts at Telefunken.

With a flick of the wrist, that Kruger was able to perform quickly and competently even in the dark, he transformed the innocent civilian radio receiver into a powerful Morse-transmitter.

It is doubtful whether Sam, the amiable "San Remo" bartender, would have chatted so freely with his regular guest had he been aware that Krueger, known as a businessman with good connections to the Acquisitions Branch of the South African Defense Department, was actually the senior ranking German agent who worked in Tel Aviv under the code name "Milton."

❄ ❄ ❄

To: Eastern Mediterranean Theatre HQ
From: Milton
Weekly Sitrep 6

Large convoys of cargo ships, accompanied by destroyers and other warships including at least one aircraft carrier, sailed along the coastal waters of Tel Aviv. They came from the north, probably from Haifa and headed south, probably to Port Said or, perhaps, Alexandria.

The British are channeling numerous reinforcements into Palestine. British units were observed in addition to the new

---

[16]short name for intelligence, counterintelligence and sabotage offices of the German military, 1920-1944

infantry and tank units from Australia and New Zealand.

The visible number of those wearing the free Polish and Greek insignia has increased.

The ATC[17] system has problems due to the amount of foreign squadrons training in the area.

In the past week, there were five alarms in Tel Aviv, but there were neither explosions heard nor flak observed. Perhaps the alarms came from lack of coordination. See above.

An unsubstantiated report has been received from a low-reliability source that a three-engine Italian bomber has crashed on the beach south of Tel Aviv, killing the entire crew.

The air defense system around the Haifa refineries has been re-enforced by at least 10 modern radar-guided anti-aircraft batteries, which are manned by experienced teams from London. Position of the batteries sent separately.

The military has expanded the restricted area around *Lod* airport; apart from the British and the South African fighter squadrons, much activity by heavy bombers and transport aircraft of the US Army Air Corps have been observed. In addition, the US Army has begun extensive construction work of a large hospital not far from Tel Aviv. Map reference sent separately.

---

[17]Air Traffic Control

Following your orders to investigate Arab commando or guerrilla activities, I went several times by bus or taxi to Jerusalem. Have not - repeat - have not seen any signs of hostile Arab activity. No anti-government resistance nests are known and, since the big Arab revolt three years ago, the Arab population has been quiet.

The traffic flows freely, even at night. Although there are checkpoints on the main roads, these are usually sparsely manned, the checks are superficial and often don't require presentation of documents.

The Jews support the British. The Jewish economy works for the British war effort, and the Jews have announced that the close cooperation with the Mandate Government will continue till the end of the war. Jewish construction companies are particularly active in the construction and expansion of military bases, especially military airports throughout Palestine, as well as in Egypt, Iraq, and even Sudan and Abyssinia.

At least 15,000 young Jews have volunteered for the British military. Only a tiny group, the "Stern Gang", continues to lead an armed struggle against the British, but they are isolated, and the British Secret Service has probably destroyed their leasership.

End.
Milton

Krueger looked at his watch and read the report again. He double checked to ensure that the last word at the end of the report had a typo – an 's' instead of a 'd', an agreed sign that the report was written of his own free will and not under pressure. "As soon as you send us a report without a typo in the last word, we assume that you are transmitting under mortal danger, while the hand of a British intelligence officer is pressing the barrel of his Webley revolver into your temple," his German handler had made clear to him at the time.

He still had a few minutes before transmitting the report.

He went to the balcony with its view of the sea and lit a strong Player's cigarette–British, however the best, and looked at the moon, which drew a magic light strip on the calm waters.

"Interesting that Berlin has once again demanded information about Arab commando activities and urgently," Krueger mused as he gently flicked the cigarette ash. He remembered, out of context, that the word "commando" was invented forty years ago by his ancestors, the Boers, descendants of immigrants who had moved from Holland to South Africa in the 17th century.

Krueger's father was a member of a Boer commando unit that had managed for months to embroil almost 400,000 soldiers of the British Empire in a war that has gone down in history as the "Boer War", despite their numerical inferiority. "History is written by winners, and therefore nobody uses the name we have given this war – 'the English War'" – his uncle had explained to him. "Your father and his comrades, excellent horsemen, outstanding snipers, native peasants, attacked British supply convoys and isolated outposts, then disappeared in the distance. But, in the end, they were overwhelmed by the huge British army, and only your father and two others survived from his commando unit."

However, not only the word 'commando' was forged then, but also the term 'concentration camp' – those terrible camps in which the British held the entire civilian Boer population captive. They were forcibly evacuated from farms and villages to prevent the supply of the commando units. The British made no effort to supply the prisoners – mostly women and children – with food and medicine. Thousands of innocent people, including many members of Krueger's family died a miserable death in the British concentration camps.

Krueger's burning hatred of the British, fueled by family-legacy stories about the horrors of the Boer War, was detected in the summer of 1936, by the German Olympic Committee official who had been assigned as a chaperon to the South African delegation during the Olympic Games in Berlin. The chaperon was actually a German intelligence officer, something the guests did not detect. Like dozens of his colleagues, he had taken upon himself the task of identifying possible candidates among the thousands of athletes and tourists for recruitment to the German military intelligence, the *Abwehr*. Krueger, who was accompanying the South African delegation as a fencing referee, responded enthusiastically to those recruitment attempts by actually offering his own services to spy for Germany. "I have a long account to settle with the Empire in general and the British people, in particular," he emphasized at every meeting with his *Abwehr* handler.

Over the years, having undergone extensive basic training, he was given the code name "Milton", and had provided excellent and reliable reports to Berlin since September 1939 – the outbreak of the Second World War– first from Johannesburg and now from Tel Aviv.

Krueger had turned to a new method of high-speed transmission, reducing the ability of the British Intelligence to locate the transmitter. He had agreed with his handler before his arrival in Palestine that the transmission time needed to be changed regularly. “But, for my own safety, it’s a good idea to shorten the transmission,” he mused while waiting for the agreed signal from the Abwehr transmitter in Belgrade. “It’s really not worth my while to be caught by the British. In that case, I have no doubt that, after a thorough interrogation, they’ll put me up against the wall, just as they did with Uncle Frederick.”

Uncle Frederick was wounded and captured during one of the last commando raids. The British held him captive for two months and even treated his wounds. Then they put him before a firing squad on the last day of the Boer War, even though they knew that a ceasefire agreement would be signed within a few hours. “The British are arseholes,” he cursed under his breath, stubbed out his cigarette in an ashtray, and went into the room to transmit the report – “a belated revenge of the fucking Brits by the Kruegers,” he muttered.

Tel Aviv Port, Summer 1938

"That's the 'Adria'. I recognize her masts and chimneys. It's the Italian passenger ship 'Adria'," shouted Hayim Cohen, a burly fellow, about 16 years old from the *Mahlul*[18] neighborhood of Tel Aviv who had dreamt since childhood of becoming either a pilot or a sailor. He and his friend Abraham stood on the hill near the port of Tel Aviv, between the Muslim cemetery and Leibowitch's leather factory, and gazed to the west onto the open sea. "I bet you ten *Grush*[19] that it is the 'Adria'."

"I don't bet with you on ships," replied Abraham, "not even on cars, motorcycles, and airplanes. You can identify them even by their engine noise. Say, you do remember that we have something happening tonight, don't you? I'll pick you up and we can go together, but I beg you to be silent as we go to the meeting with the instructor Shimon in the basement of the factory. I have a feeling that it will happen tonight," he said, his eyes twinkling. "I think the *Haganah* are swearing us in tonight – you know, blindfolded, the gun, the Bible, and so on."

❄ ❄ ❄

---

[18]At the time, a poor Tel Aviv neighborhood; today, part of its elegant beach-front promenade.
[19]Slang for a monetary unit of the currency in Palestine at the time.

Hayim was right. This was, in fact, the Italian cruise ship 'Adria', which was anchored about a kilometer off the Tel Aviv beach.

Henrietta Landwehr was one of the last passengers who had remained on board. She leaned against the wooden railing and watched her fellow travelers as they got into the big launches, which were now tied up alongside the 'Adria'.

Like Henrietta, most passengers were new immigrants from the German Reich. They looked anxiously at the boats bobbing up and down on the waves, which were there to help them traverse the last few meters of their long journey. "Don't worry, come down, we'll help you," called one of the boatmen to the frightened passengers. His cries were in Hebrew, which meant only a few passengers could understand him.

Henrietta felt a certain pride that she understood the calls, and, perhaps even subconsciously raised her head. The Hebrew sailor was aware that most passengers did not understand his calls and repeated them in English and German.

"You Jews call this the Port of Tel Aviv but between you and me, it is not a port, but rather a jetty for launches," Antonio joked in his charming Italian accent. Antonio, the nice radio officer, who flaunted a Clark Gable-style mustache, had failed during the whole trip from Trieste to Tel Aviv to get Henrietta into his cabin for an "enchanting evening." What had he not tried? He had asked her to dance after dinner, offered her a romantic walk on the bridge, and deployed all his charm. In vain. But even off the coast of Tel Aviv, he had not given up.

"Until two years ago, we were using the services of the Jaffa Port, which are run in the same way, namely, the ship's anchor in the open sea, while passengers and cargo get ferried ashore in large boats – called in jargon 'launches'," Antonio spluttered explanations at the pace of a machine gun. "But then the Arab revolt broke out. They called a general strike and paralyzed the port of Jaffa. The British allowed the Jews to open the dock in Tel Aviv. It is operated by the Jewish stevedores from Thessaloniki. They are real seamen."

He had the tone of genuine admiration in his voice. "I once saw how they unloaded goods on the high seas with huge waves," and without changing his tone of voice, he went on to another topic. "You know, in the first year at the Naval Academy in Naples, I wanted to be a radio officer, because when you arrive at the port, the radio officer's equipment is turned off and he takes a long holiday onshore. Say, shall we perhaps meet in the evening on the beach? I know all the cafes and restaurants of Tel Aviv."

Antonio's verbiage had not raised the slightest reaction in Henrietta. "How would you feel about dinner and a dance at the cafe of the Hotel 'San Remo'? The Trio Simoni is playing featuring the singer Esther Schechter. They are international class. *Alora*, what do you say?"

During this long monolog, Henrietta avoided turning her face towards Antonio but continued to stare at the beach of the first Jewish city.

"I've had enough. He should leave me alone," she mused. "Who is in the mood now for fun and dancing? He reminds me of that stupid shepherd who constantly tried to move in on me at the ski resort in Tyrol. He pressed himself close to me and I moved away, he pushed and I moved to the end of the bench; then he got a slap from me and that was that. But now I'm at the eastern end of the Mediterranean. Where are the snow-capped Alps and where am I? I wonder what will happen in the future. How will I, Henrietta Landwehr, a middle-class girl from Vienna, who speaks several languages and plays the piano, cope alone in a strange, glowing, violent, complicated country?"

Suddenly, for no apparent reason, she remembered how she was playing a few years ago with her friend in a park near her home in the eighth district of Vienna, when two girls arrived, members of the Zionist youth movement *Maccabi Hatza'ir*[20]. They did not need to make a special effort to persuade them to join the movement.

"Actually, there is a certain logic for that distant encounter to suddenly surface," she noted and drew a long bow from her then joining the Zionist youth movement to her current presence on board the 'Adria', minutes before her official arrival in Palestine.

Henrietta had been glad to join the *Maccabi Hatza'ir*. For it allowed her to escape the strictly disciplined regime of her parents for a few hours, enabling her to enjoy the company of young contemporaries her age during activities and excursions. She was less enamored of the ideological debates that were also part of the activities in the movement's center. But over time, she had learned to pretend and appeared to participate wholeheartedly. "Am I scared of what will happen to me now in Palestine?" she asked herself without reply.

Secretly, she had to admit that she was a bit nervous but was also really hoping for a positive change in her life: independence and accepting responsibility for herself. "From now on, I will compile an annual report on what I was doing, what I have achieved, and what I missed. Today is the August 9, my second birthday."

Angelo the radio operator, Antonio's assistant, posted a news bulletin at the entrance to the 'Adria' dining room every morning. The bulletin on the last day noted that the weather forecast for August 9, 1938 was "clear, maximum temperature 29 degrees Celsius, high humidity."

---

[20]Literally: the young Maccabi or the young Maccabean.

"Thank you for traveling with us, and, in the name of the captain and crew, we wish you a pleasant stay in Palestine and hope to welcome you again in the future."

❄ ❄ ❄

During the voyage from Europe to Palestine, which contained a promise of renewal, Henrietta repeated in her mind the dramatic events of the last few weeks that had brought her on board the 'Adria'. For example, the frantic chase after the coveted permit, the certificate that allowed her to escape the Nazi Reich and legally immigrate to Palestine.

Since the annexation day, the "Anschluss", in early March 1938, when the walls of the waltz capital's buildings were flooded overnight by a sea of swastikas and posters welcoming the return of their prodigal son, Adolf Hitler, Henrietta and her family had tried to leave Austria by every possible way, like most of the 200,000 Viennese Jews.

The Jewish community, about ten percent of the total population of Vienna, whose members were proud of their contribution to the life of the beautiful city – doctors, scientists, musicians, lawyers, businessmen, teachers, craftsmen – suddenly became a persecuted minority, dejected and helpless. Her older sister Elsa had received an entry visa to the United States, thanks to the affidavits and documents that Aunt Eva from Brooklyn had organized. But she, Tamar, an activist in the Zionist youth movement, longed only for Palestine.

"The fact that you have been a member of the movement since a young age and speak Hebrew tipped the scales in your favor," the *Youth Aliyah*[21] clerk explained with a serious

[21]Hebrew: immigration to Palestine/Israel; between 1933 and 1943 about 10,000 children and youths were brought to Palestine by Zionist organizations and thereby saved from the Holocaust.

expression in the office of the Jewish community in Vienna. "You're lucky because we have at least twenty applicants for each immigration certificate."

In the anxious and tense community, rumors were circulating about all sorts of bad transactions for the purchase of certificates, including the transfer of money under the table into the pockets of employees. But from personal experience, Henrietta knew that this was only malicious gossip, as these activists did their job with commitment and determination to save lives.

Her parents, too, had considered emigrating, but where? Almost all countries had closed their gates to Jewish refugees sitting trapped in the Third Reich, which had deprived them of their basic rights as human beings.

❄ ❄ ❄

Grandpa Siegfried Landwehr had the dubious honor of being one of the first on the long list of Viennese Jews to be murdered by Nazi thugs. How he was murdered, she learned in the dining room on the first night of the trip. This happened when Henrietta, alone, following the abrupt separation from her family, and scared, due to her uncertain future, heard someone say something in Viennese. Without hesitation, she overcame her natural shyness and went up to the speaker, a man of about forty, thin, bent, but with bright eyes and a look of wisdom.

Henrietta introduced herself, emphatically using the Viennese dialect and asked if she could sit at his table; she got a positive response, accompanied by a warm smile.

"Bartok, Theodor Bartok," he introduced himself. "Landwehr? Are you related to Siegfried Landwehr?" After she had confirmed that it was her grandfather, Bartok told her that he had been active in the Socialist Party and, as a lawyer, represented members who were in trouble with the law. "I often had to appear before the courts of Vienna, representing union leaders or getting them out on bail when they were arrested for violent confrontations or skirmishes with fascists."

Bartok had hardly eaten. Between courses, he lit spicy oriental cigarettes and blew smoke rings into the air, which attracted the fascinated gaze of two children at the next table.

"I knew your grandfather, who dealt with civil actions, professionally; we would sit in the same room occasionally," Bartok continued. He relayed how he met Siegfried Landwehr a few days after the Anschluss, hurrying along the *Graben*[22]. "We were both in a hurry, so we only exchanged a few polite words. He said he was on his way to the Brazilian Embassy; a rumor had been circulating that the Brazilians were issuing Jews with visas. The rumor turned out to be false. We said goodbye; I went ahead and after a few seconds, when I had reached the street corner, I heard screams. Your grandfather was surrounded by a gang of Nazi villains, led by Johann Schumacher. "

Schumacher's name was familiar to anyone in Vienna who had something to do with the judiciary; he was known as a violent, stupid thief with a rich criminal past. "I recognized Schumacher immediately. Your grandfather, Siegfried, was the prosecutor in a trial that had cost this criminal a few years of freedom. 'Bloody Jew,' Schumacher yelled. 'What are you doing in the center of our beautiful city?' Since the new era had now arrived in the city and as a seemingly pure Aryan – although, like most Viennese, he probably had Polish, Croatian, Hungarian, Czech and maybe even Jewish blood flowing through his veins – he quickly slipped into the new regime and was appointed SA group leader."

---

[22]A street in the city centre of Vienna.

Henrietta followed, with bated breath, the detailed description of the traumatic event that she knew well, but from a different perspective.

In short sentences, while smoking furiously, Bartok described in detail the violence displayed by Schumacher and his pals, dressed in brown coats with swastika armbands.

They noticed Siegfried Landwehr while they were busy trying to paint slogans on Jewish shops:

Jüdischer Laden. Deutsche, kauft nicht bei Juden[23]!

"Your grandfather, who recognized Schumacher's voice immediately, tried to ignore them and went on as if the roar did not apply to him. I also saw a cop on the beat, leaning against the baroque statue in the middle of the road. He knew your grandfather very well. But now, as he realized who was against whom, he turned and disappeared."

Henrietta closed her eyes in shock. She knew how Bartok's tale would continue and tears began to flow from her bright eyes. She felt the pain that her beloved grandfather had to suffer, with whom she had spent so many pleasant hours, ranging from discussions on issues of the heart that she could not discuss with her strict mother to clowning and fooling around.

"Schumacher and his cronies beat your grandfather, threw him on the pavement, and kicked him until he lost consciousness."

Henrietta tried to hide her tears but did not turn her eyes away from Bartok. Now she noticed a long, thin scar on his neck, which had turned dark, perhaps because these memories upset and depressed Bartok as well.

---

[23]German: "Jewish shop. Germans, do not buy from Jews."

"How can humans behave like animals? Hard to believe that someone torments someone else just because he is a Jew," Anna, a seventeen-year-old girl from Prague, quietly interrupted the conversation. She had made friends with Henrietta during the trip and had also joined the table.

"My dear young lady," Bartok responded patiently, "anyone who has not personally experienced the rampage of the Nazis cannot understand. We are now in the summer of 1938 and the Nazis have not yet reached Prague. Not yet. But it is only a matter of time until the swastika flag flies over the Charles Bridge in the Czech capital. Then the Czechoslovakian Jews, whose mother tongue is German and who have German culture in their blood, will lose their status as human beings. Maybe, one day someone will explore the love story of Central European Jews with the German culture – the Jews from *Czernowitz* being the outpost of German culture in Eastern Europe – and the horrible, deadly hatred that Hitler and his cronies have for these Jews."

Anna remained gob-smacked and did not utter a single word until the end of the evening.

Bartok continued to describe the incident. He focused on the fact that dozens of Viennese, all culture vultures, who loved to listen to Mozart and Beethoven and read Goethe and Schiller, saw all this, watched, but did nothing to intervene. "Only one lady, a well-dressed, well-known figure in the gossip columns, a member of an old noble family from imperial times, yelled at Schumacher and his henchmen. She also tried to chase them away; she hit them with her small, fashionable handbag. 'Get out of our sight before we finish you off, countess,' Schumacher made fun of her while brushing her aside."

Bartok described in a flat voice how the countess stumbled away and wept bitterly. The other curiosity seekers also moved away; none of them had tried to help the old man, who lay motionless on the pavement with blood streaming down his face. It took almost an hour until a city administration car took the bleeding, broken body of her grandfather to the Jewish hospital.

Since the Anschluss, the Jewish community hospital enjoyed a surplus of specialists due to the employment ban for Jewish doctors in Aryan hospitals – including some Nobel laureates and candidates in different categories, making it the best hospital in Vienna. Nevertheless, these doctors had to overlook stab wounds, bleeding, and fractures because they were instructed by the police to register "myocardial infarction" as the cause of death.

"You have no idea how humiliating it is to be a witness to such a barbaric attack and to know that you can do nothing," Bartok told his bewildered fellow diners. "I knew that if I interfered, they'd kill me, too. I am not only a Jew but also a paroled political prisoner, a well-known socialist campaigner," he concluded bitterly. "The fact that I'm sitting here with you this evening, traveling to the land of Israel, borders on the miraculous, although, as a socialistic atheist, I should really not believe in miracles."

He explained that, in his opinion, this was nevertheless an act of higher intervention: He was incarcerated in the aftermath of the brief socialist revolt that had broken out in Vienna in 1934. The police of fascist Austria had arrested Bartok and violently interrogated him because of his senior position in the Socialist Party and his leadership role during the rebellion. The long list of damage caused by the ongoing, brutal interrogation was two broken hands, five broken fingers, some big scars on his back and neck, a short trial and a sentence of ten years in prison. For four years, Bartok shared a cell with Franz Schuster, a bigwig in the local Nazi Party, which was at that time outlawed by the nationalist government in power in Austria at that time.

"We got along famously. Franz, a violent man, not clever, but with gut instinct, hated Jews. However, he did like me – maybe due to the circumstances. I remember that I told him the joke about the Jews and cyclists who were to blame for all the problems in Europe. So this idiot asked me, 'Why the cyclists?' And I responded, 'Why the Jews?' And he almost choked with laughter. Anyway, since we had time in abundance, we conducted long conversations. Seems to me that I expanded his world view," Bartok sarcastically summed up the strange situation.

After the Anschluss, as his Nazi pals seized power, Schuster was immediately released from prison and given a senior position in the new government.

The prison also underwent some changes; for example, within a few minutes, the former director had to trade his elegant office for a particularly smelly cell as a prisoner without any rights. But most of the guards remained at their posts and the routine had not changed.

About two weeks after Schuster had been released from prison, Bartok was urgently summoned to the office of the Director. Franz waited in the room, wearing the Nazi party uniform, a few pounds rounder in the midriff, which he had put on since his release from prison. "I have not forgotten you and am putting my career on the line for you," Schuster told him. "After all, our friendship was formed under very special circumstances."

To help his former cellmate, Schuster enlisted the help of Adolf Eichmann, whom he described as "an evil, but useful SS stooge," responsible for the deportation of the Austrian Jews beyond the borders of the German Reich. So Bartok was released from prison that very same day. Following Schuster's directives, he turned up at the SS headquarters in Mariahilfe Street to get the emigration papers.

"I was on my way to pick up the exit visa when I witnessed the murder of your grandfather. Shocked and scared, I ran through the first district, the city center, and breathlessly reached the address that Franz had given me, with a near heart attack. The porter, in SS uniform, gave me an envelope with an exit permit and an entry visa for Palestine. I have no idea how Schuster or Eichmann did it. The envelope also contained twenty Reich-marks and a small note: 'Have a good trip and don't come back. Your cellmate, Heil Hitler.' That same evening I was sitting on the train to Prague, thanks to the certificate from Franz and Eichmann, and now I'm about to become a pioneer in the Land of Israel," he concluded with an ironic tone.

"I see that both of you, Henrietta and Anna, have left a lot of food on your plates. I hope I haven't spoiled your appetite. I must express my admiration for your excellent table manners, absolutely according to etiquette. I'm afraid you will be hit by a culture shock in the land of Israel. I have heard that the pioneers, in their eagerness to shun Diaspora life, put no value on folded hands or chewing with your mouth closed. They talk loudly during their collective meals and hold their forks like pitchforks."

After this long closing statement, he was breathless. He chuckled, gasped, coughed, and lit another cigarette in a long line of what the poet Avraham Shlonsky had described as "a weed with a glow at one end and a fool at the other." A few years later, they would bring about his agonizing death from lung cancer.

❄ ❄ ❄

Arthur liked Tel Aviv from the first moment on. Before him, a city was spread with white houses that were built close together. There were less of them the further his gaze turned to the north beyond the anchorage from which the launches had come. North of that jetty, he saw a small estuary, with an imposing concrete building on its banks. White steam and smoke welled from the roof of the building, which served as a power plant. He immediately recognized the minarets and steeples, which he saw to the south, as those of Jaffa. That Jaffa, from which the prophet Jonah had sailed, through the gates of which Alexander the Great had marched, later conquered by Richard the Lion-Heart and then Napoleon, was now a bustling city, one of the centers of Arab nationalism in Palestine.

"Unbelievable, but we did it. We are in the Holy Land," said his father Herbert. Despite the strong summer heat, he wore a suit with a matching tie that was choking his neck. "It is hot here, but I have to provide the correct appearance. After all, I am a well-known lawyer of good standing," he explained in the morning when dressing for the last day on deck and their arrival in the land. "I think the climate in Palestine is wonderful," he joked, "unfortunately, it is ruined by the weather."

Arthur did not laugh.

He had heard this joke dozens and perhaps hundreds of times, with geographic adjustments of course. "Believe me, it is no small wonder that we are here and, moreover, with the right papers. We owe everything to Frank Foley." He began with the explanation, which Arthur had also heard a few times since the train to Trieste had left the Berlin railway station and the Nazi police had finished rummaging through the contents of their luggage. "We know all the tricks, how you Jews smuggle gold, diamonds, and foreign currency out of the Reich." When they found nothing, they vented their frustrations with a long series of annoying questions about visas to Palestine, which were stamped in the Weiss family's passports. After they were done with this torment, the police searched for another victim.

If someone had told Herbert Weiss in 1933 that he would be emigrating in about five years and going to where those British ruled, who had strained not too long ago to kill him, he would have sent them to an insane asylum. For months after Hitler had come to power, Herbert Weiss still believed that his personal track record guaranteed him and his family a solid insurance. In fact, he even identified himself in those distant days with some of Hitler's and the Nazis' views, especially with the need to free Germany from the dictates of the humiliating the Versailles Treaty, which the Allies had forced on Germany, his beloved Fatherland. He believed that every German patriot had a personal account to settle with those politicians who had thrust a dagger into the back of the World War I front-line soldiers – referred to as the "Great War, the war to end all wars ..."

❄ ❄ ❄

His chambers were located in a prestigious office building in the center of Berlin, across the street from the KaDeWe department store, which belonged to the Wertheim family. Herbert hung up a copy of the order-of-the-day from 1916 at a central and prestigious spot. Signed by General Gröner, it contained a commendation for Sergeant Herbert Weiss, of the 169th Prussian Infantry Regiment. "Sergeant Weiss continued to man his machine gun position, even after all his comrades had been hit," read the citation. "Despite serious injuries and under heavy fire from British artillery and gas grenades, he continued to fight bravely. Due to the effective fire from his machine gun, which he was manning alone now that his comrades lay dead or wounded around him, an enemy counter-attack on hill 372 was foiled."

The memory of the Battle for Hill 372 had now disappeared among the thousands of similar deadly skirmishes that characterized the Great War that had torn Europe apart between 1914 and 1918. Those few who did remember, were a couple of hundred German soldiers and British Empire troops, who had survived those clashes on the forgetful hill in the Battle of the Somme, where more than one million German, British, French, Australian, New

Zealand, Canadian and other soldiers had lost their lives. But the solemn presentation ceremony of the Iron Cross 'first class' in the military hospital of Cologne for his courageous actions under fire on Hill 372 and his recognition as a "combat veteran" led Herbert to believe that Hitler's wild, anti-Jewish policies were not intended for him.

"We are Germans of the Mosaic faith, we have sacrificed so much for the Fatherland, and no one would dare do us any harm. The Nazis only want to expel the *Ostjuden*[24], those immigrants from Poland and Russia. Just between you and me, you can't stand them either," he tried to joke with his wife Ruth.

Ruth thought otherwise.

She reminded him that if he had dug a little deeper at the roots of the Mendelssohn family tree, that great philosopher, due to whose privilege the Jews were allowed to settle in Berlin less than two hundred years ago, he could have found the Galician origins of the Mendelssohn family. "Yes, Mendelssohn, the enlightened philosopher, founder of the Jewish community in Berlin, was also what you call an Eastern Jew."

"Have you actually read Hitler's **Mein Kampf**? I have read it and I think that this Austrian lunatic means every word he has written. Herbert, you're so proud of your military service, the camaraderie of the veterans, that you have become blinkered. You cannot see the reality. We have no place here anymore. For the sake of our future and especially for Arthur, we have to get out of here, flee, and quickly."

Arthur, a brilliant high school student and an outstanding athlete, who was liked by his classmates because of his

---

[24]Literally: Eastern Jews, in German, a derogatory term used by German Jews to describe the visibly orthodox Jews from Eastern Europe.

gentleness and the wide smile that always shone from his round face, had been thrown out of the school following the enforcement of the Race Laws. Like all young people of the Berlin Jewish community, he was now transferred to the Jewish school system, which continued to function in the face of the difficult conditions.

Despite the expulsion of his beloved son from school and the need to deal with an increasing number of administrative regulations and legal prohibitions, Herbert still believed that this was merely a dark cloud which would clear away soon. "You see, now the situation will improve," he told his wife in the summer of 1936, when thousands of athletes and tourists from around the world flooded Berlin for the Olympic Games.

"Herbert, you may think that you have fully recovered and are healed, but the gas that you have inhaled and the British bullet in your chest have influenced you. Look, even your so-called friend, Theodor Ravel, of whom you speak at every opportunity, recounting how you saved his life under fire by risking your own, and who until 1933 was like at home with us, nattering constantly about your eternal blood brotherhood, how he has disappeared! Now he is serving as a high brass in the *Luftwaffe*. So, when you asked him for some help based on your camaraderie forged by the Iron Cross, did he even lift a finger?! What did you actually ask of him? To intervene on your behalf with the bigwigs! And what happened? Have you heard from him? Have you seen him? He has hopped it, disappeared, and why? Because we're Jewish and Jews have no friends under the new order in Germany."

Herbert tried to say something in defense of his friend, but Ruth silenced him impatiently. "Don't you see that this current relative calm is only temporary? That's only due to the Olympics. Therefore, cynically exploiting the 'family of nations', the Nazis have removed the '*entry for*

Jews prohibited' signs and are feigning the appearance of a normal state. But the instant the last athlete leaves here, the situation will only get worse."

❄ ❄ ❄

"As your mother had foreseen, not long after the closing ceremony and the extinguishing of the Olympic flame, four Nazi hoodlums come to my office, destroyed the filing cabinet and smashed the furniture," continued Herbert's description of their departure from Berlin.

Arthur knew the story by heart.

"I took the Iron Cross from the drawer and went to the police station in the district of Grunewald to complain. Police Commissioner Hoffman, my company mate during the war, was shocked and took me into his room. 'Herbert,' he begged of me with tears in his eyes, 'don't ever come back here. You don't understand how these brown barbarians, these Nazis, have totally taken control of us. I can't help you. I have been marked by them as a former socialist. In the end, I, too, will end up in Dachau. Do me a favor, take your family and get out while the Nazis still let you go.'

"A few months later, your mother died of cancer and I began to trudge all the foreign consulates in Berlin, to try to get a visa. Everywhere they fobbed me off with 'please go now and try again later'. The Americans were not even prepared to accept my request, when they heard that I was the bearer of the Iron Cross." But from the British Consulate of all places, he received a visa and that was thanks to Frank Foley. Officially, Foley was in charge of visas at the British consulate, whilst in reality he was the representative of the British intelligence services in Germany. In contrast to the official British policy seeking to limit the intake of German Jews in Palestine, Foley helped hundreds of Jews to bypass the bureaucratic obstacles. Sometimes he did it with the help of forged documents and produced the visa that allowed the Jews to escape from the clutches of the Nazis.

❄ ❄ ❄

Arthur wasn't listening to his father's explanations. All this was already part of the past. Now, on the deck of the 'Adria', off the coast of Tel Aviv, Arthur was concentrating on Henrietta Landwehr, who was leaning against the railing, where she revealed the well-formed leg, which had the radio officer Antonio so fascinated. Nor did Arthur hear his father's exclamations of admiration at the sight of the crates with agricultural equipment stacked on the quayside –"it seems that the Jews can really be good farmers. Maybe there is something to the theory, that if we want a healthy society in the Land of Israel, the social pyramid must be turned upside down with a wide, productive population segment at the bottom. But turning the theory into practice should be left to others, Arthur. I hope you're not going to join some remote kibbutz, to make the desert bloom. After we have settled down you will go to university. You're too smart to waste your brain on breeding chickens, bananas, or tomatoes."

His father's nattering did not interest Arthur at all, and not only because he already knew most of it by heart. His eyes continued to focus on Henrietta, who was standing at the bow of the 'Adria' with the Italian radio officer by her side. "Oh, Henrietta," Arthur thought and remembered the deep conversations on board the 'Adria' during the long nights of the crossing. He watched with admiration Antonio's shiny hair that resisted the breeze, thanks to a liter of scented brilliantine.

Arthur had grown up as a Jewish boy in Nazi Berlin, a formative experience of survival in a persecuting and coercive society. The sudden departure from Germany and boarding the 'Adria' affected him like a dam that burst, turning the introverted and quiet boy into a curious, fun loving young man who was looking for adventure. He and Henrietta had already become friends in the first hour on board the Italian passenger ship, even before it lifted anchor and steamed out of Trieste. They spent many hours together, finding hideouts from the wind and the prying eyes of other passengers. Arthur spread out his dream before Henrietta, to join a kibbutz in the Yisre'el Valley, to become a pioneer, despite his father's opposition, who would rather see him studying law or at least accounting. While Henrietta told him about her dream "to do something useful, to work in agriculture or perhaps as a nanny on a kibbutz in the Jordan Valley or the Galilee." The actual distance between them shrank from one encounter to the other. She clung to him and did not move or resist when he put his hand on her shoulder. But then, as he tried to kiss her, she drew back in horror. "What are you doing? What do you take me for? A slut like in the movies?" And ran to her cabin. Since then they had not spoken to each other.

As soon as Henrietta saw him at the entrance to the dining room or on deck, she would turn around and run away. But the flame of first love, which had been ignited in Arthur on the journey from Trieste to Tel Aviv, refused to be extinguished. His passionate jealousy was fueled by effervescent hormones. "If Antonio touches her, I'll kill him," he hissed through his teeth and swore the oath of an infatuated boy. "You belong to me and if not now then in the future, no matter how long it takes. But in one year, two years, maybe four years, we'll be together."

❄ ❄ ❄

Paul Roberts hated his job.

A few moments of ecstasy and gratuitous fantasies inspired by reading **The Seven Pillars of Wisdom** by T.E. Lawrence, better known as Lawrence of Arabia, had motivated him less than a year ago to join the British administration in Palestine. But from his tight little booth at the border control of the tiny port of Tel Aviv – his current job – the adventurous world of Lawrence, which had lured him from London to the Orient, appeared to him like a mirage in the desert. Paul was short, plump, quick-witted, but basically lazy. His parents had heard at every parent-teacher meeting, the same laconic summary by his teachers such as, "too bad that his marks do not reflect his abilities. He can do much better." He remembered well those nights, full of dreams, that had led him a year earlier to the dark government office in central London, where he signed forms which appointed him as a junior officer of His Excellency, the British High Commissioner for Palestine.

In the nights before signing, he experienced the longest dreams of his life. They were full of images of him riding lightly, floating on a fine camel at the head of tough, courageous Bedouin fighters; a white and golden striped *keffiyeh*[25] adorned his head while his white, loose robes were fluttering in the hot desert wind and a military document-pouch dangling from his hip. His dreams were an exact replica of the painting, which he remembered from Lawrence of Arabia's book, that British intelligence officer who had led the sons of the desert in a revolt against their cruel, Turkish oppressors.

Paul Roberts, who came from a London working-class neighborhood, was supposed to bring those eastern barbarians progress by introducing British order into the oriental chaos. At day's end, a magnificent exotic beauty in wrapped in transparent veils would be waiting for him in a beautiful, spacious tent. But the reality in Palestine,

---

[25]Traditional Arab headdress, similar to a big shawl.

the banks of which he had reached in the last days of 1937, were far removed from the scenes that had embellished his foggy, gray London nights. Nevertheless the image on the first page of his life's oriental chapter, promised a series of pleasant and thrilling adventures.

Palestine welcomed him on a clear, sunny winter day with a kaleidoscope of colors and sights that he had never experienced before. "The colors really match the paintings by the famous traveler of the last century, David Roberts," he thought, and wondered why he only realized now that they both carried the same name. "Who knows, maybe we're related. Maybe my journey here is no accident, but providence of a higher force?" From the deck of the 'London Star', which was being slowly towed into the new port of Haifa by a small tug, a spectacular view spread out before him that miraculously intertwined with his oriental dreams in faraway London.

As an amateur historian and expert on the stories of the Old Testament, he immediately recognized the Carmelite monastery, Stella Maris, to his south on the summit of Mount Carmel – that mountain where the prophet Elijah had roamed.

In front of the ship's bow, on a stretch of white sand, long-armed cranes were working on the construction of a large plant with two giant cooling towers in the form of milk bottles.

From articles in the business section of the London Times, Paul knew that this was going to be a huge refinery, the third largest in the world, which was intended to receive and process oil flowing through long pipes from Kirkuk in Iraq.

"The construction of a modern oil refinery in Haifa, a Shell Company project, is an important strategic element on the project list of the British Empire," wrote the Times commentator. "The plant is scheduled to be up and running in the summer of 1939, which will raise the strategic importance of Palestine to the next level. However, it must be emphasized, that investors in the City of London are concerned about the functionality and performance of the system, which may be a target for sabotage attacks by Arab rebels; they have already proven their skills and determination by blowing up pumping stations and above-ground sections of the pipeline, thereby delaying the entire project. To allay these concerns, General Bernard Montgomery, commander in chief of the armed forces in Palestine, has stressed that his troops are suppressing the Arab revolt with extreme punitive actions and by the application of modern methods, especially the use of aircraft and motorized patrols."

Just before the ship sailed into the large bay, a few kilometers away from the Carmel mountain-range, Paul noticed to the south the ruins of the walls of the *Atlit*[26] fortress. "This is the last Crusader castle in the Holy Land, and we speak of 1291," he explained to Victor, a young man from Jerusalem who had come aboard the 'London Star' in the port of Marseille. During the trip, a familiarity had developed between them, which went beyond the exchange of pleasantries. "The Muslims had conquered the country, including Acre, which was their capital at the time. But in spite of all their efforts, the Muslims did not manage to conquer *Atlit*, because of the massive fortifications, into which King Louis of France had pumped the royal treasury a few years earlier."

Victor listened carefully and Paul felt flattered.

"The knights fought in the hope of getting help from Europe, but they did not take into account that, after two

[26]A small coastal town south of Haifa. In the 1940s, the British Mandate Government turned their base there into an internment camp for illegal Jewish immigrants, prisoners of war and other "undesirable aliens".

hundred years of continuous bloodshed, Europe was fed up with the Crusades. After a few weeks of siege, they set sail and fled to Cyprus. It was the end of the Christian presence in this part of the world."

"Not exactly," Victor remarked nonchalantly, with a hint of superiority of a know-it-all.

"Five hundred years later Napoleon roamed here. Specifically, in 1799. He marched to Acre and contemplated attacking Lebanon." Paul did not feel offended. After all, he had read a book about Napoleon's campaign in Egypt and Palestine and his mistake about the end of the European presence was merely a momentary memory lapse. In addition, he had taken a liking to the tall, athletically built young man, who, despite his youth, had expressed himself with authority and maturity, speaking good English with a slight, foreign accent.

Meanwhile, it got crowded on the deck of the 'London Star', because many passengers had gathered there craning their necks to view the ever approaching Haifa. "That there is the German Templer Colony," Victor explained, pointing to a wide road, densely planted with trees on both sides, with their canopies meeting at the top thereby providing the two-story mansions with shade. He noted that it was the Templers who had basically made Haifa the center of the North.

"When the Germans arrived here in about 1870, Haifa was a sleepy town in a weakened Turkish province. The long building that we see on the left is the *Technion*, the largest academic center for science and technology. My father wants to send me there, but, as I said, I'm crazy about history. I devour books with historical themes, and I somehow manage to remember details without having any idea why they are engraved here," he said as he tapped his head lightly.

"So, for example?" Paul asked.

"Let's see ... oh well. Do you know what the shortest war in history was?"

"Must have been conducted with the participation of the Italians," Paul tried to joke.

"Not exactly," Victor replied with undisguised pride. "On August 27, 1896, war broke out between the ruler of Zanzibar and the UK, your Britain. The war was declared at nine o'clock in the morning. The British fleet bombarded the palace of the ruler, and at nine forty-five, the war ended with Zanzibar's unconditional surrender. Three quarters of an hour, one half of a football game, so to speak."

Paul laughed heartily, along with several other travelers who had joined them.

"In short, I really do not want to study engineering or some precise science. I'd rather learn about historical events. This is much more interesting," concluded Victor.

"Interesting and horizon-expanding," replied Paul, "but I can't remember when I last saw a newspaper ad with the caption 'Historian Wanted'. I can understand your father well, if he prefers that you study engineering or architecture at the *Technion*. By the way, where does your excellent English come from?"

Victor explained that he had been a pupil of the Jerusalem Hebrew College and added that in his extended family they spoke Hebrew, French, English and Arabic, but that he spoke Ladino with his grandparents.

"Ladino. What is Ladino?" Paul asked.

Victor explained proudly that Ladino was basically the Spanish of the 15th century, which, over time, was influenced by Hebrew and other languages. It became the language of the Jews who had been expelled from Spain and who settled in the Ottoman Empire, today's Greece, Bulgaria, and Turkey. "I thought that I had learned everything you need to know about Palestine, but it turns out that my education has holes like a Swiss cheese," thought Paul.

Victor expanded on his family history; he noted that for more than a hundred years, the Levy family was a synonym for reliable international banking, at least in this part of the Ottoman Empire. "My father met my mother in Tiberius. Her family had come to the city from Gibraltar about two hundred years ago. Thanks to my mother, I have a British passport. My father has a French passport, and because of his business, we have moved to Jerusalem."

❄ ❄ ❄

These and many other details about the history of Palestine were deposited during the past eight months in the various compartments of Paul's mind. In contrast to that pleasant winter day in Haifa, when his feet touched the ground in Palestine for the first time, he was now suffering in the hot, crowded passport control hall at the port of Tel Aviv.

Paul Roberts, dressed in the khaki uniform of the Palestine Police, had reported for duty at the port in preparation for the disembarkation of passengers from the Italian ship, the 'Adria'. He didn't just suffer from the heat and humidity that could not even be relieved by the occasional gusts of cool sea breeze. His work was simply mind-numbing but despite the frustrations and the difficult conditions in the tiny, glowing office, he persisted with the professional performance of his tasks. He insisted on casting a professional look at the daily CID list, which contained details and photos of suspects the police was searching for.

"Mr. Appelbaum, I am so pleased to welcome you again in Palestine! How nice, you have married again!!! Congratulations," he greeted with undisguised sarcasm the gentlemen with thinning hair, mid-thirties, tanned, of medium build and casually dressed, who submitted a handful of documents with unsteady hands, including a fresh marriage certificate.

Paul Roberts was familiar with this trick for smuggling immigrants, which the Jews were applying to bypass the restrictions on Jewish immigration to Palestine imposed by his government. "Legally, it is difficult to curb this phenomenon," the legal adviser of the Immigration Department clarified on a training day for border control officials. "We do not have enough staff to investigate every couple that arrives, check their documents, follow their integration in society and whether they actually live together; neither can we search all flats, open closets, and count the toothbrushes in the bathroom. It is disrespectful and inappropriate. We'll just have to accept the fact that a few hundred Jews, men and women with fake marriage certificates manage to enter the Mandate territory every year. As long as it's not a flood and only a few dozen a month, I see no reason to change the rules," he concluded.

The diesel engine clatter from the launches could be heard constantly in the background. The boats arrived every few minutes and hundreds of passengers stepped onto the pier; it was the usual human mix of the Trieste-Tel Aviv line.

Over time, Paul had learned to sort the new immigrants in his mind's eye and used to imagine where they wanted to go. From his perspective as an immigration official, there were no interesting or unusual cases among the 250 passengers on the 'Adria', except Zvi and Lina Appelbaum.

Most passengers were bourgeois refugees from Germany and Austria, noticeable by their formal clothing, including suits, ironed shirts and ties, which they persisted on wearing despite the oppressive heat and humidity.

Based on his experience, Paul assumed that most were intellectuals and professionals, among them a large number of doctors and renowned professors who would certainly try to settle in large cities such as Tel Aviv, Haifa and Jerusalem. Among the arrivals were also tourists, wealthy

Jews, mainly from the Baltic States, who wanted to explore what opportunities they might have for investments, but also for relocation.

In each group of incoming passengers, there were individual Jews with Palestinian travel documents who were returning from a business trip or studies in Europe.

Another unique group consisted of a few dozen young men and women, who called themselves "pioneers". They were almost all uniformly dressed in khaki. Everyone was excited; everyone was talking loudly, but they could not quite hide the tension and anxiety of the future that awaited them on some spartan kibbutz in a remote corner of Palestine.

As always, also this time Paul observed several girls who were travelling alone, polite and quiet, some of whom would be joining the pioneering groups and others who were going to settle in the large cities. A tall girl with black hair who had stepped on the dock among the last passengers, attracted Paul Roberts' trained eye. Her documents were in order with a valid entry permit. The name "Henrietta Landwehr" registered in Robert's brain for a few seconds, but then disappeared quickly among the crowd of faces and names of hundreds of 'Adria' passengers, whose documents he provided with an entry stamp.

The complete absence of Arab passengers was an integral part of the routine procedures at the port. This is probably explains why none of those present except perhaps Paul, would have actually viewed this as a strange phenomenon, considering that the majority of the inhabitants of Palestine were Arabs. The Arabs did not utilize the services of Tel Aviv Port. They insisted on entering Palestine through the port of Haifa or the land-border-crossings, fearing the vengeance of the Arab underground movement. Although the various Arab resistance movements fought endlessly among themselves, they made sure that the common policy of eliminating all those whom they saw as collaborators with Jews was fully implemented. Arrival in Palestine via the "Jewish" port of Tel Aviv was designated as such collaboration.

❄ ❄ ❄

The last passengers had finished having their papers checked and had proceeded into the terminal – a pretentious term for a large shed with corrugated iron roof, where dozens of frantic scenes of welcome, accompanied by kisses, hugs, tears and backslapping were being played out.

On the concrete dock next to the big crane, the only one in the port, the Thessaloniki stevedores were stacking the cargo from the 'Adria'. Besides the personal belongings of the passengers, a relatively large consignment of agricultural equipment from Poland, packaged in bulky, square wooden crates, was unloaded. The addresses in striking black color made it clear that the boxes were destined for the new cluster of kibbutz settlements in the *Yisre'el* Valley.

Paul suppressed a big yawn that had threatened to reach dimensions not fit for an official representative of the largest empire in the world. He played with the official stamp, which had landed hundreds of times during the day on documents of all types and was carrying the text "Palestine, entry, 9 August 1938" in three languages. Almost absent-mindedly, he took a piece of cloth, cleaned the stamp, and wondered if he should change the date for the next shift. "Today is Tuesday," he thought, "I don't work tomorrow. So, whoever is on duty should change the date. I have finished my shift and am done for today."

"Boring," he muttered to himself while he was cleaning the stamp; he was depressed because of the large gap between the exciting pictures of his dreams about adventures in the Orient and the gray reality of his current job. But the feeling of frustration and depression racing around in his head, was quickly suppressed by a surge of determination and initiative to change the situation.

"If a conversation with Appelbaum, the eternal bridegroom, is the highlight of my day, it is high time to change jobs. I've had it with this nonsense of border control and paperwork. Tomorrow I'll go to the police chief of the Jaffa District and enquire how one can be transferred to the Criminal Investigation Department, the CID. Actually, why not? I grasp languages quickly and speak quite good Hebrew already; I can even say a few sentences in Arabic and am quick witted. That's how I cottoned on to Appelbaum. I'm sure the CID will want me. Yes, detective, that's what I should be."

Paul's ingenuity was indeed well developed, but not well enough. He had correctly observed that Zvi Appelbaum was nervous and excited. But his assumption that it was because he, Paul, had discovered the fake marriage was completely wrong. Appelbaum's obvious nervousness had nothing whatsoever to do with the humiliating moments at the border control booth. Rather, it was the consignment of the large wooden crates, stacked on the ramp, which worried the serial groom Appelbaum. Although all actually held a variety of agricultural machinery, some of the crates contained twenty Polish-made machine guns that had been hidden by skilled hands in some deeply disguised compartments – an important inventory boost for the secret armory of the *Haganah*.

The discovery of such a supply would have meant a big blow for the procurement of the *Haganah*. But for Appelbaum the discovery of the secret cargo by customs officials or police would have cost him many years in the notorious Acre prison, following the enforcement of new, more stringent Mandate Government regulations.

No wonder then, that he only calmed down after the last box was stamped "approved" by Customs and loaded on a truck that left the port quickly.

German Air-base near Athens, Summer 1942

In-spite of the early hour, there was feverish activity on the large base, all because of a bold and unexpected visit from the British Royal Air Force. Ambulances and fire trucks, with sirens blaring and blue lights flashing, followed by trucks with rescue teams were racing in all directions. Thick clouds of smoke ascended from several points on the base, whirling in circles in a spectacular display similar to a tornado. This artificial nature display was caused by a couple of Messerschmitt 109 fighter aircraft with yellow nose cones, which were circling the airfield with engines roaring because they had arrived too late.

"I will personally see to it that the shift supervisor at the radar station lands in jail because he failed to notice the approaching bombers," said – rather, shouted Colonel Theodor Ravel into the phone connecting him directly to the *Luftwaffe* headquarters in Athens. "That idiot, this fool is apparently not able to distinguish between a flock of migratory birds and four B-25s. Thanks to that idiot, we are sitting ducks. It's a miracle that my forces have not been totally destroyed. Believe me, it was close."

The reason for Colonel Ravel's rage were four twin-engine RAF bombers, which had approached from the east a few feet above the treetops, while taking advantage of the rising sun's dazzling fireball, making them invisible to the soldiers of the base's anti-aircraft batteries.

A bombing run, lasting a mere 120 seconds, was enough to cause serious damage, including the destruction of at least ten Messerschmitt 109 fighters and Junkers 52 transport aircraft that were parking unprotected on the main runway.

Also, two fuel tanks were burning, billowing thick clouds of smoke into the air. The main runway and the side track were now pockmarked with deep potholes. Each bomber had dropped dozens of small bombs – some with a delay mechanism that made the work of the specialists in the bomb disposal squad especially dangerous.

During the attack, the British bombers were firing on anything that moved with heavy machine guns from turrets in the nose, fuselage, and tail of the aircraft.

Ravel's anger with the radar operator and the general chaos was fueled by fear and adrenaline. The attack had surprised him as well as the rest of the soldiers on the base. He had stormed out of his room to see what was happening. Why, all of a sudden, are explosions being heard, without warning or alarm?

The instant he bolted out of the building, he noticed one of the bombers flying so low that his cap was almost torn from his head, to soar away like the dead leaves that were scattered by the wind in all directions. A long burst of machine gun bullets, some with tracers, were spitting out of its tail; they came fast towards him, spraying dust and dirt, forcing him to jump into a filthy ditch full of garbage. "For the first time since the last war I'm in a crappy trench," he said with a mixture of anger and fear.

❄ ❄ ❄

"Captain, we have left the Nazis with a burning field. I see at least eight, no, ten fires," reported Hayim Cohen, the rear gunner over the intercom.

Cohen, a young Tel Avivian, who had always dreamed of becoming a pilot in the Royal Air Force, had to contend himself in meantime with the title 'Rear-Gunner B-25', because the British refused to train Jewish pilots from Palestine. "I made a Nazi officer with high-rank insignia on his shoulders jump. I saw him dive and hope the bastard was hit by my volley and doesn't come out of the hole into which he leapt."

"Keep your enthusiasm for the return flight," said Captain Bill McDonald, a tough Australian, who had accumulated thousands of flight hours in civil aviation on low-flying crop dusters. For him, daring bombing raids at tree height were mere routine.

"Red Section, this is Red Leader," McDonald said into the open radio network. "Well done. We've given them a surprise, if there ever was one. But it is too early to celebrate, because we are not done yet. Look out for German and Italian interceptors that are likely to start right now from assorted bases in the area to catch us on the way back."

Relaxed but still extremely vigilant, McDonald said a few words to his own team on the intercom: "We've copped some ack-ack shrapnel, but the plane is solid and it seems as if no critical systems are damaged. If you continue to be vigilant and dodge every *Kraut* who dares to get too close to us, we'll be sitting in the NAAFI in two hours, sipping hot chocolate, or, for that matter, even whisky. We deserve it."

❄ ❄ ❄

"That arsehole almost finished me off," cursed Ravel. He rose slowly out of the ditch into which he had jumped under the heavy machine-gun fire from the B-25, and cleaned the dirt off his uniform. "Is anyone here taking care of these trenches? They were probably dug by the Greeks way back in their war with the Italians ... unbelievable! This is supposed to be a *Luftwaffe* base."

"Where have we landed?! The trenches are full of garbage and no one cares about the rules. Everyone here suffers from exaggerated self-confidence, dangerous arrogance, lack of discipline and disregard for the rules."

Having informed the High Command in great detail by phone about his opinion of those responsible for the incident and after he and his men had finished their inspection of damage to his command area, Ravel sat down to compose a situation report for encryption by the impenetrable Enigma machine and urgent radio transmission to the *Abwehr* headquarters in a gray building on the Landwehrkanal in Berlin.

Top Secret
To: Admiral Canaris, chief of the Abwehr intelligence service.

In a daring daylight raid by the RAF, a plane of Squadron 200, which was supposed to take part in "Operation Plier Squeeze", has been damaged. The right engine was hit by shrapnel and must be replaced.

I have asked our home base in Frankfurt to send a replacement engine, but it is doubtful whether they have one in stock, so we may have to cannibalize one from another captured aircraft.

Another option is to secretly purchase an engine from the national airline of Switzerland, which uses aircraft of this type.

In my estimation, we can have the plane ready for takeoff within 24 hours of the engine's arrival, weather forecasts and moon phases permitting.

Meanwhile, I have given instructions to take advantage of the delay for additional training of the "Plier Squeeze" unit, especially to improve the parachute skills of the two foreign volunteers.

After the incident this morning, I ask for a thorough investigation of all sources to determine whether the attack of the four B-25 was pure coincidence. I would like to check the possibility whether information about "Plier Squeeze" was leaked to the enemy, so that today's attack was meant to harm our capability.

I fear that the British Secret Service has an agent in the entourage of Haj Amin al-Husseini, who is based in Berlin. I want to reiterate, that I had insisted from the start of the planning phase for "Plier Squeeze" to marginalize our Arab allies, the Mufti's people, because of the operational sensitivity here. Unfortunately, my recommendations were rejected because those higher up decided on a policy of full cooperation.

Heil Hitler,
Colonel Ravel, Commander, Squadron 200

Ravel reread the telegram, to make sure that the text was an accurate expression of his thoughts, but did not sound too sharp, in order not to harm his future promotion opportunities. He corrected a word here, a point there, signed at the bottom of the page, and handed the telegram to the radio officer.

"What I need now is to calm down with a strong coffee and a hearty breakfast," he told the officer, then left the building and walked thoughtfully toward the flight crews' dining room in the terminal building. He wondered if there was a connection between the concept of flight safety and that final word 'terminal'.

On the way to the dining room, he recalled a chance meeting yesterday at the Officers' Club with his childhood friend, Walter Rauff. Rauff, who had meanwhile moved on with his life, displaying a high SS-rank, told him some vague story about a task that had been assigned to him: "Appropriate treatment of the Jews from Egypt and Palestine." Rauff gave further explanations about a group that he managed called "*Einsatzgruppe Aegypten*[27]" that was supposed to join the armed forces of Rommel himself, who was advancing on Alexandria. But Ravel, who could not hide his lack of interest in this matter and did not want to give the impression as if he was listening, could not remember much of Rauff's explanation. However, the unexpected encounter with Rauff and his strange talk about 'treatment of the Jews' caused Ravel to remember his good friend Herbert Weiss.

His guilty conscience pricked him instantly when the name Weiss surfaced, perhaps because he was ashamed that he had ignored their courageous friendship for fear that any support for Weiss and his family could have hindered his promotion in the *Luftwaffe*. "Actually, a charming and

---

[27]German for "Taskforce Egypt". *Einsatzgruppen* were special paramilitary SS units, deployed as death-squads in the wake of regular troops, to commit mass killings of Jews and other targets of "unwanted life". Their ethnic cleansing type activities were particularly notorious in Eastern Europe.

honest man," thought Ravel, and he wondered why he needed the word 'actually'. "Weiss is not only honest and reliable, but also a German patriot and brave; so why this expression 'actually'?!"

❄ ❄ ❄

As soon as Ravel was let in on "Operation Plier Squeeze", which was to be executed by his men, who were now assembled in Hangar 12, an uneasy feeling had overcome him. It was something indefinable. A kind of feeling that was based on a combination of data from the field, the scope and objective of the mission as well as an intuitive, fundamental doubt about the ability of the Mufti's men to successfully accomplish their mission, despite their boasting about their bravery, which they spread everywhere.

So far he had actually not understood how Berlin could have been cajoled into such a big operation, including the allocation of a submarine, U-372, for the landing of supplies on the coast of Palestine. His unease increased the more he immersed himself in the operational instructions. "This is a disaster in search of a place and a time," he thought. "This place is Palestine and the time is probably the day on which we will undertake the operation."

❄ ❄ ❄

Hangar 12 was situated on the edge of the base, at the end of the second runway, partially hidden by a green pine forest. The constant presence of a military police patrol supported by a security officer made sure that only personnel with special permits could enter the closed area. "There's something mysterious happening at the end of runway 270", was a rumor spreading on the base. As is normal with supply troops, who are exposed to unusual activity, curiosity grows with every crumb of new information.

In contrast to most of the soldiers who had to rely on rumors, Hans, the driver of the base's kitchen supply truck had access to credible information. "It is totally impossible to enter the hangar," Hans shared the information he had collected during his work, with his comrades. "A paratrooper in combat gear, with a round helmet, you know, not a normal army helmet, with a loaded Schmeisser submachine gun, stands guard at the entrance. They don't even let me into the building."

According to him, the guard allows him to drive his Opel Blitz truck right up to the door of the hangar. There he unloads the provisions off the truck and the users of the hangar carry them inside. "I tried to peek through the door, but a large tarp covers the opening. Given the amount of food that I bring every morning, I estimate that there are about twenty people inside. They get the best of food, according to the food list for flight crews."

"So what are they, paratroopers or pilots?" Asked his comrades.

"No idea," Hans continued with his report, while obviously enjoying the curiosity of his comrades and his new status in the group. "Helga, the Operations officer in the control tower," Hans went on, inspired by his audience's attentiveness, "yes, the one who sucks my cock when I keep on supplying her with oranges, sausages and chocolate, told me that a twin-engine plane had landed two days ago during the night shift. The plane had not identified itself by radio contact; rather its arrival was announced by urgent telex and it got permission to land using a green fluorescent signal fired from the control tower."

Hans interrupted his rant to increase the tension in his audience.

"For those who did not understand, I'll explain it. This aircraft had its radio switched off, to avoid being intercepted by the *Tommies*. How shall I put it, something very mysterious is going on there. An aircraft lands without as much as a peep from its radio. Helga watched it from the tower with strong binoculars and could not see any identification marks. She only noticed that it was silver colored and not painted in military camouflage. The plane taxied to the end of the runway directly into Hangar 12. That's what Helga told me and I'm sure there's something going on, but who knows."

Tel Aviv, Summer 1942

The small lightbulb spread a faint light in the narrow, sparsely furnished room. It was equipped with a closet without doors, the front of which was covered with a loose curtain and a tiny table that had one leg reinforced with a thick plywood triangle at its base. Four men of varying ages were sitting on assorted chairs around the table. There was an air of exhaustion and fatigue in the room.

Three of those present wore rumpled, almost shabby, khaki colored clothing, which merely emphasized the gloomy atmosphere even more. Only the clothes of the youngest among them displayed any fashion sense. The paint on the walls varied from white in the middle to yellowish from dirt near the ceiling and the floor. Lime bubbles on the walls pointed to water damage from the rain of the last winter. The blackout curtains only partially covered the lone window frame and a gentle breeze that hardly penetrated the hot room.

"Let's close the windows and curtains, as it should be," suggested one of the participants. "It's not worth getting into trouble with some nosy civil defense inspector. He might possibly even call the police."

The scaremonger's proposal met with derisive reactions and contentions that, anyway, the window was directly overlooking the courtyard; so the probability of an inspector coming into the yard and noticing the light was zero.

"Come on," one of them ended the discussion, "look at the other buildings, you can see pinpoints of light on almost every floor. The British blackout rules and the Tel Aviv heat in July-August are incompatible."

"Have a look at that! Our people are worth an elegant apartment on Shenkin Street," joked the youngest in the group, who was absorbed in his newspaper and had shown no interest in the debate about the blackout. "Look, you can read it for yourselves." He pointed to a large advertisement on an inside page. "Here is a listing by a builder who sells a house with two luxury apartments for £1,850 in the *Allenby* neighborhood. Tomorrow I will denounce Cohen and Ronin to the police, then buy myself two homes and even keep some change."

Shimon Bahar, who, despite his relative youth, was considered the fastest runner in the underground organization, obviously enjoyed his joke and gave his edition of the Haaretz newspaper to the person on his right. "The Palestine Police have announced a reward of £1000 to anyone, who delivers one of the following fugitives: Joshua Cohen, Nehemiah Tornberg and Zvi Ronin, suspected of the attempted assassination on April 22 of Inspector Morton, Deputy Police Commissioner of the *Lod* district police," Aaron Levi read out aloud.

"Look at the beautiful photos these British arseholes are publishing of them," Shlomo Frankel tried to joke. He was stout, casually dressed, and sweating. He glanced over Aaron Levi's shoulder at the item. "I wonder if Morton and the detectives also have our pictures and I'm really curious about how we look on these mug-shots." Tired looks from his colleagues made it clear to Frankel that his humor was not quite appropriate on this occasion and at this time.

"On April 22, an attack on Inspector Morton, the *Lod* district Deputy Police Commissioner failed," Levi continued reading the report, in which the newspaper took the trouble to explain to their readers the background and the circumstances of the British police announcement. “At 8:20 a.m., a bomb exploded near *Sarona*, while Inspector Morton was travelling in his official car on the main road to Haifa. The car was occupied by Morton, his wife and another British policeman. The car and several buildings were damaged, but no one was hurt.”

“Some report!” Noted Gershon Zisovich, the oldest in the group, sarcastically. “This busy little reporter forgot to mention only one thing, namely the fact that Morton was the officer, who six months earlier cold-bloodedly murdered Yair Stern in the Svorai family home on Misrahi Street. So, neither God nor an Arab criminal planted the bomb in Guenther’s orchard, but we did. We will catch him, this son of a bitch Morton and settle with him. He is not only a murderer, but also a liar, because he claimed without batting an eyelid that he had shot Yair while he was trying to escape. Yuck!” Zisovich spat symbolically. “What a pig.”

A heavy silence descended on the room.

“Yes,” remarked Levi finally, “we have an account to settle with him, but in the meantime, it is unfortunately the CID that is winning this tit-for-tat game by putting huge bounties on the heads of those of our boys who were involved in the action against Morton, while continuing to systematically destroy our organization.” Levi’s thoughtful words annoyed Bahar. “Levi, just speak for yourself now!” He hissed angrily. “I can’t bear such defeatist talk. Never, but never, will we surrender. They can follow us to the end of the world, but we will fight to the last man.”

“Bahar, I am sorry to have to say this, but we’re not far away from this thing about the ‘last man’,” Levi replied sarcastically, “and, correct me if I’m wrong, when I think that, apart from the four of us, as well as a cell each in Jerusalem and in Haifa, plus some supporters on the streets of *Binyamina*, there are no longer any active members. We are the last, so that we are already fighting, more or less, down to the last man."

❄ ❄ ❄

Bahar did not contradict Levi's summation. He himself had realized how serious the situation was, which would clearly emerge from his deeply depressing report he had prepared for the meeting.

"The British police, the CID, are relentless; they recruit informants and sources in all areas," he reported to his friends. "The British are active in all cities and settlements. They are very efficient – like a lice comb. It is true that the British have not yet wised up to our cell, but just this week they ambushed the arms stockpile near *Givat Shaul* in Jerusalem. A member of the cell, Yisrael, had gone there to look after the weapons. The police surrounded the shed; there was a brief gunfight and Yisrael was seriously injured. He is in the Augusta Victoria Military Hospital under heavy guard. One of the nurses at the hospital told us that he is unconscious; his condition is critical and the doctors give him no chance of survival."

A dark silence filled the room.

"The three fugitives – Torenberg, Cohen and Ronin – find it difficult to obtain shelter," Baher continued with his report. "So far, none of those few who are still helping us have been tempted to go to the police, snitch on them and earn a tidy sum. But I am afraid that it will happen soon."

"How do you know? Why do you think that?" urged Zisovich.

"Look, I'm reluctant to admit it, but I sense a serious weakening in the level of support for us," Bahar tried to explain. "Those who sympathize and support us have difficulties in understanding the principles and methods of our organization. You have no idea what palpitations I have when I call on someone who is registered with me as an activist. I don't know what to expect when I come to a meeting – do I expect there a Jewish sympathizer who offers me a cup of tea, or a disgruntled Jew who has alerted the police, so that Morton and his detectives are waiting for me in his living room."

Levi nodded. "Bahar's not the only one who thinks so."

"Wait, I'm not done yet," Bahar continued. "Shmuel Cohen, the shoe retailer from *Ramat Gan*, was happy to help us wholeheartedly until recently, support us financially, provide alibis and find hiding places. Now he assaults me with screams. 'You're worse than the worst criminals! You have evolved from freedom fighters to simple robbers. Heartless Jewish gangsters. Two weeks ago, one of your people tried to get a donation from my uncle Shlomo Prinz, who has a large shoe store on Nahalat-Binyamin Street. He refused, and bang! That same night you broke into the store and stole his entire stock. Prinz is not insured and you have not merely destroyed his business, but also his life. You are criminals,'" he yelled. "Say, Levi," Bahar turned to Aaron, "that shoe shop, Prinz, on Nachalat-Binyamin, was that your handiwork?"

Levi identified with the bitter words of the *Ramat Gan* businessman. In recent months, more and more difficulties in raising funds had to be overcome; thus the organization was forced to extort money from wealthy merchants and even break into banks or rob post offices.

All eyes turned to Levi, because fund-raising, even by force, was his domain. "Prinz? Nahalat-Binyamin? No, why?" he countered. "It is neither my work, nor that of my unit. I can't help it, that we don't have a monopoly on the Tel Aviv burglar-and-thieves market. We compete with real criminals. Bona Fide bandits".

Laughter broke out in the room and everyone urged Aaron to proceed with stories of his squad's adventures. In these difficult days, which the organization was going through, such stories were probably the only way to put a smile on the faces of the most persecuted members of the Jewish population.

"Listen to this joke," Bahar continued in an attempt to maintain the more relaxed atmosphere. "A visitor to the Jerusalem zoo sees a little girl leaning into the jackal enclosure. Suddenly, the jackal grabs her by the cuff of her jacket and tries to pull her inside his cage, right under the eyes of her screaming parents. The guy runs to the cage and hits the jackal with a powerful punch square on the nose. Whimpering from the pain the jackal jumps back letting go of the girl, and the guy brings her back to her terrified parents, who thank him profusely. An English newspaper reporter has watched the whole event. He says to the visitor, 'Sir, this was the most gallant and brave thing I've ever seen a man do.' The visitor replies, 'Why, it was nothing, really. The jackal was behind bars. I just saw this little girl in danger and did what I thought was right.' The reporter says, 'Well, I'll make sure this doesn't go unnoticed. I'm a journalist, and tomorrow's paper will have this story on the front page. So, tell me something about yourself.' The visitor replies, 'I live in Tel Aviv. I arrived from Poland recently because I am a Zionist, but am currently unemployed.' The journalist leaves. The following morning his paper reports the story under the following headline:

"RIGHT-WING ILLEGAL IMMIGRANT ASSAULTS NATIVE PALESTINIAN AND STEALS HIS LUNCH."

The thoughtful chuckles in the room made it clear that, at least for the moment, the depression, which had threatened to engulf the remnant of the *Stern Gang* had turned into determination.

❄ ❄ ❄

The voice of the newsreader that came from a radio in the adjacent apartment through the open window in the room was a little louder than good neighborly relations would usually have allowed.

"What, it's a quarter past eight already? Let's hear the news," Frankel called out.

The news headlines were mainly about reports of fighting around the world:

In Russia, the Nazi troops were marching on towards Stalingrad and had also reinforced their positions in the south of the country.

The Chinese government reported a massive attack by the Japanese army and appealed to the US and the UK to provide them with urgent food supplies and military equipment. The report noted that supplies to the Chinese military were already on their way, with the help of an air bridge over the Himalayas and convoys of trucks and porters on the "Burma Road", a path of about 1300 km, which connected British India with western China.

Two more British warships were sunk by the German *Luftwaffe* in Malta; meanwhile an Italian naval commando had entered the port of Gibraltar and blown up an American tanker.

In the Pacific, the Americans and the Japanese continued to fight over an island with such a strange name that even the announcer had trouble pronouncing.

In the western desert, it was relatively quiet; the new commander of the 8th Army, General Bernard Montgomery, expressed confidence that the front-line British Empire armed forces, who had just received new American equipment, would be able to stop Rommel's *Afrika Korps*.

In Madagascar, British forces had completed the conquest of the island from the French Vichy troops in order to prevent a Japanese takeover of that strategic island.

And in local news, the announcer reported dryly the end of legal proceedings against Yitzchak Trachtengut, one of the leading wholesalers in the country, who had embezzled enormous quantities of commodities to be sold on the black market. According to the indictment, Trachtengut had managed to spirit away 7 tons of sugar crystals, 276 kilos of sugar and 1.5 tons of wheat. Given his advanced age of 65 years, the judge imposed a penalty of £600 or six months imprisonment.

"I'm so glad that they caught Trachtengut," Levi commented. "What a stingy miser. Of such people, my grandmother used to say, 'One who expects support or a donation from a miser is like an angler trying to catch fish in the desert.' Truth be told, it isn't an original quote from my grandmother, but I think she took it from Shlomo Ibn Gabirol[28]. "No matter. Six months ago, we turned to this millionaire with a request to donate something for our struggle. He stubbornly refused and even threatened us with a police complaint."

"Do you know what makes me mad," interrupted Frankel. "Look how Tel Aviv celebrates as if there is no war in the world. The billboards are full with posters for theater performances and concerts. In cinemas, people fight over tickets and cafes are packed; all seem happy and content. Despite the alleged scarcity of different items, there is a shopping frenzy!"

"Speaking of shopping frenzy," Zisovich suddenly piped up, "Bahar, you look like a male model. Tell me, have you raided a clothing store?"

Bahar stood up, bowed, turned around and walked like on a catwalk during a fashion show. "Nice, what? I'm tired of dressing like a poor Kibbutznik who is dependent on the

---

[28]Famous Jewish philosopher and poet, 11th century Spain.

collective clothing storeroom. So I popped into 'Klausner' on Ahad Ha'am Street. He now sells long trousers for 30 *Grush*, shorts for 25 and thin corduroys suitable for summer, for only 49 *Grush*. A bargain." Bahar twirled around once more to the amusement of his friends.

"By the way, have you noticed that there is something unique in Tel Aviv? Does anyone know what I mean?" Asked Zisovich. His friends looked at each other, Levi raised an eyebrow, but no one answered. "Look at what is happening in playgrounds and on the streets. This is a young city. You see many children, many young mothers, but really rarely do you see grandparents walking with their grandchildren."

Audible consent was heard in the room.

"Well, what do you want? This town is just a little over thirty years old."

The conversation about Tel Aviv and the few minutes of radio news broadcast had been sufficient to disperse the tension in the room.

"You know, every morning at five twenty-five, the radio station broadcasts a special news bulletin for the Australian troops," Frankel recounted. "Just think about it. Tens of thousands of men leave their families and businesses to be on the other side of the planet to fight in the name of a king, who had transported their ancestors to Australia on convict ships. It's a crazy world."

"How should I be able to distinguish at night between British and Australian soldiers without their big hats on their heads, only displaying regimental insignia on their shoulders, or have we even declared war against the nice Australians," Levi asked himself aloud, trying to guide the discussion back to the matters at hand. "Should we regard the Australians as enemies just because they are wearing British uniforms?"

His provocative words were met with silence.

"A wise philosopher once said that war is not about who is right, but who is left," Levi added as an attempt to penetrate the wall of hostility, which he had built with his own words.

Question marks on faces were looking at him from three directions.

"I don't know what to make of that," Bahar said in a mocking voice.

After about ten seconds of silence, the other three broke into loud laughter simultaneously.

"Bully for you, our historian and philosopher," noted Bahar and applauded.

Again, it was Zisovich who steered the conversation in a different direction. "The radio broadcasts news in Hebrew, English, Arabic, French, Turkish, Romanian, and Serbo-Croatian during the day," counted Zisovich proudly. "In winter, when I was hiding in the Dizengoff Street apartment, the one attorney Kahanov had made available to us as a safe house, I was forced to become their constant listener from five o'clock in the morning until midnight. Since then, I know their schedule by heart."

"Speaking of lawyers," interrupted Bahar, "I think Kahanov is the only normal lawyer I know. There is something in this occupation that attracts crooks and shitheads. Kahanov told me a joke making the rounds in their circles. A rabbit walks around in the forest. Suddenly a big lion appears and licks its bum. 'Leo, what are you doing? You should be ashamed of yourself,' the rabbit yells at him. 'Sorry', replies the Lion and licks his arse once again. 'Stop it, you're crazy!' screams the rabbit. 'Awfully sorry,' apologized the lion, 'but the last prey I ate was a lawyer and I'll do anything to get rid of this taste.'"

Laughter broke out in the room and echoed off the walls of the surrounding buildings. "Guys, jokes aside, but we need to concentrate and go," Levi said, wiping a laughing tear from his right eye. "We are not here to tell jokes and gossip like old spinsters in the cafes on Hayarkon or Ben Yehuda streets."

Levi ignored the cool reaction and continued with his instructions. "I would ask that you pay attention to safety. We are together here for too long, which is dangerous for all of us." We'll meet again in a week. It is also important to avoid being tailed. If necessary, don't hesitate to roam the streets, even for half a day as if you are unemployed and time does not matter; just be sure that you arrive at the meeting without a tail and leave it without a tail. We can hold the next meeting of our diminished movement on a single paving stone opposite Dr. Frank's hotdog stand on Mughrabi Square. You know, that *Yekke*[29] sausage dealer who sells the best sausages in the whole country. So, stick to the rules, don't be careless and remember the old adage: 'It is the invisible detective into whose trap you'll fall.'"

A few minutes later, after the completion of details, the distribution of funds and the allocation of tasks, the participants left, separately of course, and each went his way.

Before he left the apartment, Levi made sure that his small Smith & Wesson pistol was secure in its little holster on his right calf. In recent weeks, his feeling intensified, that a fatal CID ring was drawing ever closer around him. "I won't give Morton and his henchmen the pleasure of gunning me down like a duck in a shooting gallery," he told his colleagues, "and a calf holster is a classic place to hide a weapon, especially now that the trouser legs are so wide."

Levi had originally planned to take a *sherut*[30] run by the *Kesher* Company on Rothschild Boulevard, but at some point during an attempt to shake off a potential tail,

---

[29]Yekke was and is a nickname for a Jew of German cultural background
[30]Collective taxi.

a slight suspicion began to gnaw at him that someone was really following him. "Suspicion causes fear," Bahar, the surveillance expert had explained at one point.

To be sure, Levi walked to the bus station, convinced himself that he was "clean" and caught the second last bus to Jerusalem. "If everything goes according to plan, tomorrow afternoon I'll get together with Tamar, whom I haven't seen for two weeks," he mused, and dozed off. His sleep was restless on the hard wooden bench of the bus and he wondered when *Esched*, *Shachar*, *Hamekascher* and *Drom Yehudah*[31] would amalgamate into a cooperative, so that we would finally get buses with comfortable, padded seats, like the ones in American movies.

---

[31]Public Transport companies, operating busses in various parts of the Palestine, later to merge into Egged, a huge nation-wide bus company.

Jerusalem, December 1938

Tamar stood in the middle of the polished dance floor of the Cafe “Rehaviah”, happy, cheerful, hot and sweaty. Her stormy applause expressed her enthusiasm for the “Blue Ribbon Swingers” band, which had just finished a set of fast, dizzying melodies. “What rhythm, what harmony. How I love Swing! And this band is really great. It was so much fun, I could start all over again,” she shouted in Wolfgang’s ear. Wolfgang gave her a look he had practiced for many hours in front of the bathroom mirror while gently embracing her waist. In the last film he had seen during a matinee in the “Zion” cinema, a similar look had helped Clark Gable melt the hearts of three women, which had impressed Wolfgang tremendously. The Clark Gable look required a slight raising of his right eyebrow, an almost invisible move of the head to the right and a big smile that exposed two rows of white teeth.

From the other side of the dance floor Alisa gave Tamar a wink. She was looking over Nabil’s shoulder, who was embracing her affectionately.

“You move and dance like a goddess,” Wolfgang shouted over the noise of the revelers, after he had accomplished the Gable look. “Leni Riefenstahl is an ironing-board by comparison.”

"Yikes! Leni Riefenstahl is a lousy Nazi-bitch. If anything, please compare me with Marlene Dietrich," laughed Tamar. The warm embrace and passionate kiss on the cheek proved that she liked the compliment as well as its author.

Who knows, maybe the Hollywood-style look had helped.

Tamar had enjoyed every minute. The bustle of the revelers, the rousing music, Wolfgang's love and affection; four or five glasses of alcohol that flowed in her veins, had also helped paint the world in optimistic pink. This momentary happiness made her forget her deep concern about the fate of her parents, who had remained in Vienna.

"Henrietta, my dear, the situation is getting worse. The decrees against the Jews get aggravated and every day new injunctions are issued," her father had written in his last letter, which was provided with a stamp featuring Hitler's head. The letter had just this week landed on her desk. "We had lodged applications for entry permits from dozens of countries, but all were rejected," he wrote in his precise style, which he had adapted while serving in the military of his Majesty, the Emperor Franz Josef, during the First World War. "One possible solution is a boat ticket to Shanghai, where you don't need a visa, but now there is a war raging between China and Japan, so that all ship voyages to Shanghai have been canceled. We are now considering immigration to Rhodesia. Can you imagine your old father, the textile merchant, as a farmer in Africa? But the chances of obtaining the necessary documents are minute. We console ourselves with the fact that you are in Jerusalem, your sister is in Brooklyn and that you are both happy and secured."

The letters arrived once a week and each one hit Tamar hard. When her eyes darted between the lines wandering back and forth, she was again Henrietta Landwehr from Vienna, who empathized with the suffering of her parents;

her powerlessness, not to be able to help them in their hour of need caused her despair.

Four months had passed since she had left Vienna.

Again and again, the image of her parents surfaced in her memory – two small, elderly people dressed in gray, waving goodbye to their younger daughter, whom they might never see again, on the platform of the Vienna Central Station where the walls were decorated with Nazi flags.

In the long letters that she had sent them, she tried to report only joyous events. She avoided descriptions of the hardships, ignored the frustrations and long moments when she had been on the verge of collapse. During these months, far away from home, she realized how much she missed them and how deeply she loved them. She had grown up in a strict home, full of restrictions and prohibitions, where feelings were rarely expressed. Nevertheless, it was filled with lots of love.

Now, because of world events, she and her sister had left their home, leaving behind old parents who were tired and exhausted from the constant struggle for existence, under a hostile regime, in an environment where they had become undesirables. These four months of independence in Palestine, far from home, had toughened her up. The spoiled Henrietta from the eighth district of Vienna had become the assertive Tamar from the nursing school. "Necessity is the mother and the father of all inventions and changes," Grandpa Siegfried used to say. The reality of her new life without parents, without support, and the need to shape her own life, had only accelerated her personal development.

She replaced her natural suspiciousness, which she had inherited from her father, with cautious optimism. "I think the best of everyone until they prove otherwise to me," she once told Alisa. She had quickly discovered that a small smile could open doors. But she had also learned to insist on her rights and to defend her position – a useful trait in a hierarchical institution such as a nursing school. But during the short nights between tedious work shifts and long studies, Tamar felt the burden of the physical and emotional price she paid. "I am glad that I have a loving man like Wolfgang," she pondered. Just the thought of him spread a mischievous smile on her face. "It's great that you can occasionally interrupt the grinding and grueling routine with a good party."

❄ ❄ ❄

Many of the regulars in the Cafe "Rehaviah", who had come to enjoy their usual Friday afternoon "five o'clock tea", were among the growing community of immigrants from Germany, the *Yekkes* as they were called. This Friday was, coincidentally, the seventh day of Hanukkah, which this year occurred two days before Christmas thereby contributing to the festive mood. A few of them – including Tamar – could speak Hebrew fluently. But most of them preferred to speak German, after failing in the attempt, to get on top of this difficult Semitic language, written from right to left, with its guttural sounds and letters. This explains why the German conversation between Wolfgang and Tamar attracted no particular attention.

The idea, to celebrate Christmas and Hanukkah in the Cafe "Rehaviah" with a noisy afternoon dance party "like in Europe," came from Wolfgang.

"Sure, lovely," responded Tamar to his suggestion. A free weekend, that interrupted the tedious routine of the Hadassah nursing school, where Matron Landsmann dominated the lives of the students almost 24 hours a day with her Prussian style, was a rarity, a gift from heaven for Tamar and her friend Alisa.

"I finish classes one hour before you, and I'll catch up with you later in Cafe "Rehaviah". I have a date with Nabil, to meet him at the Nashashibis in *Sheikh Jarr'ah*,"[32] Alisa arranged with Tamar.

Wolfgang was waiting for Tamar at the hospital exit, beside the "*Hamekascher*" number 9 bus stop. Heavy black clouds were drifting slowly in the icy wind above Mount Scopus and the Mount of Olives. They floated towards the Jordan Valley and the Dead Sea, while sometimes hiding the sun, so that they painted the city in a gray winter coat, which so charmed the painters from Europe.

"This cloud looks like a rabbit" Wolfgang repeated a game from his childhood. "Here's one that looks like the roaring MGM lion."

Those waiting for the bus were a mixture of many young and older students, faculty and administrative staff. All huddled together in the half-open shelter, looking for refuge from the cold wind. Two female students – one pretty, her friend a bit chubby, but still absolutely appealing – studied Wolfgang with appraising glances; he was standing slightly away, disregarding the weather. Their glances admired his tall figure, his broad shoulders in the old leather jacket and the sloppy woolen cap that had seen better days. In the strong Jerusalem wind, the cap barely managed to reign in his shock of fair hair.

In the not too distant past, before he had met Tamar, such a situation would have embarrassed him. But the events of recent months and his beautiful, pleasant love story with Tamar had made him mature, so that he simply accepted what his father had been claiming for years – that he was a young man, handsome and attractive. He looked at the two young women with a tiny smile. "Until recently, I would

---

[32]An East Jerusalem neighborhood, with a predominantly Arab population

have lowered my eyes humbly and been embarrassed, only risking a glance from below," he thought with satisfaction.

The two giggled behind their hands and mumbled something unintelligible about the steel-gray eyes and the pretty profile of his face. Then they rushed to the end of the queue of passengers who were about to board the bus that had just arrived. The bus drove off and disappeared in a white cloud of smoke. Wolfgang recognized immediately that it had a problem with excessive oil consumption. He noticed the smiling faces of the two girls who were sitting in the back row and looking at him through the slightly dirty window until the bus was gone around the next bend. He was alone again and continued to wait for his Tamar until she would come out of the hospital.

The Old City of Jerusalem, the dome of the Omar mosque on the Temple Mount, as well as a variety of church spires and minarets were clearly visible from the summit of Mount Scopus. A cacophony of chiming bells and muezzin calls rose up from the old city. Scattered groups of houses, some new and shiny, stood out from the fields between Mount Scopus and the Jerusalem within the walls. A few brave, early flowering cyclamen grew among the rocks on the roadside, giving the cold air some beautiful purple flowers. Wolfgang watched the light vehicle traffic on the road to Jericho. Some police officers and a contingent of soldiers, supported by an armored car with two machine guns, were checking vehicles and passengers. A little congestion had been building up, but was moving slowly and steadily forward.

Last week, when he took a spontaneous trip with Tamar to Jericho and the Dead Sea, the checkpoint at *Abu Dis* was manned by soldiers of the Scottish "Black Watch" regiment. Wolfgang and Tamar noticed immediately that, in contrast to the tense and nervous behavior the soldiers usually displayed at this checkpoint, they smiled this time and were incredibly friendly. "Where are you heading? To

Jericho?" Asked the sergeant who had stuck his head into the spacious Packard which Wolfgang had borrowed from his father. "Have a look at this," the sergeant said with genuine admiration, after he had checked Wolfgang and Tamar's identity cards. He noticed the radiant faces of the two young people, where every look they exchanged, every gesture, clearly made it obvious that they loved each other. "Here we have a pair that is a little different than usual. It's nice to see that there are some like you in this crazy place."

He returned the documents with a wide gesture that suggested, "Go ahead and have a good trip," accompanied by an even wider smile. "Take good care. Although the road is open, try and connect anyway to a military lorry or some other vehicle. Just the other day Arab terrorists had laid an ambush on this road near the slope to the Hostel of the Good Samaritan. The driver, incidentally an Arab, was seriously injured. Not that it mattered to these bastards. This gang was eliminated, but maybe there are others in the area. Well then, keep your eyes open and have a lot of fun," he said, tapping on the thick tin roof of the Packard, as if to indicate "on your way".

"Excuse me, Sergeant," Wolfgang turned to the sergeant in perfect English, "You look as if you're, well, having a bit of fun and celebrating. What's up?"

"We are going home to Scotland. We've completed a year's combat mission against Arab insurgents. We've already finalized the transfer to the Royal Artillery Regiment and this is our last shift in this cursed place, where, for some reason I don't understand even if you kill me, every crank in history – from Moses to Jesus – traipsed around. Take care and enjoy yourselves."

They did actually have a good time in Jericho and made sure that they perpetuated every happy moment with photos taken by Wolfgang's small Kodak camera; often they even asked passers-by to photograph them together as a couple. They had lunch – sliced chicken on fresh, warm Pita bread, with a big salad and delicious lemonade, which was freshly squeezed before their eyes from large, juicy, fragrant lemons – in a typical garden restaurant in Jericho next to a brook. Unlike other couples who were sitting across from each other, Wolfgang and Tamar sat on the same side of the table, holding hands, cuddling and whispering. They skipped the visit to the *Tel*[33], which contained the oldest city in the world, and drove straight to the new hotel on the north shore of the Dead Sea, the *Kalia* beach, which was known in Jerusalem as a haven for lovers who were not necessarily married to each other.

Though the sun was already setting in the west and cool air was blowing from the mountains, they changed into swimsuits, ran into the cold water, bopping like corks on the oily Dead Sea water, shouting for joy but also with a little pain from scratches and minor wounds which burned like fire because of the high salt content. But that was a week ago, which had quickly faded away, accompanied by some grief; "Such is young love," his mother commented with a smile.

Now Wolfgang was on Mount Scopus, in the shadow of the number 9 bus shelter where he sought refuge from the wind gusts that had developed into a winter storm, as he waited for his beloved Tamar, who for him, would always be Henrietta.

"I'm sorry, but I need the car tonight," his father had reacted somewhat annoyed at his request to borrow the Packard again tonight. "Tomorrow is Christmas Eve; I have a thousand and one things to do, not only for the midnight mass, but also in general for the festival on Sunday. By the way, we are planning a picnic with our relatives from

---

[33]An archeological hill, containing ancient settlements.

Sarona, the Wennagels. It would also be very nice, if you could help me with the Christmas preparations, instead of going out with your girlfriend."

But Wolfgang insisted on spending every free minute with Tamar, whose limited free time was squeezing their love story into a straightjacket of time pressure dictated by the nursing school. He recognized her steps as soon as she came out of the building. Even in the thick woolen skirt, wrapped in a heavy, military style coat, Tamar appeared to him glamorous and beautiful like a movie star. He caught her with a long, strong embrace from which they had to free her forcefully, not in anger, but with love. "Careful, you are crushing me."

In the meantime, the bus stop was filling up with passengers, but until the arrival of the bus Wolfgang and Tamar remained standing at the side of the bus shelter, snuggling and hugging as he had his back to the wind, wrapping Tamar in his open coat, her hands tucked under his jacket, stroking his back.

On the second to last wooden bench in the bus, as it slowly went down the winding road from Mount Scopus, they exchanged reports about the events of the past few days between whispering sweet nothings.

"Enough already with German. Here, in the land of Israel, the Hebrew speaks Hebrew," stated, almost scolded a youth who was sitting in front of them dressed in khaki pants, white shirt and leather jacket.

"My Hebrew is so-so" Wolfgang responded in Hebrew in a serious tone of voice, leaving his hand casually on Tamar's shoulder. "I'm barely two months in the country."

Tamar could hardly suppress her laughter, which would have betrayed her opinion about the dialogue between Wolfgang and someone who was apparently a member of an organization determined to realize the vision of the founders of Zionism. Among other things, they worked intensively to get Hebrew generally accepted as the everyday spoken language in the country. Pushing her hair aside, she buried her head in Wolfgang's chest, so as not to burst out laughing.

Wolfgang's slow response had an almost magical effect on the nag in the leather jacket. Spontaneously, he gave up his hostility and began a friendly conversation. "Say, aren't you from Breslau? Aren't we casually acquainted from the *Blau-Weiss* Center in Breslau?" The promoter of the Hebrew language wanted to know. Now, after Wolfgang's explanation, he had switched to German.

"I doubt that," Wolfgang replied. "I come from a small community in Baden-Baden, you know, on the other side of Germany. Also, I am a member of *Maccabi Hatza'ir*. Interesting that you are not the first who confuses me with someone from Breslau. But I'm told that the one I am being confused with is not a *Yekke*, but a Polish Jew, one of those *Ostjuden*."

Tamar pushed her face deeper into his jacket to hide, as much as possible, the huge smile that was spreading across her face. Despite her best efforts, she let out a laughing snort, which could have sounded like a sneeze or fart to the ears of unsuspecting listeners. Anyway, after a few short sentences, the annoying advocate of the Hebrew language left them in peace.

The tired bus engine howled and moaned on its way down from Mount Scopus to *Wadi Joz* and *Sheikh Jarr'ah*, uphill to the Russian Compound[34], back down into Princess Mary Street and then again uphill to the elegant Palace Hotel in the direction of *Rehavia*. A light, but cold rain began to fall. They ran hand in hand the last few meters to the entrance of the brightly lit cafe.

❄ ❄ ❄

[34]Government area of Jerusalem

About an hour later, after they had already enjoyed countless turbulent rounds on the dance floor, they noticed Alisa and Nabil, who had come into the hall late. "Nabil has just led me through the old city and took me by a side entrance into the Church of the Holy Sepulchre to watch the preparations for Midnight Mass," she shared her experience with Tamar, after a round of kisses on the cheeks French style. "I wasn't aware that two Arab families – Nusseibeh and Jodi – whom Nabil knows well of course, had been the custodians of the church keys for centuries, ever since the Muslims expelled the Christians from Jerusalem. The reason is that the various churches constantly quarrel among themselves and so it is the Muslims who open and close the church, an open and shut case – I mean church – you might say."

She wanted to continue to talk about her adventures with Nabil in the old city, but her partner, who was eager to enjoy himself, took her hand and led her to the dance floor for a tight dance to the sounds of a romantic melody.

❄ ❄ ❄

The party, which had begun so harmoniously ended in discord.

The attempt to reconstruct the course of events while they were enjoying a cup of real, steaming, hot chocolate in the more relaxed atmosphere of the Cafe "Allenby" brought up several versions. "Suddenly this ugly guy pushes through – wavy hairstyle like Jean Gabin, average height, built like an ox – and begins to curse at me," Nabil aired his version. "He yells at me in Hebrew with breath reeking of booze, that he would not celebrate Hanukkah, the Feast of cleansing the Temple in the land of Israel, with dirty Arabs. Then he claimed that this festival symbolizes freedom and independence of the Jews, and that I'm spoiling the celebration and the mood. He poked me with his finger and began to push me towards the exit."

Nabil, with black hair combed back, a prominent Greek nose in his face, took another sip of cocoa and continued: "He knew that I am an Arab because we know each other. His name is Hanan and he is a customer of my father's. This Hanan owns a hardware shop in the upper part of the Maalot Street, not far from the Mahne-Yehudah market. It is claimed that his brother is a member of *Etzel*[35] and has been sitting in jail since the wave of arrests following the attack on the Arab bus in the *Rosh Pina*[36] area." Tamar and Alisa nodded, but did not answer, perhaps because they had both noticed that the others present had their eyes turned to the group that talked in a mixture of Hebrew and English.

Wolfgang sipped the remainder of his chocolate through a straw, finishing it contentedly with a loud slurp. "Look, there will always be hot-heads, but fortunately they are still a minority," he said while lovingly stroking Tamar's head. "I somehow thought that everything had started because someone had stepped on a lady's foot. Her partner was angry and lost his temper because he had, like all of us, drunk too much of the new, concentrated, nine percent Christmas Beer, which this chemist, what's his name, Rosengarten, brewed in his bathroom. A little rant, a little push and it degenerates straight away into racist slurs."

Tamar liked Wolfgang's attempt to downplay the incident, but in her heart she knew that he underestimated the gravity of the situation which was much worse and more threatening than it appeared. "It makes me very sad that even very talented and cultured people are caught in the trap of chauvinism," she said softly with carefully chosen words and slightly downcast eyes, taking refuge in checking her fingernails. According to hospital regulations, they had

---

[35]A Zionist, paramilitary organization which was agitating against the British Mandate 1931-1948; also known as the *Irgun*.
[36]A small town in the upper Galilea.

to be clipped down to the fingertips. "I wish I could paint everything pink like Wolfgang does, who always sees the good side of things. But, unfortunately, the reality is quite different."

In a low voice she described how, while all attention was focused on the dispute between Nabil and Hanan, a man she had never met or seen before, approached her and whispered in her ear: "Stop seeing this Nazi, you slut. I'm warning you in the name of the Committee for Chastity of the Daughters of Israel; stay away from this Nazi before you get hurt."

Wolfgang looked at her with wide eyes, shocked, almost offended. "Why didn't you tell me? I would have clobbered him, taken him apart, made mincemeat of him," he said and hugged Tamar warmly.

Secretly Tamar was considering seizing the moment and revealing all her doubts before Wolfgang. But they were together with Nabil and Alisa – not alone. So she pushed the personal things into a far corner of her mind and referred only to the current incident. "Beating does not solve anything," she said softly, "It's not the first time that I was threatened. In the eyes of these extremists, all Germans are the same. They also believe that all Arabs are the same. They are convinced that Jews, who are not of their opinion, must be attacked. It is assumed that they *think*, but in reality they only refocus their prejudices. People can be so cruel, so cruel." She wiped her forehead and eyes, smudged her mascara and burst into tears. Her tears left a dark trail as they flowed in an almost straight line down her cheeks.

In the Woods by *Mishmar Ha'Emek*, Summer 1942

"Attention! Stop rocking back and forth like a praying Jew. Head up, chin forward, back straight, chest out, arm high and outstretched, proud Aryan look in your eyes, as befits a soldier in the army of the Thousand-Year Reich," bellowed the sergeant," and now I want to hear you greeting our providential *Fuehrer* and me, your sergeant in Berlinese."

"Heil Hitler!" shouted Asher with perfect execution of his sergeant's instructions.

"Heil Hitler," replied the sergeant. He was visibly pleased, but suppressed a blatant demonstration of satisfaction and turned his attention to the nearest soldier.

Asher remained standing at attention, his eyes directed at the big picture of the Nazi leader that hung on the wall in front of him. From the corner of his eye, he noticed the squad leader whispering with one of the officers who had gathered the NCOs by hand signal.

"Attention! Listen!" shouted the sergeant in a strong Bavarian accent. He was short and red-faced from the heat. "We are now going on a forced march to the sounds of our Fatherland's best hits and I will personally deal with anyone who just hums instead of singing."

A few minutes later, the sweating soldiers were quick-marching in single file on a dirt road, hollering enthusiastically at the top of their lungs, "when Jewish blood spurts from the knife" and "against England we advance."

After a few kilometers through yellow fields, exhausted from the summer heat, the column reached a fork in the road with small road signs—one pointed toward Kibbutz *Mishmar Ha'Emek* and the other to *Dalia*. The signs were in Hebrew.

"Look at this – what a joke! They pretend all day 'as if', but forget about the Hebrew signs," whispered Asher to his friend Erich, who marched panting and breathless beside him, silently cursing the thousands of cigarettes he had smoked over the past few years. "Yet we are always threatened that, if anyone expresses a word in Hebrew, he'll get kicked out of the group."

This conversation was conducted in German.

Asher, who was born in Berlin, where he was called Arthur, fled in 1938 with his father from swastika-covered Germany. Almost two months had passed since he had interrupted his studies at the Hebrew University to join a British commando unit to fight the Nazi enemy. Now he was marching in this stupid, German-military style single file to the sound of Nazi songs, salutes with raised arm, wearing a Wehrmacht uniform.

❄ ❄ ❄

"Welcome to the German Section," the commander welcomed the ten new volunteers who had arrived by British military lorry from Tel Aviv at a secret camp, hidden in a dense forest in a small valley not far from Kibbutz *Mishmar Ha'Emek*. "My name is Simon Koch and I am the commander of this unit. You have been recruited to this special force following the warm recommendations of your *Haganah* commanders and I hope that you are really as good as your promoters describe you. I trust that you will settle in quickly and get to know the older recruits." The official registration process was carried out thoroughly and completed within a few minutes.

"Asher Weiss? Let's see. The last name is not bad, but this Asher we must get rid of," remarked the sergeant, who was responsible for recruitment and registration. "A borderline case, but possible. What was your first name? Arthur? Then you're Arthur again. Weiss is not really a Jewish name, so keep it. You're lucky compared to the guy whose turn was before, Erich Salomon ... We changed his name to Fritz Schweinestall[37]."

Arthur's face remained expressionless, although the idea that a name like pigsty would be given as a code name to a Jewish fighter in an anti-German commando unit seemed to him exaggerated and even absurd. "Anyway, Weiss, here is your personal number in the Wehrmacht," the sergeant continued with the registration process. "Memorize this number very well. If your commander awakens you in the middle of the night, you respond automatically, without thinking with this personnel number, as if you were born with it. Sit down somewhere alone and revise your CV a little, to bridge the gap of almost four years since you left Germany."

Arthur was not quite aware and took little notice of what was happening around him while he listened attentively to the sergeant, who was advising him on how to construct a good cover story; he recommended sticking with details as much as possible to the truth, for example, date of birth, address, name of father and mother, provided of course that they were not originally called David, Moses, Sarah, or Rachel. "So far everything clear?" Roared the sergeant.

Despite his confusion over the many details that had flooded over him in the last few minutes, Asher-Arthur

[37]German: Pigsty

jumped to attention and said loudly whenever necessary, "Yes Sir."

"In German, you fool," yelled the sergeant.

"*Jawohl, Herr Feldwebel.*"

"Very well. So let's move on. You should be highly motivated to construct a good cover story. Just think of the interrogations in the Gestapo cellars. Imagine what the interrogators do with you when they discover that you have not only impersonated a German soldier, but are also a *Yid*. Then sit down and build yourself a cover story that fits you as close as the chastity belt, with which medieval knights outfitted their wives before crusading to Jerusalem to liberate it for Jesus."

The admin officer was satisfied with his successful creative description and put the required stamp on the document with one quick motion. Then he raised his head. "Dismissed," he barked at Asher-Arthur. "Next! Lotz! Where's Wolfgang Lotz? That's a great name for a spy. Where the hell is this Lotz?"

❄ ❄ ❄

From the first day in the new unit Asher-Arthur and Erich-Fritz had become friends. "It's funny how you with such a Jewish name as Erich Salomon look so totally Aryan. Exactly like the Nazi propaganda poster. Tall, blond, blue-eyed," laughed Asher-Arthur at his new friend.

"Believe me, it just proves how absurd the Nazi race-theories are," responded Erich-Fritz: "My father had immigrated to Dresden from Poland and my mother came from Galicia. But I remember how, as a small child, even before the Nazis came to power, my father one day took me to the stand of an Italian who made the best ice cream in town. Just then, a Nazi parade ended and some thugs, you know, in boots, brown shirts, with trumpets, flags and stuff lined up to buy ice cream. One of them turned to me and said, 'Look here, this is an example of an Aryan boy' and asked me my name. With my first name, he had not yet understood the bind he was in. But when I said 'Solomon' and all the people in the queue laughed – and again, that was before the Nazis seized power – that oaf almost choked, muttered something under his neat Hitler mustache and stormed away in rage."

Asher-Arthur almost killed himself laughing about this story of the ice cream and the young Aryan.

Erich-Fritz continued to relate humorously how after 1933, especially after the enforcement of the race laws, he had continued to take advantage of his appearance which was a "godsend".

"I was often stopped on the street by fanatical Nazis who said that I was an ideal Aryan example of the racial purity of the master race. I learned from experience and in response to questions for my name, I would feed them with complicated German names. Funny, what? You know, the poster of the typical Aryan soldier that appears on the title page of the ***Signal***, the official journal of the Wehrmacht? It so happens, I know the guy. His name is Werner Goldberg. He is what the Nazis call a 'half-Jew' or 'half-caste'; however, according to their race-laws, he is a Jew. But that's not all. Some say, that there are many 'half-castes' at the top of the military and even in the SS."

"Sure," contributed Asher-Arthur a relevant fact: "My father claims that General Helmut Wilberg, one of the Air Force commanders, is a 'half Jew', and that Hitler had personally issued him with a certificate as an 'honorary Aryan'."

"There are thousands of such 'half-castes'," Erich-Fritz continued, "who prefer to present themselves as loyal Germans and ignore the persecution of the Jews, in the foolish belief that their insistence on German heritage and their loyalty to the *Reich* will protect them from persecution and attacks."

Asher-Arthur knew exactly what Erich Fritz was talking about. He knew the feeling of this German patriotism from home. Even now, that detailed reports about pogroms and Nazi massacres against European Jews and other atrocities in the occupied territories reached Palestine, and despite the great concern about the fate of the Weiss family members, who had remained in Germany, his father, carrier of the "Iron Cross" from the previous war was occasionally moved to declare what he would have continued to do for his country, if only the Nazis had not been in power...

❄ ❄ ❄

At the end of the recruitment procedure, on the small parade ground in the middle of the small camp that was hidden under pine trees, Koch informed the newcomers about the history of the unit and its functions. "You represent here the determination of the Jewish, Zionist *Yishuv*[38] in Palestine to fight the Nazi enemy. Allow me to quote at this difficult time a Roman named Seneca. Maybe he's known to some of you. 'Lack of boldness does not emanate from difficulties, but difficulties arise from lack of boldness' he said two thousand years ago. We have adopted this way of thinking. The leaders of the Jewish community decided to form this unit in response to Rommel's rapid advance eastward from Libya to the heart of Egypt," Koch began his overview, "and you're here with the blessing of the British Army. This is important because such recognition speaks for

[38]Hebrew literally: Settlement. This was the term used by the early Jewish community in Palestine to describe itself.

itself. The unit was founded after full coordination with the 'Special Forces' High Command of the British army, namely those who are responsible for commando operations. The objective is to create a trained operational force for guerrilla activity behind enemy lines."

A murmur of excitement ran through the ranks of the new soldiers.

"You are all volunteers from Germany, Austria, Czechoslovakia and Gdansk. You speak German as your mother tongue, with matching Aryan appearances and you are in good condition. Josef Goebbels, if you can remember what he looks like and how he walks, would not have been accepted in this unit" he said, smiling at the laughter of the recruits. Everyone had seen the Nazi propaganda minister in newsreels, how he preached the Aryan race theory and superiority from the height of his dwarfism, with his prominent limp and his black hair shining with brilliantine.

"Your German is the main weapon of this unit. Anyone who dreams in Hebrew or even utters one word in Hebrew will find himself kicked out of here immediately. Even if someone is not feeling well and goes to the doctor, he does it in German. Remember, even if you're boiling with fever, are worn down by toothache, scream in German, not in Hebrew. It sounds silly, but this is the only way you can get used to the new reality of your life."

A new murmur rose from the ranks of the soldiers. Koch waited a few seconds until it was quiet again.

"We, the High Command of the *Haganah*, are prepared for all eventualities, even a breakthrough by German forces from Egypt through the Sinai desert into Palestine. We have already started with the construction of the defenses. The slogan for this project is 'Masada on Mount Carmel.' "

The short break in his address only increased the tension.

"The entire Jewish armed force, *Haganah* units and

Palmach[39] companies, founded a year ago, whose members had received combat experience kicking the *Vichy* army out of Syria and Lebanon, as well as thousands of Jewish soldiers from Palestine have been mustered on Mount Carmel and in the Yizra'el Valley along the line that stretches from the Carmel, via the Megiddo road to Jenin and to Tiberias. The goal is to conduct a decisive battle to the last bullet."

Again, a murmur spread through the ranks.

Koch waited a few seconds before he continued. "You shall operate behind enemy lines in Wehrmacht uniforms. For those who have not yet understood: the Geneva Convention rules do not apply to you. A firing squad awaits the soldier who wears the uniform of the other side, and then he is captured. Those are the rules. There is no mercy and this is the best-case scenario. What really awaits those who fall into captivity, is torture and very painful elimination from the Gestapo's best gamut. Your task is to sabotage the supply routes, cut off telephone lines, ambush small units and lay mines. In short, you are Jewish partisans inside the Land of Israel."

Koch's remarks shocked the young volunteers.

"Anyone who believes that he is not suitable for this type of operation may request a transfer to an administrative post in HQ, which requires no field operation. Here's your chance. Anyone who wants to leave, step forward."

No one moved, partly because of the paralysis that had taken hold of at least some of the new volunteers.

❄ ❄ ❄

In contrast to the explicit instructions by supervisors who had issued the order not to tell anyone about the existence

---

[39]Hebrew acronym for *Plugot Mahatz* = Task Forces, the elite forces of the *Haganah*.

of the secret unit, Asher already revealed to his father during his first leave, where he had spent the last two weeks. He did not go into details, but what little he did reveal, gave his father a very good idea of what it was all about. They were sitting on the balcony of the apartment on Ben Yehuda Street in Tel Aviv. Due to the recent increase of *Yekkes* living in the street it began to be referred to as Ben Yehuda Strasse.

"They are nuts! Your commanders are just crazy," Herbert laughed with obvious contempt. He was busy removing watermelon seeds out of his mouth in the most polite way. "Did your commanders, who have never seen a tank up close, have even a glimmer of a clue what an armored division of the Wehrmacht looks like? Come on boy, let's start counting."

He rose from his chair with a quick movement, took a large sheet of paper from the chest of drawers and drew with the precision of a seasoned field-sergeant the battle formation of an armored division with the associated vehicles, consisting of six tank battalions, two mechanized infantry battalions, one field and anti-aircraft artillery battalion, an engineer battalion and other units that fit into this framework. The numbers were impressive. Hundreds of armored vehicles, more than ten thousand soldiers.

"Rommel has currently four such divisions, not just one! Don't you see? These figures are only of one division! Apart from the German units, Rommel has ten Italian divisions, which may not be of comparable quality, but at least some of them are not bad. It is likely that, if Rommel conquered Egypt, he might get reinforcements from bases in Greece directly into Alexandria and Port Said. Then he will press forward with reinforcements along the northern Sinai route to Gaza and Tel Aviv. These are vast quantities of tanks and hundreds of weapons of all calibers. They are really stupid, your superiors."

Herbert put down the piece of paper and focused on the elimination of another slice of watermelon while continuing with his analysis of the situation between each bite.

"Rommel defeated the French army with a lot less in 1940, although they were much larger than the Wehrmacht and equipped with better tanks. We have not yet even mentioned the air support by the *Luftwaffe*; and all of that the *Haganah*, *Palmach* and your tiny unit want to stop? How many are you? Thirty rookies? Fifty volunteers? And with what are you equipped to fight Rommel's tanks? With Mills grenades? This thing that is powered by a spring and can allegedly penetrate armor? What do you call that, 'PIAT'[40]?" He remarked sarcastically, while a derisive snort accompanied his remarks. "Rommel's 88 mm guns will perforate the nebulous fortifications of *Solel Boneh*[41] on the slopes of the Carmel like a sieve. The tanks will completely pulverize these ridiculous concrete blocks which your so called defense experts had distributed quasi strategically – defense experts, my foot! They might be able to drive tractors, but what do they know about tanks? Don't make me laugh!" Herbert went on with his analysis, which, to a neutral listener, might have sounded almost pro-German. "Let us pray that Montgomery succeeds in stopping Rommel with his 8th army before he manages to reach the Suez Canal and Palestine. But now, son, do you know why I am not stopping you from serving in that funny unit? Because I personally believe that Rommel has reached the limit of his operational capability and that his threat to Egypt and Palestine is mainly psychological."

---

[40]Projector, infantry, anti-tank. A kind of rocket propelled grenade fired from the shoulder.

[41]Building cooperative (founded 1921), responsible for the large building projects during the period of the Mandate and for a while after creation of the State.

Asher looked at him with wide eyes. He was not sure whether his father's words made sense, or if he may have lost his mental balance.

"You don't need to be a field marshal. Even a simple soldier can reach such conclusions," Herbert went on. "A glance at the map shows that Rommel's spearhead is more than a thousand kilometers east of its main supply port. Do you realize what that means, a thousand kilometers? A Wehrmacht Tanker that departs from Benghazi to the front uses for the round trip half the amount of fuel it carries! In addition, the RAF also ensures that not all of Rommel's supply convoys reach their destination. And we have not yet even talked about the Royal Navy, which dominates the Mediterranean and keeps sinking a large quantity of all deliveries intended for the *Afrika Korps*. For some reason I have a feeling that Montgomery, who of course knows these things far better than I do, consciously builds up Rommel's image as a great general."

At this point in the conversation, Asher became convinced that his father had consumed too large a quantity of *Schnapps* in the afternoon, but he said nothing. He stared at his father, who displayed a peculiar type of delight, and he continued to absorb the information, which his father fired at him with the staccato of a machine gun.

"Why, you might ask yourself, does Montgomery want to build such an image for Rommel," continued Herbert passionately. "Because the moment he defeats Rommel and dispatches him to Libya, he who has conquered a great general will automatically get the reputation as an even greater general. Maybe that will get him promoted to field marshal? Don't you see?"

Asher's face made it clear that he did not quite accept his father's analysis. "This amuses you, huh?" Herbert responded. "Just wait and see. The genius who manages to stop the clock has not yet been born and over time you'll see how right I am."

On Saturday night, Asher managed to spend the last few hours of his furlough with his girlfriend Braha Szold. It was billed as "an evening of humor and satire" by the "Moghrabi" cinema with dance, acrobatics and a satirical skit featuring Goland and Klatschkin. "The advertisements promised two hours of laughter and good humor, but in fact there was not much going on," Braha summed up the presentation. She was a few years younger than Asher and her mother insisted that the "child" get back home before midnight.

"What exactly do you do on that mysterious base of yours?" she asked as they were walking hand in hand along the Rothschild Boulevard while enjoying the sea breeze.

"Something similar to Wingate's special forces during the riots[42]," he intoned the official line. "We are to secure the oil pipeline from Arab insurgents. The British Secret Service fears that, with the approaching Nazi army, the mufti's supporters will again raise the banner of revolt."

❄ ❄ ❄

It must be said in Herbert's favor that he kept his word and did not prevent his son from returning to his base at the end of his weekend leave.

Although he was in excellent shape, the daily intensive training demanded greater efforts from Asher-Arthur. Apart from marches to improve their fitness, the volunteers learned to disassemble Mauser rifles, Schmeisser submachine guns, MG34s with closed eyes; to throw German stick grenades, to lay mines and to use Siemens and Telefunken radios.

---

[42]Word used to describe the attacks by the Palestinian Arabs against Jews and representatives of the British Mandate, 1936-1939.

Of course, under strict maintenance of the Wehrmacht's communication protocols.

The process of their "Germanization" was carried out thoroughly. The morning began with waking up to the sound of a German march and brushing teeth with toothpaste that was probably captured in one of the previous rounds of the battle for *Tobruk*.

The training routine was interrupted only once, when all the soldiers were ordered to the parade ground without warning or explanation. "We have in our midst a big pig," thundered the Sergeant in the Saxon dialect, which pointed to his hometown being somewhere between Dresden and Leipzig. "Yesterday, the British military police arrested one of our soldiers, who was caught committing a crime. The soldier was summarily sentenced to sixty days jail in a military prison and of course kicked out of the unit, but not before he was warned not to talk about what happens here if he doesn't want to rot in jail till the end of the war. I repeat and emphasize again the obligation of secrecy. As for the theft, I guess that one bad apple does not represent the whole bunch."

The Sergeant and the other officers refused to reveal more details about the offender and his offense.

"That must be Seidenberg, I'm sure it's Avri Seidenberg, that Viennese liar," shared Erich-Fritz with Asher-Arthur. "From the first moment, you know, from the first second he boarded the lorry in Tel Aviv, I could not stand him. I can't quite explain it, but there is something crooked about him. My grandmother used to say about people like him: 'He's lying even when he asks a question'. But I could not figure out what he had done wrong and what had led to his conviction. According to rumors he was supposed to have stolen food supplies from the kitchen and sold them on the black market in Afula."

The excitement about Seidenberg's arrest had abated by the evening. Unlike other nights that were used for night exercises or memorization of material, the recruits were free that evening.

"Not bad, this meat," muttered Erich-Fritz at dinner, which consisted of German military salt beef rations in cans labeled **AM**. The instructor explained that the Wehrmacht soldiers designated this product cynically with an acronym for "*alter Mann.*"[43]

"It tastes much better than the British field rations of Bully Beef. It can't be helped – these German buggers know how to make canned meet. The British Bully Beef gives me terrible constipation," concluded Asher-Arthur.

"Listen to this joke," said Erich-Fritz. "A wolf walks through the woods and sees a pair of huge eyes behind a bush. 'Is that you, Little Sheep?" he asked hungrily. 'What do you mean sheep, I am a rabbit', said the rabbit. 'Then why do you have such big eyes'? 'Because I am having a crap,' replied the rabbit."

Asher-Arthur looked surprised at Erich Fritz. "Not very funny," he said. "Maybe in a different language, you know which one, it does sound funny," Erich Fritz consoled himself.

❄ ❄ ❄

The next day, the training program was interrupted by the ringing of a brass bell that a former naval officer had attached to the front of the parade ground. The ringing was a signal for the recruits to line up for parade in rows of three.

"Due to an emergency, our training program will be temporarily suspended," Erwin, the duty officer announced. As usual among soldiers, they all appreciated the break in the training program before they knew the reason.

---

[43]German: old man.

"We will now undertake a combat mission. Really. I repeat, combat! No exercise but support for British military and police units," Erwin continued loudly. "From this moment on, you forget all about the German project that you have taken on and rehearsed during the last few days. You will return to being regular soldiers; therefore you must avoid an over-zealous British soldier accidentally bayoneting you because he takes you for a real Wehrmacht soldier. Now listen well to the intelligence officer who will outline the reason for this action to you."

The intelligence officer's briefing was detailed and to the point: The RAF radar post on *Stella Maris*[44] had spotted a suspicious, unidentified aircraft late at night that circled in the area of Jericho and then disappeared. Simultaneously, military intelligence received unconfirmed reports concerning an unknown number of Nazi agents who had parachuted during the night near Jericho.

A chorus of excited voices rose from the ranks of the soldiers. Among other comments you could clearly hear in Hebrew, "unbelievable" in defiance of the regulations.

"Police scouts have discovered traces of at least five suspects," continued the intelligence officer with his situation report. "But later they lost the trail. Apparently, the Nazi agents tried to reach Jerusalem via *Wadi Kelt*. Their mission is still unknown. But because they might indeed be Nazi agents, the British High Command had requested that the German unit take part in the pursuit, because we are supposed to be experts who know the German dodge-and-camouflage tactics firsthand."

The officer paused, took a deep breath, scrutinized the soldiers with a piercing glance and continued.

"I think that the British high command exaggerates somewhat in their assessment of your capabilities."

---

[44]Strategic position on Mt. Carmel, named after the Carmelite Monastery there. It overlooks Haifa bay.

Dozens of soldiers laughed loudly, which infected the officer and the rest of the commando personnel.

"So perhaps the HQ chaps went over the top," Erwin went on with his instructions, "but we are going to prove to them that it is only a small exaggeration and that they are not wrong in principle. We shall split our troops into squads; eight soldiers with a corporal or sergeant in each squad. I expect of you, that one of these squads will be the first to capture the Nazi agents. The interrogation will than start immediately, in German..."

Erwin reminded them of the basic rules of the prisoner interrogation that they had learned in the previous week. "Remember that the Germans are at a disadvantage if you capture them. They fear for their lives. Exploit that. But we want the Nazis alive. Is that clear? I have no problem with a slap or a shove, but nothing beyond that. You are not a judge seeking justice. Remember that we need accurate information. The truth. Torture and beatings persuade people to confess things they did not do, or to provide explanations adjusted to the interrogator's questions in order to stop the torture. Clear?"

A tense silence reigned now, apart from the chirping birds in the trees around the parade ground.

"Woe to him who does not follow these guidelines. We must interrogate them immediately after their arrest, to find out what their mission is, whether they are to join anyone in Palestine and why on earth *Wadi Kelt*? Is it a single operation or are we to expect more commando groups to end up here? So, you now have half an hour to get ready, including getting changed into regular uniforms of the British army. Then you sign for weapons and get on the lorries. Dismissed!"

Apparently no one, except Asher-Arthur, was wondering about the fact that even this entire briefing was actually held in German.

Mount Scopus, Spring 1939

Tamar found it hard to concentrate on reading **The Forty Days of Musa Dagh** despite the fascinating story. This difficulty had nothing to do with the quality of writing. The writer, Franz Werfel, had described with talent and drama the events of the First World War, when the Turks massacred the Armenians away from the flashlights of the international media. Werfel had placed in the centre of his action the history of 5000 Armenians, barricaded on a high mountain in southeastern Turkey, who were desperately hungry and sick, waiting to be rescued by the Western Allies.

Grandpa Siegfried had given her this book three or four years ago, accompanied by a critique of Werfel and his writings, including an explanation why the Nazis did not like them and especially this work. According to him, the negative attitude of the Nazis did not only refer to Werfel's Jewish origin, but because he dealt with an incident of ethnic hatred which could have encouraged readers to make comparisons with their anti-Jewish policies. So they declared Werfel as "undesirable" and banned the sale of his books in Germany.

Tamar closed her eyes and remembered how her grandfather Siegfried had explained, that, in his personal opinion, the critics had exaggerated a bit. "Can one ever compare the Turks with the Germans? Come on, that's ridiculous!" he concluded emphatically.

Since then four-years had passed, during which Hitler had re-established the German military, entered the demilitarized zone in the Rhineland, annexed Austria, dissolved Czechoslovakia and had introduced an extremely anti-Jewish campaign, depriving them of all civil rights in the Third Reich. This process culminated in the "Crystal Night" during which hundreds of synagogues were torched, shops looted, hundreds of Jews killed and thousands transported to concentration camps. Grandpa Siegfried, who had believed so strongly in the existence of a huge moral gulf between the backward Turks and the sophisticated Germans, was murdered in cold blood by Nazi thugs on the street of the oh-so-cultured Vienna.

Tamar also had a copy of the book in Hebrew next to her bed – as the result of an impulsive decision that was never implemented, to utilize the description of the sufferings of the Armenians to improve her Hebrew language skills. Although she was bothered by Joseph Lichtenbaum's less than flowing translation, if truth be told, it was her laziness that led her back again and again to the German original. Despite all her efforts, she did not manage to concentrate on reading; she was honest enough with herself to realize that her absent-mindedness was related to concerns about the fate of her parents and the latest developments in her relationship with Wolfgang.

There was silence in the long corridors of the nurses' home. It was interrupted only by the occasional banging of a wooden window shutter on the upper floors. A pleasant warmth spread from the iron ribs of the central heating making the small room cozy.

Her thoughts drifted far away to the distant Vienna which was awaking right now from the cold of winter, beginning to green in anticipation of spring with flowering trees on her well-groomed wide boulevards. "What is to become of Mom and Dad? Why must they suffer so much? Where does this terrible hatred of Jews come from?"

The last letter from Vienna, which had arrived the day before yesterday, now lay on the spartan bedside table. Her father described their horrible life in measured, simple sentences, which he had written in the knowledge that the Nazi censorship was looking for reasons to blot out whole rows with black ink. Each week there was a new restrictive regulation, a prohibition of practicing this or that profession, the nationalization of property, seizure of savings accounts and acute risks of arrest by SS thugs whenever leaving the house. Between the lines she felt the despair arising from the constantly unsuccessful scouring of foreign missions in an attempt to obtain an entry permit. "How have we reached this point where the gates of all the countries are closed for Jews only because they are Jews?" her father was wondering.

Tamar could not refrain from imagining how the Nazi censor would have smiled when he was reading this line. In his last letter her father had indicated a new way: to leave Austria on a barge along the Danube to Romania and sail from there on an illegal immigrant ship to Palestine. "Oh god, Mom and Dad are not young and healthy. How can they survive such a journey," she asked herself in frustration because of her powerlessness to help them. She had put the book down, as she lay on the simple iron bed, her legs covered with a thick blanket stretched over a white sheet with the emblem of the Hadassah Hospital.

Tamar stared at the ceiling. "This ceiling needs a new coat of paint," she thought, and let out a pained sigh that came from deep within her chest.

The three other beds in the room were empty, placed exactly according to the instructions the students had received on the first day of classes from matron. The building, usually buzzing at most hours of the day with a flurry of activity like a beehive at the peak of nectar collection, had now emptied of its residents for the Passover holiday. Some of the students whose families lived in the country had left to spend the festival with their loved ones. Many of the students, new immigrants and refugees from Europe whose families had remained on the old continent, contented themselves with visits to relatives – if they had any – or with friends in settlement groups that were scattered all over the country.

Tamar was one of the unfortunate girls in her class, whose name was drawn in the raffle for "*Matzo-Service*"[45] as they called it.

"I'm sorry, girls," declared Matron Landsmann. "Ten girls from each class must remain in the hospital grounds to support the staff during the Passover week. But don't be so sad," she began with words of comfort in reaction to the grim faces of those remaining behind. "As a reward for your staying here over Passover, you get an extra week of leave in the summer."

"A bird in the hand is worth two in the bush. More to the point, to leave now would beat vague promises for the future," one of those left behind vented her opinion of Landsmann's proposal.

In contrast to the demonstrative expressions of disappointment by her friends, Tamar remained indifferent. "To be honest, I don't mind being stuck here over the holidays," she thought. She rubbed the scar that remained on her left hand as a souvenir of the blows she had received from a group of Jewish thugs, who had been sent to "take care of her" because of her affair with Wolfgang. She tried again to focus on reading the book, but her thoughts wandered far away from the heart-wrenching tragedies, the

---

[45]Matzo in Yiddish, Hebrew: Matzah, the unleavened bread eaten by Jews during the Passover festival.

small joys and shattered hopes of the besieged Armenians on Musa Dagh.

Only five days had passed since she had finally separated from Wolfgang; he was the first man with whom she had been through the emotional and spiritual experience that moves the world and is known in every language on earth as "love". In contrast to her defiant demeanor that men often mistakenly interpreted as encouragement for flirting – and she did attract members of the opposite sex like moths – her romantic past was banal, even boring.

Prior to her love affair with Wolfgang she had had two brief, unsatisfactory love affairs with two members of her group in the youth movement. During the second one, a few days before her 18th birthday, she was also deflowered. That was on the eve of her departure from Vienna and her old life. The sexual act itself was not filed in the memory portfolio of her experiences as particularly pleasant. In intimate conversations with her girlfriends, some spoke of fireworks that suddenly lit up the sky; stars that appeared in the firmament or butterflies in the stomach. She had not experienced any such things, but only felt Paul's heavy, panting breathing. Paul was a member of her group in the movement, but had remained in Vienna voluntarily, despite the entry certificate in his name, which had reached the offices of the Jewish Agency. He had done this to help organize the emigration to Palestine of the group's other members.

While he was courting her before they went to bed, he behaved like a Don Juan with a lot of experience. But when it came to action in the dingy back room of his parents' apartment, it became clear that, for him too, it was the loss of virginity and he reached his climax seconds after penetration.

With Wolfgang it was different.

From the beginning.

From the first moment, she experienced this unique and special feeling, which is commonly referred to as "love" – accompanied by fireworks, explosions and stars in the sky. At their third meeting, when he took her in his strong arms, rocking her like Pharaoh's daughter had once done with baby Moses, she abandoned herself to him with heart and soul. The many hours they spent loving, stroking and giving mutual pleasure, defined for her the term "paradise" anew. The physical relationship between them strengthened over time in an ascending curve, which stood in stark contrast to her growing awareness of their problematic affair and their very different characters. Despite his uncomplicated ways and his ability to drive her to new limits of pure pleasure, a certain uneasiness crept in. Sometimes he surprised her with an unexpected ability to understand, to feel, to express emotions and bring them forth from the depths. Usually, though, he displayed emotional shallowness. On an intellectual level, too, the differences were becoming stronger.

"It may be that over time, even without the intervention of external influences, our fairy tale would have been over because of these differences. But who knows how things could have developed," she wondered.

Either way, the initiative to separate came from her. She also took the helm and steered the events relatively indifferently, almost without hesitation towards separation.

However, what had seemed logical and appropriate in the evening of their separation, melted within hours into a sea of nostalgic memories and renewed dramatic outbursts of love for Wolfgang. During the long nights, when she was not scheduled to work in the various hospital departments, she spent hours mainly shedding a sea of tears which were absorbed by her pillow, leaving whitish salt stains on the fabric. At a certain point, when the pain of love was at its height, Tamar even considered going into town, knocking on the door of the Schwartes and throwing herself into Wolfgang's arms, as if they had never parted. But these nightly dreams were never carried out. Although there was no hour that passed without her spontaneously reaching a new decision to renew the relationship with Wolfgang, Tamar held back, sometimes at the last moment.

❄ ❄ ❄

Tamar was missing the family celebrations of holidays. Her family was among the secular, almost assimilated sector of the Viennese Jewish community. Only Grandpa Siegfried occasionally visited the neighborhood synagogue and even that only during the High Holidays or on special occasions. Her father, Meir, a firm, resolute atheist who was also equipped with a good dose of Zionism, made a point of keeping far away from any activity related to organized religion, starting with religious synagogue services to keeping kosher.

At every possible opportunity he would explain to anyone willing to listen, that he had lost his relationship with God over the many years wearing the uniform of His Imperial Majesty, Franz Joseph, in his unnecessary military service during the frenzied campaigns of the First World War.

"I remember the precise moment when that happened, in a remote field in Galicia before another senseless battle," he declared in every debate on issues of religion and tradition. "We, the chosen ones of God's creatures, slaughtered each other with machine guns, cannons, gas and any other destructive weapon. If God had only been aware of our existence, he would have destroyed us like he incinerated the priests of Baal on Mount Carmel. But what was the strangest thing of all? Before any crazy attack on the Russian lines, the regimental priest would come over, pray and send us all 'in the name of God' to death by the Russian machine guns –

including us Jews and Bosnian Muslims who served in the Regiment. By the way, similar ceremonies were also held in the Russian trenches before the start of the massacre."

It was only out of esteem and respect for Grandpa Siegfried that Tamar's father used to assemble the family on the Jewish holidays. On *Rosh Hashanah*[46], they ate a festive meal with fish-heads, apple and honey. "*Sukkot*[47] I can do without, although I consider it to be an important holiday," said Grandpa Siegfried, thereby releasing his son from making a decision. The grandfather explained his attitude in relation to *Sukkot* with the remark, that the children of Israel had received the divine instruction to celebrate the festival by dwelling and eating in temporary huts in the pleasant heat of Egypt and Sinai, and not in cold Vienna. "Here, in October, one needs the skin of an Eskimo to sit in the *sukkah*," he joked. Hanukkah candles were lit and the *dreidel*[48] spun. On Passover, *Seder-Night*[49] was celebrated more or less properly at the family table, with some slight skipping of the *Haggadah*[50] pages before the meal and giant leaps to the final song at the end of the feasting.

Now, in the empty dormitories on Mount Scopus, far away from her family, her loneliness on the eve of Passover lay heavily on her shoulders like a thick, heavy eiderdown. She was staring at a tiny stain on the ceiling and losing herself in the beautiful memories of happy days and family celebrations.

---

[46]The Jewish New Year.

[47]The festival of Tabernacles. When the Israelites were wandering in the desert after the Exodus from Egypt, they dwelt in *Sukkot* – temporary huts. The festival is celebrated in the same way today, when Jews build such huts and dwell in them for eight days.

[48]Yiddish: Spinning top, *sevivon* in Hebrew, with which children play during the festival to learn more about the Maccabean revolt.

[49]Hebrew *Seder* – order; the traditional way to celebrate Passover eve, in memory of the Exodus from Egypt.

[50]Hebrew: The narration. A book used to celebrate the traditional *Seder*.

Finally, **The Forty Days of Musa Dagh** slipped out of her hands. As if she was sitting in the cinema watching the big screen, a movie was playing in her head, packed with pictures from the last holiday she celebrated far away from her family. It was a holiday to commemorate the birthday of none other than Jesus.

"It's a bit ironic that this was the very first holiday I was spending in the bosom of a family in the Holy Land," she giggled, and sank in the reconstruction of her experiences of the humble and peaceful Christmas rituals celebrations with the Wennagels, together with Wolfgang and his family, as well as with a nice British family, whose name she could not remember for some reason.

She recalled very well how the charming and warm celebration, which was held in the spacious Wennagel home in *Sarona* had brought tears to her eyes. All guests were gathered around the decorated Christmas tree and sang "Silent Night, Holy Night" and all the other traditional Christmas carols.

Tamar knew the songs well from the time when she was called Henrietta, the happy days of the old Vienna before the Anschluss. Martha, her best friend since third grade, used to invite her every year to celebrate Christmas with her family in their elegant villa in the 19th district. "After all, Jesus was born a Jew," lectured her father, a wealthy industrialist, a devout Catholic, but with socialist tendencies – a combination that granted him a certain flexibility between rival political camps at the time. "So there is no reason in the world why you should not celebrate his birthday with us. You are also welcome at New Year's dinner, because this then is actually our Savior's circumcision ceremony on the eighth day." But Martha, her best friend, suddenly disappeared from her life in the first week after the Anschluss, when the Nazis had marched into Austria. And she was not the only one. Of all her school friends, only one, Ingrid, dared to continue to talk to her in the schoolyard during recess, and to accompany her home from school, thereby preventing harassment by the fanatical neighborhood louts.

The other 24 girls in the class, some of them true friends, ignored her as if their classmate had suddenly vanished into thin air or metamorphosed into a particularly transparent glass figure. The headmaster called her and two other Jewish girls into his room to make it clear in a few dry, direct sentences that, thanks to their good grades, he was willing to be flexible and let them finish the year. A little over a month after receiving her annual report, she took the train to Trieste, which brought her to the harbor where she boarded the Italian passenger ship 'Adria' bound for Palestine.

In the empty rooms of the nurses' home on the eve of Passover, Tamar recalled her experiences during the trip on the 'Adria' and the choices she had made on the hot, humid day of their arrival in August 1938 in front of the white buildings of Tel Aviv. "I wondered how life would go on. Never in my life would I have imagined, that half a year later I would celebrate Christmas with a boyfriend, a Templer, in the house of his uncle in *Sarona*, the German Colony at the edge of the Jewish city Tel Aviv. And not only Christmas, but also Joseph's birthday, Wolfgang's grandfather. It almost sounds like the beginning of a fairy tale."

Christmas Dinner at the Wennagels was delicious and enjoyable. Tamar instantly bonded with Joseph, Wolfgang's grandfather. Despite his advanced age, he had kept clarity and a sense of humor. "You know you're getting old when the candles on the cake cost more than the cake itself," he joked in view of the birthday cake, which was decorated with dozens of glowing sticks.

"Come on, Grandpa, you're still young," Wolfgang told him. "Everyone knows how some young ladies in *Sarona* and a few Tel Aviv beauties pant after you."

"You exaggerate, my dear grandson," Joseph said. "I'm getting old, precisely according to the formula I have heard from someone: first you forget names, then you forget faces, after that you forget to close your fly and, finally, you forget to open it." With an emphatic gesture, he leaned forward and looked down.

Roaring laughter filled the room.

"My grandfather is an amazing person," Wolfgang boasted, whispering in Tamar's ear. "There is no corner in Palestine, he does not know. Even Lawrence of Arabia has appreciated his knowledge. He knows amazing stories about what had happened here once. Right, Grandfather Joseph?" The words of this question, he said aloud.

"But you're exaggerating again, my dear grandson," Joseph replied, visibly happy with the bustle around him. "Actually, I started from zero and it took decades before I came to nothing."

The British official, whose name Tamar had forgotten, laughed with his open mouth full of cheesecake crumbs and almost choked. Grandfather Joseph smiled with delight and ran a hand through his thick white hair. His eyes twinkled mischievously behind the thick lenses of his glasses.

Following one attempt and then another, Joseph Wennagel yielded to persuasion to relate his exploits and to roam into adventurous tales, which originated in part, from the time when the Turks were still masters of the land. And what stories!

"Well, those were the days," Joseph started with a series of memories. "The Turks ruled the place. It was a corrupt, messy administration. For them, Palestine was a distant province, a part of southern Syria. Only in the second half of the last century, and only thanks to the economic initiatives and funding from both the Templers and the Zionists, something began to move here."

He stressed to his listeners, and no doubt Tamar's presence in the room had inspired him to raise the issue that, in the beginning, the relationship between the Templers and the Zionists was characterized by mutual respect and cooperation.

"The elders of the Colony in Haifa told me that they were invited as guests of honor to the inauguration of the synagogue in *Samarin*, today's *Zichron Yaakov*," Joseph wandered into distant realms. Heckling from those listening, who feared that Grandfather Joseph was deviating into irrelevant stories, brought him back to other memories.

"Alright, let's leave *Samarin*. In the days of the Turks, I was a builder and worked with Yosef Treidel. Have you heard of Treidel?" He asked Tamar.

A quick head movement, which swung her flowing hair from side to side – a sight that awakened in Wolfgang a sudden desire to hug her – made it clear that the name meant nothing to Tamar.

"Ah, those were the days. We were the top team in terms of everything that had to do with construction in this part of the world. Yosef and Joseph! He, the Jewish hydraulic engineer did the planning and I, Joseph Wennagel, the Templer, did the building. We received countless orders and contracts that earned us a lot of money. We didn't just hang around in Palestine. We worked all over the region. There was no place that we did not know."

"Lawrence, tell of Lawrence," Wolfgang begged of his grandfather before he could stray again.

"At that time I made friends with Lawrence who was roving about here, I think between the years 1912 and 1914," Joseph said. "Thomas Edward Lawrence. This Briton, somewhat eccentric, but a great intellectual, who mastered Greek and Latin, claimed to be an archaeologist, visited all kinds of places and crawled into every possible nook and cranny. I believed him that he was an archaeologist, but the

German engineer who, inter alia, had designed the railroad to Baghdad for the Turks, what's his name? Oh, Meissner. So Meissner, with whom Treidel and I had worked together in many places, once told me that across from each strategic location where he built a bridge or dug a railway tunnel, a camp of British archaeologists showed up. And who was in each of these camps? Lawrence!"

"How does this relate to you and Lawrence?" Wolfgang asked again.

"There is a connection. At the time, the then two world powers Britain and Germany sought ways to increase their influence in the Ottoman Empire. 1914, on the eve of the Great War, before his return to England, I was asked by Lawrence to store for him a few capitals and other finds he had collected on his travels here. I put these things in the yard and had almost forgotten about them. Meanwhile, the war broke out, the Turks joined our side – the Germans – and together they tried to occupy the Suez Canal and failed.

"Then the British army advanced from Egypt and conquered Palestine. One day, about two years after the war, when our lives had returned to normal, Lawrence took a special trip to *Sarona* to visit me."

The British guest whose name she could not recall, uttered a cry of admiration. "Lawrence in *Sarona*? Only for you? I didn't know that. Good for you!"

Joseph nodded in gratitude for the compliment. "Lawrence came in an elegant military staff car, followed by a lorry with some Indian soldiers. Lawrence drank tea in this living room, ate one or two biscuits and was interested in what had been happening to us all these years. Then we went to the yard, identified the capitals and antiques that I had kept for him and he carted them off on the military lorry."

"But you are digressing again, Grandpa," Wolfgang remarked.

"I am allowed, I'm enjoying myself," Joseph said playfully, but then returned to the essence of the story. "Years later, though the contact between us was apparently severed, a big package arrived from London. It contained an elegant copy of the bestselling book **The Seven Pillars of Wisdom** with a personal dedication."

The effort of speaking had dried Joseph's throat and he paused to slurp a sip of tea.

"But that's not all," he continued with renewed energy. "I read the book that Lawrence had given me and suddenly I realized that actually his entire activity in the Middle East before the war was for the British intelligence service. We had been made to believe that he was in search of antiques and was inspecting biblical sites, but he was collecting information and charting maps. The joke is that, one day during the war, I showed Lawrence's antiquities to General Kress von Kressenstein, the German commander of the Turkish army. Yes, the one who had made two attempts to occupy the Suez Canal. Von Kressenstein fought against General Allenby, who used maps which Lawrence had drawn and with whose help he defeated the Turkish and German armies. Life is full of surprises, or if you like, the way of the world is amazing, right? There is an Arab proverb that I have translated as 'life is like manure on the wheel – sometimes up, sometimes down'. Originally in Arabic, it speaks of a cucumber that one day is in the mouth and another day here," he said, tapping his bum.

A new wave of laughter flooded the room.

"But let us return to my friend Treidel, undoubtedly the best engineer who had ever worked here. Treidel designed the first houses in your first kibbutz, *Deganiah*," he said, looking at Tamar "and I built them. He designed the large bridge over *Wadi Gaza* and I built it. Listen, I'll tell you something that not many people know. Long before the war, I think in 1909, Treidel and I were building the houses in the Jewish settlement of *Kineret*[51]. Treidel fell in love with the place and designed a beautiful big house for his family. I not only invested my soul in the construction of that house, but also all the knowledge that I had acquired. I personally measured and checked every one of the hundreds of black basalt stones that I have bricked into the walls of that house, right on the beach by the lake. An amazing house. The family lives there to this day."

He paused and took a sip of tea, which had cooled in the meantime.

"One day, several years ago, before the Arab uprising, I went to Tiberias and visited Treidel's son in *Kineret*. He was delighted with my arrival, brought up-to-date about the family and said, 'Joseph, you are not going to believe this, but the house that you and father have built, is now famous throughout the entire Jewish community. Members of the Zionist youth movements around the world sing enthusiastically about how wonderful it is!"

Another pause for a sip of tea; Rudolph Wennagel and Dieter Schwarte, Wolfgang's father, who already knew the story, exchanged a slight smile.

"Then Treidel Junior led me to the big gramophone, you know, His Master's Voice, with the large horn and the picture of the dog that listens."

"The dog is called Nipper." This information was contributed by the Briton, whose name Tamar had forgotten.

"What, Nipper? Very well then, let it be Nipper. Treidel Junior turned the crank of the gramophone, put a record on, and a Hebrew song floated through the room." Grandpa Joseph closed his eyes and sang with his hoarse voice in perfect Hebrew:

"*Al Sfat Yam Kineret, Armon rav Tif'eret*[52] ..."

---

[51]*Yam Kineret* is the Hebrew name for the Sea of Galilee.

[52]The stanza translates as: "*The Sea of Galilee had on its shore, a palace-so superb in splendor...*"

Tamar's eyes became moist as she accompanied Grandfather Joseph humming.

Applause rewarded the song's performance. Grandfather Joseph humbly bowed his head, like an opera singer at the end of a particularly successful performance of a long and complicated aria. Later in the evening he brought more memories, but the history of the house in *Kineret* fascinated Tamar and when she returned the next day to the Nursing School in Jerusalem, she immediately went to the library and searched the shelves to find material about the song. When her search was fruitless, she turned to the nice librarian and asked for help.

"I'll be happy to help you. I am an amateur singer and sing every Thursday evening in the Arlosoroff Centre Choir." It took several days until the librarian came back to Tamar with blueprints of some documents and confirmation of Joseph Wennagel's story.

"Yes, this is the Treidels house" she told Tamar. "I could not find anything about Wennagel, but apparently it's true, because he and Treidel were really known as the efficient and reliable twosome in the *Yishuv*, 'Yosef and Joseph build the Land'.

"Now about the song. It was originally written as a song of redemption, but because of the location described in the song, you know, *sfat yam kineret*, it became known as referring to the house over time. Since you are really so interested, the words were written by Jacob Fischman and the melody by Hanina Karchevsky."

Since that magical Christmas Eve, she kept hearing the song '*Al Sfat Yam Kineret*' in her head almost every time she thought of Wolfgang. Even now, in the small, warm dormitory room on Mount Scopus it was echoing in her mind.

Templer Colony *Sarona*, Tel Aviv Summer 1942

Commands, engine noise, and the rattling of tank-tracks penetrated from the street into every room of the spacious Wennagel house through the windows, which were open because of the heat.

"Rudolph, why do they do this to us? Why do they drive us out of our house?" cried Vera. She wrung her hands, interrupting momentarily the nightmarish work of selecting things that could fit into the small suitcase allocated to her for the expulsion from their home.

Rudolph Wennagel could barely hear his wife's desperate question, which had reached him in the basement from the bedroom on the second floor. Having measured angles and directions, he carved a cavity in the wall above the cellar door with a hand drill, hammer and chisel. Despite the severe heat and oppressive humidity, it was cool in there, almost European.

"I can't hear you very well, Vera, I'll come up shortly."

After a few minutes of chiseling and measuring, he decided that the spot was suitable. He took a cloth made of thick fabric in which he placed a number of shiny gold coins, he had removed from an elegant wooden chest. The

English sovereigns were from the last century with an image of Queen Victoria on one side and St. George, fighting the dragon, on the other. He counted the coins and wrapped them in the cloth, put the package in the hollow, which he filled with skilled movements sealing it with a layer of plaster and grout.

He put the tools on the floor, on a double page of an old German settler magazine. "We Templers must never forget that we live in a non-German country, among a non-German population, and that our task in Palestine must not have any political character" was the message of the article on which now lay a hammer, chisel and drill. "It would also be a mistake if those of us who have accepted the principles of National Socialism, despise or harm those who are still hesitating. No doubt we are, all of us, still good patriotic Germans and will remain so."

Rudolph reflected on the headline of the article that had caused such a storm in the community.

"We were already deported once after the First World War and then we came back," Rudolph tried to convince himself that he was acting correctly. "Maybe we'll also return to our beloved colony after this madness and then we'll find a suitable use for this little treasure of 23 gold coins in the future."

❄ ❄ ❄

"Attention, residents of *Sarona*" came a sharp metallic voice from a loud-speaker mounted on the roof of a military lorry.

"This is Colonel Thompson of the King's Royal Rifle Corps. According to instructions of His Majesty's Government and the authority vested in me, I have declared *Sarona* a closed military zone. I remind you that you are citizens of Nazi Germany, a hostile state, and any resistance attempt will be considered rebellion and ruthlessly suppressed by armed soldiers of the Corps, who are spread all over the Colony with their weapons ready to fire."

A metallic click ended the announcement, which repeated itself with another click after a few seconds of silence. "In two hours, at midnight, you have to leave your homes and gather in the school yard. You may bring one small suitcase per family member. Any other surplus baggage will be confiscated."

Perhaps Colonel Thompson had wanted to take a break here and turn off the microphone, but forgot to press the right button. Or maybe the Colonel had planned in advance to leave the microphone open to let the local Nazis know what he thought of them. "Any such excess stuff will be sent to the unfortunates in London and Coventry, whose homes were destroyed during the bombing by the *Luftwaffe*. Fucking Nazis." The remark, which he made to the officers around him could be heard clearly.

"Military police will be searching the buildings," he continued the official announcement with a normal and authoritative voice. "They will carry out a final check to ensure that all buildings are empty and will lock them. The sick and disabled may proceed already now to the schoolyard and the medical staff of the British Army will take care of them."

A further metallic click signaled the end of the announcement and immediately afterwards the old clock on the school tower chimed ten times. "This clock has been a part of us since 1877, awakening the industrious and lulling the insomniacs to sleep. Will we ever come back and hear it ringing again," mused Rudolph while climbing the wide staircase to the first floor.

The Wennagels' house in Christoph-Hoffmann Street, was typical of the architecture of the *Sarona* Settlement: wide basement, ground floor with spacious kitchen, dining room, study and a second floor with living rooms. The house was covered with a red, sloping tiled roof. The roof was a German design, apparently meant to protect the house from thick layers of snow that would never fall on it in the Palestinian climate. The house was surrounded by a flourishing garden, maintained for over 70 years by three generations of Wennagels from the time of the Turks. The house was built by Johann, one of the first Templers to have settled in 1871 on the hill a few kilometers northeast of Jaffa, on land bought from the Greek Patriarchate.

Grandfather Johann could not survive the harsh conditions. His name appears on the list of 28 of the 130 first settlers, who had succumbed to Malaria right at the beginning. In order to contain the disease, a parishioner who had lived for a while in Australia, proposed to utilize the good properties of the Eucalyptus tree. Parishioners planted 1,300 trees. Their roots along with extensive drainage work dried up the swamps and malaria was eliminated. The information about this successful solution quickly spread among the Zionist settlers and inspired them to adopt the method and plant these trees in their new settlements.

"Somehow the Arabs call the Eucalypt 'Jews tree' whilst we are its true pioneers here" thought Rudolph and wondered, if he could find comfort in the fact that he was remembering such trivial details during the most difficult moments of his life.

The weeping voice of Peter, the eldest son of Vera and Rudolph was heard from the living room upstairs.

"Just born and already driven from his home." Rudolph felt waves of anger welling up inside him and growing stronger.

Vera saw her husband coming up the stairs and snuggled between his shoulders while her bitter sobs mingled with the cries of their baby. "Why Rudi, why? Why did God do this to us?"

Rudolph wanted to tell her that they owe this misfortune to Karl Ruff, this silly dealer from the Haifa colony, who already recognized in 1932, which way the wind was blowing from the old country and speedily founded the first branch of the Nazi party in Palestine. And also because of her uncle, Kornelius Schwarz, head of the Nazi party in *Sarona*. Also, because most members of the Templer community were attracted by the great dreams of glory and Adolf Hitler's ideology, marching foolishly into the abyss like a flock of silly geese.

Now that Rommel and his *Afrika Korps* stood at the gates of Alexandria, the British rulers of the country, decided with some justification that it was time to drive out the local Nazis. "If the situation had been reversed, the Nazis would have stood the settlers against the wall and massacred them," thought Rudolph. He also wanted to remind her how their neighbors were defiantly flying the swastika flag in front of their houses on each April 20th, Hitler's birthday. He was also thinking of how the colony's boys were marching almost every week from the Hitler Youth hut through the main street wearing their uniforms with swastika armbands, provoking the inhabitants of Tel Aviv, many of whom had fled the Nazi Reich as refugees. But Rudolph decided that this was not the right time for detailed explanations and stuck to a somewhat more simplistic response.

"You know Vera," he said, stroking her head. "I do not believe that God is doing this to us. It is us who have brought this disaster on ourselves. God is not exactly a football referee. I think he is more like a referee at a hundred-meter sprint. He merely pulls the trigger of the starter's pistol and lets us determine the result."

A tired smile spread over Vera's face, who, in her youth, had reached first place in the 100 meters race at the first Track and Field Championship ever held in Palestine. "I love you," she whispered. "I love your wisdom, your humanity. Since Hitler came to power nine years ago, I have so often quarreled with you about your stubborn attitude. You've never tried to hide your disgust with the Nazis or to moderate your opposition to them. I will never forget how you made clear to the milkman William, Schwartz's deputy, why under no circumstances were you prepared to meet with this Nazi bigwig, who had arrived here four years ago with the mission to spy against the Jews and whom the British deported after two days. What was his name? "

"Eichmann, Adolf Eichmann. It is said that this Eichmann has now come a long way and that he is now one of the bigshots in the SS."

"And I also remember how you fought all these years with all the members of the community."

"You exaggerate when you say all the members of the community," Rudolph tried to interrupt his wife's gush of words. "After all, there were a lot who thought like me."

"Well, almost. But the majority was against us. Our doors were smeared with feces. Our windows were shattered and all that on the orders of my Nazi uncle, Schwartz. I remember how you went to him to complain about this vandalism and how this idiot replied that he would rather not investigate it because 'if I open this Pandora's box, who knows what Trojan horse will jump out', he said."

The silly answer of that stupid uncle sounded even sillier now.

A combination of laughter and tears mingled with her words. "You stuck by your guns and you were right. But if there really is a God, he would now at this precise moment, send to our door a British officer with an official declaration by the High Commissioner that the extradition order does not apply to us but only to the Nazi party members."

"We Templers were already driven out in the past. Then, at the end of the last war, in 1918, General Allenby's Brits deported us to Egypt. This happened because we were allies of the Turks." He hugged her and led her gently into the bedroom. "We returned from this exile. Did you know that it was actually the heads of the Jewish population, who exerted pressure on the British after the First World War to bring us back from the internment camps in Egypt? Believe me; we'll be back. Come on, I help you pack."

On the wide double bed, with its wooden frame for hanging a mosquito net, that had served previous Wennagel generations, there was a mess of clothes, books and pictures.

"I don't know what to take, Rudi. How can you cram a lifetime into three small suitcases?" With thoughtful and measured movements that hid the state of his agitation, Rudolph sorted out some summer and winter clothes. "You will be deported to Australia, where it is winter now," they were told a few hours earlier.

On the wall opposite the bed, hung a large colorful painting by Johan Gustav Bauernfeind, who had succeeded so well in capturing the specific colors of Palestine with his brush. When the German Kaiser Wilhelm II visited Palestine in 1898, the Templers gave him four paintings of local landscapes by Bauerfeind in an expensive and elegant cover. The painting on the wall was the fifth in that Bauerfeind series.

"The German Colony, Jaffa 1898", read the inscription on the small brass plate in the corner of the frame and Bauernfeind had given it as a gift to Vera's grandfather. "I have no choice, but to leave the painting behind; who knows where it will end up," thought Rudolph. From among the books, he grabbed only two he had selected from hundreds of volumes that were lined up like soldiers in the spacious library in the adjacent room. One of them was the family Bible, the cover page of which listed all births and deaths of the Wennagel family over the past hundred years. The other was **The Seven Pillars of Wisdom** by Lawrence of Arabia with a dedication to Joseph, Rudolph's father, which read "to a dear man, who loved the land and its people; builder, craftsman, artist and a true friend. With appreciation, T.E. Lawrence".

He opted for a few family photos, and, to save space and weight, he removed them from their heavy wooden frames. Vera sat down heavily on the bed, which caused one of the pictures to slip and shatter on the stone floor. She let out a cry of anguish.

"Look how symbolic this is," Rudolph said, showing her the plain photo without its glass cover. "It's a photo of the trip we took together with my relatives, the Schwartes from Jerusalem and the Blackbridges, the government's education inspector during the Christmas holidays in 1938. Here dad is leaning on the fender of our old Ford. You're sitting there on the back seat. Only the silhouette of your favorite straw hat is visible. I am holding the steering wheel like a little boy, and John Blackbridge is pointing at me and laughing. And that's Wolfgang, hugging the waist of his girlfriend, that pretty woman who sometimes intentionally spoke German with an ostentatious Viennese dialect, because she knew that it caused us fits of laughter. Oh, what a complicated love story that was. Our Wolfgang with a Jewish woman and, moreover, a refugee who had fled from Hitler. Do you remember? Her name was Henrietta, but she insisted that we call her Tamar."

But his consolation attempt only triggered a flood of tears from Vera. "It looks like a scene from another world," she whimpered, "Germans, English, a young German and a young Jewish woman who are head over heels in love and it makes everyone happy and all are enjoying themselves. Now, everything is shattered, destroyed, finished, exactly like the picture. Blackbridge was murdered by Arab insurgents in *Jenin*." She pointed to the image of the Englishman. "His family returned to London immediately and now they might be sitting in an air-raid shelter because of the continuous bombing by the *Luftwaffe*. Wolfgang went to study in Germany half a year before the outbreak of this damn war. He has probably been drafted and goosesteps now in the uniform with the swastika that he so hated. And Henrietta? Who knows what has become of her. And we, the descendants of those hardworking people who had brought progress to this part of the world, have been declared enemy aliens, whom the British Empire must expel to the other side of the globe. We are all small balls on the Creator's playground, the one whom you have appointed referee for the hundred meter race." A mixture of laughter and tears shook her body.

German Colony Jerusalem, Spring 1939

"I love her so much, I want to jump over the moon," Wolfgang shouted. "I don't care what people in the congregation and in the colony think of me. What is it to you or to them that she is Jewish? First and foremost, she is a human being. Unlike many of our ignorant neighbors, she is well educated and has not only heard of Goethe, but can also quote entire passages of his works by heart."

That last sentence about Goethe brought a faint smile to his father Dieter's face. "Wolfgang, you know how much I love you and that I actually also like Henrietta," he said with his pleasant baritone voice in the southwestern German dialect that was ingrained in him, even though he was born in Jerusalem and had never trodden on German ground, not even for a visit. "But, to my great regret, circumstances have arisen which make it necessary to terminate this relationship," he continued, mustering all his self-control, in order to respond calmly and not to yell; he told his son that he and Tamar were still young, and that they may not yet be able to see the whole picture – of what is at stake – and would possibly only understand it all in a few years.

"Love is sometimes the very essence of trying to turn part of a dream into reality. But trust me, in the reality of 1939

Palestine, stuffed with conflicts and in view of a world war, which unfortunately I see looming, you have no chance to realize your personal dream."

Dieter paused and looked at the distressed face of his eldest son. Through his memory flickered a different image of Wolfgang, all of ten years old, as he proudly paraded a large cuckoo clock, which he had managed to take apart, repair, and put together again. He also recalled his son's first driving lesson when he was only 14, letting the eager boy hold the steering wheel of the old Ford van on a deserted stretch of road from Bethlehem to Hebron.

But that was long ago and now Dieter was wondering how he had missed that phase when Wolfgang, the boy, had turned into a young man who was strong, handsome like a movie star, attracting admiring glances. "Based on what I have said so far, you have to finish this affair with Henrietta," he concluded. "There is no choice, because you are endangering the future of your mother and your younger brother Willi. In short, the whole family".

The fireplace of the living room in the small Schwarte home in the heart of the German colony in Jerusalem contained a cozy fire that displaced fragments of the Jerusalem cold that had snuck in through hidden crevices. Apparently these were the last vestiges of the winter wave this year, and the flames now cast a reddish light on the heavy furniture. Through the wide, clean windows – Jerusalemites used to joke that the Templer women spent half their time cleaning windows – one could see the big garden with flowering fruit trees and manicured flower beds, from which ornamental shrubs thrust green shoots upwards waiting patiently for the morning sun, which was to open their flowers.

Angela Schwarte sat sunk in a deep leather armchair, knitting diligently. "I know that winter is already over," she said, "but nothing is lost; this scarf will wait a few months and warm someone next winter." She watched with pain and interest the discussion between her husband and her eldest son. She really liked Tamar, or Henrietta, as she preferred to call their son's beautiful girlfriend.

But in her own way, quietly but rigorously, it was Angela who had prompted her husband to confront Wolfgang about ending his fiery affair with Henrietta-Tamar. She did this because this matter had long exceeded the boundaries of a conventional love story between young people.

The immediate cause of family conflict was sparked by a personal conversation she had had two days earlier with her boss, Helmut Schwarz, Director of the Jerusalem branch of the Deutsche Bank. "Mrs. Schwarte," Director Schwartz began in an officious tone, whilst letting her – the Chief Accountant – stand in front of his heavy desk, which was meant to convey authority. "It's a touchy subject which I have to sort out with you," Schwartz opened the rebuke with almost no preamble.

"I'm not sure whether you are aware of it, but in conversations I have with our regular clients, members of the community, the name of your son Wolfgang crops up frequently."

The rest of the conversation, including hidden threats that her position at the bank was compromised, she described in great detail to her husband Dieter that night. Angela and Dieter Schwarte knew that she must not lose her position at the bank. Dismissal would have destroyed their quiet life.

Not that Angela Schwarte loved her work or enjoyed her position as Chief Accountant of the bank. She found it uninspiring to add columns of figures or calculate exchange rates of Reichsmark and Palestinian pounds. The education she had received from her liberal and enlightened parents, as well as the character she had developed over the years, made it difficult for her to accept the official policy of the bank, which for the most part quite obviously benefitted from the exploitation of Jewish refugees from Germany.

"Sometimes I can't understand the financial reports of the bank myself," she said one day to her husband. But she gritted her teeth and stuck to her job, because it was only due to her weekly wage, which she received in cash every Friday in a small envelope, as was customary in the British banking system, that they successfully maintained their property and did not drift into deprivation and loss following Dieter's dismissal from his position as Chief Architect of the Templer Association.

Dieter's opponents at the top of the organization – and there were many – had accused him of negligence that could have harmed the extension work of the Templer headquarters. There were even those who claimed that his negligence endangered the community's relations with the British authorities. Everyone understood that the campaign against him had nothing to do with his professional skills, but it was a convenient excuse to sack him because he had dared to step out of line and express his opinion against the mass mobilization of the Templers for the Fatherland, the Third Reich and the ideas of the Nazi Party.

In the months since his dismissal, Dieter had found it difficult to find a new job, despite his reputation as one of the most experienced and best professionals in the planning and construction business in the land. Hundreds of excellent architects, both Jewish refugees and immigrants, many of whom were graduates of the Academy in Dessau – from where the message of the Bauhaus was disseminated in the world and which was closed by the Nazis immediately after seizing power – had managed to reach the coast of Palestine during the last years. They were willing to accept any job and to be content with a pittance, only to preserve their professional skills.

Dieter did not give up.

He scanned the newspapers in all languages and answered all relevant job postings. He had called John Michael, the director of the State Surveyor's Department, whom he knew from the time when they had both worked with Austin Harrison, Chief Architect of the Mandate Authority on the planning and construction of the magnificent High Commissioner's residence, Government House, on the *Hill of Evil Council*[53]. "I really appreciate your abilities," Michael said politely, but with painful honesty, "and I also know that, unlike many others in your community, you are not crazy about the Austrian corporal who made *Führer*. But it is out of the question that, a representative of His Majesty's government in Palestine would hire the services of a German architect in these difficult times while clouds of war are gathering over Europe. This is hopeless from the outset. However, just this week a committee was constituted to select new candidates and, in spite of everything said here, I will try to put your name on the list."

He had also received negative reactions from Jewish colleagues. Even his Arab friends, including some of the leading contractors in Jerusalem, who had intervened and tried to obtain work for him, had failed.

The good and reliable Packard was the first victim of the austerity measures instigated by the Schwartes as a reaction to the recession, which had descended upon them. It was sold quickly and at a good price to a rich Arab meat merchant from neighboring *Katamon*[54]. But this money also disappeared quickly and the longer Dieter's unemployment lasted, the faster the family savings melted away. Old investments were cashed in. Angela, who always was a capable housewife, now had to muster all her skills to reduce their living-costs to a minimum. In view of this poverty, Dieter realized that he had to act quickly.

---

[53]A hill in Jerusalem. According to Christian tradition, the house of Caiaphas in which Judas betrayed Jesus was located there.

[54]A Jerusalem neighborhood, populated at the time by wealthy Arabs.

"I went to Canossa," he told Angela one evening with a long face in which the tension of the last few weeks was reflected in every wrinkle. "I turned to Ludwig Buchhalter." The name Buchhalter was known to every member of the Templer community. Buchhalter served as head of the Nazi party in Jerusalem and had founded the Palestinian branches of the Hitler Youth.

"Given the longtime friendship of our two families, I asked him what I would have to do to get my job back."

Angela's heart ached with Dieter's humiliation, that he had been driven to take such a desperate step for lack of choice and by the desire to support his family.

"Buchhalter looked at me with his little piggy eyes," Dieter described the conversation, "and barked something to the effect that I would have to prove my loyalty by joining the party and bringing Wolfgang along. 'Of course,' he added sarcastically, 'Wolfgang will have to give up his relationship with his Jewess.' When this happens, he promised, he would recommend that I be reinstated in my former position. 'After all, we are good Christians, not only loyal Nazis, and we can forgive, at least the members of our community.' That's precisely how he said it and you should have heard and seen the arrogance and gloating that dripped from his stupid sentences."

❄ ❄ ❄

That current conversation in the living room was a continuation of Dieter's humiliating meeting with Buchhalter. In such a charged atmosphere, it was little wonder that the family reunion, which had started quietly, increased rapidly in volume. Prior to this evening Wolfgang had never raised his voice against his father. But when Dieter came out with the requirement for Wolfgang to leave Tamar immediately, break up any relationship with her and join the Nazi party, harsh words were thrown around in shrill tones and from all directions.

"How can you ask such things of me? I'll never salute with raised arm and these Nazis can kiss my arse," screamed Wolfgang crudely. The last words were still reverberating in the room, when Willi, his younger brother, appeared on the doorstep. He wore the Hitler Youth uniform with swastika armband.

"You're a traitor to Germany. You're a traitor to the Aryan race," Willi joined the stormy yelling with the breaking voice of a pubescent boy who was parroting the demagogic crap he had absorbed for three years as a member of the Nazi youth movement. "You're screwing around and your affair with your Jewish whore defile the Aryan race."

"Willi, how dare you speak like that?! I'm not prepared to hear such words in this house. Stop it right now," his father said angrily.

But Willi was not to be pacified.

"I'm being teased and mocked because of you. Comrades come and sniff my arse like a crappy dog. And because of your mucking about, I get clobbered. At first I thought that my name was not on the list of applicants for the trip to the troop-leaders camp in Germany, because I'm not good or active enough. But now I know that I owe it only to you. It is only because of you and your damn Jew-whore that I get stuck here in the summer in Jerusalem while my comrades are having fun in the camp in the Black Forest."

"I have had enough now," Dieter got angry, "Willi, shut up and leave the room. I don't want to hear you anymore."

Willi, a 16-year-old boy as big as Wolfgang, of equal stature, with burning red acne on the face, stood on the threshold. He turned to his father, mother and brother, made the sound of spitting – but did not spit, because even in this upheaval he knew the limits – raised his arm, shouted "Heil Hitler" and slammed the door so hard that the plaster from the last century crumbled and covered the doorstep with a thin layer of dust.

❄ ❄ ❄

That very evening Wolfgang left the house.

He took the shabby backpack given to him years ago when he joined the Boy Scouts, stuffed into it a couple of shirts, a pair of trousers, underwear, socks, and a Swiss army knife that his great-uncle, Joseph Wennagel had given him years ago for his birthday. With a quick movement he emptied the numerous coins and some bills that had accumulated in his piggy bank, put them in his pocket and went out into the Jerusalem cold.

"I'm going now to Mount Scopus, to the hospital; I'll find Tamar and convince her to run away with me to Australia or Argentina or wherever," raced his thoughts as he walked with quick steps along the main street of the colony. He went in the direction of the Jerusalem train station and was very excited. "We are both young and healthy, have language skills and I have a trade. I'm a decent car mechanic and she is already half a nurse. Although we quarrel sometimes, we love each other. We'll make it anywhere." The last part of this defiant determination related to the nature of their relationship. There were ups and downs – long moments of happiness followed by disputes and tense silences.

From the first day of their acquaintance, Wolfgang had not given much thought to the substantial differences in their personalities. For him it was a simple story: he loves her, she loves him, and that's it. Emotional deliberations, deep conversations into the night, veiled glances, all these things he considered "feminine" and unnecessary. Sensitivity was not his strong point. Neither was intellectual activity. He was strong, loved sports, and, as a child, had a reputation in the colony as having been responsible for countless pranks.

As a young adult, he was almost in trouble with the police because of a spontaneous shooting competition with his friend, Helmut Schönfeld.

It started when Helmut was given a small air gun for his birthday by his father. The gun, which was operated by air pressure, shot small, round metal pellets that Wolfgang and Helmut frequently fired in all directions from the improvised shooting-range they had constructed on the edge of the colony.

Admittedly, their accuracy improved quickly, but not before some windows in the colony were smashed and at least two pellets got stuck in the inner wall of the Schwartz's kitchen. Horst Schwartz, seething with anger, threatened the two young men, whom he called "uncivilized louts with no respect for the property of others," with reporting to the police. Only thanks to the intervention of community elders, emotional apologies and begging for forgiveness by the two rascals, who had to pay the cost of the glazier and plasterer for the repairs out of their pocket money, tempers calmed.

Learning was not a priority for Wolfgang. Even in third or fourth grade, towards the end of each school year, he was forced to focus a bit more on memorizing material so as not to be kept back a year. This continued in the small village high school, where students were grouped into two forms in total. Wolfgang did well in mathematics and physics and got good marks without great effort. The agriculture teacher and his colleague, the frustrated artist, who had changed his profession and now taught crafts and mechanics, had also only good things to say about the student Wolfgang Schwarte. But in the humanities, especially in German literature, he found himself in the bottom third of the class. The leaders and teachers of the strict small community's education system were not sorry to see him depart after 12 years, armed with a minimum school leaving certificate, to compete with life.

These circumstances led to numerous large and small conflicts and disputes with Tamar, who was a bookworm and loved classical music. Even a simple decision, like what movie to go and see, led to discussions. When he wanted to go to a football match between the military and the police teams, she insisted on going to a chamber concert.

Truth be told, when the initial excitement of being in love was over and their relationship had settled down, Wolfgang felt some discomfort. He felt that Tamar expected him to polish his behavior which she had described one evening as "cutely proletarian, but sometimes annoying – needs to be spruced up."

But he was not offended and persuaded himself to appreciate the full half of the glass. He felt flattered by the fact that, despite his intellectual limitations – and he was aware of his inferiority – such a beautiful, intelligent and witty girl like her wanted him. He cherished in his heart the scene from a movie they had seen together, where the hero – he remembered that it was Leslie Howard – looked with a veiled glance into the eyes of his beloved and told her, "it's not the perfect couple who have a successful marriage, but actually the odd couple, because they learn to enjoy their differences."

"Yes, that's appropriate for us. Never in my life will I give her up," he hissed between clenched teeth as he walked away angrily from his parents' house in the German Colony of his childhood on his way to his beloved.

A last cold winter wind blew through the empty streets and a light rain drenched the world and Wolfgang.

A man and a woman, drawn in bright colors, stars of a romantic Italian film, exchanging a loving glance with each other, looked at him with moist eyes from the big poster on top of the Orient Cinema on the edge of the residential neighborhood. A young man and a young woman were hugging under the poster. "Once again, these Jews are sticking up illegal posters" chuckled Wolfgang, because he knew that the young man was apparently embracing the girl when in fact he was bill-sticking. "It must be easy to find volunteers for this task. Hugging, as well as snuggling while still serving the nation. What more can a boy and a girl want to enjoy an evening of a different kind."

The girl noticed him, but signaled the boy to continue gluing, after she had come to the conclusion that the approaching young man was an innocent pedestrian. When they were done with the bill-sticking, they jogged away while a faint scent of glue and a giggle accompanied their disappearance. Wolfgang had difficulty reading Hebrew, and except for the words "*Haganah*" and "fight the *white paper*[55]," he could not decipher the content of the moist poster at the edges of which the makeshift glue made from flour and water had accumulated.

The headlights of the few cars on the road from *Emek Refaim*[56] illuminated briefly the walls of buildings and smooth pavements, enlarging the shadows and projecting them like a magic-lantern show. From a distance, the voice of a British soldier was heard from the small unit that guarded the railway station. The soldier shouted something unintelligible to his mate in the next position. All Wolfgang could understand was half a sentence with the words "off duty" and "Orient Cinema."

Wolfgang had planned to run down into the valley of *Hinnom*[57], near the Scottish Church and St. John's Eye Hospital, circumvent the walls of the Old City from the east,

---

[55]The official document, published in 1939, outlining the British Government's policy in Palestine which was strongly biased against the Jewish population.

[56]A valley south of Jerusalem constituting the Templer colony's main street.

[57]Hebrew *Gai Ben Hinom*, generally known as Gehenna; a green valley, surrounding Jerusalem's south west.

climb up the narrow street to the churches on the Mount of Olives and from there to the saddle of Mount Scopus. He had often gone this way alone and with Tamar, proudly pointing out to her the magical sights of Jerusalem, impressing her with his knowledge, calling flowers by their name and taking her to beautiful and mysterious places. Wolfgang calculated that it would take less than an hour's fast walk to reach his goal, the Hadassah Hospital gate on Mount Scopus.

The sharp squealing of brakes interrupted his thoughts. From the corner of his eye he noticed the emblem of the British Palestine Police on the door of the patrol car which had stopped next to him: "Young man, what are you doing here in the middle of the night and, moreover, with a thief's backpack on your back," asked the policeman in a tone that did not make it clear whether this was the beginning of an investigation or a matter of interest with a touch of humor.

"I'm not a thief. My name is Wolfgang Schwarte, I live in the village and I'm going to visit my girlfriend," he answered in English the question that had been asked in Hebrew.

"Schwarte? You're actually from an *anständige*[58] family," remarked the officer. He stressed the German word for "decent" to clarify that he really meant it.

Wolfgang had instantly recognized the police officer. "You are Lubor Krummholz, chief of the German colony police station," he said with awe and curiosity. "I've seen you patrolling the streets, and heard a lot about you."

"It is very good if residents know the police chief of their district," Krummholz said, amused. "And what have you heard about me?" He asked, seemingly naive. He knew exactly what the Germans of "his" district thought of him. Inwardly, he had no doubt that many residents of German descent longed for the day when a large brick would fall

[58]German: decent.

from the sky directly on his head and it was likely that some even fantasized about what they could personally do to bring about this happy day.

Krummholz came to the *Emek Refaim* precinct according to his own expressed wish, after he had coincidentally walked along the road one day and saw swastika flags fluttering in the Jerusalem wind. He was shocked. Swastikas in Jerusalem?

This sight drove Krummholz, a Jewish immigrant from Poland, to voluntarily apply to join the police force so that he could combat this phenomenon. At the end of the training, he received the Best Police Recruit Award and was offered the opportunity to choose his own posting. "I would like the *Refaim* precinct," he requested and got it.

Krummholz focused on collecting information about Nazi activists and tried, within the legal framework, of course, to curb the Nazi presence on the streets in the neighborhood that drove many inhabitants of Jerusalem to anger, not just the Jews.

"You are the focus of countless debates," Wolfgang said. "The Nazis claim that the British had evil intentions when they appointed you especially, a Jewish policeman, chief of the precinct in this district. They did this to humiliate us Germans."

Krummholz smiled under his mustache, which grew in the lower third of his face. This hairy feature had great similarity with the mustache that decorated the face of Adolf Hitler. Although this mustache was one of the Nazi leader's characteristics, it was still acceptable in many circles. It was not until the outbreak of the Second World War that the "Hitler mustache" went out of fashion.

"It's pouring down with rain," said the policeman. "What are you waiting for? A special invitation? Get in. I'll drive you wherever you want, or at least part of the way. But tell me, young man, what do you think?"

"About what," asked Wolfgang, grateful for the unexpected lift. He took his pack off his back, put it on the floor and sat in the car.

"What do you think about my appointment as chief of the police precinct in this district?"

"I don't know. Maybe it's true that they have posted you here to annoy the residents. It certainly enrages the Nazis. But the Nazis see a conspiracy and action against them in almost everything. They're insane, these Nazis."

"So you are one of the few who does not shout 'sieg heil'. But why should that surprise me? You are the son of Dieter, the architect who created tremendous turbulence in your community," remarked Krummholz, scrutinizing his passenger. "Very well. Talk to me, young man. I'm a policeman and it is my job to ensure that everything is alright. However, one need not be a policeman to realize that something is wrong when a young man hangs around in the middle of the night, in heavy rain, with a backpack on his back. What's going on? Where's the fire?"

This simple question, or perhaps it was the sympathetic tone of Krummholz's words caused a kind of emotional dam-burst in Wolfgang, who was still flustered by the heavy discussion that had taken place in his parental home. Now he was glad to unload the stress that had accumulated during the last months and that had led to the family quarrel tonight.

He described in great detail to the police officer not only the confrontation with his parents, but also selected items of his almost impossible love story with Tamar. Absorbed in his own agitation, he had not noticed that the policeman Krummholz had stopped the car at the roadside and was listening, his face expressionless.

"I'm fed up with everything," Wolfgang described how he felt. "I want to run away from here with Tamar. I don't care where. We'll start a new life, and if necessary, change our names."

"Very romantic," Krummholz responded sensitively. "But it is not so easy. You have to weigh up very carefully before you act hastily. By the way, in terms of name change I can attest first hand that it is quite simple. I myself, Lubor Krummholz, have applied for my name to be changed into something more Hebrew."

"Why?" Wolfgang asked, more out of politeness than out of interest in the efforts of a Jewish policeman in Palestine about his name.

"What name did you choose?"

"Canaan, Haviv Canaan," Krummholz said. "This is a Hebrew name, a little unusual, but I like it. Sounds really Hebrew and somewhat Oriental. What do you think?"

Wolfgang shrugged and nodded his head in a gesture indicating "sounds good."

The police car took fifteen minutes to cross the empty and wet streets of Jerusalem at slow speed – the distance that Wolfgang had planned to run in one hour. During the whole trip, Krummholz did not stop trying to convince him to give up the idea of escape. But he failed in this task and therefore contented himself with driving Wolfgang – as promised – to the hospital gate.

"It's all right. He's with me," Krummholz said to the zealous gatekeeper, who refused visitors access at such a late hour.

"I can only wish you much success," Krummholz said in parting from the excited young man. "And don't forget, before jumping hastily into anything, think about my advice: before any major decision, go to the fence and pee. No hasty action, think twice and only then make a decision, especially when it is a fateful decision."

Armed with ardent love, angry about the difficult conversation in his parents' house, equipped with the desire to prove to himself and to the world that he can move mountains, and, with the blessing of the policeman Krummholz, who had helped him at the gate to get through onto the Hadassah site, Wolfgang positioned himself under Tamar's bedroom window. After the third stone he had gently thrown – these were tiny pebbles he had chosen for fear that he might break the window – the fourth window from the left on the second floor opened and out peered the curly head of a young woman.

"Who are you?" She asked, surprised by the shadowy appearance of the young man who was almost swallowed up by the darkness.

"I am Tamar's friend. I'm looking for her," Wolfgang said in a loud whisper, "Do me a favor and call her please."

"Tamar, here is a gentleman. Although he has no guitar, he gives the impression as if he had a serenade in his heart," the girl reported to Tamar, who was lying in bed cramming study material, on ways and means of treating burns. "Although I don't know him, I suppose it is your Wolfgang."

Tamar did not hear the last part of the sentence, in which you could detect a hint of jealousy even without being an expert. She ran to the window and thrust her head out with a movement that was too fast and inaccurate. It caused her a painful scratch on the upper part of the forehead.

"*Wolfgang, was machst Du hier?*" she uttered with an anxious voice while pressing her right hand to her head, without being aware that she had blurted out the question "what are you doing here," in German.

"I need to talk to you. It's important. Please come down."

"Are you crazy? I'm not allowed to leave the building. The main entrance is locked and the Warden keeps the key. She might appear any moment and punish me."

Despite the wind, rain and locked windows, rumors about the romantic events going on in the backyard under Tamar's room had spread rapidly among the student nurses. An increasing number of windows opened into the cool night and the cold wind, the frames being filled by young heads – some giggling, others shutting up their fellow students in an attempt to better follow the exchange of words.

"Wait for me in the grove," Tamar said. "I'll get a coat and come to you."

"How can you come down? You said that the main entrance is closed."

"Don't worry, there are other doors. Now just go! Go into the woods. Don't just hang around like a *Potz*[59]."

❄ ❄ ❄

The musty smell of rainwater that had been absorbed by the thick carpet of pine needles was wafting in the air. The trees in the grove on the edge of the Hadassah compound – a mixture of pine and cypress trees, blocked the wind and softened the sound of the raindrops. The drops that did manage to run down and hit the ground with a muffled thud, were swallowed by a carpet of leaves and needles covering the ground and the few pine mushrooms that had escaped the knives of the hikers and started to flow slowly towards the parched Jordan Valley.

"Like an angel! She looks like an angel," the thought flashed through his head at the sight of the approaching figure of his beloved, silhouetted against the light from the hospital buildings.

From the first day, Wolfgang and Tamar had liked to hug, kiss and cuddle. But the long embrace at the beginning of their meeting in the grove, was undoubtedly of unusual intensity.

"I love you," she whispered in his ear. "I don't remember where I read it, but someone had once said that if any

---

[59]Yiddish pejorative for the male organ.

separation is a little like dying, each reunion is like a resurrection."

They stood for a long time in a tight embrace and kissed, his right hand stroking her hair, her neck. His left hand dug love furrows in her back while Tamar's arms clasped his strong body.

"I cannot live like this. Come with me. Let's escape from this damned place," he said in a choked voice.

Tamar increased her hug and gave him dozens of kisses during the few minutes in which he described the stormy debate that had taken place earlier in the evening at the Schwarte home.

"Where shall we flee to? How shall we escape? Which country will even let us into their territory?" Tamar broke loose from their embrace and replied with a composure that stood in stark contrast to their passionate cuddling. "Wolfgang, I love you with all my heart, with my whole body. I love you because of the little things. Your hand stroking me in difficult moments. Your generous compliments when I wear the terrible red dress that hangs on me like a potato sack. The Anemone bouquet that you had picked in a field and brought to me before my big anatomy exam. Your ability to share my pleasures, to forgive my weaknesses, to encourage me. And your smile? It is said that a smile is the shortest distance between two people and when you smile, I am drawn to you, like iron to a magnet. But," she took a deep breath, "but someone up there has decided that we cannot be together."

"How can you say such horrible things," Wolfgang reacted completely shocked. In sharp contrast to the enchanting moments of love at the beginning of the meeting, Tamar described in detail, with no shortcuts or omissions, the extent of the hate and slander that she had had to take in the last few weeks and the numerous threats that she had had to endure.

She repeated calmly and in a businesslike tone, the attack of thugs, the threats to slash her face, the curses, and the hate letters, which arrived almost daily in her dorm's letterbox, "Wolfgang, I'm afraid; I'm really scared," she whispered. A slight tremor in her voice indicated that she had lost some of the self-control she had exhibited at the beginning of the conversation. Her body trembled after her brain actually recorded all she had poured into his ears. "This will end badly. I'm going to get my face slashed, maybe even some bones broken and left crippled. And you will be killed either by Nazi or Jewish villains. Oh, if life were only like a Hollywood film. There, everything ends after 90 minutes with a happy ending and even to the sound of violins. No way can our story have a happy ending. Just bad luck. Do you remember the British soldier at the Abu Dis checkpoint on the road to Jericho during our trip in winter? Yes, that nice Black Watch guy, who couldn't hide his astonishment about us being a couple. Being together. Why? Because in this country, which is plagued by holiness and madness, our love affair is a synonym for 'impossible'. So I have to call it off, not because I don't love you, but on the contrary, because I love you so much."

Weeks later, Tamar often repeated with an aching heart their last conversation in the dark, wet grove on Mount Scopus. With each repetition, she was amazed again at the calmness and judiciousness she had displayed.

"At that time I had not yet realized that awareness had already matured earlier deep inside me, that the bells of life had been ringing and announcing the end of our love story. It seems that I still loved him at that point in time, but less. Otherwise there is no explanation for why it was I that had really broken off our relationship," she tried to summarize it for herself. But that did not mean she had not cried that night.

Wolfgang wailed uncontrollably. Her resolute tone, the logical structure of her arguments hit him like an avalanche of huge rocks. He was aware of the differences of opinion between them on various issues. But never for one second had he doubted the strength of their love. Suddenly it became clear to him that she loved him, but with reservations and restrictions. This fact came to light just then, when he exposed himself emotionally to her, revealing his boundless love for her with his desire to tie his life with hers forever! He found it incredibly difficult to gather his thoughts. As a rule, he was not afraid to quarrel with her, even though Tamar had an innate ability to argue. He had often wondered why she had chosen to attend nursing school instead of law school.

"To argue with you is like reading a newspaper in the wind," he demurred in a previous debate.

"We love each other, but a little differently," she snapped.

"So, here I am. Take me and teach me. Teach me to love."

He could not hide his anger.

"My darling," Tamar said in a sweet voice while stroking his neck, which sent shivers through his body. "You cannot teach love. You can infect someone with love, you can cherish love, but you cannot teach love."

"You don't understand the error you are committing," he told her before they parted. "The mistake of your life. Until your last day you'll never get rid of the feeling that on the summit of Mount Scopus you made the mistake of your life." He spoke this sentence under the lantern, which spread yellow light at the entrance gate to the student dormitory of the nursing school. "I love you for all eternity, and we will meet again. *Don't know where, don't know when, but I know we'll meet again ...*[60]"

---

[60]Allied soldiers used to sing these opening words of the hit made famous by Vera Lyn during WWII.

For some reason he had said the last sentence in English. In a rational moment amid the heartbreaking drama, he remarked to himself that this phrase sounded great, like a vibrant love song.

❄ ❄ ❄

A small Jackdaw, gray and ugly, shrieked its first calls into the clear morning sky, when Wolfgang returned home to the German colony. He slowly turned the key in the lock of the front door, trying not to wake the occupants. He tiptoed into the kitchen. "I'm glad you're back and I won't ask what you've been up to in the last few hours," his father welcomed him softly.

Despite the early hour, he was sitting in the kitchen, next to the window overlooking the landscaped garden, a steaming cup of coffee in his hand. "I could not sleep after our debate. I'm sorry about what I said to you," he said gently, noticing the stoop of his first-born, with his red eyes and drooping lines around his mouth on the verge of tears. For the first time in years, Wolfgang and his father embraced at length.

"Dad, I know you're going through a terrible period," Wolfgang said, "and I'm sorry that I was so selfish lately only focusing on myself and what is important to me." Aware that, contrary to the expressed words of greeting, his father did want to know the details of the night, Wolfgang reconstructed the events of the last few hours – from the lift he was offered by the Jewish police officer to the break-up talk with Tamar in the night-shrouded grove on the top of Mount Scopus.

"Dad, on the way here from Mount Scopus, I made a decision about what I'm going to do."

Dieter drank his coffee and lowered his head, as if to say, "I'm all ears."

"I love Henrietta and will love her in the future. But you once told me that it always takes two to love, like to tango. She's scared and is determined to end our relationship; so I can't go on living in Jerusalem, aware that she lives and breathes, maybe even builds a new life for herself, and all that just a few miles from here."

With thoughtful and measured words, Wolfgang described his plan to go to Germany to study automotive engineering in combination with work. One of the owners of the garage, where he was working, knew the directors of the Ford factory in Cologne. He assumed that he only needed to ask its director to get him employed as an apprentice.

"Not a bad idea, Wolfgang. You are choosing exactly the right career," interrupted Dieter. "You know that the girls nowadays have no ear for music. You could spend hours standing under the window of a pretty girl and serenading her, without getting a reaction, but if she only hears your car horn, she falls straight into your arms."

Wolfgang smiled. He appreciated his father's attempt at improving the atmosphere and dispersing a little the heavy clouds and heart ache floating around in the kitchen. "You've always had a special spark," Dieter said, "of the mischievous sort, the making out type. Do you know what I mean? There are those who pray every night, as children, to get a new bike, until they realize that God in His wisdom does not function that way. Then they steal a bike and pray that God may forgive them."

Two weeks later, Wolfgang was looking back at the disappearing Mount Carmel from the deck of a Greek passenger liner. He waved to his family, who was left behind on the dock in Haifa – including his younger brother Willie – who even now insisted on wearing the brown Hitler Youth pants. But even Willie, who was intoxicated by the mindless slogans that he had heard from his leaders, understood, that it was better to leave at home the second part of his favorite uniform, the brown shirt with the swastika.

He had not seen Tamar since that fateful night. For days, he had fought with himself about whether he should write her a goodbye note but had finally given up on the idea.

"I'll never return to Palestine," he vowed. He glanced at the vanishing Haifa and a second later had already lifted his vow in his mind. "But I love her so much. I will never forget her. What's with this stupid oath I'm swearing here? I have told her myself, 'we'll meet again'. I do not know where and don't know when, but we'll meet again."

❄ ❄ ❄

While she was making the beds in the hospital's surgical ward, Alisa hummed a tune softly. Only when she noticed Tamar's tears, did she realize that the soft sounds coming out of her mouth were the first verse of "*al sfat yam kineret*". Suddenly Tamar began to cry her eyes out, bolted out of the room, ran into the bathroom and locked herself in one of the stalls.

"What's the matter with her? She behaves like a madwoman," murmured Naomi, her classmate. "What's happening to her? The cheerful Tamar, who had blossomed like a palm tree on the Sea of Galilee, has become a nervous wreck in recent days. Maybe she's even pregnant?"

Alisa shot her a dirty look.

"A broken heart Naomi, that's the havoc a broken heart wreaks. Yesterday she found out that her boyfriend has left the country."

"But they had already split up, right?" Naomi was wondering. "They are no longer friends."

"Maybe they have parted company with words, but not in their hearts. And I hope that you never have to experience something like what Tamar is going through now. Believe me, I know from personal experience what I'm talking about."

Hangar 12, German *Luftwaffe* Base near Athens, Summer 1942

Despite the closed doors, a wind was blowing in Hangar 12, accompanied by a whistling sound, which grew louder with the intensification of the airstream. A row of large holes marked a line along the roof of the building, like soldiers on parade, resulting from dozens of American produced half-inch machine-gun bullets. In the middle of the big, dismal building stood a DC 3 aircraft, also known as a Dakota, painted in neutral khaki color, without markings.

"We have quickly repaired the holes that the Brits shot into the wings three days ago, but the engine has given us a lot of grief," muttered the gray-haired, middle-aged man. Before the war, he was Chief Mechanic at Lufthansa and had earned the reputation of having "golden hands".

"Just give him an engine and a propeller and he can turn even a closet into a reliable aircraft," his colleagues used to say in awe.

"Four rounds hit the engine, smashed four of the 14 cylinders, ripped through the hoses and all that deep inside, where making repairs is most difficult."

He was standing on a high ladder with another mechanic for whom his murmuring about the problematic engine was meant. They were examining the repair work meticulously using flashlights. The senior technician was poking about inside the engine, accompanied by the recitation of technical details and stating that, thanks to the original maintenance manual of the manufacturer – Pratt & Whitney – which had probably arrived via Switzerland, the engine was re-assembled according to instructions.

"Otherwise we would still be busy with putting it together. And I am not even talking about mounting the additional fuel tanks to extend the flight range of this plane, which, between you and me, and maybe I shouldn't say this out loud, is much better than our so glorified Junkers 52."

Along the walls were stacks of equipment boxes and parachute containers.

Other mechanics and soldiers were running around in the hangar, some busy checking equipment, others were relatively successful in practicing the technique of hectic idleness, known to soldiers of all the armies in the world, to provide their commanders with the impression that they were frightfully busy. In a remote corner of the hall, lay two men, stretched out on thin military mattresses, wrapped in gray army blankets, their heads draped in *keffiyes* against light and noise; they were sleeping, or maybe just napping.

"I need help to unload the lorry," called a plump sergeant from the entrance of the hangar.

"You, you and you, come here. And you there, sentry, watch out that the driver of the van, who appears to me to be quite inquisitive and intrusive, does not stick his head into the hangar."

❄ ❄ ❄

In a small area, shielded by a tarpaulin, three officers were sitting at a rickety table on which a tin cup, a plate of half-chewed sandwiches and various devices were spread out.

"Wolfgang, excuse the question, but I've noticed that you're carrying a colorful civilian scarf in your backpack, and, a woolen one to boot," said Captain Kurt Wieland. "Hello, it's summer now. What exactly is this scarf all about?"

"It's a long story that has to do with my mother's knitting passion. But for me it means something very personal, so for three years I have been carrying it around everywhere, ever since leaving Jerusalem. Summer, winter, whenever," said Lieutenant Wolfgang Schwarte.

"Yes, everyone has their own little quirks," Wieland said. "With you it's just the scarf. Whatever."

Captain Wieland was of average size, whose receding hairline and large ears made him look much older than he was. At first glance, he looked like a bored and sloppy postman. Contrary to regulations and standing orders, he had not buttoned his uniform jacket up to his neck. Stains on the collar of his white shirt, which he wore under his jacket, were clearly visible.

"Please go to the other end of the hall, wake Hassan Salame and Zulfikar Abu Latif, and take them through an additional drill," Wieland commanded Schwarte. "Repeat the landing, so that they don't break their legs on the ground."

Wieland and Schwarte knew that the planned landing site, at the mouth of *Wadi Kelt*, near Jericho, was to be marked with fire torches by the reception unit who would be waiting for them. However, as experienced veteran soldiers they prepared for unexpected problems.

"Given the competence of our two muftis, it's a safe bet that both will finish the jump with at least one broken leg – each – or even worse," Wieland explained. Wolfgang Schwarte smiled, saluted casually, got up from the bench and, one second after he had begun to move in the direction of the two sleeping men, he stopped and turned to Wieland. “Look, Kurt,” he began in a very unmilitary style, disregarding the rules of distance due to the years of their personal acquaintance. “I’m worried about a few things.”

Wieland responded with a tired smile, but did not reply and listened quietly. “I have no problem with the fact that our operation has no time limit. I am also aware that it might take months for Rommel to have accumulated enough provisions to break through the British defenses in Egypt and reach Palestine. It’s true that a rendezvous with a supply submarine is planned. Nevertheless, it can take months until the *Afrika Korps* can cross hundreds of miles from the Western Desert and the Sinai. Who knows when he can join us?”

A slight nod indicated that Wieland, the team commander, was listening to every one of Wolfgang’s words, wondering whether it might be advisable to interrupt him and say something about this. But Wolfgang beat him to it and went on with his questions. “Well, that does not bother me; but to be honest, do you really believe that fairy tale the Mufti sold Canaris and Himmler about the two divisions of Arab freedom fighters battling the British Army in Palestine and Transjordan? Do you really think that we are joining some force of Arab partisans, training and leading them in commando actions behind British army lines in Palestine?”

Wieland raised his right hand halfway up, opened it and made a quick movement to the right and left, which meant “more or less, not necessarily.”

“Unfortunately, I tend to agree with you,” he said in a tired voice, “and not just because of a gut feeling.”

Quietly, so that his words reached Wolfgang’s ears only, he informed him of new details. “After the briefing at the headquarters in Berlin, Wilfried Hause took me aside. Perhaps you know him. He is also a Templer, but older than us, from Jaffa, from Walhalla. Hause now serves with Intelligence and is responsible for the region of Syria, Lebanon, and Palestine. In short, because we are both almost compatriots, Hause departed from the field-security regulations and told me that *Abwehr* agents in Palestine, who have, as far as I know, at least one particularly successful agent operating in Tel Aviv, have been unable to confirm the Mufti's assertions about the scope of his people's activities in Palestine." Wieland took a deep breath and continued with the report of the details known to Hause, and especially the fact, that not only the *Abwehr* was unable to find any confirmation of the alleged anti-British Arab commando operations. Throughout the entire German intelligence community there was no glimmer of a report on this subject.

"Anyway, Wilfried tends to think that all this talk of an Arab guerrilla army in Palestine is part of a British S.O.E[61] ploy."

Instead of being worried about Wieland's reply, Wolfgang laughed briefly.

"I laugh, although I should be concerned that we may be jumping directly into a trap. Berlin has apparently no idea of oriental fantasies," he grinned and continued in a serious tone: "I imagine how the Mufti is sitting in front of Himmler, selling him Arabian Nights stories about the Arab underground; how his daring warriors are laying mines at traffic junctions, setting ambushes for British Army patrols, blowing up the Iraq-Haifa oil pipeline, sniping at Jewish settlements and causing headaches for the Brits; how this paralyzes tens of thousands of soldiers in Palestine who are pursuing his people in the Jerusalem hills and the Jordan valley, instead of occupying positions in the western desert opposite Rommel and his *Afrika Korps*."

Wolfgang's amusing description made Wieland smile.

---

[61] Special Operations Executive.

Wolfgang paused in order to take out a cigarette, but remembered that he was standing near a fully fueled aircraft and put it back in the box. “Personally I don’t believe a word that Mufti Haj Amin al-Husseini utters,” he said emphatically. “He tells stories and can’t distinguish between reality and fantasy. Even at the peak of the Arab revolt under his leadership, when he used leaflets to call for the ‘burning of the Holy Land’, life went on more or less as usual in Jerusalem. Do you remember any differently? We were not only going to the Orient Cinema in the colony, but also to the Edison, Zion and Rex, went for walks in the city, ate ice cream on Ben Yehuda Street and were hiking in the *wadis* outside the city. During the winter months, we’d go to Jericho almost every weekend. We were playing soccer in the fields between the colony, *Talbiyeh* and *Rehavia*; we’d go to *Sarona* and on weekends to the beach in Tel Aviv. It is true that I remember a few weeks of tensions at the beginning of 1936 when I was a boy, but then everything calmed down more or less, and the revolt by the Mufti and his people expressed itself primarily in the mutual murder of rival clans.”

Wieland, who was busy with meticulously cleaning his Luger, looked up at Wolfgang, wondering where this conversation was going.

“I still can’t believe that we might be seeing our homes again in a few days,” Wolfgang continued going off at a tangent to the description of his nocturnal dreams of Jerusalem, the *Emek Refaim* colony, the church bells, the Sunday rest. He also dreamt of a beautiful girl he had once painfully loved. Lately, having been given the new assignment of parachuting into the vicinity of Jerusalem, she reappeared in the forefront of his memories, but this part he kept to himself.

“I still remember our Boy Scouts and the Hitler Youth jaunts. Do you remember our hike along the train tracks, built by the Brits at the end of the last war? From the train station in Jerusalem, through the hills of *Talbiyeh*, the San Simon Monastery, then through *Lifta*[62] to the outskirts of *Ramallah*[63]? And how many times were we in *Wadi Kelt* and *Ein Fareh*? At least three times! And I see the Monastery of St. George like a postcard in my mind's eye. In color. And the Inn of the Good Samaritan with the Crusader castle across the road, and how John, the British scoutmaster, fell from the *Wadi Kelt* aqueduct. John, you may remember, wanted to keep us in the scouts at all cost and continued to lead us, even after our activities in the Hitler Youth had begun, in the hope that we could be persuaded to remain in the Boy Scouts."

"Oh," Wieland let out a sigh, either because of the memories, or as a hint to Wolfgang that he had been talking too long. "How long ago was that? Five years, six? You were three intakes behind me, weren't you? But it all seems like something from another world."

Wieland examined the gun closely, looked into the polished barrel, and blew into it, as if to remove an invisible speck of dust. "Honestly Wolfgang? I find it strange to hear how you invoke memories and relish nostalgia. In my head I have an image of you which, to express it politely, differs a bit from what you describe here. I won't mention that in the neighborhood they said of you: 'he never let school interfere with his education.' You were naughty, rebellious, quarreled with teachers and with everyone who had a whiff of authority. Correct me if I am wrong here, but you were really never thrilled with the Hitler Youth activities, the torch parades, and the loyalty-oath to Führer and Fatherland." In a matter-of-fact tone, with the intention of avoiding sounding critical,

---

[62] An Arabic village at the outskirts of Jerusalem

[63] An Arab town, about 15 km north east of Jerusalem. Today, the Capital of the Palestinian Authority.

Wieland pointed out how Wolfgang had already left the Hitler Youth in the early days of the movement. "You fell by the wayside quite early on and willingly chose to become socially isolated," Wieland said. "Later you even found yourself a Jewish girlfriend. Her name was Henrietta, wasn't it? And an Arab soulmate, what was his name? Nabil, Nabil Nashashibi. To further complicate the whole thing, he also had a Jewish girlfriend. The four of you insisted adamantly on staying together, on spending time together, as if that was the most normal thing that could happen in Palestine – a Jew, an Arab, and a German with a Jewish woman going out together as a group. Honestly! That sounds like the beginning of a joke."

From his expression, it was easy to see that Wolfgang Schwarte did not like the new direction of the conversation at all.

"How they gossiped about you and your family! On Sunday, after the service in the community one would hear 'Schwarte, Schwarte, Schwarte' from all directions. Likewise, in the queue at the counter of Müller's grocery store, at Schmidt's butcher shop in the city and in Ludwig's dairy. The Schwarte family in general and especially you were a popular topic of conversation. What a troublemaker! You were as stubborn as a mule. Heaven help us."

Wieland poured a decent measure of *Schnapps* into his glass of tea from a metal flask in his pocket, took a careful sip and looked with amusement at Wolfgang, who tried to keep a blank expression despite the nervous twitching at the corners of his mouth.

"As to your question, which I had almost forgotten, because I got carried away," Wieland continued, "one of the reasons why I was happy to join this operation – although I realize that there is no division, not even a battalion, a platoon or even a squad of Arab freedom fighters who are loyal to the Mufti and are attacking the British enemy from behind – was that I would thereby somehow manage to see my family again." The level of *Schnapps* and tea in his glass had sunk in the meantime. He took a deep breath and continued. "It's been three years since we were last together and over a year since I've heard from my family. I have no idea how my parents are, what's going on with my two sisters, my uncles and aunts. Nothing. On the first Sunday of the war, in September 1939, the police came to the Colony led by Krummholz, the Jewish policeman, who was then chief of the police precinct – didn't you say that he was called Canaan, not Krummholz? How do you know? Never mind. Doesn't matter. So, the police came to the town hall, waited until the service was over and then arrested Imberger, head of the Templer community in Jerusalem and the Nazi Party branch in the city. At the same time they also detained his wife and his son and took them to jail in the Old City."

"This Imberger was no small bastard," Wolfgang remarked.

"And a great fool," Wieland added with a smile. "It is said that Imberger, on his way to prison in the police car, saluted with his arm raised, shouted Heil Hitler, yelled at the police and threatened them that it was only a matter of a few weeks, until the German army would reach Palestine, when they, the police, would be the ones to have to salute him, Imberger ... "

Wolfgang who had earlier expressed his opinion about Imberger, enjoyed Wieland's narration, and laughed heartily.

"Anyway," Wieland continued, "the last Red Cross postcard, which reached me in 1940, came from a prison camp in *Atlit*. My parents wrote that with them, in the same camp, behind the barbed wire fence, were Jewish prisoners from Vienna, Prague, and Gdansk who had tried to immigrate to Palestine illegally. What a world, eh? Jewish refugees from Germany who took refuge in Palestine are locked up together with Germans who were born in

Palestine. The Brits wanted to deport all illegal Jews to Mauritius, but the Jewish underground movement sank one of their deportation ships and the explosion killed at least two hundred of them. The British then agreed to let some of them stay in Palestine and the rest – about 900 or so, including children – they still expelled to Mauritius." Wieland drank the rest of his fortified tea quickly. "But why am I bending your ear with this; after all, you haven't heard from your family either since then. Dinninger!" Wieland turned to the third soldier: "What's happening with you in the north, in Waldheim?"

"Six months ago I received a letter from my parents through the Red Cross," Fritz Dinninger said softly. "Actually, not really a letter, rather a postcard, a censored document, a few lines written in pencil, with minimal details. Because they used the names of friends and family members who live in different places, I realized, reading between the lines, that the British had arrested all the men of military age at the beginning of the war. If we had stayed in Palestine, they would have arrested us, too."

Wolfgang shook his head, hesitated, but interrupted Dinninger nevertheless. "Listen, taking into account all the shit we have eaten since the outbreak of war, our recruitment to the *Abwehr* unit because of our special background, all the battles from Poland to Russia, I'm not so sure that it wouldn't have been better, to sit in a British prison camp in Palestine, eat Jaffa oranges, flirt with the female prisoners and at least smell our home."

A slight twitch that could be interpreted as consent for Wolfgang's words ran along Wieland's face.

Dinninger went on with his analysis and stressed that he personally believed that the goddess of fortune was on his side and on the side of two the hundred other young men from the community who had traveled to Germany a few days before the outbreak of war on what was described as "family visits". "And you, Schwarte, had even been sent long before the war to Stuttgart and Cologne to study," he continued, "and as to our families in Palestine I have deciphered from the postcard that part of the Haifa, Jaffa and Jerusalem community members are held in several places, especially in *Atlit*, but also in other small camps."

"We know that. Give us something new," demanded Wieland.

Ignoring the remark and without altering the volume of his voice, Dinninger continued softly. "The agricultural settlements, Waldheim and Bethlehem in the Galilee in the north, Wilhelma and part of *Sarona*, have been surrounded with barbed wire by the Brits. But the guards, Indian soldiers and Jewish watchmen, let the residents work the land and sell the produce on the markets. It is claimed that the Red Cross is working on a huge deal to exchange our families with British Empire nationals stranded in Europe because of the war. But honestly, I can't imagine either your parents or mine leaving Palestine voluntarily. My 77-year-old grandfather arrived as a child, at the age of just over two years, with the first group who had already landed in Haifa in 1868. He doesn't know Germany at all, because he had left it before it was united. What would he be doing there? He would not want to go home to the Reich."

"Do me a favor Kurt," Wolfgang tried his luck, to change the order he had received from Wieland, which had led to the last conversation. "Let Dinninger drill those two muftis. After all, he is fluent in Arabic, and even in the original Galilean dialect. Thus, at least Salame cannot shirk carrying out the instructions for allegedly not understanding what we want or demand of him."

"*Yalla* Wolfgang, *yalla imshi*[64]," Wieland said, using the first Arabic phrase that every child in the German colonies had learned. In the current situation, his words caused all

[64]Arabic: come on, let's go or get a move on.

three to smile. "Schwarte, stop looking for excuses. Go ahead and be done with it. And after you have finished" he stood up and walked over to the pile of equipment, "join Fritz and me to put some things in order."

"What is there left to do? I thought that everything was packed and ready," Wolfgang wondered.

"Rule number one: tidying up has no end. There's always something new," Wieland laughed. "There is a big package with a new chemical material that I have received from the technical department; they claim that it drives sniffer dogs mad. 'You scatter a few grams and the dogs lose their sense of smell' they explained. I want every one of you to have a small amount of this powder in your equipment and scatter it as soon as we leave the landing area after the jump. The problem is that this stuff comes without a label." He pointed to a large brown paper sack, which was marked only with a skull as a warning against poison. "If the Brits catch us, they will malign us by inventing some story about how we had come to poison wells, or something like that."

Fritz and Schwarte exchanged amused glances.

"In addition, here is the operation-fund with a thousand gold coins, we have received from headquarters. We will divide them among us and keep the fund away from the eyes of Salame and Zulfikar who don't need to know that there is such a fund, lest they get some silly ideas. I would like everyone to stash few coins in his equipment for emergencies. It seems to me that we can expect many emergency hours in the coming days. *Yallah* Schwarte, come on, stop wasting time and take care of our two muftis."

❄ ❄ ❄

Wolfgang had barely gone a few yards when suddenly a loud shout echoed through the hangar. "*Achtung*," yelled the guard who stood at the entrance to the building.

Colonel Ravel, dressed in the *Luftwaffe* full dress uniform, came in at a fast pace, accompanied by his personal aide and four officers. With a flick he returned the salute of Wieland and his men. "Captain Wieland, Lieutenant Schwarte, and Lieutenant Dinninger, please come. It seems that Berlin decided to change some important details of 'Operation Plier Squeeze' and I want to bring you up to date," he said, giving his adjutant a sign to spread a large map of the eastern Mediterranean on the table. "Let me introduce the teams that will take you to your destination."

The paratroopers shook hands with the crew members – two pilots, a navigator, and a flight engineer – exchanged a few brief greetings and gathered around the table.

"We've received new details," Ravel began, "and I am pleased to inform you that apparently the flight to your destination will run a lot smoother than we had imagined."

Dinninger or maybe it was Wieland, let out a small sigh of relief. Or so it seemed to Wolfgang.

"To make you realize how important your operation is and without going into all the effort and resources that have been mobilized to ensure its success, I can tell you that the *Luftwaffe* Intelligence Department succeeded in obtaining fairly current, detailed aerial photographs of the intended landing site," Ravel continued, having heard the sigh, but decided to ignore it.

"Excuse the question," interrupted Wieland, "if you say, fairly current, what does that mean?"

Ravel, who never tolerated this kind of interruption, shot a cold look at the questioner. "I can't go into the operational details of the photo reconnaissance," he said dryly, "but please remember that we are dealing with a remote, sparsely populated desert region. So, even if this is the result of a mission last year, the data about hidden caves, water sources, locations of telephone lines and so on are still relevant. You need to memorize the photos very carefully. Our decryption experts have marked several points on the photos that you should remember."

He gave Wieland a large brown envelope with the words "top secret."

"Now, to the flight details. You will take off from the base after dark without any contact with the control tower. The entire take-off procedure will be carried out with the help of flares. The *Tommies* are listening in on us and we don't want to make their lives easier, right?" Ravel returned to the briefing, "You will be flying eastwards at low altitude and reach Turkish airspace here," he said, pointing to a spot on the Aegean coast. Ravel's instructions went to the smallest detail. He explained that in parallel with the penetration of their plane into Turkish airspace, ten Junkers 88 bombers would also be taking off from this base and some Italian bombers would join them from Rhodes, to run a diversionary attack on the British base of Castellorizo and take out the radar stationed there. He reminded them that he is talking about an island, located just a few miles off the Turkish coast opposite the town of Kas which was being bombed by the *Luftwaffe* every few weeks, so that such an attack should not arouse any British suspicion. "Apart from this distraction, our *Abwehr* comrades have received a reliable report from a sympathizing Turkish Air Force officer, that the new radar system, which was recently installed in the mountains of *Antalya*, works only partially and leaves large parts of the coast unguarded. Even the Turkish air traffic control barely works. You will exploit these holes by advancing eastward at low altitude."

"What do we do if the Turkish radar identifies us nevertheless, demands identification and even dispatches a warplane to check?" asked the co-pilot, a wiry little lieutenant.

"You ignore the radio calls, if there are such. The Turkish Air Force seldom lets planes take off at night. In addition, there is no reason for the Turks to make a special effort or that your cargo plane should somehow increase the vigilance of their air traffic control," Ravel said, this time good-naturedly, probably because this questioner belonged to the *Luftwaffe*, just like him.

After a very brief pause, which was used to pull out the plane's design plans, Ravel emphasized that, due to the additional fuel tanks installed in the aircraft, the Dakota could easily cover the distance from Athens to Palestine and back.

"We have checked the systems of these tanks several times. They are functioning perfectly," he said.

"You continue to fly low along the Turkish coast and turn south near the Syrian border. There is really no one to disturb you. The few units of the French Armee de L'air, which had joined de Gaulle's troops, are described by the *Luftwaffe* Intelligence as only 'partially operational.'"

"What do we know about the radar in Lebanon?" asked the copilot again.

"You need not worry about that," Ravel said patiently. "The French radar system on Mount Sannine above Beirut is inefficient, only operational sporadically and it is doubtful whether it is actually connected to the central British air traffic control system." Ravel had assessed the performance of the British radar facility on Cyprus and concluded that it was too far away to be relevant to this operation. Another British radar station on Mount Carmel in Haifa could detect the plane, but as the Dakota was flying in from the north, from friendly territory, without evasive maneuvers and at an acceptable altitude for transport aircraft, it would be registered as a routine flight.

"Most likely, the duty air traffic controller will come to the conclusion that it is a French plane or one from the many air forces that operate there under British auspices. I, myself, have read the account of an *Abwehr* agent who sits in Tel Aviv. He reports that the British do not actually control everything that moves or is flitting about in this part of the Middle East. According to him, their control system is suffering massive problems of coordination between the many foreign entities active there, and had recently almost eradicated a squadron of Polish aircraft due to erroneous identification. So, that's it. Any questions?"

There were none.

"You enter the air space of Palestine here," he pointed to the valley between Mt. Hermon[65] and the Galilee Mountains. "The British look mostly to the west, but since you are already in Palestine, and I stress this once more, the air traffic controller will assume that this is a friendly plane on its way to Amman or Iraq. You will fly south along the Jordan River, across Tiberias, whose inhabitants are not very disciplined in adhering to the blackout rules as far as we know, so that it is easily identifiable by its light. You then continue south to the jump site, about five kilometers west of Jericho."

It was again the co-pilot, who was wondering, whether they would recognize the drop zone by signals or lights, or whether the crew must establish radio contact with the reception unit on the ground.

Ravel let out a breath that could have been understood as a sigh to express his discontent. "So far, all attempts have failed to establish radio contact with the Mufti's people who are active in the area. Moreover, we have no confirmation that they even know about your coming and the exact time of your group's parachute jump."

Wieland and Schwarte exchanged glances.

Wolfgang was amazed at Wieland, that as the unit's commander, he did not interrupt the briefing at this point

[65]A mountain in the Golan Heights with its summit stretching along the borders of today's Lebanon, Syria and Israel.

to clarify this issue and get more details, because it was ultimately also his arse that was parachuting into Palestine. But Wieland was silent and Schwarte decided that it would be better for him to keep his mouth shut.

"To ensure an accurate jump and prevent the dispersal of the unit, the pilot will perform two overflights," Ravel said. "All of you, all five will jump as one cluster. The pilot makes a second overflight and drops your equipment at exactly the same spot. He then turns around and flies back to Athens along the same route."

The briefing went on for a few more minutes.

Ravel's assistant handed the pilot some weather reports, a list of frequencies for radio contact, and other necessary operating details for the long flight.

"Gentlemen," concluded Ravel. "You are embarking on a difficult task, which requires the full use of all your fighting skills in the field. This is a historic operation that will be added to the textbooks of military academies. The German army now extends from the Arctic Circle in Norway to the Caucasus and the gates of Alexandria, from suburban Moscow to the Atlantic Ocean. Our comrades in the Navy claim to have landed units on the coast of faraway Greenland and set up weather stations there. So, in this huge area you will be pioneers of the Wehrmacht in Palestine and, moreover, at the lowest point on earth. Admiral Canaris asked me to express his appreciation and to convey his best wishes for the success of the operation."

Ravel straightened up, clicked the heels of his boots, and shook hands with the pilot and the three paratroopers, only one of whom – Wieland – saluted with the raised arm of the Nazis.

Ravel returned his salute in the traditional military style.

"Of course we'll meet before departure," the colonel said, and walked with quick steps to the door of the hangar, followed by his aides laden with bags.

It was again only Wieland, the faithful and active member of the Nazi party, who believed that it would be appropriate to end such an event with 'Heil Hitler'. But given the indifference of the remaining group members, he decided not to make a fuss about it. Within seconds, he was absorbed in the fine-tuning of various details with the pilots, the never-ending work of equipment preparation and the cramming of all details for the deployment.

Jerusalem, Spring 1942

Nabil liked Boutros' coffeehouse, which had been in business from the Turkish period, in a narrow alley in the Christian Quarter, not far from the Church of the Holy Sepulchre. The coffeehouse was very popular with the residents of the old city, in part due to the owner Boutros' skill in catering to the needs of his customers. For his Muslim patrons whose religion forbade them to drink alcohol, Boutros, a Copt, had in store brandy bottles with colorful medicine labels. Because these brandy bottles were labeled "MEDICINAL" in big letters, many Muslim customers occasionally permitted themselves a small glass without feeling guilty about any infringement of the fundamental principles of Muhammad. Boutros had another way of meeting the needs of those guests who wanted to hide their love of liquor even more. He sold them "French Tea", i.e. brandy or whisky, poured from a traditional jug into tea glasses.

Nabil's cousin, Jawad, asked to meet him there, under the pretext that this place was near his office. Nabil accepted gladly. "It's noisier than ever here," Jawad stated, having arrived ten minutes late as usual.

"Some of the customers here appear rather suspicious to me – peasants of the Husseini mob. Come; let's sit closer to the entrance, so we can get some fresh air." Nabil had whispered his assessment of the clientele quietly, ensuring that it did not reach the ears of strangers, all the while continuing to spread his smile in all directions. He used this occasion to share a little joke. “What’s the difference between a peasant of the Husseini clan and a roll of film,” he asked Jawad, who screwed up his face with an expression of “buggered if I know.”

“A film can be developed,” he said.

The answer amused Jawad so much that he almost choked with laughter, whilst trying to stay calm, so as not to attract attention. He gave a snort, which turned into a heavy smoker’s cough.

In fact, every joke about the Husseini clan automatically received positive acclaim from any listeners in the Nashashibi family. Similarly, vice versa, because of the decade long struggle between the Husseinis and Nashashibis for supremacy of the leadership among the Palestinian Arabs.

For example, the conflict between Rajeb Nashashibi and Haj Amin al-Husseini. Rajeb, Nabil, and Jawad’s great uncle, who was sitting in the Turkish Parliament as a representative of Palestine in the days before the British occupation. He also served as mayor of Jerusalem from 1920 – 1934. His bitter political opponent was Haj Amin al-Husseini, the nationalistic Mufti of Jerusalem who accused Rajeb of a conciliatory policy towards the Jews and pandering to the new rulers, the British. Husseini’s followers pasted the walls of cities with insulting caricatures of Rajeb in a degrading position with his face turned upwards towards a British officer’s behind, with the words “fifty thousand British steamers cannot manage to pull Rajeb’s mustache from the arse of the Englishman.” In Arabic, the words *Tisi* and *Inglisi*[66] rhyme very nicely. Husseini also loathed Rajeb’s idea of establishing a Palestinian Legislative Council.

[66]Arabic: Tisi = arse. Inglisi = Englishman

"We are the majority, so that we can block the settlement enterprise of the Zionists in a democratic way," Rajeb had tried to explain the political wisdom of his proposal to his people. But Husseini was totally against any manifestation of moderation and took the majority of the Arab population with him, so that the idea of a Legislative Council disappeared in the annals of history. When the great Arab revolt under Husseini's leadership broke out in 1936, Nashashibi supported the idea of an economic boycott of the Jewish community, the struggle against the British, and a general strike. But when it became clear that the strike would fail and the Jewish community would only grow stronger, the leaders of the Arab states advised the Palestinian Arabs to end the strike and to seek a solution by negotiation.

Nashashibi supported the proposal.

Husseini objected vehemently to any compromise with the Jews and the British, and his men began with the elimination of anyone who dared to express a different opinion. Among the hundreds of murdered victims by the Husseini gangs, were Nashashibi men and women. Although the Arab Revolt was suppressed by the British army and Husseini had fled Palestine, the disputes of the past continued to demand blood sacrifices. The relative calm that had taken hold in the land, did not affect the determination of extreme elements to settle accounts, according to the well-known Arab proverb: "After twenty years, when the Bedouin has completed his revenge, he said: I have hurried."

The mass migration of rural dwellers to Jerusalem, which was caused by the economic flourishing of the city, had also influenced the fashion. Most of the guests in the Cafe "Boutros," those who had appeared to Nabil as peasants supporting the Husseini camp, were dressed in the usual style of villagers – a combination of traditional wide pants and jackets that had seen better days. In contrast to the two cousins from the Nashashibi clan – who were elegantly dressed in European suits and walking around without a hat – the vast majority of men who were drinking coffee, reading newspapers, smoking hookahs, playing backgammon or dominos, were wearing a fez or covering their heads with black and white or red and white *keffiyes*.

Nabil and Jawad had a special, very warm relationship and not only because they belonged to the prestigious Nashashibi family. They had spent their youth together, attending the same classes at the prestigious Terra Santa School, which was proud of its student mix – Arabs, Jews and children of British officials. Their special love for Jewish women – Alisa and Esther – reinforced this relationship even more.

"In the end you cracked, huh, Nabil," teased Jawad, "you couldn't bear up. How long did you go out with this nice Jewish nurse, what's her name, Alisa? Two, three years? You were a beautiful couple. Pity that you split up."

Nabil closed his eyes, raising in his mind images of a wonderful, but impossible love affair. Pictures of running hand in hand, free and sweet, in the colorful sea of flowers that covered the open ground on the rocky hill between *Mishkenot Sha'ananim*[67] and *Talbiyeh* and from there along the narrow train tracks to Ramallah. His memory raised images of watching romantic movies together in the Rex Cinema. They preferred the Rex to other cinemas because of its layout, whereby the end-seats were a bit hidden. Lovers took advantage of that to hug and cuddle in the dark.

Nabil and Alisa loved movies. They identified with the characters, knew full sentences by heart, even silly ones, that Hollywood screenwriters had woven into the dialogue of the characters on the screen. In his mind, Nabil drew their naked bodies, his and Alisa's, writhing, entwined passionately on

---

[67]The first Jewish neighborhood built in the 19th century outside the old city of Jerusalem.

the big bed in the spacious room of the Pilgrims Hotel, which they used to rent regularly, at least once a week, in Mamilla Street, not far from the Tonus-House.

He also remembered how he sometimes had to quiet Alisa when she forgot her European manners in moments of pleasure and passion, uttering loud moans and cries of jubilation that disturbed the almost holy silence in the corridors of the hotel. He would calm her with soft words and a loving smile, reminding her that, after all, the guests had come from all over the world to visit the Christian holy sites and not to hear a young couple's lively lovemaking.

"The first ones to crack were my friends Wolfgang and Tamar," Nabil replied, shuddering at the memories, thoughtful, introspective. "Who knows better than you that relationships between Arabs and Jews are not so unusual, although it is interesting that I've rarely heard of a Jewish man falling in love with an Arab woman. However, a Jewish woman and a German Christian, a Templer, that was truly exceptional. They drew flak from all directions. Do you remember how I told you about the incident at the dance party in *Rehaviah* when a Jewish extremist attacked me? At the same time, Tamar was also threatened."

"There are threats all the time. You know what my Esther had to go through," Jawad showed empathy.

"Yes, but in the case of Tamar they were put into practice. One evening, after she was done with her studies and had finished her work shift, three thugs attacked her brutally even within the guarded Hadassah compound. One of them violently held her mouth shut, while the others were beating her up, all the while cursing and insulting her. After they had abused her, the apparent gang leader, a little nervous teenager, pulled a razor and threatened to slash her face and leave her scarred for life if she didn't stop 'hanging out with that Teutonic Nazi and an Arab' – as he put it."

"And, presumably, the police, found no suspects, as usual" remarked Jawad.

Nabil made a small movement, like saying: "Sure, of course not," and noted that Tamar had not even bothered to go to the police. What could the detectives have done? Go searching among the young Jews of Jerusalem for three unknowns, of whom even the description was missing?

This attack had scared Tamar to death. She tried to dodge all danger and continued to meet Wolfgang secretly in hidden places. But it all came to an end when Wolfgang's parents also put pressure on him to break off the relationship. His parents were actually isolated in their community for various reasons and the affair of their eldest son with a Jewish woman earned them no brownie points. Therefore, they forced him to stop meeting with her."

"And he capitulated under that pressure?" Jawad persisted.

"You have met Wolfgang and could get your own impression of him. He is one of those types who keep banging their heads against the wall and the wall breaks. In this case, too, he had refused to recognize the reality and spoke about eloping together to Australia or Argentina. But it was actually Tamar, who realized that their love affair had no chance, and it was she who broke off the relationship. But he, who wanted to flee with her to some remote hole in the world, had a broken heart. I saw him one day in the city and he looked exhausted, shattered. He did not even try to hide it. 'I gave up,' he said to me and told me that he had decided to go to Germany and study automotive engineering."

Nabil then went on to describe to his attentive cousin the crisis that Tamar had been through. Despite her initial determination, driven by rational reasons to part with Wolfgang, she was not able to remove his image from her life and continued to love him. But now they were separated by thousands of kilometers. Then the war broke out and any opportunity to communicate, even if only in writing, was lost in the whirlwind of the dramatic events that shook the world.

❄ ❄ ❄

Jawad dragged pleasurably on his cigarette and tapped off the ash that had extended quickly at the burned end. "What are you smoking? I can't identify the smell," said Nabil surprised. "What, is it something imported?"

"So what can I do? Esther only smokes Emir and I was so impressed with them that I am now addicted to this shit," he whispered and looked away. "Don't ask what problems this causes me. They're actually Jewish cigarettes, produced by the Maspero Company in Tel Aviv. All I need is for someone to see me. A Jewish woman and Jewish cigarettes!" With deft movements and accompanied by giggles, Jawad told his cousin, how he was getting rid of the "incriminating evidence" after each purchase of an Emir packet: he would remove the cigarettes from their original packaging, put them in a silver case given to him by his grandfather and throw away the "incriminating" empty box.

The two cousins laughed, relaxed while sharing a little secret in a complicated world full of hypocrisy, where even smoking cigarettes – a seemingly normal activity – marked someone as a member of one or the other camp and could actually endanger his personal safety.

"Two days ago, I overheard a conversation between two young Jews. One of them was smoking," Jawad continued with the topic of cigarettes and smoking, "and the other one asked him: give me a 'line'. Don't you see? He did not say give me a 'drag' as one would usually do."

"Do you know the origin of this expression 'give me a line', which is common here, both among Jews and Arabs?"

Nabil teased him. He was known among the Nashashibis as a walking encyclopedia.

Jawad shook his head.

"It dates back to the Turkish times when everyone was rolling their own cigarettes manually. The paper was purchased in rolls marked with lines so that the shopkeeper could easily measure how much paper he had sold. So when they rolled their cigarettes they had lines and if someone took a cigarette from a friend, he actually told him how much he wanted to smoke, namely from one line to the other."

Jawad's facial expression made it clear that he was not convinced.

"If you don't believe me, you can even ask Boutros. He was already selling tobacco here during the Turkish era."

Nabil gave his cousin an amicable pat on the back. "Now it's your turn to tell me something. Basically, I know your story, but I like to listen to you tell it. As I understand it, she is not a girl who goes to parties or belongs to a circle of those spending time in cafes. As far as I've heard, she rarely leaves the house. So, tell me again how you got to know her. Where did you meet?"

Jawad lit another cigarette and leaned back, stretched his legs, blew a cloud of smoke and began to chatter away "Boy, oh boy! What a story. Like in the movies."

"So tell already. I love movies and I like your way of telling stories, and a film story is exactly what I want to hear."

Now it was Nabil, who relaxed. He settled back to listen to his cousin's portrayal.

Neither Nabil nor Jawad had noticed the young man at the next table sit up, turn his stool towards them, and move a little closer.

"It's all Aunt Jamila's fault with her irrepressible love of shopping, shopping, shopping," Jawad began with the intricate story of how he met Esther Wiener, daughter of the furrier Moritz Wiener, the niece of the famous writer S.Y

Agnon. "We're getting married," Jawad shared his sweet secret. "She has agreed to convert to Islam and we will start a family. I want to have at least three children."

Nabil let out a whistle of admiration.

"You see, for you it worked out well. My story with Alisa blew up, partly because she insisted on remaining Jewish and wouldn't even consider converting to Islam. Without this step, there was no way in the world that Papa would have agreed to such a marriage."

Nabil had just uttered the last syllable of this sentence, when Ali Husseini, the young man at the next table who had been listening so attentively to the conversation of the two Nashashibis, jumped up, screamed "*Allahu Akbar*", grabbed Nabil from behind, and, with a swift move thrust the knife he had just recently purchased for this purpose between his ribs.

"*Allahu Akbar*! This is what the traitors get who sell land to Jews," yelled Husseini, without regard to the horrified looks from Jawad and the other guests of the cafe. Ironically, this was a steel blade that had been forged in the twenties in the German town of Solingen, brought to Palestine by Jewish refugees from Nazi Germany, who, for economic reasons, had been forced to sell it together with other possessions. It penetrated between the ribs and hit the heart. Nabil was killed on the spot.

Ali Husseini fled from the coffeehouse. He was almost caught a few hundred meters away, near the New Gate, by the police, who had been alerted by witnesses to the murder. But he managed to escape into the maze of alleys. Merely two weeks later, after an intensive investigation by the Jerusalem police and their detectives, he was arrested at the home of his uncle in a small village on the road to Ramallah, tried, convicted, and hanged in the Akko prison.

In the police statistics of Palestine, Nabil's murder was registered as yet another victim of the endless chain of murders, assassinations, and revenge attacks in the long struggle between the Nashashibis and Husseinis. The detective, Paul Roberts, who had led the murder investigation, received an award and a cash prize of five Palestinian pounds for the arrest of the murderer.

Jerusalem, Summer 1942

Something about the overall modest structure of the Hebrew University campus gave Aaron a feeling of inexplicable tranquility. The buildings of this academic institution, covered with bright Jerusalem stone, conveyed an old established, almost ancient, dignified presence. Nevertheless, even for the oldest building, twenty years had not yet passed since the laying of its foundation stone.

Having arrived too early and with an hour to spare until the counseling session in the History Department – "We would like to talk to you about your further academic career," explained the letter that had landed in his parents' mailbox – Aaron purchased a sandwich in the canteen, added a bottle of juice and, with those provisions, seated himself in the last row of the amphitheater on the edge of the campus, on the saddle between the Hadassah and the Augusta Victoria compounds. He internalized with pleasure the stunning scenery of the Judean Desert, bounded on the southeast by a glittering strip of water, the Dead Sea.

The magic silence was disturbed after a few minutes. An annoying buzzing noise was rolling up the *wadis* with increasing intensity drowning out the soft chirping of mountain birds with metallic brutality. A few seconds after the first buzzing sound, Aaron noticed a small black dot in the sky, approaching from the northeast, which was growing larger, until he could clearly discern that it was a light reconnaissance aircraft. "Looks like that new American aircraft, Piper," Aaron noted to himself. In his mind he reviewed the amazing development of aviation in the 39 years since the Wright brothers had succeeded, for the first time in history, to fly in a machine that was heavier than air, in the Kitty Hawk Dunes.

"The funny thing is, that the only witnesses of this historic event were four anglers from the nearby Coast Guard base and a boy who was vacationing with his family nearby," remembered Aaron, who was known from childhood on as an "airplane nut". This passion, combined with his love of history, made him a competent expert in aviation history. He collected and built model-planes from balsa wood, bought foreign brochures about aviation, joined a youth group of flight enthusiasts, practiced flying gliders from the *Hamoreh*[68] Hill and dreamed of becoming the Zionist Charles Lindbergh. Even in high school, he was known as an expert on aircraft and other flying machines; he wrote a few articles on the subject for two newspapers in Tel Aviv. His proud father hung the framed newspaper cuttings on the walls of his office, with emphasis on "our correspondent Victor Levi."

But it was actually his cousin, Shimon, who fulfilled the Levi's dream of flying. He had volunteered for the Royal Air Force, completed a pilot's course, and was assigned as co-pilot to a squadron of heavy Wellington bombers. During his ninth combat mission only four months ago, his plane was hit over the German city of Kassel and since then he had been listed as "missing".

Unlike Shimon, Aaron had never considered the possibility of voluntarily registering with the air forces of the country he described as "Albion the Conqueror".

---

[68]A hill at the edge of the *Yisre'el* Valley, north-east of Afula.

With a wistful glance, he was now following the flight of the Piper.

"After the war, when civilian air traffic returns to normal, I'm taking an aviation course. It's expensive, but my father can afford a private pilot's license for me."

The small plane circled low over the ground as if it was looking for something. Then it made a turn to the north. Aaron thought that it was circling above the gorge of *Wadi Kelt* and its magnificent views. He envied the pilots and imagined the excitement floating in the air, high above the ground like a bird. He was wondering if it was a reconnaissance flight or a routine training flight. The plane sank deeper and disappeared from Aaron's field of vision. The humming of the engine continued to be heard for a few seconds and then there was silence.

❄ ❄ ❄

Aaron had gone to the University in order to consolidate – or actually save – his cover story as a diligent student of medieval history. "At the beginning, in the first year, it was not a cover. I really enjoyed studying," he recalled. "I loved the lectures, debates, and atmosphere."

Lively debates had taken place in the spacious Levi home in *Rehaviah* when Aaron announced his decision, to devote the coming years of his life to the study of history. "What kind of a subject is history," thundered his father, the banker and took advantage of the opportunity to show off his broad general education by quoting a saying by Napoleon: "What is history if not a fable, agreed upon and written by the victors. Victor, you need to learn a profession," his father changed tactics and continued in a calmer tone. "Well, it's clear to me that you have no palate for business, but you're good with numbers. So, become an engineer, study architecture, or even accounting comes to mind. Then you come out of there with a more practical degree."

"Dad, first and foremost stop calling me Victor. You know that I don't like this name. It sounds like Diaspora and I don't care that Grandpa was called Victor. I am a Hebrew, live in the land of Israel and my name is Aaron, not Victor. As to my studies, I want nothing practical. I love history and this is what I'm going to study."

"But history, why history of all things? Study geology! This is the history of nature and is a profession with a future. Groups of geologists traverse the country in search of oil and other natural resources. You have no idea how much money the British and American companies are pumping into these explorations," his father said passionately.

To his credit, it must be said that Aaron, at least at the beginning of his student life was trying to respect the wishes of his parents and took geology in the first year. But after a month in the small, intimate Geology Department, he had trouble keeping going. These thoughts increased with time and finally erupted, when one of his lecturers showed, with satisfaction, his impressed students a stone he was holding in his hand, claiming that it was more or less a million years old.

"A million years more or less" rebelled Aaron's shocked historian soul, which demanded exact dating. "A million years more or less!"

Scarcely another month passed and his rather brief career as a geologist was finally over. This occurred during a particularly boring lecture, when a chemistry lecturer pointed out excitedly how the combining of two matters, produced a third substance and Aaron blurted out loudly, "so what?"

"The professor glared at me angrily," Aaron described much later to Tamar the scene that finally removed him from the Faculty of Science student list. “He looked me up and down and said, in the tone of a kindergarten teacher: ‘Do you want to repeat your comment, Mister Levi’? I looked at him; he looked at me like two stray cats in a struggle over a dustbin. ‘I’m glad that the new substance you have created makes you happy. Congratulations! But I’ve had it with geology’. Having said that, I left the lecture hall, slamming the door and went directly to the secretary of the History Department.”

Luckily for him, it was the last day on which it was still possible to change courses. Thus, Aaron Levi was admitted to general history studies at the Hebrew University of Jerusalem.

❄ ❄ ❄

Aaron settled down quickly in the new department. He gained his BA with honors mastering the study material with minimal effort. This ability allowed him plenty of free time for extracurricular activities. At the beginning of his life on campus, he was able to gain a foothold in the student body, where he became known as a great joker at parties and the kingpin of all boisterous student activities.

At a particularly joyous celebration a few months ago, his eyes fell on a pretty young woman. It was impossible to overlook her proud gait, straight back, head raised at a defiant angle, nice breasts, and long legs. A quick inquiry revealed that the girl was Tamar Landwehr, a young nurse, working in the Hadassah Hospital. The gossips in the group knew to tell that she was “hard to get”.

“There is no young doctor in the hospital who had not tried to make a play for her,” his friends informed him. “But apparently no one has managed to progress one step further after a second date in a cafe.”

One of his friends even knew to report that he had heard from someone who knew somebody who had studied in the school of nursing with Tamar, that the heart of the young woman had been broken during a complicated love affair in the past – probably before the war.

Aaron loved challenges and difficult tasks. "I want her and I'll get her," he said to himself, and planned to achieve his goal like a military operation.

In the bourgeois circles of the Jerusalem establishment, Aaron was known as a real lady-killer who knew how to conquer the hearts of the most beautiful *Rehaviah* and *Ein Kerem* girls. "I'm not bad looking, the head works well, pearls flow from my mouth, and I have a talent for dancing. In short, God has given me everything that's necessary and my father, the banker, contributes the rest," he concluded sarcastically after one of his successful conquest campaigns.

This also made an impact on Tamar. He asked her for a dance, then another, told a little about himself, dropped a few names, and mentioned events that made it clear he was not exactly living in a workers' hostel. He passed, with flying colors, the second-meeting-test with Tamar during a romantic dinner at Fink's, the legendary bar in Jerusalem.

That, which had begun with him as a routine hunt, had evolved into a love affair.

Tamar too, who initially did not really know how to behave towards the handsome romantic suitor let things develop. "*Panta rei*, everything flows," she told her friend Alisa, who could not hide her envy about Tamar's new, perfect friend.

"I feel good with him," she explained to Alisa. "Aaron is a bon vivant and has the financial means to do so. He is warm and intelligent, very knowledgeable and has an insatiable curiosity. We talk for hours about all the problems of the world." With the exception of the one big story.

The story of her love for Wolfgang Schwarte she kept in her heart and stubbornly refused to let Aaron into the sanctuary of Wolfgang's and her personal memories, in spite of his persistent pleading. Aaron had also never heard from her about Ronen, her own little baby, one of about twenty young children who were growing up in Zimmerman's orphanage in *Talpiot*.

❄ ❄ ❄

The almost unbearable ease – from the perspective of his fellow students – with which Aaron overcame the academic hurdles, enabled him to meet with Tamar whenever she was off duty from the hospital. On the days when he was a "grass widower", he hurled himself enthusiastically into the turbulent activities of the Jewish Students Debating Society in Jerusalem.

He soon earned a reputation as a right-wing exponent on the political spectrum and someone who did not shrink from the verbal onslaught by representatives of the traditional Zionist establishment, who occasionally appeared as guests at club meetings. Aaron attacked hard all those who would advocate political moderation.

"The Arabs are against us. The British support the Arabs and are against us," Aaron shouted at every meeting. "The British have betrayed the mission which they have taken upon themselves of creating a Jewish National Home here. They are now merely occupiers and therefore there is no other choice but to begin a struggle for a Jewish state. Let us learn from the Irish. Looks like they have managed to expel the representatives of the British Empire and establish their own state, Ireland."

The fact that his views were considered extreme only reinforced with Aaron his "obstinacy" and his belief that he was right. His friends, none of whom supported the extreme opinions that Aaron advocated so passionately – "unbearable, and, translated into German this sounds like excerpts from a speech by Goebbels" his fellow student, Asher Weiss, once admonished him – would say in his favor, that he knew how to separate politics from everyday life.

Tamar also disapproved of the positions Aaron took. He had only once managed to drag her into the debating society, and what she heard there was enough for her to form an opinion. But she knew that his right-wing radical zeal broke out only in debates and that in real, everyday life he would never have chosen his friends according to their political views.

"I have no problems beating you with arguments," Aaron told Asher Weiss. "But when it's over and we have to cram for an exam, or we go to the movies together at the Orah or Zion cinema, I'm with you. A friend and nothing but a friend."

He displayed this composure outwardly, helping him to dodge the tentacles of the British Criminal Investigation Department, when detectives were trying to find activists among the students and to arrest suspected supporters and operatives of what the British designated as the "*Stern Gang*". None of the police informants, neither the paid ones, nor those who passed seemingly innocuous information when questioned by detectives, pointed to Aaron Levi as a right-wing activist.

He was described as a "pugnacious windbag" by some of his friends who were convinced that Aaron's involvement in radical right-wing activity was confined to fiery speeches, which he gave regularly. No one, including Tamar, suspected in the slightest that this enthusiastic and passionate orator was among the small group of senior leaders of the most extreme right-wing organization in the Jewish community.

"And if Tamar knew? Or Asher Weiss, if he knew what has become of me, he would go mad," thought Aaron.

"Interesting; where has he disappeared to lately? I actually was going to suggest to him to come to Jerusalem to have a bit of fun. Strange, that he has not yet met Tamar. Both are, after all, *Yekkes*. They would certainly find topics of conversation in common."

In the meantime, without the knowledge of his fellow students, Aaron was sucked into the ideological turbulent vortex, which threw him into the heart of "*Etzel*" led by Yair Stern. He followed and still believed in Yair Stern, even when he began to lead a small group of activists who had preferred to separate themselves from the *Etzel* organization and establish an even more radical framework.

Aaron belonged to the small camp of a few dozen activists who had gathered around Yair Stern. He was enthusiastic about Stern's political vision, but had a few reservations about some of his revered leader's ideas. He was particularly disturbed by the hostility towards the Palestinian Arabs, which most members of his movement had developed and fostered. "Personally, I feel sometimes more closely connected to the Arab neighbors of my mother's relatives in Tiberias than with some new immigrant from Germany or Poland, who had just arrived yesterday, not because he is a Zionist, but because he was driven out of Europe," Aaron described his feelings.

To his delight, he discovered allies. It turned out that some of the leading members, including Natan Yellin-Mor and Eliyahu Beit-Zuri shared his view. Despite the debate on this issue, the activities of the organization continued. "Right now, we have enough problems with the British, so let's defer the debate on our dear Arab cousins for better days," joked Stern. The more Aaron's commitment to Stern's organization increased, the more he tried to soften his traditionally fiery arguments during the debates that raged in the student club, in order not to attract undue attention.

"The fact that you have reduced your profile is not enough, unless you are definitely keen to familiarize yourself with the living conditions in the prisons of His Majesty, the King of Great Britain," warned Eliyahu Beit-Zuri and advised him to consider resigning from the club. And so, one fine day, Aaron announced his resignation from the student's debating society, "because I have exhausted the topic and have nothing new to add. I prefer to concentrate on my studies."

This did not mean that he had stopped debating. He only changed the setting from student evenings to underground meetings. Even within the small secret organization, his reputation as a relentless debater solidified. He used his best arguments to express his strong opposition to the initiative of the organization's leaders to collaborate with Nazi Germany against the British occupation. He also objected loudly, to the dispatch of Naphtali Lubentchick to Beirut. Lubentchick had been sent to Beirut before, at the time, when the city was under the control of the Vichy government, which had collaborated with the Nazis, and consequently had an official German representative working there. He had met in Beirut with the Nazi diplomat Werner von Hentig and proposed in the name of the new organization, to collaborate in order to drive the British out of the country.

This initiative received no response from Berlin.

Nevertheless, in late 1941, Stern attempted to renew the contact with Germany.

"That's enough," Aaron insisted sharply. "I am ready to die in the struggle against Albion the Conqueror, but I will never consent for it to be done in collaboration with Hitler and his gang of murderers. The enemy of my enemy is not necessarily my friend." Because of Stern's "German politics", Aaron quit all activities at the beginning of 1942 and focused on his studies and deepening the relationship with his new girlfriend Tamar Landwehr. But two months later, shocked by the brutal murder of Yair Stern at the hands of British Police detectives, he returned to the organization and quickly climbed to the top of the command structure.

❄ ❄ ❄

Aaron left the meeting in the History Department nervous and tense and not because of the things that were said in the room. The committee members – two professors and a management representative – were really nice. They unfurled before Aaron the path that, in their opinion, could lead him to academic glory, or at least to a career with material and intellectual rewards, if only he decided to make the study of history the center of his life.

"You are very talented and also have a great general knowledge – and with regard to the history of the Crusades, you are an absolute star. You have excellent analytical skills and a fluent writing style, a winning combination in the academic world," they praised him. However, at the same time, they expressed admonition about a marked neglect in his studies and research that was being observed of late. "If you want to pursue an academic career, you need to decide where you want to go and adjust your lifestyle accordingly."

It was this last sentence that had caused Aaron's nervousness and tension. While he continued to look at the panel seriously, giving them the impression that their words were well received by him, his thoughts were drifting into other realms. "The world explodes, the future of Jewish settlement in Palestine is in danger, and I'll be sitting in the library looking for old documents about the adventures of Raynald de Chatillon? It would actually not be a bad idea to explore this Chatillon's crazy endeavors sometime around 1175, when he dismantled ships transported them on camels through the Negev desert to the Red Sea and tried to conquer

Mecca. But this is not the appropriate time to deal with such things," he decided deep down.

Since he was dealing with himself, he formulated his thoughts in the second person: "To be honest, you should admit to yourself at least that the studies have lost their appeal. The academic world does not offer you the thrills you get in the underground life. True, you are indeed tense, are under pressure, rarely sleep and feel like a hunted fox in the park of an English lord. But you are already addicted to the activities of the organization. You can no longer pass your days without the excitement and the adrenaline. This applies also to the feeling of satisfaction that you enjoy at the completion of an operation. While there are moments of fear, you feel as if you are living in a movie. Imagine Tamar's surprise when one day she'll discover that her boyfriend, the cute student who apparently can't hurt a fly and has only crusaders and archives on his mind, is actually one of the leaders of the struggle against the British occupiers."

The interviewers had difficulty in assessing what exactly the meaning of the light smile was which had spread all over Aaron's face. They could not imagine that this was a spontaneous reaction to the idea of withdrawing from the academic world.

"By the way, Mr. Levi, we hear that you speak several languages, which of course is a big advantage. Would you please tell us which languages they are?"

"Hebrew, English, Arabic, French, and Ladino," Aron said promptly.

"And which language, may I ask, do you like most?" asked one of the interviewers who clearly could not find a better question.

"The language of the waves. Most of all I love the sound of the sea and that's where I am tempted to go now," Aaron replied somewhat haughtily. His face was beaming at the looks of astonishment that came from the other side of the table.

"Gentlemen, thank you for your time, your patience and your willingness to support me," he fired at them his further thoughts, "but I'm withdrawing from academic life. Currently, I have more important things to do."

That extraordinary finale he had performed in the conference room lifted his spirits only for a few minutes. The feeling of elation, which accompanied him when leaving the meeting, was quickly replaced by dark gloom. With quick steps he crossed the long, cold corridors of the Faculty of Humanities building, feeling the level of tension rise in his body with every step that brought him closer to the exit gate.

"The situation is shitty," he heard himself mutter. "We have the British on our backs, the Jewish community doesn't want to know us, our coffers are empty – and, worst of all, it seems as if Tamar is no longer so enthusiastic about me. This is my fault. What does she want on the whole? Love, attention, or as my mother's Hungarian doctor would put it, TLC, tender love and care, but instead of stroking and hugging her, or giving her my full attention, I'm stuck in the organization. Admit it, Aaron, face facts. Lately you have neglected her, so you should not be surprised if you get to hear some strong words from your Hadassah beauty on your date at the Cafe 'Vienna'. Come on, the bus will not wait for you. So get a move on."

❄ ❄ ❄

While Aaron was explaining his language theory to the representatives of science, Tamar and Alisa stepped off the bus at its stop opposite the *Sansur*[69] building at the end

[69]An office building in the centre of Jerusalem, built by a wealthy Arab entrepreneur in 1931.

of Ben Yehuda Street. Two military policemen, sitting in a shiny Jeep, assessed their curvy figures from top to bottom with long, unconcealed glances.

"Ignore them," Tamar said. "They're just trying their luck. I'm actually glad that the military police have stepped up their patrols. That's good for us."

She was referring to an incident a week ago when, in the early hours of the evening, four unknown assailants attacked three Hadassah nurses, who had decided not to wait for the bus, but to walk through the new town to Mount Scopus via the *Shimon HaTzadik*[70] neighborhood.

The girls, second year nursing school students, suffered blows and bruises, but an approaching vehicle had fortunately forced the attackers to flee before they could satisfy their nefarious urges. They ran away and disappeared among the courtyards. Police investigators assumed that the attackers had been drunken soldiers, but could not identify their origin – an understandable result, when considering that the barracks around Jerusalem were at that time housing units from at least ten different allied armies. "We have arrested and interrogated suspects, but nothing, zero, zilch. We were unable to identify anyone," the investigators reported. "Jerusalem has become a Babylon of uniformed men, including serious problems with deserters from foreign armies who have joined criminal elements in Jerusalem and other areas."

"Jerusalem is nothing compared to Cairo," Paul Roberts told his colleagues in the Investigation Section. "Just yesterday a surprising report arrived from Field Security headquarters in Cairo. Two officers of the unit dressed in uniforms of Rommel's *Afrika Korps*, with the palm branch on the swastika badge and walked around for six hours in Cairo. They took pictures of each other in front of the

[70]North Jerusalem Suburb.

pyramids, sat in the Cafe Groupie that is so popular with the British soldiers, went to the movies and nobody gave them another look. And all this is happening, while Rommel is sitting one hundred and twenty kilometers from Alexandria. It's unbelievable, what?"

❄ ❄ ❄

"So what have we decided? Movie or concert?" Alisa asked, standing in front of a bill- board skimming over the different offers.

"Do you think Aaron may prefer a movie?" She asked. "There is a historical film showing in the Orah cinema, in color, about the Roman Empire, with plenty of romance."

"I will never in my life watch a historical film with Aaron again," Tamar responded in a determined voice, which contained a touch of impatience. "It's impossible with him. He constantly, really obsessively, finds logical or historical errors in the script or the staging and ruins my viewing experience."

This happened, for example, two weeks ago. Tamar was actually rapt in the film. She followed the story with interest until Aaron began with his remarks. He laughed at the scene of a dramatic cavalry attack by the Romans on their enemies, the barbarians. "What kind of an idiot is this director," he whispered in Tamar's ear. "The horsemen in the film ride with a saddle and stirrups like cowboys in the Wild West. But in fact, no one in Rome ever had the idea to combine stirrups and saddle, even though they had invented so many things. So they rode like the Indians with their feet hugging the belly of the horse. Think about it. Alexander the Great had ridden around half the world with dangling feet and sore balls."

Cries of "shush" were heard from the other viewers, but Aaron ignored the protests and continued his historic speech. He took advantage of the darkness of the cinema to occasionally breathe a gentle kiss on Tamar's ear.

"When I met him he was nice, friendly, welcoming," she tried to explain to Alisa, who, with her keen senses, recognized a cooling of her best friend's love. "But in recent months, something is wrong with him. He is pale, nervous, disappears for days without leaving a message and comes back dirty, stinking of sweat and machine oil, lies down on the bed and immediately falls asleep."

Tamar took a deep breath.

"A few times I've been looking for him in the library or in the History Department, but even there they told me that he was absent too often. It is not clear to me what he's doing. He is not willing to volunteer to the British Army. He cannot stand the *Haganah* and therefore the *Palmach* doesn't interest him either. If, at least, he were to take advantage of the his father's connections, in order to get himself a regular job and to earn some money, as so many good people are doing these days..."

"It really doesn't sound good," Alisa analyzed the matter carefully and began to count on the fingers of her hand, "I see three possibilities."

Although she tried to look casual, Tamar followed Alisa's analysis of the situation with interest.

"The first, most logical and rational possibility is that your Aaron has another, or let's say an additional love."

"Not on your life," Tamar said angrily and stomped lightly with her foot like a schoolgirl, while wondering if Alisa was displaying some jealousy, because she could not hide her affection for Aaron.

"The second possibility is that your young man has just lost his way. I don't want to gossip, but you know that there are all sorts of things happening in their family. His middle brother, Ezra, is suffering from depression, and he wastes his father's money on endless treatments by

Vienna psychologists who have fled from Hitler and Freud to Palestine. Sometimes he is also hospitalized in a public institution."

Tamar had not responded and Alisa saw this as confirmation to proceed with her analysis.

"The third possibility is that your Aaron is involved in something unlawful. For example, trading on the black market. Who knows, maybe your Aaron has even taken up with the *Stern Gang*."

Tamar's eyes widened. "Aaron? In the Stern Gang? Do you think so? It is true that he is in something of a study crisis and has neglected his research into the Crusader attack on Damascus or the events of the Hundred Years War, but how can you even think that he is active in the underground? Do you think it's possible? Can you imagine, then, that he plants a suitcase with explosives in a British army camp? No, that's simply impossible."

The last sentence was uttered as the two were climbing the three steps leading from Jaffa Road to the terrace of the Cafe "Vienna".

"Let's have a drink," suggested Alisa. "Maybe they finally have real coffee and then we can decide what we want to do later tonight."

Above the Aegean Sea, Summer 1942

White clouds were floating by in that sliver of sky, which was framed by the open door of the Dakota.

"Have a look," Wieland remarked before boarding the plane, via its narrow oval opening that he could barely squeeze through because of his kitbags and equipment. "Have you noticed what side we are boarding on? An airplane should be the ultimate in perfection and the peak achievement of human technology, shouldn't it? But we get in on the left. Why? Because it's still a tradition dating back to the cavalry whereby one used to climb into the saddle from the left, combined with the maritime tradition, according to which cargo is loaded from the left side."

"Yes, and therefore 'port' in English means both 'left' as well as 'harbor'," Wolfgang added the completely trivial detail which Wieland and he had acquired during the German Scouts activities in Jerusalem.

Dinninger gave them a puzzled look, expressing wordlessly, what he thought of his comrades, who now, of all times, found time to make a long and illusionary statement on the subject of "the left side in the light of history."

But since then, half an hour had passed and the plane, which had taken off after receiving clearance from the control tower – a green flare – was moving forward at a steady speed and an altitude of about one thousand meters above sea level. Both engines were humming monotonously and in tandem, as if they had always worked together harmoniously, a testament to the high technical skill of the mechanics at the base, who had replaced an engine only less than two days ago.

A deafening noise, a combination of howling wind and the rumble of engines penetrated loudly into the passenger cabin.

After a few minutes flight, Schwartes' eyes had gotten used to the faint red light that was spread by three small lamps on the ceiling. He stared through the door and wondered how he was keeping so cool on the way to this mission, which he had considered unnecessary and foolish from the outset with the potential of cutting short his temporary existence on this earth within the next few hours.

"There are only two things which are infinite," he recalled one of the conversations he had had with his father, "and these two things are the universe and human stupidity. But the universe I'm not so sure about." In his memory it also remained stuck how his father had stressed that this was a quote from Albert Einstein, "one of the smartest people that Germany had ever produced and whom Hitler and his thugs had driven away, just because he was a Jew. Who knows what this genius, who is now sitting in America is planning for these Yankees. Probably a doomsday weapon as a revenge on the Nazis."

Wolfgang looked at the passenger cabin, which was flooded with dim red light. "Once again, these two Muftis are ignoring instructions and doing what they want", he noted at the sight of Salame and Abu Hassan Latif laying stretched out on a canvass bench that straddled the entire cabin, having shed their equipment, which was stacked in the aisle.

Wolfgang was impressed that Salame and Abu Latif were conducting a lively conversation in Arabic in spite of the noise. They were shouting alternately into each other's ear and, from the smiles and giggles, he assumed that their conversation was also peppered with jokes and wisecracks.

Dinninger who sat to Salame's right, appeared detached from what was happening around him. He squatted, leaning forward and was busy writing on a piece of paper that rested on his knees. "It would be interesting to know what he is writing about – maybe a letter to his girlfriend or possibly his last will and testament. Who knows?"

Wieland, displaying indifference or perhaps toughness – the result of his accumulated combat experience – took the time for a catnap while his body was occasionally shifting to and fro in search of a comfortable position. The members of "Operation Plier Squeeze" – three Germans and two Arabs – wore combat uniforms of the Brandenburg Regiment, paratrooper boots, and round paratrooper helmets, which differed from the steel helmets with neck-guards worn by the Wehrmacht.

"We're not taking any chances," Wieland had declared before takeoff. "According to direct instruction of the High Command, we jump in German uniforms. The plainclothes initially remain in the backpacks. The uniforms are necessary in case it is the British army, which awaits us on the ground instead of the Mufti's partisans. I am not prepared to provide the Brits with an excuse to shoot us as spies. They are entitled to do so if we wear British uniforms or civilian clothes."

Dinninger asked whether it was intended to wear the German uniforms throughout the entire deployment, because "I have only one uniform, and, after a few days of action in the terrible heat of Jericho we'll stink like pigs."

"We'll stick to the German uniforms as long as necessary. After we'll have landed in one piece and met the Mufti's fighters, we'll decide. We might possibly dress up as Bedouins; perhaps even as ordinary citizens. It's all open. The decision will be made according to circumstances and conditions," concluded Wieland.

He and Schwarte were equipped with a Schmeisser submachine gun, six magazines per weapon and a Luger pistol. The two Arab volunteers and Dinninger, who was also responsible for the radio, contented themselves with pistols. Many additional weapons, including an MG 34 machine gun and some novel powerful explosives, "to blow up the Haifa oil pipeline", were packed on special pallets, neatly stacked beside the door.

In addition to the Task Force, a *Luft*waffe sergeant, a loadmaster also responsible for the parachute jump, was walking around in the cabin. "Would you like some hot tea," he yelled into Schwarte's ear while pounding on a big thermos flask in his hand. "Tea with sweetened condensed milk. Export quality. Captured Canadian field rations."

Wolfgang smiled at the offer made in the style of a waiter or steward and made a sign with his thumb that he was not interested. "Tell me; are there any women in your task force?" The sergeant wanted to know while looking with obvious admiration at the little fabric ribbon on the paratrooper's jacket. Despite his slim figure, the ribbon made it clear to all that its wearer was the recipient of the Iron Cross II. Class.

Without asking permission, the sergeant sat down next to Wolfgang and waited for an answer.

"What a nuisance," Wolfgang whispered to himself, but relented in view of the sergeant's broad smile. Each line in his face expressed genuine curiosity.

"Of course. Without women, it is difficult to carry out certain tasks" Wolfgang took on the role of a friendly, obliging soldier. "Do you know how they are selected?"

The sergeant moved a few centimeters closer to hear better.

"You know that we select only the best of the best. Once, we tested two men and one woman. The chief instructor told the first man that, in order to prove his preparedness to perform any task, he would get a loaded gun, go into the next room where his manacled wife was sitting, and shoot her in the head."

"Impossible," said the sergeant.

Wolfgang ignored him and continued with his description of the event. "The first man thought for a minute, told the instructor that he was unable to fulfill the task and left the room.

"The instructor turned to the second candidate and again explained the procedure. The man thought for a moment, then another two minutes, followed by five and finally said he couldn't just murder his wife and went home."

"This is a joke, right?" asked the sergeant, with tone of disappointment in his voice, but he still showed a desire to hear the end of the story.

"Now it was the woman's turn. The instructor told her to go into the next room with a loaded gun and kill her husband, who sat tied to a chair in the middle of the room. The woman did not hesitate, took the gun and went into the room, locked the door and after a few seconds we heard loud screaming and yelling and the sound of blows from behind the door. We didn't understand what was going on. We tried to burst into the room, but it had an iron door that the candidate had locked from the inside. We knocked on the door, but the woman did not answer, and the screams just continued. After two minutes there was silence, the door opened, the candidate who, incidentally, was very beautiful, came out bloodstained and radiant. She explained to the instructors 'the gun was loaded with blanks, so I had no choice, other than to beat the son of a bitch to death.'"

Despite the dim lighting, Wolfgang noticed an expression of amazement spreading over the sergeant's face.

"Not true," shouted the sergeant. "This is a joke. I don't believe you."

"Maybe yes, maybe no."

"How can I know?" Urged the sergeant.

"You are flying back to Athens; there you can go on asking. Eventually you'll find someone who can give you an answer."

The sergeant was about to answer when the lamp above the cockpit door began to flash. It was a signal that he needed to get there urgently. "Are you sure you do not want a cup of tea?" asked the sergeant, who got up from the bench and went to the cockpit while shaking his head in disbelief about the story he had heard from the tough paratrooper.

Wolfgang laughed briefly and turned his attention back to the cotton-wool clouds floating past before his eyes outside of the door frame.

❄ ❄ ❄

He had seen exactly such clouds a year ago, but back then he was lying on his back near the border of the Soviet Union. Why, of all places in that part of the world? Because, with typical military logic, he was assigned to the second company, which was composed of ethnic Germans from the Baltic States.

"But, with your permission, Sir, I'm a Templer from Palestine. What have Latvia, Lithuania, and Estonia to do with me?" he pleaded passionately to the company commander.

Wolfgang was smiling now as he remembered the company commander's shrug of his shoulder and his ironic response. "I don't understand either, why they have assigned you to me, but go figure the military logic. After all, we are supposed to sneak across the border disguised as Red Army soldiers; your knowledge of Arabic doesn't seem to me to give us an advantage at this section of the front, unless our intelligence is totally fucked and no one has taken the trouble to inform me that our target – the main bridge over the Daugava river – is somehow guarded by an Arabic speaking Red Army unit," the commander replied sarcastically, not meant personally for Wolfgang. He scratched his head, winked, and congratulated him on his successful and "logical" transfer to the Baltic Company of the Brandenburg Regiment.

While Wolfgang continued to stare into the clouds, he sank into brooding. "Damn, who would have thought," he said in a monologue tapping lightly the trigger guard of the Schmeisser. "At least be honest to yourself, Wolfgang. Don't hesitate to admit, that you are not exactly suffering in your military service. On the contrary. How come and how did it happen, that I, Wolfgang Schwarte, who was never enthusiastic about the Nazis and to whom the speeches of Hitler and Goebbels appeared bloated and silly, enjoy wearing the uniform now in the service of the Fatherland and these gentlemen. All that, despite hating the moment when I was drafted. When war broke out, I realized that my dreams were shattered and all the future plans I had pictured in my imagination, had gone up in smoke. When was that? September 1939. I had just settled everything, erased Henrietta Landwehr from my memory, got a job at the Ford plant in Cologne, was about to begin my studies of automotive engineering at the Technical Institute within a week. And then suddenly, WHAM!!! The Poles attack a German border post. The war breaks out and I'm drafted; and, moreover, into an elite unit, following orders like an idiot and risking my life in the name of an ideal of Greater Germany, in which I do not really believe."

The *Luft*waffe sergeant, who had returned from the cockpit and had renewed his efforts to serve tea from his thermos flask, noticed a big smile on Wolfgang's face.

He waved at him, as if to say: "What's happening, what's funny?" Wolfgang's smile widened and he signaled that everything was fine.

❄ ❄ ❄

Already on his first day in the Brandenburg Regiment, while he was looking for his new platoon and carrying his heavy backpack crammed with supplies, Wolfgang met dozens of young Templers. Some were his age and lived in Haifa, Jaffa, *Sarona*, Jerusalem, Waldheim, Wilhelma, and Bethlehem in the Galilee. Of those who came from Jerusalem, he did not have good memories. For example, Hans Friedrich, a burly thug with few brains. Wolfgang despised him as a loud activist of the Jerusalem Hitler Youth cell and because he constantly badgered him about his affair with Henrietta while always looking for opportunities to beat him up.

"Wolfgang, what a surprise," Hans greeted him joyfully at the unexpected encounter, reinforcing his words with a warm hug that almost broke Wolfgang's ribs, a gesture of reconciliation meant to begin a new chapter in the relations between them. "Are you still mad at me, because of everything that happened in Jerusalem? Forget it. That was long ago. It's ancient history, *eili fat mat*[71]," he said in Arabic. "What's done is done. I'm glad to see you here."

"Me too," Wolfgang said honestly, quickly calculating the time that had passed since the start of their animosity in Jerusalem and with genuine happiness about meeting a familiar face so far from home in *Emek Refaim.*

The cotton wool clouds, which were now floating by the Dakota's doorframe, resembled remarkably those that had

---

[71]Arabic proverb: The past cannot be recalled. Something like let bygones be bygones.

been hovering above his head on the eve of the attack in Latvia. The actual raid on the Daugava had lasted only a few minutes, during which not a single shot was fired.

Wolfgang was among those in the spearhead, who stormed the bridge in Red Army uniforms. In the first order of the day for "Army Group North," their commander, General Wilhelm Ritter von Leeb, praised the soldiers, without going into details that could identify the secret unit. They were the ones who had taken the Daugava Bridge, paving the way for his tanks to advance on Riga.

Wolfgang's personnel file contained a copy of the order together with a small certificate attesting to his bravery. In that operation, the soldier Wolfgang Schwarte, from Jerusalem, was awarded the Iron Cross II. Class. Together with the Iron Cross, he also received an elegant pilots' watch, produced by Lange and Söhne. "This is a donation from a wealthy Dresden merchant, a descendant of the first Templers, who is bestowing the gift of a watch on any Templer who is awarded the Iron Cross," the regimental adjutant told him.

"Why are you bothering to sew the decoration ribbon to your jacket?" Asked Wieland, who had been watching Wolfgang tinkering with the ribbon during the preparations in Hangar 12. "You are going on a combat mission, not a party."

"This is exactly the reason," Wolfgang said softly. His words were directed more to himself than to Wieland. "If the British catch us, they will probably hand us over to the interrogators of their intelligence service. Interrogators the world over hit first and ask questions later. So they might treat me a little differently if they know that I am a carrier of the Iron Cross. The British appreciate bravery."

❄ ❄ ❄

A sudden nosedive, the result of the plane unexpectedly hitting an incidental air pocket, shook the aircraft and its passengers.

Dinninger looked up impassively, peered left and right and continued to devote himself to his intensive writing.

"Hey man. Pilot, get us to *Falastin*[72], not to the ocean floor," Salameh yelled in Arabic and laughed out loud, which hardly hid his nervousness at the sight of the dark sea that had suddenly become visible through the door.

Wieland had woken up immediately. He shook his head, got up, yawned, went to the cockpit, returned after a minute and sat down heavily on the bench. "The pilot says that we expect overall good weather conditions and that the air pocket is unusual," he informed Wolfgang loudly. "Pretty scary to see the sea race past a hundred feet below the cockpit."

"How long until we jump?" Inquired Wolfgang.

The conversation was held at high decibels.

"At least five hours. And then only if the pilots are able to comply with the planned route. Say," Wieland turned to Wolfgang changing the subject, "I've been meaning to ask you for a long time and believe that this is a good opportunity. How did you actually meet your Henrietta? "

"How much time did you say we have? Three hours? Five?" Look, it's a long story which begins in the center of Jerusalem on a pleasant autumn day in 1938, but I can give you the abridged version in less than three hours, provided of course that I don't lose my voice."

"All right then. If you can make it interesting, I'll try not to fall asleep," teased Wieland.

❄ ❄ ❄

---

[72]Arabic for Palestine.

"Excuse me, I'm new in town and don't know my way around yet. How do I get from here to Mount Scopus?"

Wolfgang, who was on his way to Wolf's Electrical Goods Store on Ma'alot Street, only caught part of the question that had been put to him. The "I'm sorry, I'm new in town," was the bit he had heard, while the rest of the sentence was deleted by a flash of infatuation, that hit him like a romantic scene from the movie **Gone with the Wind**.

Even before the questioner – a slim, beautiful girl, with high cheekbones and wavy hair, wearing a full skirt and white, shiny blouse – had finished the question, Wolfgang was head over heels in love.

"Sorry, I did not quite catch that," he answered slowly in Hebrew. "What exactly did you ask?"

"How to get from here to Mount Scopus? I had been told, by bus number nine, but I see no stop for number nine." She had a pleasant voice and a hint of an undefined German accent colored her Hebrew.

"Do you speak German?" He asked.

"Yes," she answered in Hebrew, while scrutinizing with interest the handsome young man. She had already determined at this point that, clearly, he must also be an immigrant of *Yekke* origin and, who knows, perhaps they even have friends in common.

Until that moment of the unplanned meeting in downtown Jerusalem, Wolfgang had justified the label "shy", with which his mother used to describe him. In spite of the substantial qualities he was endowed with by the creator, he was not able until now – and he was already 18 years old – to develop a close, intimate relationship with the opposite sex.

With a somewhat childlike faith, which was mainly fueled by scenes from movies, that everything depended on the first impression, he used to practice for hours in front of the bathroom mirror catchphrases that were meant to melt the hearts of the girls in the city. However, his daily life did not offer him the opportunity to apply these catchwords. But now, in the course of this accidental conversation on a beautiful morning in early autumn in the center of Jerusalem, Wolfgang behaved as if the famous movie star and heartthrob, Errol Flynn, was hovering directly over him and was whispering the right text, at the right pace, with the right catchword in his ear.

Five minutes after Tamar – as she introduced herself – had turned to him with the question of the way to Mount Scopus, they were already sitting like two old friends in the Cafe "Atarah" on Ben Yehuda Street. He drank a cherry soda and she was enjoying a cup of chocolate with whipped cream.

"Do you remember our first meeting? If you had only known that it was the first time in my life that I had gone to a cafe with a girl," he admitted months later.

"Either you're a good actor or someone has trained you," she said, giggling. "You behaved as naturally as if you were a regular at that table there every day. During the first moments, I was wondering if you weren't one of those bourgeois hedonists who was spending his days lounging in cafes and restaurants, whilst the pioneers were risking their lives for the reclamation of one more *dunam*[73] and the drainage of yet another swamp during times of the Jewish national struggle. Until you told me who you really were, it would never have occurred to me that you were not a Jew, but a Templer, third generation in the country. Your smile! It was your smile that grabbed me from the first moment. So shy, but so heartbreaking. It is said, that a smile is the shortest distance between two people..."

As it turned out, the lightning that had struck him, had struck in both directions, which confirmed the ancient folk

---

[73]Turkish: Dönüm; an agricultural field measure of 1,000 sqm.

wisdom that true love begins where one expects nothing in return.

His spontaneous proposal to nip into a nearby cafe, was accepted with pleasure. At the entrance to the cafe, where he opened the door for her like a gentleman, he quickly checked the contents of his pocket to ensure that he had enough money for this unexpected treat.

From the moment they sat down, they drew the attention of the other guests, as it was impossible to ignore the sight of the two attractive young people who were smooching in the middle of the day, whispering and laughing, without being aware of their surroundings.

"I didn't know that there were cherries in Palestine" she remarked at the sight of the tall glass full of red, bubbling soda, which was served at the table. "There is almost everything," Wolfgang was ready to praise the country. "It is written in the Bible that this is the land of milk and honey, but there are no cherries. Sometimes, in winter, a load comes from Lebanon and then, cherries are worth their weight in gold. About the cherry soda I can tell you only one Jerusalem story: the owner of a firm for the production of juice concentrates, a religious Jew from *Mea She'arim*[74], was laying on his deathbed, summoned his sons and said: 'I need to reveal a big secret to you'. The boys approached him and with his last breath, he managed to say: 'You should know that cherry concentrate may also be made from cherries.'" She bared perfect white teeth as she laughed merrily.

That day they had spent nearly three hours in the cafe.

The "Atarah" waiters, who would usually hint to meandering guests that they should either order something else or vacate the table for more profitable customers, were infected by the magic of being in love, which enveloped the

---

[74]Ultraorthodox neighborhood in Jerusalem

table of the two young people. Only after almost two hours had passed, which they had spent over a glass of cherry soda and a cup of hot chocolate, the headwaiter cleared his throat – a thin man with a forced smile – and asked in a friendly voice: "Would you like to order something else?" He had to settle for a further order of cherry soda and hot chocolate.

Tamar briefly told Wolfgang the story of her life and what she had experienced since coming ashore from the deck of the Adria a few weeks earlier, her feet touching the soil of the Land of Israel for the first time.

Wolfgang listened attentively and with the exception of an occasional nod, he did not say a word. "I was shocked," he explained to her later why he was almost speechless when they first met. "Your stories about what you had gone through in Vienna, how your classmates disappeared from your life, the regulations of the Nazis against the Jews, and especially the story of your grandfather's murder!"

Wolfgang knew that terrible things were happening in Germany and all this hoopla about the Hitler Youth and the Nazis in the colony disgusted him. But he had no idea what was really going on in Germany. At this point he had also not yet told her that he was a Templer so she spoke freely from the heart without restraint.

"After all, I was already in love with you," he admitted. "I was afraid that, if you had discovered my true identity, you'd have gotten up, given me a slap in the face and disappeared out of my life. Forever."

At that meeting in the Cafe "Atarah", Tamar had not noticed any of this. She was engrossed in her story, relieving months-long tensions, succumbing to the desire to speak with someone, without being aware that she had completely dominated the conversation. She even forgot, if only out of politeness, to be interested in the life story of Wolfgang; to try figuring out, where this young man, who was now sitting opposite her with an open mouth, eagerly lapping up her experiences, had appeared from.

Tamar described in minute details the difficult daily events at her aunt's, who had invited her to stay in her tight little house in *Rishon Lezion*[75]. The aunt, who was not really a direct aunt, but a distant maternal relative, was constantly complaining how difficult it was to live in Palestine. She was bluntly tapping Tamar in an attempt to extract from her a few pounds of the money which she – the aunt – was convinced the new immigrant from Vienna had hidden in her luggage.

"It was horrible. After two days, I packed my things and went to Kibbutz *Givat Haim*, which some members of the youth movement had joined in Vienna last year. I arrived in the kibbutz with high hopes, but despite all attempts, I did not really manage to adapt."

Tamar explained, with an apologetic voice, that the reality of kibbutz life did not match all her dreams of pioneering spirit and self-realization that she had imagined in Vienna. One week's accommodation in a small tent glowing with hot summer heat and mosquitoes swarming around, brought her to despair.

"Perhaps you know that in order to keep mosquitoes away, one hangs at the entrance of the tent a shirt soaked with sweat belonging to one of the members who, for some reason, had not been stung by the mosquitoes, in the hope that the smell of his shirt will keep that disgusting vermin away? After one week in this boiling tent the first heretical thoughts entered my head."

The term "heretical thoughts" Tamar had said in Hebrew. Wolfgang did not know this expression, but at this point

---

[75]One of the first agricultural villages south of Tel Aviv. Founded in 1882, it is a thriving city today.

preferred not to interrupt the flow of her words and did not ask for an explanation.

She actually managed the heavy physical labor quite well. When necessary, she dug water ditches in the citrus groves, held a hoe in her hands, and sometimes dug with a bent back up to eight hours non-stop in the marshy ground.

"No problem. I regarded it as physical exercise to strengthen the back and arm muscles. But something the passion of the kibbutz members, whose ideological debates lasted until the early morning hours, did not suit me. So a young man stands up, waves his arms about like an airplane propeller, brandishing a book by Borochov or Rosa Luxembourg and talks and talks and talks, showering with praise Mother Russia and Stalin, this genius of a man. How boring! But woe to anyone who dared to yawn. The movement's fanatics would pierce with burning eyes any participant, who displayed an expression or even a hint of indifference."

She emphasized her words with exaggerated widening of her beautiful eyes, accompanied by a deliberate yawning and a crescendo of sparkling laughter, which caused some of the guests to become interested in what was going on at the young people's table.

"They are jealous, I feel that they envy me," a fleeting thought shot through Wolfgang's head.

But Tamar took no visible notice of their temporary status, as the main attraction of lunch-time customers at the Cafe "Atarah", at least outwardly. She continued with enthusiasm, to describe her experiences on the kibbutz.

"What made me particularly mad? The fanaticism with respect to communal ownership. I just could not tolerate this Marxist intransigence about 'absolute equality – everything belongs to the collective'. What! Should I wear the big, ugly and not very clean shirt that they gave me from the supply store? Why can't I have a blouse? The beautiful blouses that

I had brought from Vienna, I had to give up to the clothing store and, believe me, it is contrary to feminine nature, to walk around in a shabby khaki shirt from the communal clothing store, whilst seeing some huge, ugly female strutting about in my elegant blouse – and not to react! It is simply inhumane. And I have not yet even mentioned the slogans and pronouncements which seemed so hollow to me."

What had enraged her most was the "claptrap" about equality at work. The members spoke nobly about equality, constantly declaiming egalitarianism, parity, but who drove the tractor, which brought the workers on the trailer to the citrus grove? A female comrade? A Woman? No chance! And who was working in the laundry? In the kitchen? Men? Of course not.

"Equality, equality, but apparently there are some who are more equal than others," she summed up her opinion.

The kibbutz episode in the life of the young pioneer, Tamar Henrietta Landwehr, was over quickly. The disillusionment from the revolutionary ideas occurred simultaneously with her chance encounter of a nice, cheerful girl, whose name suited her perfectly.

"You know that this is not always so. There are stupid Sofias, cowardly Leons, and Victorias, who are total wimps?! However, every rule has an exception, and in this case, it's Alisa[76]. She reflects her name. She is cheerful, an incorrigible optimist, a bit of a chatterbox, but absolutely goal-oriented and knows exactly what she wants. I hope that you'll meet her and judge for yourself."

Alisa had arrived in the kibbutz two months before Henrietta-Tamar from Poland. Already at their first meeting in the queue outside the clothing store to exchange work clothes, Alisa sensed the indecision of the new immigrant

---

[76]Hebrew feminine name, meaning cheerful, jolly, happy.

from Vienna. Alisa's gradual disillusionment with the ideals of the labor movement corresponded exactly with Tamar's growing disappointment, albeit a bit slower. So it was only a matter of a few hours acquaintance for both to become an inseparable pair.

The "Keepers of the Seal" on the kibbutz, those types who saw themselves as guardians of the collective morality, held it against Alisa long after she had left there, that it was she who had persuaded Tamar to sign up together with her at the nursing school in Jerusalem and had thus hastened her departure, which they considered "apostasy".

One evening, just before another long and dreary meeting, Alisa hugged Tamar, took an envelope from her pocket and pulled out a typed sheet of paper bearing the letterhead of Hadassah, containing the joyful news that both were among the small group of lucky people who had been accepted to receive training.

Only three weeks after she had walked through the gate of the kibbutz for the first time, she was now leaving in the opposite direction – this time in the cab of the kibbutz milk wagon, penned between Alisa and Abrascha the driver, who was happy to take them to Tel Aviv. During the long trip to Tel Aviv, he switched the gears of the truck – an old and creaky workhorse made by White – with exaggerated movements he considered particularly masculine, in the hope of attracting the attention of one of the two passengers. Had Abrascha known the whole story, some unnecessary gearshifts would have been spared the old truck. But at this point, neither Abrasha nor the other members could have been aware, that this journey to Tel Aviv would finally end the chapter of Alisa and Tamar's life on the kibbutz.

❄ ❄ ❄

"Do you know the story of Ida Pfeiffer?"

The sudden question surprised Wolfgang. No. He had never heard the name Ida Pfeiffer and his strong head movement made that clear.

"Listen, I don't believe in fate, but sometimes events happen that are hard to explain and you will see how all these events now happening to me connect with the adventures of Ida Pfeiffer. This is a somewhat long story; I warn you," she said cheerfully, "but be patient, because in the end it connects to my story."

Tamar took a deep breath, like before diving into deep water.

"Before I left Vienna, my neighbor, Maria Himmelstadt, a nice non-Jewish woman, a bit stupid, but honest and decent, gave me a parting gift. It was a travelogue by Ida Pfeiffer, with a dedication. 'To our Henrietta, a child of the Eighth District, on her way into the adventure of a lifetime to the remote Palestine'. From reading the dedication. it was clear that the term 'genius' did not fit Frau Himmelstadt. She actually believed in her ignorance that I was making a carefree journey to remote Palestine and did not understand that I was actually a refugee and had to flee to save my life."

Again, her laughter resounded through the cafe.

"This book was in my luggage throughout the journey to Palestine, without me reading it. Only on the kibbutz, when I remembered, did I open it and could not put it down until I had finished it. The next day I met Alisa, but the continuation of the events, you already know."

Wolfgang did not quite understand the connection between the book, her story, and what Tamar was driving at, but he decided again not to ask. Although they had known each other for less than an hour, it was clear to him that she would expound on the story without his assistance.

"Oh," Tamar gave a sympathetic sigh. "What a fool am I? You don't yet know the story of Pfeiffer, so how could you understand then, what I mean? Listen, the story of Ida is amazing."

The next ten minutes of his life Wolfgang devoted to interested listening about the adventures of a 19th century Viennese housewife in Palestine, told by a Jewish refugee from the Vienna of the 20th century.

"After more than twenty years in an unhappy marriage, after her two sons had grown up and left the nest, Ida decided that it was time to fulfill her childhood dream: to see the world", Tamar began with the story that fascinated Wolfgang.

"Ida, an energetic and determined woman, small, round – not to say plump – went to the bank, drew her not very considerable savings, bought a ticket to an exotic destination, and went, at the age of 45 years, on a journey full of adventure and challenges, which lasted nearly six months. So far, this story doesn't have too many surprises. It sounds pretty banal, right?" said – asked Tamar, "but the little difference that made Ida Pfeiffer a sensation, lies in the fact that all this happened long ago, in 1842, to be exact. At this age, most of her peers would begin to think about their survival. In those days it was only aristocratic ladies who could indulge in travel around the world, while she, a simple housewife, had done something unbelievable until then: alone, without help, with a particularly meager purse, she traveled on her own from the heart of Europe to Jerusalem to stroll around there?!"

There was something about Tamar's manner of speaking that fascinated Wolfgang as well as the two women, sitting at the next table who had been gossiping, until the arrival of young people, about the elegant clothes worn by some of the prominent Jerusalem society ladies to the last Philharmonic concert in the Edison Hall. The two exchanged silent glances, trying not to appear rude, by pretending not to be listening, which is precisely what they were doing.

"So what has your Ida really done?" Wolfgang asked with the most authoritative voice he could muster.

Tamar got carried away by the description of Ida's adventures, how she reached the most remote places in Turkey and Syria, rode all the way to Jerusalem and arrived safely at her destination.

Wolfgang thought that she was somewhat stretching her description, but realizing that this was not the right response at the first meeting with a girl, he indicated with a strong nod "No, no, please go on", whenever she stopped to ask if she is not digressing too far into details.

"Well, I see that I do get carried away. So, in a nutshell, Ida continued to roam Palestine. Despite the difficulties, lack of money, illness, and blazing hot weather, she visited Cyprus, toured Egypt, and returned triumphantly to Vienna half a year after she had departed from there.

"After a number of warm hugs from members of her family, she went straight to a well-known publisher and handed him the detailed diary she had written while travelling. In those days, it was not common for a simple woman of low background to publish a book, so it was printed without the name of the author. But the book, ***The Travels of a Viennese Woman in the Holy Land***, became an instant hit. So later they published further editions, this time printed with full recognition of the author, which enabled Ida to continue traveling around the world. Now she had money and did so under much better conditions. She crossed the Arabian desert on a camel, climbed the peaks of the Andes in South America, visited the ruins of Nineveh, struggled with robbers in Kurdistan, toured China, made friendships with famous scholars such as Alexander von Humboldt, went deep into the jungles of Sumatra, was captured by a tribe of cannibals and was on her way to discover the inside of a huge cooking pot, when she managed to convince the chief that it was not worth cooking her, because her meat was old, dry and lean."

Wolfgang's amused roars and Tamar's uproarious laughter mingled with the genteel snigger of the two eavesdroppers at the next table and that of at least two other guests who, as it turned out, had also been listening to Tamar's exciting story.

"Why am I telling you all this?" Tamar asked and leaned closer as if she wanted to tell Wolfgang a secret. But before continuing with the sentence and with a quick movement that caught him off guard, she gave him a quick kiss on his lips.

"I'm telling you this," she said, as if nothing had happened, but a little quieter, which prevented the rest of the audience from listening to her words, "because I read this book, which I received on the eve my departure from Vienna, during the nights of my despair on the Kibbutz. When I had finished reading it, I decided that if Ida, a housewife from the conservative Vienna of the past century, proved that you do not have to bend to the constraints of society; and if she was travelling on her own in distant Palestine – then I, Tamar Henrietta Landwehr, can take my destiny into my own hands and don't need to submit to the Marxist and socialist ideas that do not excite me. With astonishing coincidence, as if someone had read my mind up there, Alisa suggested the very next day the idea about the school of nursing! So, say yourself, is this not a coincidence?" And pressed another surprising kiss on Wolfgang's lips.

❄ ❄ ❄

"You're smiling like an angel who has encountered a bevy of sweet, flying cherubs," Wieland brought Wolfgang back to reality, in a tone that prevented him from forming an opinion whether the words were sarcastic or compassionate. "It's amazing how the memory of a kiss can move the muscles of the face of a tough fighter and even four full years after the event."

"You know why I smiled?" Wolfgang improvised a brief explanation. "First, because her kisses were really sweet. But most of all, because I suddenly remembered, how, at our first meeting she was so engrossed in the story of her life that she did not have the faintest idea who I was. Do you get that? Henrietta was sure that I was a Jew, a new immigrant from Germany, a member of the youth movements, the devil knows what they were called, *Maccabi Hatza'ir, Blue - White, Hashomer Hatza'ir*[77]. Just imagine, only after we left the cafe, and I accompanied her to the bus, she found the time to ask me: 'So, Wolfgang, who are you really? Judging by your accent, you probably come from the South, Stuttgart or thereabouts."

"Oh boy," whistled Wieland sympathetically. "What an embarrassing predicament. Not an easy situation! How did you get out of it?"

"I took a deep breath, then a short one and, in a split second, made the best decision of my life."

"Well, spit it out!"

"I told her the truth."

"What do you mean by truth?" Wieland persisted. "Did you tell her that you were German, a Templer – not a Jew but a Christian?"

"Yes, that's exactly what I told her. Then her eyes swelled to the size of plums, her mouth opened wide in surprise, while a strange noise of air could be heard coming out of her lungs."

Wieland's roar of laughter caused Dinninger to raise his head despite the engine noise and look up from the paper on which he was writing, in order to catch what was so amusing.

---

[77]Early Zionist youth movements in Europe.

"Joking aside, but from that moment on, my life was like a movie. Believe me," Wolfgang went on, "a combination of a romantic film with a thriller. And what a strain!"

In the first two weeks of their friendship, Henrietta was not sure how to digest the fact that she had fallen in love with a Christian in Jerusalem of all places. In the beginning, she even tried to hide his true identity from their friends and acquaintances. "May I introduce Wolfgang from Stuttgart, now in Jerusalem," she would present him as a rule, without going into unnecessary detail.

"And how did the story get out?" Wieland was interested.

"Oh, on the whole Jerusalem is a small town. One of the administrative staff at Hadassah was married to a draftsman, who sometimes worked with my father. She knew me through a chance meeting of families on a Saturday walk in the city center. As I said, Jerusalem is a small town. Henrietta and I were in the queue at the ticket office of the Tel-Or cinema precisely in front of this woman. We behaved freely, felt nothing unusual or anything. We had not noticed her and I did not recognize her at all. I had met her once or twice in all my life maybe. A few minutes only. But she recognized me. Well, you can imagine. She identified me right away as the son of Dieter Schwarte, told one of her friends and the rumor that Henrietta – everyone called her Tamar already – had a boyfriend, a Templer, a German Christian, was running like a wildfire through the corridors of the Hadassah dormitory."

"Henrietta did not understand why there was whispering behind her back and why every time she entered the dining room, a sort of clucking like in a henhouse could be heard from the tables, as they gossiped about her. But then after a few weeks of denying and squirming – and perhaps because of her character, you know, this tendency to defy – she decided to face facts and ceased to hide my origin."

"Got it. You loved her, right?" Wieland came out with a banal question.

"Loved her, what? I was crazy about her and told her all the time 'I love you, I love you,' One day, she replied with a mischievous smile, 'if someone says: I love you, he really means I need you'. Gosh! Was I offended?!"

Wieland smiled and fired another question. "But this story has another side. Your family."

"Can you imagine what I went through until I decided to tell my parents and invite her home to us?! Do you know what was going on in the Schwartes' home in *Emek Refaim* when finally, after nearly three months of going out with her, I dared to invite her home just before Christmas?"

Wieland was actually interested in how this meeting had ended.

"I had butterflies in my stomach. Really. I had a concrete feeling in my stomach as if I had eaten a kilo of beans and my stomach was jumping back and forth from sheer bloating.

"I need to give you the background. The events of *Kristallnacht*[78] were still a fresh memory. Although Henrietta longed to meet my family, she was really afraid to go to a Jerusalem neighborhood with the reputation of being a Nazi district, where the residents were saluting with raised arms and the swastika flags were fluttering from almost every window. But because she knew from my stories that my parents had slightly different views, she pulled herself together and came anyway."

"I know that she came to your home. But you are digressing and I'm still waiting to hear how the meeting went," insisted Wieland.

"A version of Jerusalem's *veni, vidi, vici*[79]. She captured them," Wolfgang was enthusiastically reliving this incident,

[78]So called night of broken glass. The night of 9 November 1938 when Synagogues were torched and Jewish shops destroyed.

[79]According to tradition, a phrase from the report by Julius Caesar to the Senate after the battle of Zela, about 47 BCE, "I came, I saw, I conquered..."

which he described as one of the most successful moments of his life. Even Willie, his younger, nagging brother who, from a young age had been quoting whole passages from Hitler's **Mein Kampf** like a drunken parrot, felt drawn to her after a few minutes.

"Later, he developed a deep hatred for her, but that's another story," Wolfgang said. "But my mother! An instant Love Story. Almost from the first moment. My mother hugged Henrietta and took her into her heart, as if this was the daughter she never had."

After this successful meeting, Henrietta went to the Schwartes in the German colony at every opportunity, whenever she received permission to leave the hospital even for a few hours.

"She felt right at home. On the very first night she blurted out. 'Oh, how I missed that' when she saw the festive Rosenthal set my mother had laid the table with; 'though I grew up in a socialist youth movement I will never betray Rosenthal'. My father almost choked with laughter when he heard those words. But they had much in common anyway."

"What for example?"

"Sometimes Tamar would come out with such utterances like 'life is not measured by the number of breaths that we breathe every minute, but the number of those minutes that took our breath away' and all sorts of observations, which considered life differently. That appealed to my father immediately."

The humming of the engines, the red light, the vibrating bench and his efforts to follow Wolfgang's descriptions, had exhausted Wieland, but he continued to listen while fighting against gravity, which threatened to lower his eyelids like shutters.

"One evening, in January 1939, on a Saturday, we were all sitting in the living room, drinking coffee, and eating my mother's cake. Man, how I miss her *Gugelhopf*." The memory was accompanied by deep breathing and loud snorting through the nostrils.

"As you know, you could look from our living room window through the trees to see a part of the school yard and parade ground. The Hitler Youth were just holding a parade, with trumpets, drums, and flags, marking the sixth anniversary of the power seizure by the National Socialists in Germany."

Wieland smiled in spite of his fatigue. He had spent many enjoyable and pleasant hours as a leading member of the Drummers of the Jerusalem Hitler Youth Tribe. "Because of the cold, my mother ensured that windows were closed, but muffled sounds did penetrate into the room and the flames from the ranks of the torchbearers spread streams of red on the window glass. My father watched the parade with worried eyes and said. 'Look, how they are marching in step, blindly obeying all the orders. Just like those from the Guards Regiment, who had blindly followed the '*Hauptman of Koepenick*'."

Wieland didn't really like this description. He remembered very well the parade, of which Wolfgang was speaking now, because he was marching at the head of the procession, drumming enthusiastically. Wolfgang's unflattering descriptions annoyed him, but he decided not to respond.

"As soon as my father mentioned the Captain of Koepenick, Henrietta came out with one of her long sentences. Something like 'who would have believed that good Christians from southern Germany, who had come to the desert of Palestine as a result of high ideals, would lose all traces of reason and really behave like the Köpenickers, who blindly obeyed someone just because he was wearing a uniform he had bought at the flea market.'"

Wieland was familiar with the amusing story of the Captain of Koepenick, which had taken place before the First

World War in imperial Prussia. The alleged captain was in reality a cobbler and petty criminal. He commandeered a squad of disciplined, but stupid Prussian Guard soldiers, marched them to the Köpenick Town Hall, arrested the mayor 'on the orders of the highest authority', 'confiscated' the city treasury, signed a receipt, remanded the mayor and the cashier in custody, ordered his Guard Regiment troops to continue to guard the Town Hall and made off, with the money of course.

"It sounds like a made-up story, but it really happened," recalled Wolfgang, "but in the Germany of Kaiser Wilhelm, and, much to the delight of the satirists, that was also the name of the little crook. Wilhelm, Wilhelm Voigt. In short, Henrietta and father were wondering together, how it could happen that none of the soldiers or police officers who had blindly obeyed Voigt, thought of stopping and asking: 'Wait a minute, what's going on? Does he even have an official document that confirms what he claims? Who is he and where is he leading us?' My father summed up the matter and said that it was an amusing incident at the time, which became a successful play, but now all Germans obey blindly the corporal from Berlin – including the Templer Community in Palestine – only that this time it will not end as a joke, but rather a tragedy."

This part Wieland had not heard and maybe it was better that way.

Wolfgang's last remark had exceeded the limits of criticism levels acceptable in the Third Reich and Wieland, the captain, who was loyal to the party ideology, would not have let it pass quietly. But the terrible fatigue, coupled with the relief of the tension that had accumulated during the weeks of preparation, made him yawn rudely and noisily, then again a bit weaker, lulling him into a deep, pleasant slumber a few seconds later.

Wolfgang felt a wave of indignation swelling in his chest, like a cloud bank seconds before a downpour accompanied by a thunderstorm. But a deep, controlled breath calmed him, like the effect of raindrops falling on a cloud of dust. "This is not the appropriate time to feel offended," he calmed down. "Actually, I did get carried away with rambling descriptions and details. Why should my story fascinate Wieland at all? This is not the right occasion for a nostalgic story in the style of 'Once upon a time'. He is right. One should use every free minute to sleep." His mouth breathed an even bigger yawn than Wieland's into the Dakota's passenger cabin, which continued to fly safely at low altitude towards Palestine.

Wadi Kelt, Summer 1942

A strong smell of shepherd's camps, typically known to all those who have ever roamed the desert – a combination of burnt wood, smoldering embers, the aroma of goat and sheep droppings mixed with the vague smell of unwashed clothes – wafted into the cave.

Salim Abbas did not mind the smell. Actually, he was not even aware of its presence. This multi-layered vapor cloud was an integral part of his life from birth. His grandfather had herded the family flock from the time of the Turks; and Salim had been doing the same thing for as long as he could remember, from the moment he could stand on his own feet. First, with his father and in the last few years alone. At times, straddling a period of several years, he had served as a scout with the British police and was awarded several medals and decorations. However, he could smell very well the fragrance of coffee, which was slowly cooking in an old, black, dented kettle, standing in a small pile of glowing charcoal. "How I love this silence, this blessed quiet," he thought. "In the middle of the desert, a clear starry sky, the herd safely in its enclosure guarded by alert dogs and a small cup of excellent coffee. The only thing missing is a hot, passionate woman."

It was cool in the cave. Its walls had long lost their natural rock tinge, having been blackened by the smoke of thousands of campfires lit by generations of shepherds over many years. And it was quiet. Apart from the occasional call of a nocturnal bird of prey and a short, nervous barking of a guard dog that only wanted to go back to sleep.

But slowly some other noise, not belonging here, began to penetrate the subtle sounds of the desert stillness. It began with a faint hum, like the sound of the frenzied buzzing of the wings of a bee, grew stronger, hovered over the barren hills, plunged into the deep ravines and penetrated the silence of the cave.

"These crazy English, practicing night flights again," Salim murmured softly. For some reason he remembered the question a drunken British soldier had once asked him: "Tell me, mister super tracker, if a camel lying in the middle of the desert with no one around him for miles, blows off an enormous fart – does this fart come out loud or quiet?"

This annoying buzz was an indication of a relatively recent phenomenon disturbing the silence of the night, caused by increased RAF activity. Every night, except Saturdays and Sundays, twin-engine Mosquito planes flew past above him with engines roaring. They circled at low altitude and even appeared sometimes in the canyons and *wadis* almost grazing the ground. As a rule, they would appear from the Dead Sea and fly west towards Jerusalem.

Salim knew that they were Mosquito aircraft, because one of these training flights ended in a fatal collision with a hillside in the crook of *Wadi Kelt*. He was the first to reach the crash site. Then he waited nearly an hour next to the remains of the aircraft and protected the burned body of the pilot from the teeth of the jackals that had followed the scent, until a small convoy of military lorries reached him.

"The plane had crashed at high speed against the slope and was completely burnt," he reported to the unit commander. That was an officer in a blue uniform who looked puzzled at the Arab, wearing traditional clothing, from the upper pocket of which poked out a thick English language paperback in the typical design of the Penguin publishing house. Salim told the officer that he was a former police officer, a scout who had resigned from the service three years ago. He said that the police in Jericho knew him well and repeated the description of the accident.

"Yes, it is usually the ground that kills pilots," the officer remarked dryly, thanked Salim, inquired where he had his fluent English from and explained why only the canopy, the engine and small metal parts were left of the plane.

"This may seem incredible to you, but this airplane is built of wood," he said. "A Mosquito, a fighter and reconnaissance plane, fast, agile, and easily combustible."

"Uh-huh, its humming is actually reminiscent of mosquitoes," remarked Salim.

But the buzz that now came from the Dead Sea and had increased to an angry roar, did not sound like the engine noise of the Mosquitos that Salim had learned to identify without fail and for lack of choice. He also noted that, unlike the mosquitos, which were usually practicing low-level flying, this noise came from a plane that was circling high above the desert.

"Damn it, these motherfuckers and their noises. Enough already," he sent a curse to unknown recipients. "Let them kill each other – Brits and Germans, Germans and Brits, Husseinis and Nashashibis, and all of them the Jews as long as they stop waking the dead here with their racket."

As if his words had just reached the heavens and were absorbed by open ears, the annoying noise disappeared in the distance and was replaced once more by the soothing sounds of the quiet desert. A slight smile of joy spread over Salim's face. He was obviously pleased with the impressive success of his curse and the return of drowsiness which caused the closing of his eyelids. In the final seconds before falling asleep, all kinds of thoughts were running through his head from the last book he had read which contained an interesting chapter about the theory of a famous scientist named Darwin. "So that's the scientist who claims that we are descended from apes," he muttered to himself, "but if the monkeys have evolved into humans, then why are there monkeys in the world?"

A broad smile spread across his face, as the fog of sleep veiled his other thoughts. If he had not fallen asleep, but instead had put his head out of the cave, he would have thought that he was dreaming: eight dark objects were floating with big gaps between them over the silent desert, sailing with a gentle swoosh through the air. These were large parachutes. The first three parachutes were carrying elongated objects like thick cigars. Among the five other objects approaching the ground, movements of arms and legs were visible. The parachutes sank slowly into the little valley, not far from the cave Salim was sleeping in.

The cigars were the first to hit the ground with a dull thud. The muffled sound of the impact accompanied by the crackling of shattering wooden boards rewarded one of them for its encounter with mother earth. In contrast to the cigar-shaped objects which had come down close to each other, the paratroopers landed at considerable distances from each other. The first two managed to reach the valley floor, executed a perfect paratrooper's roll, and, immediately on reaching the ground, hauled the parachutes in with a few practiced movements, hand over fist. The third and fifth were driven to the rocky mountainside, but they also succeeded in carrying out a relatively soft landing. The fourth parachutist landed hard on the ground.

A loud cry of "bloody hell", accompanied by painful moaning and groaning announced the somewhat unconventional return to Palestine of Zulfikar Abu Latif, a leader of the Arab revolt against the British and one of Mufti Haj Amin al-Husseini's most senior officers.

❄ ❄ ❄

"These bastards; to hell with the fat, bloated Goering; may he burn in hell together with his fucking *Luft*waffe," Wolfgang let out a juicy curse while dangling under the canopy looking with anxious attention at the black object, which was approaching him with menacing speed. To the west, on the crest, he thought he could make out some individual lights – who knows, maybe the lights of Jerusalem. In the south, the vast area of the Dead Sea was reflecting the dim light of the narrow crescent moon which had risen over the mountains of Edom.

His spontaneous curse uttered while still hanging in the air, was meant for the Dakota pilots of squadron 200, who had just set course for the long flight back to base in Athens, where hot chocolate, a good meal, a soft bed with white sheets and cuddly blankets were awaiting them. Wolfgang's expressions of anger and rage stemmed from the large discrepancy between what had been said during the pre-takeoff briefing in Athens and the actual execution in practice.

"The aircraft will be circling at a low level above the jumping-off point, while trying to find the flat field that appears here on our maps; incidentally – and I'll be honest with you – we don't know how up to date they are," said squadron commander Reval during the detailed briefing. "After checking the area, the plane will turn around, throw off the equipment in the first run, and drop the group as close as possible to the landing place of the equipment during the second run. You have at least two hours until first light. So, get organized, find cover, and send Salameh out, to locate the Mufti's command post."

During the debriefing with the crew after their landing in Athens, the pilot will probably report to his superiors that

that's exactly what he had done over the landing site. No one would be able to contradict him, because everyone who knew a different version had bailed out of the aircraft hours ago above *Wadi Kelt*.

But in reality, the entire parachute jump proceeded completely differently. It started already during the last stage of the long flight, when the sergeant informed Wieland that he was asked to come into the cockpit for an urgent consultation. Wieland reacted quickly; followed by Wolfgang, he stuck his head through the door and listened to the verbal exchange.

"We don't have enough fuel. There are some problems with the transfer of fuel from one of the spare tanks," the captain informed Wieland by pointing to one of dozens of instruments that all looked the same to Wieland. "The difficulty is, that we need to maintain an even speed and height, as if we are a routine flight so as not to alert the British radar stations. Due to the fuel problem, I have to limit the time of circling above the target to a minimum."

Wolfgang shook his head in disbelief and saw Wieland's nod, indicating that he didn't like the change of plans either.

"I will already start the circling maneuver before Jericho," shouted the captain, to drown out the noise of the engines. "Above the Dead Sea, I will rise to 800 meters above the ground, not above the sea level. Above the ground. That's the height of my return flight to Syria. I will make only one run, so you need to jump together with the equipment."

"Shit," cursed Wieland. "We will be scattered over a huge area. It will take hours to find the equipment. And it would suffice if one of the muftis hesitates when jumping to open a huge gap on the ground."

"I understand your problem, but I'm sorry, I have no choice, unless you want to abort the operation and fly back with me to Athens," said the captain in the full knowledge that this was not a realistic option. The usual punishment for insubordination, was a short court-martial and execution for “cowardice”.

Cursing softly and boiling with rage, Wolfgang returned to the passenger cabin. A minute later Wieland arrived too, and noisily vented his displeasure at the *Luft*waffe and the reliability of its commanders, which was mainly subsumed by the aircraft noise.

“That captain is as stubborn as a mule,” he informed Wolfgang. “I threatened him with court martial and do you know what this bastard answered me?’My problem right now is, how to get the plane safely back to Athens. The court-martial, with which you threaten me, I can handle, assuming of course, that you return from this operation in the near future and find someone who is willing to listen to your complaint’. What a fuckwit! Never mind that before takeoff he was sounding off about camaraderie and what an honor it was to participate in such a prestigious operation. Yuck!” Wieland spat symbolically on the ground, a habit from his childhood walks through the markets of Jerusalem, Bethlehem, and Jaffa. “I wouldn’t be surprised if he hadn’t invented the whole story about the lack of fuel, just to experience flying low over the Dead Sea, the lowest place on earth to see how the altimeter needle plunges under the zero line.”

“You really can’t stand him, can you?” Wolfgang replied. “How did you ever get the idea about the negative indication of the altimeter?”

Wieland made a gesture like “never mind” and in the few minutes that remained until the jump, he also called Dinninger and reorganized the squad, in light of the unexpected change.

“We throw the equipment boxes off quickly, one after the other. Watch out, a southerly is blowing – weak, but nevertheless from the south. Schwarte jumps first, then I,

Salameh third, Abu Latif follows him and Dinninger – you take the spare radio, jump last and then we're rid of the *Luft*waffe."

With an authoritative voice, Wieland explained to his men that, although they would jump from much higher altitude than planned, the parachutes remain on automatic opening. "Although that might increase the risk of us spreading out a bit, but, trust me, based on experience, automatic is preferable to unregulated manual opening at varying heights. In this case, the result would be for everyone to end up on the other side of Palestine, not to mention the possibility that one of our Arab companions could forget to pull the lever and end up planted deep in the soil of the Holy Land. So, remember what we practiced. You jump out strong and sideways, because I don't want one of your chutes to get tangled up with the rear wheel of the plane above the Holy Land of all places."

Wieland did not bother to inform Salameh and Zulfikar of the changes. He merely re-emphasized the need to jump out as far away from the fuselage as possible, asked Dinninger to translate this for the two Arab volunteers and ensure that they understood. "All Clear? Any questions? No? Then let's go. Last equipment check."

The paratroopers were preparing to jump with hysterical equanimity.

"One minute. All up," yelled the sergeant, who stood at the open door of the Dakota checking the line connections for the automatic opening of the parachutes. The squeaky buzzer sounded three short beeps and the green lamp over the door flickered. With deft movements and short intervals between them, the sergeant pushed out the three packages. Even before the last one was gone, Wolfgang stood already at the door, and, without waiting for the dispatcher to tip him on the shoulder, jumped through the door with his arms outstretched as he had learned it in the parachute school. "The Yanks and *Tommies* jump with arms folded on the chest and legs squeezed tightly together, but we, and, incidentally, the Ivans of the Red Army, do it like men – with outstretched arms and legs," explained the trainers.

Personally, Wolfgang felt that the American method contains a certain logic since jumping with outstretched limbs had no special advantage – except maybe to deliver nice shots for the propaganda films of the "*Wochenschau*[80]" from Joseph Goebbels' "educational institutions", shown in thousands of cinemas in the Third Reich. But when it mattered and he had to leave the relatively safe space, falling through the air, he relied on the familiar way he had learned during his parachute training.

The sudden transition from the incessant noise of the aircraft to the silence of the desert caused loud ringing in his ears. Below and ahead of him he saw the large parachutes with the equipment boxes. A quick turn of his head brought another parachute into view, probably Wieland's.

"Where are the others, where have they gone?" he was wondering, but looked down again focusing on the encounter with Mother Earth, which it had always managed to surprise him during night jumps. "Legs together, mouth shut, teeth clenched," he repeated a second before he hit the ground and executed a perfect roll. Almost. A sharp pain shot up his left leg. "Shit, it got me," he groaned and patted his leg. Waves of pain came from his lower leg, the section between the top of his paratroopers boot and the knee.

Wolfgang was a mechanic, not a doctor, but the accumulated experience of his childhood, which was filled with all sorts of broken bones, made it clear to him that this time it was not broken. At worst, a severe sprain. Having also examined the other leg and his hands, he began to haul

---

[80]Newsreel

in the parachute, which had started to re-inflate in the light breeze that was blowing along the ground.

"Three years. After three years, and in spite of everything, even after I've fucked up my leg, I'm returning to Palestine and thinking of what?" echoed the thought in his head – "of my Henrietta. Yes, Henrietta, whom I had tried so hard to erase from my memory."

❄ ❄ ❄

Scattered dots of light flickered in the darkness.

Wolfgang took a deep breath of desert air, a combination of absolute pleasure in its purity in contrast to the number of undefined odors floating around in the Dakota's passenger cabin mixed with the scent of anxiety and tension arising from his situation. "John the Baptist was hanging around here and Jesus fasted here," he recalled, when he saw the straight line of Mount *Qarantal*[81] rising above Jericho. His nostrils flared at the faint smell of the shepherds' camps which wafted in the air. He lay on his rolled-up parachute and looked around in all directions. Only after he had convinced himself that his fall from heaven and his gathering up of the parachute had not disturbed the peace of the desert, he rose slowly, taking care not to transfer too much weight onto the left leg. Using the small shovel, which he had drawn from his belt, he dug a shallow hole, put the parachute in, covered it with a layer of sand, and sealed the small hole with a big stone.

"The plane was flying from south to north; the wind blows south. Therefore, according to the wind direction, Wieland and the rest of the group must be over there," he decided,

---

[81]Known also as the Mount of Temptation, it is the place – according to Greek Orthodox Tradition, where Jesus fasted for 40 days to withstand the temptations of the devil.

as he looked up at the mountainside. "The equipment came down a little earlier in the opposite direction. But first, the other team members have to be found. Equipment? It can wait."

He walked with a slight limp and small measured steps, due to the injury to his left leg. Almost without thinking, he loaded a magazine into the Schmeisser, "just in case, for all eventualities."

After less than fifty paces, his ears picked up a sound.

"One more step and you'll stumble over me," Wieland said quietly but cheerfully, probably due to the successful jump. Like a wildcat, he came out from behind a large rock, with the barrel of his Schmeiser facing sideways.

"Are you alright?" asked the commander. "What's with the limp?"

Wolfgang gave Wieland a brief report.

"I see," Wieland said. "From experience, the pain is now still weak, but it will grow stronger later. The same thing happened to me a year ago in Iraq, when they dispatched us to support Rashid Ali in his rebellion against the English. But, in spite of the injury, I hobbled up to the Persian border, where Canaris' agents took me home. Believe me, Iraq is much more remote and barren than Palestine, and if I could return from there, you will come back safe and sound from Palestine."

Thrilled by his rousing impromptu speech of encouragement, Wieland stood on the spot and looked around. "Let's see where we are. That's the road from Jerusalem to Jericho. A matter of a few kilometers from here and I can already see that the blackout provisions in Palestine are not strictly adhered to," he said, pointing south towards shimmering headlights of vehicles driving in a convoy. "I will go to the west towards the mountain to find Dinninger and the two muftis. You go back in the other direction towards the east, locate the equipment pallets, release their parachutes so that they don't drift in the wind and wait for us. I guess we will all be together in half an hour."

A long and loud barking of a bored or lovesick dog could be heard in the distance.

Wolfgang turned and walked slowly because of the increasing pain in his left lower leg. After he had gone a few yards, he came across a lowly desert tree. He noticed that a bunch of rags was hanging on a rope from one of its branches. He knew that this was a makeshift Bedouin storage area, or that at least was an explanation given by one of the Scout leaders in the German colony in a past life. "The desert dwellers tend to hang various items on trees – such as clothing, for example – knowing full well that no one will take them."

The bunch was hanging on the chunkiest branch of the tree, precisely the one Wolfgang liked. He shifted the bundle of the unknown Bedouins to another, smaller branch, drew his commando knife, cut off the thick branch, and removed its leaves and small branches, turning it into a crutch. While he was limping along, trying it out, the Schmeisser slung over his shoulder, one hand on the strap of his backpack, he tripped over a small pile of silk which had belonged to the cargo parachute. Its edges were fluttering in the desert wind. A small briar had become entangled in its lines thus anchoring it to the ground. "Holy shit," Wolfgang cursed whilst viewing the pile of splintered planks and pieces of equipment that were scattered over a wide circle. A quick check showed that apart from the field rations that had remained intact upon impact with the ground, most of the equipment was in pieces. In spite of double and triple padding, the radio had received a blow, which left a deep dent in the rear side of the device.

Wolfgang picked up the unit, shook it violently, and made a long face at the sound of rattling from the interior that contained the message "totally kaput". He pressed the mode button. The little light that should have flared up remained off. Wolfgang turned to the volume setting in the hope of hearing any sound, even if it was just static. But the unit remained quiet, like a lump of metal, which it actually was. Wolfgang cursed again the *Luftwaffe*, Goering, the quartermaster, who had delivered the pallets – "a new product development, just arrived from Berlin," he had boasted proudly on the night prior to packing - but actually his curses were addressed to all those who had anything to do with this operation.

"Somebody up there does not like this operation," Wolfgang mused. "We were chucked out and scattered contrary to the agreed plan. On the ground, there is no trace of a 'welcoming committee'. The big 10 watts radio is shattered. Meanwhile, we don't even know how to communicate to the base that we have landed safely, because it is the only unit with a suitable transmission range from such a low place as Jericho. I just hope that Dinninger has landed well with the second unit. His unit is weaker, only 3 watts, and, to establish contact with the station on Rhodes or Rommel's HQ in *Marsa Matruh*, we have to climb to a mountaintop and pray that any Wehrmacht relay station picks us up so that we can at least report that we are alive."

Wolfgang's mood did not improve either when he discovered the other two pallets had actually landed in one piece. He did not bother to open them, because he remembered that they contained some weapons, ammunition, clothing, and a number of other supply items, which were not required at the moment.

Wolfgang sat up and listened to the sounds of the desert. It was quiet.

Despite the painful leg, he went to work. He buried the cargo parachutes, dragged the intact pallets close to the remains of the smashed ones, and gathered them all at one point. He lay down on the ground after having carefully removed small stones and sharp rocks, looking to the west hoping to see the approaching shadow of the rest of the squad. He looked at the watch. The hands shone bright and indicated three o'clock Athens time.

Nearly an hour had passed since he had left the door of the Dakota. "Where the hell are they? Soon the night will be over. Now all we need is to be stuck here in daylight. We must collect the equipment and hide."

Just then, he noticed a slight movement to the west. An agreed whistle indicated the approach of the rest of the squad. Up front Wieland, Schmeisser at the ready, followed by Dinninger and Salameh, who half supported – half carried Zulfikar. "As I feared," Wieland hissed grumpily to Wolfgang. "Zulfikar had landed with his legs spread like a Berlin hooker and has probably broken his right foot. He almost passed out on the way here. It's beginning to get late. We have to find a cave or a hidden crevice. Let's send Salameh out to search for his friends whilst we spend the day in hiding and continue at night."

Wadi Kelt, Summer 1942

The heat rays emitted from the *wadi* rocks, dried Asher's throat, threatening to scorch his lungs.

"Just a few hundred meters further and we reach *Ein Fouar*[82], the stuttering well" Asher comforted the soldier marching in front of him. "It is so called because it stops flowing every few minutes. According to a Bedouin tale, Allah created the well for two goblins, Khouri the good one and the evil Abed. When the good Khouri wins, the spring flows. If the evil Abed wins, the flow stops."

"Well, now you are exaggerating a bit with too many details", Wolfgang Lotz answered wearily his neighbor in the column, which was moving slowly forward; it should have been a vigilant, combative patrol, but due to the heat and fatigue, it was just a long line.

"Tell me, how do you know all these details?"

"When I was in high school, I used to hang out with hikers – I especially loved to go trekking with *Zeev Vilnai*[83]. We reached every corner of the land. Almost."

Lotz was no longer interested in this explanation. He was wiping the sweat flowing like a waterfall from his forehead.

---

[82]A spring in *Wadi Kelt* which alternately empties and refills on a regular basis, therefore also known as the "stuttering" well.

[83]Geographer, archeologist (1900-1988), one of the country's greatest explorers.

"Say, Asher, how can one live in a place like this. The brain shrivels up. I can hardly think clearly how to put one foot in front of the other at the next step; but I'll be damned if I understand, how Moses, Jesus and all the other eggheads who had fled here, not only did not keel over dead from the heat, but even emerged from the desert with new messages and ideologies for humanity," he was wondering aloud.

"Well, they probably did so in the winter. Imagine if Moses had fled into the wilderness, was hit by sunstroke and died. Or Jesus would have faded away. Interesting, how mankind would have developed, had this really happened in the summer heat. On the other hand, one can perhaps discard this theory altogether. Because as you can see, even we let slip a few words of wisdom despite the heat."

Lotz and the soldier behind him, who had also heard Asher's witty explanation, let out a muffled, tired laugh. There were ten of them: seven soldiers of the German *Palmach* section, a sergeant, a Bedouin tracker, and an English police officer from the Jericho precinct. They reached *Ein Fouar* after a few minutes of marching through the deep, hot ravine, just like Asher had predicted. Tired and exhausted they scrutinized the square concrete pool, in the middle of which was a round, open building, its entrance partially barred by wrought-iron rods.

"The pool is almost empty," noted Asher, who had climbed down the steps that led to the pool. "A sign that right now evil Abed is winning." He had barely finished speaking when suddenly a gurgling sound was heard inside the circular structure and a water stream was gushing out of the well.

"Yes, I know. Now it's Khouri," laughed Lotz and washed his face with the cold water.

"Five minutes of rest", the officer announced in heavy, Scottish accent, regretting that he was in the middle of a military operation, which made a jump into the refreshing water out of the question.

"Lotz, you stand guard, because you were the first who laid down his arms and washed his face, unlike the biblical warriors of Gideon, who took care of their weapons." The Scottish officer did not hide his delight at the fact that he remembered the story of Gideon and his thirsty people and ordered Lotz in a smiling tone, to position himself at the side of the *wadi*, to ensure that his small squad would not be surprised by robbers.

"Who knows, it might even be German commandos," he concluded jokingly.

Tired laughter from the soldiers demonstrated that the latter part of the officer's reasoning appeared to them unlikely.

"What's happening with the fucking communication," roared the officer at a burly soldier, carrying a heavy radio on his back.

"Sorry, sir," said the radio operator. "Only static and interference. Sometimes I also receive some Morse, which is very strange. The Morse is transmitted in groups of five letters, but it's probably encrypted, because I can't recognize a single word."

The sound of falling stones could be heard around the bend just before Lotz reached that point of the cliff and brought them all back to reality, including the loud cocking of weapons.

"Don't shoot, I'm unarmed," someone shouted in Arabic and English. "I'm coming from behind the bend."

A few seconds later the caller appeared – a slender and athletic Bedouin – and turned directly to the officer in perfect English: "My name is Salim Abbas, former police tracker."

"That's you, the legendary Salim?" enthused the officer. "In the Jericho precinct everyone is still raving about your exploits. I'm honored to meet you. However, I don't understand how an experienced tracker like you can generate so much noise. We heard you coming for miles."

"I deliberately kicked off stones, so you wouldn't shoot me," Salim said dryly, noting that if only he had had a good weapon and had wanted to, "believe me, your entire unit would now lie with their heads deep in the sand. You make a racket like a herd of cows on their way to the well after two days in the desert without water."

The officer smiled.

"I suppose that you are looking for the paratroopers," continued Salim without further ado.

The officer looked at him in surprise. He was wondering how come, that a Bedouin, even if he was a former police tracker, was initiated into this mysterious spy episode.

"It was me who discovered their tracks yesterday morning," said Salim, noting that he had been minding the family flock. "They landed not far from the cave where I slept. In the morning, I saw their tracks and the area where they had regrouped after landing; I also found few buried parachutes. I ran to the road, stopped a bus which had come from Jerusalem and instructed the driver to report to the police in Jericho. From the fact that I see you here, one can conclude that he did the job. But I don't understand why it took so long."

The officer did not really like Salim's critical tone, even though he knew deep down that the experienced tracker was right.

The first report about the presence of suspects in the area had already reached the police yesterday, but was received with disbelief by his colleagues in the Jericho police station. Only as a result of a stream of additional reports of unusual activity in *Wadi Kelt*, someone in the Jerusalem headquarters recognized that this was neither a joke nor the imagination of Bedouin shepherds and ordered a search and destroy mission. But in the meantime, the unknown paratroopers had been given a whole day to organize and leave the area.

The Scottish officer, a generally cranky and bitter man, this time exercised self-control. Therefore, even though he did not like Salim's critical tone, he kept his temper and even found a few good words for the tracker.

"Excellent. Well done."

Salim was pleased with the praise. It reminded him of days gone by, full of activity and adrenaline.

"I think I know where they are hiding."

"So what are you waiting for? We have been running around for hours in this desert swallowing sand. How far are they?" began the officer with a number of questions, while barking short, irritated orders at the radio operator, to keep trying to establish communications with headquarters.

"Severe blocking. It's impossible, I get only static and occasionally this mysterious Morse code," said the radio operator and expressed the hope that maybe later, when the valley widened and a path to the top would be found, he would try some more.

Salim pointed to the map and put his finger on the paratroopers exact landing spot.

"Here I found a pile of broken and splintered wood. If it is a spy unit, which is supposed to blend in with the terrain, then they are complete fuckwits. The boards are tagged with writing in the German language and bear markings of swastika with wings. Could be provision chests," he told the Scottish officer and, indeed the rest of the squad members, who had gathered around the map. "Not far away, I found a shallow pit in which they buried their parachutes. Meanwhile, Bedouins had arrived who were after the silk of parachutes; don't ask. Knives were drawn and it was only due to the presence of Sheikh Abdullah, who organized a more or less fair distribution of the material that it did not end in murder."

Salim took out a piece of khaki colored cloth. "I cut off a big square from one of the parachutes because I thought it might be of interest to headquarters in Jerusalem," he said and handed the cloth to the officer. "On the ground proper, I recognized many suspect tracks in different directions."

"How many of them are there?" asked the officer quickly. "Can you estimate that?"

"No," Salim said. Noticing the signs of disappointment which were beginning to spread over the questioner's face, he corrected himself quickly, accompanying his words with a broad smile. "I have no estimate, but know for certain that there are five of them, all marching in military boots with soles that leave tracks in the sand, which I've never seen in my life. According to the tracks, I believe that one of them is hurt, because they have left traces of two people walking side by side and in the center is a set of tracks with a lot of pressure on one leg and almost no pressure on the other leg. In addition, one of the five is limping. It's nothing serious, but he limps."

"Excuse the question," Asher interjected, "You can deduct all that from the tracks you found on the ground?"

Salim did not answer. He only looked up at the questioner and was wondering if this was the right time to give a brief discourse about tracking. He decided against it, ignored the comment, and continued his explanations for the officer. "Four soldiers, including the wounded one, were moving in this direction and I am convinced that they are now hiding in one of the larger caves scattered here."

Salim pointed to a specific spot on the map and the officer quickly marked the spot with an X. "One member of the group went in the opposite direction, to the west. I did not follow his trail, because I had decided that the four were of greater interest. I have a feeling that the one going west had some knowledge of tracking because he was making a special effort to walk on the rocks and avoid treading on the sand, as if he was trying to cover his tracks."

"Oh," muttered the officer. "He probably wanted to call for help or try to contact someone. What the hell is wrong with the communications?" He yelled at the sweating soldier, who was carrying the heavy radio on his back. With a regretful shaking of his head, the radio operator indicated that he had not yet been able to overcome the blockage.

"Okay, the party is over; let's cut the bullshit and go find these arseholes," the officer ordered the soldiers who had crowded around the map, attentively following Salim's remarks. "Salim leads, along with Abdallah our tracker; you and you," he pointed to two soldiers with tommy guns, "advance guard with Sergeant Stevens; everyone else in the march formation as before; remain alert. As you heard from the report of this honorable gentleman, who has appeared before us in the desert, we are now not talking about a picnic in *Wadi Kelt*, but hot pursuit of German paratroopers. And you," he added, pointing at the sweaty radio operator, "will continue with this fucking machine and try to establish communications."

❄ ❄ ❄

"Can you hear anything?" Wieland asked in a whisper, as he knelt beside Dinninger who was sitting bent over the little radio, earphones on his head, which he had tilted slightly to the left, the side of his better ear.

"Zero. Zilch. Only static noise," Dinninger said. He folded the sheet of paper on which he had previously encoded a Morse message that they had landed safely at the destination. "I also tried to transmit fiver batches in Morse code, but it does not surprise me. To be sure, I have drawn the antenna to the bush outside the entrance, but even so, we're in a ravine, at least 200 meters below sea level. It's almost impossible for our message to arrive in *Marsa Matruh*, let alone in Belgrade or in Rhodes."

"All right, keep trying every half hour," Wieland ordered.

"Psst! Hey, I need someone to relieve me," Wolfgang interrupted softly from his vantage point where he stood guard at the broad entry to the cave. He looked over the rock that partially blocked the view of the *wadi* and the small valley. "I'm sorry, but I've got to take a crap."

Even before he had finished the sentence, a moan of pain could be heard from the direction of Zulfikar, who was lying unconscious on his back. One leg was bandaged with a provisional splint and was elevated on an ammunition box.

Wieland went to Zulfikar, felt his pulse and wiped the sweat that had accumulated on his brow. "I'm going to relieve Wolfgang for a few minutes," he said, looking at Dinninger who had now finished folding the radio notes, had begun to nibble on a thin, long sausage, which he had taken from his backpack, pretending not to have heard Wolfgang's remark.

"Schwarte, don't go too far and don't dawdle. And don't forget to bury your shit according to regulations. As you know, this is necessary not only because of the flies."

"Since we took off from Athens, I've not had a crap, so I warn you in advance that this time it may take a little longer than usual," Wolfgang said, smiling at Wieland. He raised his hand with a slight movement meant to express: "Don't worry, I know what to do."

Before leaving the cave, he hesitated for a moment whether to take the Schmeisser, but put it next to his backpack. He ascertained that the Luger was secured in its holster on his belt and left the cave. After the darkness that had prevailed in the cave, the bright light of the summer sun hit him like the searchlight of an anti-aircraft gun.

"Shit," he uttered his favorite curse. "I should go back into the cave and get my sunglasses," he muttered. His eyes were half-closed to narrow slits, as a reaction to the strong light. But he stayed outside, clung to the side of the mountain and waited a few seconds before his eyes could adjust to the blinding light rays that hit him from all directions.

Gradually his field of vision expanded beyond the narrow frame he had seen from the cave opening during his watch. Lone, bent trees with spiky leaves that threw almost no shadow on the ground were spread over the *wadi* floor. He noticed moisture stains on the northern side of the gorge. They pointed to a trickle of water. "Water in the desert, even in small quantities will immediately attract plants and animals. A moisture stain indicates the seeping of water through the soft layers to the hard rock layer. Thus, a raindrop in the desert can come out after months of slow leakage. By the way, this is also the source of springs," he recalled wistfully the tour guide's explanation on the Easter trip in the year 1937.

"37 or 36? But does that really matter now?" He asked and replied, while scanning the area for a large rock, preferably a shady area that could meet the minimal requirements of a provisional field latrine. He turned right, stepping carefully bent forward while dragging the injured leg. After a few dozen steps, he found it. "Excellent," he murmured at the sight of the small square in the shade of the north side of the valley, which appeared to have been made to order. It was hidden by a few large rocks, some of which were themselves hidden by bushes with broad leaves, of which he was aware that they were carrying toxic fruit, the name of which he could not remember now.

Wolfgang unbuckled his belt and put it aside, pulled out a sheet of paper from his pocket, opened his pants, squatted with a short moan – a reaction to the waves of pain that raced through him from the injured leg – and began to tear it into small squares.

"They sold us some cock and bull stories, the mufti and his cronies," he mused while continuing to prepare the paper squares required for the next phase. "Let's see what has happened to us since the jump? We are already the second night in Palestine and no trace of the Mufti's partisans." His gaze swept automatically over the entire area. "Apart from bats and desert animals, we have not seen anyone. And Salameh, who, immediately after the jump, set out towards Jerusalem on his way to connect with their headquarters, has disappeared. Like a ghost. I don't understand what Wieland is still waiting for? The water is getting scarce. Tomorrow there will be no more morphine and Zulfikar will begin to scream in pain like a pig before the slaughter. If there are really Arab fighters in the area, how long can it take before they reach us?"

Wolfgang became engrossed in the reconstruction of the past 30 hours when all squad members had gathered around the shattered equipment pallet. While he and Dinninger were trying to bandage Zulfikar's leg, Wieland and Salameh agreed on a series of signals for the meeting of the German paratroopers with the Arab fighters whom Salameh had promised to bring to them.

"I'll be back in a few hours with our armed forces and lead you to a safe place between Ramallah and Nablus," Salameh said proudly, noting that the Arabs had actually occupied the mountain during the Great Revolt in their fight against the British. "Our friends are not far from us; I can feel it in the air. You know, instincts of a desert son," he boasted, shook his squad mates' hands and went on his way – but not before he changed from the Wehrmacht uniform into civilian clothes.

Wieland and Dinninger supported the injured Zulfikar during the short walk to look for safe shelter until their anticipated extrication. "You are exempt from carrying Sulfi," Wieland said, thus bestowing on the Arab paratrooper a nickname, which raised a smile on the faces of his comrades. "You mustn't put too much weight on your injured leg." They were moving slowly in search of a cave that, according to the aerial photograph that Wieland had memorized, should be around the next bend. And there, indeed, it was.

They spent the remainder of the night and the entire daylight hours in the small, musty cave after they had cleaned it a bit from the goat and sheep manure, left by former "tenants".

All attempts to contact headquarters had failed. The adrenaline-soaked tension decreased with every minute that had elapsed since their landing and was replaced by a cloud of anxious irritability. During the day they remained hidden in the cave, strictly observing total silence, which was only broken by the occasional moans of the injured Zulfikar. Wieland, the commander, forbade them to leave the cave and so they had to relieve themselves in a corner, directly into the empty cans that had been thrown into a makeshift pit after use. Around noon it appeared to Wieland as if they were being watched by someone from behind a rock on a nearby hill. He calmed down only after careful inspection of the area with the help of strong field glasses, but except for a lone rock hyrax, he didn't see a single living being.

By this time, due to the unpleasant odor that had spread in the cave, and following his realization that no one was watching them, Wieland loosened the disciplinary measures and allowed them to alternately go out to relieve themselves and to get some fresh air – of course only after repeated, careful scanning of the environment. But all in all, they spent the daylight hours waiting listlessly, slumbering and taking turns to guard the cave entrance. Improvised cold meals from field rations – Wieland had refused on principle to light a fire – interrupted the routine.

"Look at the fools who are sitting in headquarters," remarked Dinninger, while examining a can of applesauce he had just emptied. "They gave us clean field rations – that is, no wrapper with German inscription – so as not to leave any traces on the ground as befits a secret operation, but they forgot to check the can itself and here the name of the manufacturer is engraved; in German of course. Naturally, the producer added that he is a limited liability company, GMBH. Only a fool doesn't know that this is a common German label."

Towards sunset, Zulfikar's pain increased.

Wieland and Dinninger changed his bandage, supported the broken bone with a makeshift splint, and sedated the injured man with a double dose of morphine.

"Come on, let's use the opportunity while our Mufti is dreaming of his Asisa" whispered Wieland. "I have a feeling that he and Salameh know something of the gold, so I'd rather not walk around with all this golden treasure I 'm carrying with me. Everyone takes twenty coins and adds them to his escape kit. This is also an opportunity to check the equipment overall. Make sure that you have a compass, a small map of Palestine printed on silk, and five Palestinian pounds in notes and coins. Dinninger, continue to guard the exit. Schwarte and I will dig a hole and bury most of the gold coins here near the wall of the cave. A kind of piggy bank for emergencies."

❄ ❄ ❄

With nightfall Wieland decided to improve the waiting conditions despite Zulfikar's severe condition and move to a nearby cave that seemed to him larger and more comfortable; he also remembered its location from the air photos. Before setting off, they sedated Zulfikar again so that he would not utter a sound and carried him alternately, "piggyback", to the new cave, which was about a kilometer away from the first shelter.

Their second night in the Holy Land passed slowly, as if every minute had a few more seconds added, and every hour lasted longer than 60 minutes. Around midnight Dinninger climbed with his radio to the top of the hill and tried for a long time to zap all frequencies. Occasionally, he also transmitted the call sign of "Operation Plier Squeeze". Their call sign received no answer. He also tried to send Morse code, but the result remained the same: only annoying static.

An enormous fart, which almost stirred up a cloud of dust, interrupted the flow of his recollections and cheered Wolfgang up, who was squatting in the shade of the rock. It seemed to announce the end of the troublesome constipation, from which he had been suffering for the past two days. "Maybe it is caused by the damn field rations," he mused. His thoughts focused for some reason on the canned meat, which he had eaten at night. He glanced at the watch on his right arm, because he felt that this obstruction had detained him too long in the open.

For years, ever since he got his first wristwatch, he insisted on wearing it on his right arm. "Wolfgang, why are you wearing it as opposed to what is customary? It's uncomfortable to wind up the watch like this. It is not coincidental that one normally wears the watch on the left arm," his mother admonished him. But he persisted, with a kind of youthful stubbornness or perhaps because he wanted to be different from others, to wear the watch on his right arm. Having grown accustomed to it over the years, he was wearing the A. Lange & Söhne watch he had received along with the Iron Cross, on his right arm.

But now, in the heat of the *Wadi Kelt* day, as he was looking with almost instinctive movement to the watch on his right arm, he noticed from the corner of his eye a movement at the crook of the gorge, accompanied by the flash of a blinding ray of sunlight dancing on metal. He lifted his head to the left, in a gesture that reminded him of some funny creatures from Madagascar – the name "lemur" came to mind, but he was not sure and now was not the time to consider this – which were the main characters in a nature documentary he had once seen as a supporting film at a matinee in a Jerusalem theater.

He swore briefly during the seemingly simple process of pulling up his pants, which was complicated because of the squatting position and the necessity to avoid protruding from behind the rocks. With a rapid movement he grabbed the belt, buckled it up, and pulled the Luger from its holster while he was rebuking himself with all epithets for having left the Schmeisser machine pistol in the cave. Now he was stuck in the desert alone, with a weapon that might have been enough for a bank robbery, but not for more.

"Three, six, nine, eleven," he counted quickly, processing the information that he had managed to perceive. "Two unarmed trackers, an officer with a revolver, two soldiers equipped with automatic weapons up front, the rest have rifles. They are moving in from the left, about two hundred meters from the cave. I'm stuck right in the center of their visual field. How the hell do I warn Wieland? In a few minutes they will reach the entrance to the hideout in the cave."

In almost invisible slow motion, with the movement of a sleepy lizard trying to avoid being seen by a hawk circling overhead, Wolfgang raised his head a few centimeters until he could identify the silhouettes of the approaching soldiers through the leaves of the bushes. They were moving according to the three-foot rule towards the cave. They were walking slowly, carefully.

The pace was dictated by the two trackers, who were excited by the boot prints the paratroopers had left in the *wadi* floor. One of them raised his hand and the column stopped. The soldiers – "with a lot of practice," remarked Wolfgang to himself – adopted a kneeling stance and surveyed the *wadi*, the ravine walls, and the crevice that surrounded them.

Schwarte estimated that the distance between the trackers and the entrance to the cave had shrunk to less than fifty meters. He ducked his head, shortened his neck while trying to breathe more slowly even though the adrenaline was already racing through his veins and his heartbeat increased. "My God, they are sure to discover our footprints at the entrance to the cave. And I have no way to warn the comrades."

Now that they had decreased the distance, he heard how the two trackers were quietly deliberating. He realized that they were speaking Arabic, but could not hear exactly what was being said there. He also noted that one of the trackers turned to the officer in English. But again, because of the distance, he could not decipher the conversation other than a word here and there.

❄ ❄ ❄

"Here it is, end of the line. They are here, in this cave" determined Salim and showed the officer the tracks in the loose sand. The markings were weak, but for Salim's practiced eye, they were as clear as footprints of elephants in mud. He also seemed to note that occasional footprints ran out of the cave to the west. "Worth examining later," he said softly to himself.

Salim was careful to stand behind a rock, which hid him from the opening of the cave, as opposed to the officer who did not bother to take cover, positioning himself in the middle of the *wadi* in the posture of a Hollywood General.

"I see nothing. How do you know that they are in a cave and which cave exactly are you talking about?" asked the officer grumpily, which was not least due to the severe heat. In his eyes, the stones and all the marks in the sand looked alike. He also had not recognized the cave, which was blocked by a big rock.

"They are in the cave. The tracks don't lie," answered Salim, who tried to adopt a matter-of-fact tone, but had had enough of the snide remarks he was made to swallow in the last twenty-four hours from the representatives of His Majesty's police force.

"It's all because I wanted to be a good citizen," the thought ran through his mind. "Idiot, let this be a lesson to you. Next time don't offer your services and don't poke your nose into the affairs of others."

This episode of the good citizen, which he had meantime come to regret, had begun in the morning of the previous day, when he discovered the mysterious tracks for the first time. His years of experience made him realize quickly that this was not a matter of yet another smuggling gang of sugar or coffee from Transjordan. After all, he had an unwritten agreement of "live and let live" with the smugglers, whom he occasionally met along the paths in the wilderness.

He did not report to the authorities the smugglers, whose businesses flourished, who were always armed, but who appreciated that he did not meddle in their affairs and simply ignored him with his little flock. But this time he was convinced that this was a serious security incident that had nothing to do with smuggling.

"It could be an exercise of a British task force. Should this really be the case, I will be laughed at by the Jericho police at worst. But I know the tracks of British soldiers and boots such as these I've never seen in my life. These must be connected to the war that rages in the world."

He left the flock after he had made sure that the door of the enclosure was locked, ran onto the main road, stopped a bus that was driving along the road, ordered the driver to swear that he would report to the duty officer at the police station in Jericho that "Salim, the former police tracker, had found suspicious footprints in *Wadi Kelt* and requests that you send out a patrol to check the area."

Salim knew the mentality of his people, and assumed that the driver had performed the job of reporting. Nevertheless, the British took almost a whole day to take up the pursuit. During the long, hot hours Salim was waiting in the area, he collected evidence and only took time out to quickly take care of his flock, leaving it in the enclosure guarded by only two faithful dogs. Now, just a few meters from their objective, the officer is behaving like an idiot, asks stupid questions and does not understand that perhaps an enemy soldier hiding in the cave, has his head in his cross hairs.

Salim took a deep breath, exhaled slowly, trying to calm down. "Look here. Do you see the footprints that we have been following for almost one kilometer? Three pairs of legs belonging to three men," he told the officer. "One walks normally, one is lame and one carries a particularly heavy load. The footprints lead directly to the cave."

"I thought that you spoke of five," insisted the officer.

"There were five. One of them left the group and went alone towards west, north-west. I had already told you that at the beginning of the pursuit. The other, with the heavy load is probably carrying the fifth."

"Okay, you've convinced me," admitted the officer. He corrected the angle of the cap on his head after he had wiped away the sweat with a tiny handkerchief and turned to the soldiers. Softly, but clearly, he began to give orders, based on his military knowledge which he had acquired as a young officer in His Majesty's Service during dozens of chases in the lawless border areas of northern India.

But maybe it was due to the many years that had passed since this adventurous period of his life that he had forgotten the principles of weapons security; thus he gave the orders while brandishing the barrel of his Webley revolver, which he held in his hand, in such a frightening manner, that Salim and the soldiers ducked instinctively each time the barrel was pointed at them.

"Sergeant, you sneak carefully to the *wadi* wall, crouch against it, then advance to the distance of a grenade throw and take cover. On my command you throw a hand grenade and we fire a volley. You and you, yes, you two with the Tommy Guns, make your way to the other side and fire rapid bursts into the cave. I want you to shoot first and empty your magazine with a few long bursts. While he replaces the magazine, you empty yours. In this way, each one of you fires two magazines. Clear? All remaining soldiers, fire single shots and aim at the cave entrance. I repeat: no one opens fire until I give the order. Clear?"

"Sir, maybe we should rather try to call for them to surrender," interjected Salim. "Innocent civilians roam around here, even young girls who tend the herds of their families living in this area. They may even be holding civilians in the cave, threatening them with weapons."

The officer's eyes widened with amazement. He scratched his head and Salim noticed how his Adam's apple jumped up and down several times. "Okay. Go on, Salim. It doesn't matter. If you want to risk your neck for a few fucking Nazis, then come on, try talking to them and persuade them to surrender."

Salim did not consider it necessary to respond. He rose from his cover, went straight for the cave, leaving a gaping officer, an indifferent tracker, seven bewildered Jewish soldiers, through whose heads confused thoughts were racing in Hebrew and German, a combination of fear of the unknown and youthful eagerness for the fight.

"We know that you are in there," Salim shouted in Arabic and English. He crouched behind a large rock, about ten meters from the entrance of the cave.

Silence.

"I repeat. We know that you are in there," Salim repeated his call, this time in English. "You are surrounded and if you don't come out of the cave, we will open fire."

Silence.

"I'm sure they are inside," Salim reckoned. "I'll try once more and then I'll let the stupid officer run the show."

❄ ❄ ❄

"I can simply blow him away as well as the two soldiers with automatic weapons, but then that'll be the end of me," Wolfgang analyzed the situation as it appeared to him from his hiding place. With slow, practiced movement, he surveyed the area and was considering the possibility of hitting as many soldiers as possible, and doing so quickly. Again and again he cursed, but softly, his stupidity, that had brought him at the end of a flight of thousands of kilometers and a parachute jump from a great height into a superior position relative to the enemy, but only with a 9 mm Luger and eight rounds. "What kind of a fool you are. If you had at least taken the Schmeisser," he swore at himself.

The tracker, who by now had approached the cave entrance, repeated his demand for a third time. Again, only in English. "Attention. We know that you are in there and we know exactly how many you are. We are a strong special unit, equipped with automatic and heavy weapons and have surrounded you. We can destroy you with bursts of fire or besiege you and wait until hunger and thirst overwhelm you. You now have 30 seconds to come out without weapons and with your hands above your heads; we promise you that you will not be harmed. As soon as I have finished this demand, you have 30 seconds to surrender. Then we open fire."

Wieland and Dinninger exchanged glances. They lay next to the cave entrance, hidden by large stones and were trying to estimate how many soldiers they had to deal with and where they were positioned.

"Wieland, where did they suddenly appear from? What should we do?" whispered Dinninger. "Schwarte is gone and we are just the two of us, with one Schmeisser and two pistols. What the hell are we going to do? Do you see them? How many are they? Do we have a chance of doing something?"

"Shhh! We have a chance. If Schwarte is behind them, we have an advantage over them. We can eliminate them."

"Yes, but we have no idea how many they are. It must be a big unit; otherwise, they would have done nothing. They would have surrounded us and waited for reinforcements. And Schwarte? Where is he? Maybe he has fled? Perhaps they got him?" said Dinninger with a strained voice.

A hubbub of orders and the sharp clicking of loading weapons penetrated into the cave.

"Your 30 seconds are up. This is your last chance," cried another voice with a distinct British accent.

"I'm not giving up," uttered Wieland, pursed his lips, took the Schmeisser magazines from his belt and arranged them for quick loading. "We have an advantage. They don't know that Schwarte is out there. I have known Schwarte from our childhood. He is not the type to run away. He is probably waiting for our fire, to let them have it from behind."

Neither of them had noticed Zulfikar's faint stirring. He was lying in the back of the cave and had woken up when the effect of the morphine was wearing off.

"But what can Schwarte do," Dinninger whispered in horror, pointing at Schwartes' equipment which was lying to the side with the barrel of the Schmeisser poking out from behind the backpack. "He's outside with the Luger and a magazine."

At the end of Dinninger's explanation, a sharp command in English could be heard.

"Aim directly at the entrance," the officer ordered loudly. "Fire!"

A long burst of an automatic weapon opened the cacophony of battle. After a few bursts the second Tommy gun joined in, accompanied by single shots from the Lee-Enfield rifles of the other soldiers who aimed much more accurately. The first hand-grenade landed next to the entrance, exploded, sprayed glowing shrapnel inside the cave and spread the particularly deafening noise of a pressure wave. Most rounds that were fired landed in the outer walls. Some odd ones got inside, sprayed splinters of stones and rocks, bounced off of one wall to another, fragmented into small, blazing parts that scattered throughout the whole, narrow space of the gloomy cave.

A cry of pain, followed by a curse in Arabic, indicated that Zulfikar's healthy leg had been hit by a fragment. Another tiny chip hit Dinninger's cheek. He cursed and quickly opened a field bandage. Within the same second in which he pressed the bandage on the non-lethal wound in the cheek, Dinninger was killed by a Tommy gun bullet which penetrated his chest, crushed one of his ribs, pierced his heart and remained buried in the opposite rib.

From his hiding place in the cave, Wieland located only one of the attackers. A short burst from his Schmeisser crossed in a millisecond the distance of several dozen meters that separated them.

At least three bullets had shattered the skull of the tracker, who, contrary to Salim, had not taken cover behind a rock and, moved by stupid curiosity, stuck his head out to see what was happening. His limp body fell to the ground next to Salim. "Dead, Allah have mercy upon him," Salim determined at once. Due to the volley of bullets from the Schmeisser, one didn't need to be a doctor to be so certain.

"Why isn't Schwarte shooting," Wieland yelled, firing off another salvo. "I can't see the arseholes. They are well hidden." He noticed a round metal object rolling towards the hole.

"Grenade!" cried Wieland and pressed himself against the rocks, as if to break the stone and creep into it. He held his hands automatically to his ears. The hand grenade exploded right at the threshold of the cave, scattering hundreds of lethal fragments and filling the interior of the cave with a cloud of dust and smoke.

The attackers had stopped firing.

A terrible ringing in the ear was pealing in Wieland's head. The thunder of the explosion had caused him temporary deafness and instantaneous shock. In that situation he could not hear the officer ordering his men to cease firing.

"Attention, this is now really the last chance for you to surrender. It's hopeless. I give you my word as an officer and a gentleman, that you will not be harmed," he shouted.

This sentence Wieland did hear. A bitter smile spread over his face at the word "gentleman" which the British officer had woven into his surrender proposal. "He has seen a lot of movies, this officer" the fleeting thought crossed his mind. "It seems that 'Operation Plier Squeeze' has come to an end," he said, without being aware that he was actually shouting because of the ringing in the ears. "What do you say, Dinninger? We will spend the rest of the war in a POW camp. Who knows, perhaps even in Australia together with our families."

Dinninger did not answer. Wieland looked back. He saw Dinninger lying on the floor of the cave, his gun still in his hand, eyes wide-open, staring at the ceiling.

Wieland crawled quickly back, checked Dinninger's pulse, beat nervously on the cave floor, and mumbled something incomprehensible with a lot of "shit" interwoven among the words.

"Don't shoot. I'm coming out," he shouted in English, waited 10 seconds and repeated the call twice. He stood up, brushed the dust off, straightened his shirt and windbreaker with the instinct, which he had acquired during the three years of military service, tossed the Schmeisser out through the opening, raised his hands, folded them behind his neck and step forward.

The blast of a single shot thundered through the cave, accompanied by the cry of "Allahu Akbar! Oh traitor, you must die," shouted Zulfikar. He held the Luger pistol with both hands, his eyes wide in a fit of madness.

Wieland was pushed forward by the impact of the bullet that hit him from such a short distance. His body began to collapse, but before he reached the ground, Zulfikar squeezed the trigger again. "Allahu Akbar, death to the traitors!" He roared. Then, ignoring his broken leg, he stood up at the back of the cave, staggered to the entrance and rapidly pressed the Luger's trigger repeatedly.

Tel Aviv, Summer 1942

The battle was engraved in Asher's memory as a long and exciting event, although it turned out in retrospect, after the debriefing, that since Salim's first warning till the end of the battle, less than ten minutes had passed. During the weekend holiday, two weeks after the encounter in *Wadi Kelt*, he shared his experience of the bloody incident with his girlfriend Braha Szold. Like all the other inhabitants of Palestine, she, too, was exposed to the many rumors of a mysterious incident in the Jericho area.

Representatives of the military censorship in all the newspapers and, of course, in the broadcasting service of the Mandate Government, made sure that not even a smidgen of a news item would be published in the media. Due to the lack of official details, the scope of the incident was inflated to ever larger dimensions from one narrator to the next.

"You are pulling my leg," Braha reacted to Asher's first sentence. "I don't believe you. German paratroopers in Jerusalem? I thought they were a gang of pro-Nazi Iraqis who had infiltrated through Trans-Jordan. A classmate told me that she had heard from her father, who in turn was informed by his uncle, the police officer, that there had been a battle with the remnant of the Ka'ukji gang, who, after years of hiding in caves, had raised the banner of revolt again."

"It's amazing how rumors spread," Asher laughed. "One more week and the story would go that Hitler personally parachuted over Jericho, because he felt like visiting the Church of the Holy Sepulchre."

Before going on his short leave, the unit's sergeant had reminded all the soldiers of the official secrecy classification which had been imposed on the entire event. "*Oy vavoy*[84] if anyone raises this topic. Not even at family reunions," he instructed with his loud voice. It took a second, until he understood why his remarks had sparked an outburst of roaring laughter among the troops: the combination of the sharp order given in German of course and the Yiddish words, which had diminished their fear of his authority.

But now, in relaxed, serene Tel Aviv, as if there was no war in the world, Asher ignored the orders to keep the event a secret. He was hoping that his heroic story would increase Braha's passionate desire for him and told her of the sudden departure from the base, the reconnaissance in the scorching heat around the *wadi* bends and the brief battle. "I fired eight times," he boasted, remembering the excitement that had gripped him when he pulled the trigger for the first time and then the rapid fire until he finished the ammunition in the gun. Then the fast reloading of new bullets and the continuation of the shooting.

"The noise was terrible because the echo from the *wadi* walls even doubled the volume. The Nazis returned fire and one salvo swooshed a few centimeters past my ear. Like this," he indicated the distance with his hands. "I felt the wind on my face from the salvo which hit the tracker, who had taken cover three feet from me. But, together with all the other guys, I continued firing. Only after the second hand grenade was there quiet."

---

[84]Woe to the one who…

"What, they were killed? That's it?" questioned Braha.

"No, of course not. Maybe some were wounded by our fire, but we were not able to eliminate them. Then we heard someone from inside the cave shout at least three times in English, 'don't shoot, don't shoot, I'm coming out'."

"Then they surrendered," Braha enthused.

"That's just it. It's still unclear what exactly happened there. A few seconds after the third call, we heard a shot from inside the cave and a cry that sounded like 'Allahu Akbar'. But no one is willing to swear to that. Then another shot and followed by one more shot after which a body rolled to the cave entrance. One of us – I think it was Lotz – was startled by the shots from inside and opened fire. All of us joined in. The officer stood behind a rock in a movie-star posture and threw a hand grenade directly into the cave."

Asher stood up and demonstrated how the officer threw the grenade. "After the fight, he told us proudly that he had played cricket in his youth, which explained how he was able to throw the grenade directly into the interior."

"So then it was the grenade, which ended the fight?"

Braha'a last question appeared somewhat tiresome to Asher, but he continued with the description. "We don't know yet, because then it turned out that the Nazis had a large supply of a novel and powerful explosive in the cave. So, you can imagine what happened when the hand grenade exploded inside. This was a fragmentation grenade – one that scatters hundreds of fragments – and not a stun grenade that only makes a lot of noise. In short, the grenade explosion caused a number of massive explosions inside the cave. A cloud of dust shot out of the opening like a plume of smoke from the chimney of a steam locomotive. And then, half the mountain slowly collapsed over the cave, rocks tumbling from above, fragments flying through the air. What can I tell you, it seemed as if someone in heaven had decided to punish these Nazis and they were buried under hundreds of tons of earth and rocks."

"Wait a minute," Braha stopped the enthusiastic description. "How do you know altogether that these were Nazis?"

"Aha," Asher said, raising his eyebrows and wagging his finger. "After the dust had settled which took a few minutes, we found at the edge of a heap of rocks, a bruised and battered, but still easily recognizable submachine gun. A Schmeisser. This is an automatic weapon, standard equipment for the Wehrmacht. Next to it lay a charred and somewhat dented German helmet. The main tracker, who spoke English and had led us to the cave, found the Schmeisser and the helmet. He immediately suggested to the officer to scour the area within a radius of several hundred meters, to ensure that actually all the Nazis were in the cave."

"Makes sense, doesn't it?" wondered Braha.

"Does it ever?! There is nothing that makes more sense, but, for some reason, the officer got shitty with the tracker and told him, that if he knew so well what needed to be done, and if he was such an excellent tracker, he should go and scan the area himself."

"Interesting. So what did the tracker do? A scan?"

"I just happened to be standing nearby and could see the contemptuous gaze with which the tracker looked at the officer. Then he said to the officer in a very quiet voice, which was hiding much suppressed anger, that he had done his part and had to look after his flock of dozens of hungry sheep and goats. He shook hands with each of us and left. So what do I mean by 'left'? After all, we were in the middle of a desert canyon, not in Tel Aviv. But he simply climbed up the wall of the gorge, as if it were a flat field and disappeared over the ridge. "

"So what did you do?"

"We thought that they would get us out within an hour, two at most. Nothing doing! The sun was setting and we were still alone in the *wadi*. We also spent the night there, guarding a heap of stones and hoping for relief, which only arrived mid-morning. The famous British Army did not exactly enhance its reputation as a competent and well-organized force. This, too, is an understatement. The officer who arrived in the morning explained that headquarters had given him the wrong coordinates!"

"They were a squad of a Sudanese unit led by a British officer and a sergeant, with the task of removing the debris. Along with them, some senior officers had also arrived. They looked like staff- or intelligence officers and strutted like peacocks around the area," Asher explained. "They actually did not like it at all that it had been a squad of Jewish soldiers who had stopped the Nazi unit, but they found solace in the fact that the squad leader was a British officer."

After a brief explanation of the battle, the soldiers of the German section of the *Palmach* were granted permission to leave the area and return to base.

The soldiers marched quickly and proudly to the lorry that was waiting for them on the Jerusalem – Jericho road. No wonder, as they felt confident that they had passed the baptism of fire and won their first battle. The army lorry, which brought them back to their base at *Mishmar Ha'Emek*, drove through Jerusalem and needed about half an hour for the trip to the city centre. Asher and his friends were behaving like soldiers who had known no civilian life for several months. They sang obscene songs, whistled after girls, and cheered the well-endowed among them. As the lorry was driving along Jaffa Road, he saw a familiar figure sitting on the raised terrace of the Cafe "Vienna". "Wow, she looks like Henrietta Landwehr" the thought darted through his head. "But why Henrietta. She had insisted that I call her Tamar. She looks exactly like four years ago aboard the Adria, when she made my head spin and drove me nuts. Interesting if it is really her and what has happened to her. I've heard that she had an affair with Aaron Levy, that indefatigable debater from the Department of History. At the first opportunity I will investigate what's going on with her." Meanwhile, the lorry had moved on and the image of the girl who so resembled Henrietta disappeared from his view.

A few days later, when they were back training in *Mishmar Ha'Emek*, the sergeant updated them on the latest developments in relation to the incident. After two days of continuous work, the soldiers of the clearing unit got through the rubble to what had once been the interior of the cave. The chief pathologist of the Mandatory Government's Health Department was urgently dispatched to the scene with his assistants and a mobile laboratory unit. A series of tests revealed that an estimated three or four people had occupied the cave at the time of the explosion, which is what Asher told Braha.

"Three or four? Don't you not know exactly?" insisted Braha.

"You can't imagine what kind of a blast happened there. Everything collapsed, burned, evaporated. There was hardly anything left of the human bodies in the caves. Everything was disintegrated, incinerated and reduced to ashes. Besides human bones, they also found sheep and chicken bones. But it makes no sense that animals had been in the cave. The investigators believe that these are the leftover bones of meals that the shepherds sleeping in the cave had buried in the ground. The enormous explosion blew the sand from the cave floor in all directions and also laid these bones bare. The investigators were able to identify the remains of iron pieces of what could have been a radio, another Schmeisser submachine gun and three Luger pistols."

The mention of guns offered Asher the opportunity to impress Braha with his great knowledge – he was still considered one of the most outstanding students of the history course at the Hebrew University – and began with a brief explanation of this weapon, which was originally called *Parabellum.*

"The inventor of this pistol – an Austrian called Luger – named it after the Latin proverb '*Si vis pacem, para bellum* – if you want peace, prepare for war'. And this weapon..."

"Good grief, stop bragging already. What else have they found?" Braha interrupted him sharply.

He hid his disappointment and went on to describe how the investigators found remnants of food cans, which were easily recognizable as a German production, because of the manufacturer's imprint on the lid. "And then the ultimate – the investigators found dozens of gold coins scattered on the ground, obviously money the Germans had brought with them, God knows why – possibly a reserve for an emergency escape fund or perhaps for other purposes."

Asher noticed the admiring look that Braha was giving him and continued with his heroic descriptions in the hope, that only a small effort was needed to make a breach in the wall of her shyness and modesty so that they would really finally do it. Like adults.

"I'm sick of this snogging, which is very pleasant but leaves me with aching balls," the thought raced through his head, which caused him to tell her yet another detail of the secret investigation. "If this time I get nowhere with Braha, I'll split up with her and look for someone else. Tamar? Why not, actually?" But in the meantime he continued with the description of the heroic struggle in *Wadi Kelt.*

"One item that troubled the investigators most was discovered by chance, at the farthest end of the cave under a large boulder: remnants of a white powder, the purpose and exact chemical composition of which could not yet be fathomed by any of the tests. You cannot imagine what discussions took place in our unit. Some people think that one of the orders of the Nazis was perhaps to poison the water sources in the Jewish settlements."

Braha responded with a negative gesture. Despite her young age, she knew something about chemistry and by a quick calculation, she realized that to poison a whole water source – even for the smallest settlement – a huge amount of poison would be required, however deadly.

The difficult situation at the Western Desert front, coupled with the progress of the Nazi army in the Caucasus Mountains, intensified the power of the rumor mill in the Jewish community. Half-truths, half-baked stories, and rumors spread quickly. This explains why Braha hastened to inform her schoolmate Osnat, from the parallel class of the *Herzliya*[85] *College* as they stood in the small line, which had formed in front of the most famous Tel Aviv kiosk on the corner of Allenby Road and Rothschild Boulevard.

"You wouldn't believe what I've heard," Braha began excitedly with her report in a relatively loud voice, so that all around them would get it that she "is in the know". "It is said that a group of Nazi spies parachuted in the Jericho area, but all of them were captured or killed. But that's not all. It is alleged that a huge amount of poison was found with which they had planned to poison the water sources of Tel Aviv."

Osnat's eyes widened. "What, Nazi paratroopers? In Jericho?"

"Yes, but the story of the poison is one big nonsense," Braha continued. "Do you know how much poison you need to spread in the water source to poison the water of an entire city?! One shouldn't spread stupid stories." She took the soda and the ice cream cone.

"Sorry, only fruit sorbet. I have no more milk powder to make real ice cream," said the nice seller.

---

[85]Despite the name, it is the first ever Hebrew high school in the world, founded 1905 in Tel Aviv

Braha vacated her place at the stand to a corpulent gentleman in a summer suit.

"What bothers me is the fact that the Nazis can parachute so close to Jerusalem. Who knows, maybe they can even land spies from a submarine."

The two had spoken Hebrew, of course.

Hendrik Krueger, who had come to the kiosk to buy a cold and refreshing drink for the immediate relief of the heat and humidity, had just stepped out of a *Sherut* taxi from Jerusalem. In recent days he had gone three times to Jerusalem and Jericho at the request of his secret employer in the Berlin headquarters of the German Intelligence Service. "Require urgently even the smallest spark of information you hear about the landing of a German intelligence unit in the Jerusalem region and the activity of the Arab underground by Mufti supporters. These reports have top priority," it said in the brief, urgent items transmitted to him every night.

Despite his efforts, Krueger did not manage to compile a clear picture. To show Berlin that he was active, he would even transmit smidgens of information, most of which were completely unfounded, as it turned out later. As usual, it was his friend Sam, the nice bartender from the San Remo, who provided the first clue and then more details about a mysterious battle in one of the *wadis* between Jericho and Jerusalem, which ended in the destruction of the paratrooper unit. But even Sam had no additional details on the composition of that unit and the fate of its members, whether they had been captured or killed.

In fact, Hendrik Krueger had eventually stopped trying to figure out exactly what had happened there. His thoughts were occupied with other problems that had directly to do with his personal security. "Sometimes you're an insect, and sometimes you're the windshield on which the insect is squashed," he recalled somehow a saying which he had heard as a child.

While he had no concrete evidence, he had begun to feel insecure in the past few days, *accompanied by a sense of uneasiness that he was under surveillance.* For several days, when leaving his hotel, he had noticed a street cleaner eagerly sweeping the pavement opposite. In addition, two technicians from the telephone company had been working for three days on the distributor box on the street corner and they were still there whenever he came back to the hotel. Twice he was watching a gray car, a Morris, with two men sitting in the front seats, from the corridor window, which provided him with a view of Hayarkon Street. The car was parked at the corner, but in a spot that allowed its occupants to peer into Hayarkon Street.

"You don't need to be paranoid to believe that someone is out to get you," Krueger recalled the favorite saying of Klaus, the *Abwehr* instructor, who had taught him the basics of securing secret meetings and the shaking off of tails. "It's either my age, I'm getting tired, or I'm really being followed," he thought and was seized by fear.

Memories of family members who had been killed by the British played a major role in his dreams. He found it difficult to fall asleep at night, even though he had increased his amount of whisky consumption. He also became aware of the involuntary movement he had acquired recently, of putting his hands around his neck, "like the hangman, who takes measurements for the size of the loop."

"Calm down, Kruger," he told himself, whilst standing in line at the kiosk behind the two pretty girls talking fast in Hebrew. "Switch off, don't be conspicuous, stop behaving like a suspect, then no one will catch you. A little more patience and Rommel will get here." Krueger did not understand Hebrew, and therefore he could not follow the conversation of the two lovely girls. However, he had picked up the word "Nazis" and wondered if it had something to do with the incident, which was of such great interest to Berlin. But he had agreed with himself that he was through with this matter, which is why he focused on drinking the cold, delicious soda and enjoying the sorbet which was nothing special, but at least cooled his throat.

The Mountain Slopes of Jerusalem, Summer 1942

The tense and frightening hours that he had spent lying motionless in his hideout, which was originally intended to be his temporary latrine, were the longest of his life. Wolfgang had been watching with horror and dismay the brief battle that took place in front of the cave. "I need to join in and save my comrades," his conscience told him.

Slowly, he worked the Luger's slide. But it was logic that prevailed and led the left hand to put the safety catch on. As soon as the shooting started, the soldiers took cover and, in their current position, he could make out only four soldiers. "Even if I kill these four, the rest will hunt me like a rabbit and with only one magazine my situation is worse than that of a rabbit."

His ears heard fragments of shouts exchanged by the soldiers – and Schwarte observed that these soldiers were well trained and disciplined. To his surprise, the exchanges among the soldiers were not in English, but in a foreign language with guttural sounds, which somehow reminded him of Hebrew. "Hebrew? Can it be?" He wondered: "What, the British are now also recruiting Jews? That's unthinkable. Whilst it is true that most of the world is fighting against

Germany, I must surely be hallucinating. It's probably a unit from one of the British Empire armies, perhaps Boers from South Africa?"

When the noise of firing had stopped and the call to the besieged to surrender had abated, it seemed to him that he heard Wieland shout something in English, which began with "don't". He assumed that Wieland had decided, correctly under the circumstances, to surrender to the British. But then a single shot was heard, followed by renewed exchanges of fire. "What bastards, these Brits are," he raged. "They have a sniper who dropped Wieland although he wanted to give himself up."

Wolfgang felt the powerful explosion, which had taken place in the cave after the grenade was thrown, with the intensity of an earthquake. Rocks fell from the cliff into the *wadi*. He rolled over in one quick motion, which again caused pain to the leg he had injured during the landing. Two particularly large boulders landed a few meters away from him with a terrible noise upon shattering and drove a cloud of dust into the air, which slowly spread through the silence that had enveloped the *wadi* after the shootout and the huge explosion.

"That's it, finished," he thought, trying to assess calmly and cold-bloodedly his new situation. Wieland, Dinninger, and Sulfi had fallen. Certainly, no one could survive this massive explosion. "What the hell do I do now? Get up and surrender? If the Brits do an area search – probably the first thing they will do – they'll find me; then they'll immediately, on the spot, put a bullet through my head or capture me. Headshot is the greater likelihood," Wolfgang assessed the situation. Carefully and slowly, waiting for the dust to settle, he looked through the cracks of the rock, bracing himself for the inevitable end.

The minutes passed quickly.

But the British did not scour the environment. They stayed put in front of the entrance, a few dozen feet away. He noticed the radio operator, who was accompanied by another soldier; they climbed up the side of the gorge, apparently in an attempt to increase the reach of the radio transmission and report about the battle. A few minutes later he watched the accompanying soldier come down or rather slide down as he ran to the officer and reported excitedly.

Following the report, the officer looked happy and content and gave a few brief orders which resulted in a guard being posted at the cave entrance, while the rest of the soldiers sat under a lone tree in the middle of the *wadi* – several hundred meters from his hiding place – opened field rations and appeared to be settling down, waiting to be relieved.

"So, let's see what happens," Wolfgang reassessed his situation. After all, it was quite clear to him that his unit's comrades had undoubtedly perished. All, that is, except Salameh, who had left before this incident, to contact the Arab fighters. "Salameh has disappeared. Theoretically, it's possible that he is on his way here with a group of Arab fighters. Theoretically, they could also be brave enough to attack this squad. But this theory has no basis in the reality of the Orient. Clearly Salameh is already sitting in a tent, smoking his hookah and telling his friends Baron Munchausen stories in the Arabic version, *mabsut*[86] – and interestingly I've chosen the Arabic word – that he's home again and has no intention of carrying out his original mission."

Wolfgang noticed that despite his impossible situation – stuck alone behind enemy lines, in a *wadi* teeming with soldiers, thousands of kilometers away from his base, without water, without food, without a game plan for moving on – he was in a kind of euphoria.

---

[86]Arabic: Happy; satisfied.

Clear, vivid pictures from the adventure books of Karl May, whom he had loved reading as a child, projected themselves suddenly into his reality and made it tangible. He, Wolfgang Schwarte, a soldier in the Wehrmacht Regiment Brandenburg, played the role of Old Schatterhand. "Maybe that comes from proximity to the German colony, to Jerusalem," he philosophized.

"Moshe, you schmuck, come, relieve me at last; stop leaving me stranded here. It's your turn now to keep watch," the soldier at the cave entrance shouted to his comrades, who were sitting under the shady tree. He had done so in a voice, loud enough for his words to clearly reach Wolfgang's ears.

"Hebrew? They speak Hebrew? Then these are Jewish soldiers serving in the British Army," he marveled. "When I left Palestine, there were some Jewish policemen, such as the nice policeman from *Emek Refaim*, the one that had driven me to Mount Scopus, at the time of my great crisis with Henrietta. But soldiers? They're clever, these Brits, recruiting Jews for the fight against Nazi Germany. Look at this crazy world. They seem to be my age, and, in the end, it'll turn out that I even know some of them."

He gathered together his entire military prowess, acquired during the three years of service in the elite Wehrmacht unit, to escape out of their sight. At the same time he wanted to explore closer the possibility if, by an ironic and rare capricious fate, Jewish acquaintances from his youth in Jerusalem had been sent to him in this remote *wadi* on the eastern slopes of Palestine. He waited for the darkness, saved his strength, and fought helplessly against the headache that he got from the heat and the thirst. Each heartbeat pounded in his temples like the rhythm of a tom-tom drum, which simultaneously covered up the pain of his leg injury.

It wouldn't have taken much more for his hideout to be discovered.

Two bored soldiers, who had received permission to leave their assembly point under the big tree, to see what was on the other side of the *wadi*, almost stumbled over him. But he lay as still as a stone and was not discovered, although they were passing less than ten meters away from him. After long minutes, when the sound of their steps and their casual conversation had subsided, he dared to raise his head making sure the coast was clear.

The last rays of sunshine flooded the wadi gorge and painted everything in red and orange tones, their intensity constantly decreasing until they were swallowed up by the darkness. The soldiers of the squad – Wolfgang thought it very odd that they had not yet received reinforcements – were now improving their positions, all gathering together near the cave entrance round a bonfire, that had been lit with collected branches and which was casting long shadows.

He heard the soldiers singing; it sounded like Hebrew. He recognized two of the melodies, which spread a smile over his face. One of them was about the charming house on the lake of Galilee, which his grandfather had built decades ago for the Treidel family. "It's silly, but I feel at home," he chuckled. "Here I am in the middle of nowhere and it feels like home ... in half an hour total darkness will prevail here and then I'll bugger off. I'll find water at the entrance to the *wadi,* with food I'll manage, but most importantly, I must get rid of this uniform. I'll keep the Luger for now; and there I was, thinking, that the Iron Cross ribbon could have made my life easier."

Wolfgang analyzed his situation from all angles and came to the conclusion that his best bet was to reach Jerusalem hoping that the British had not expelled all the inhabitants of the German colony. "If I find even only one of them, they will help me. How exactly? Only God knows."

Crawling slowly, which seemed to him like an eternity, but had lasted merely a total of 30 minutes, Wolfgang traversed the short distance between his rocky site and the *wadi* bend. Only then he dared to stand up. He walked cautiously, but steadily to the west while humming the song "*Behold, we are going up to Jerusalem*", that he had learned in his childhood and which was annotated in the hymnals distributed on the benches of the congregation's prayer house for Sunday worship as an anthem of the Christian pilgrims at the time of the Crusader Kingdom.

Cafe Vienna, Central Jerusalem, Summer 1942

The sudden fainting of the nice woman, who had been enjoying a cup of good coffee and a carefree conversation with her friend only a moment ago, startled the guests of the Cafe "Vienna".

"Ambulance, someone call an ambulance," shouted Alisa, while pouring cold water on Tamar's face. "And tell them that it's for a Hadassah employee. It'll get the ambulance here faster."

Paul Roberts, the detective who had been sent with his younger colleague, Lennon, to the Cafe "Vienna" to observe Tamar Landwehr's movements – the girlfriend of Aaron Levi, according to unconfirmed sources, a leader of the *Stern Gang* – used the opportunity and the turmoil. Under the pretext of coming to the aid of the lady in distress, he pushed his way into the human circle that had closed around her – the kind of circle consisting, as usual, of some individuals who want to help and the vast majority just idle curiosity seekers.

"Very distressed," he remarked to himself with unsentimental, professional detachment, at the sight of the unconscious young woman's facial expression. From the corner of his eye, he noticed how his young colleague also took advantage of the commotion, elegantly removing her handbag, looking at him for approval. Lifting his eyebrows almost invisibly, he instructed the young detective, Jim Lennon, to proceed with picking through the handbag, quickly and discreetly.

"The bag is okay, nothing suspicious," Lennon indicated by pursing his lips and ever so slightly shaking his head left and right.

Roberts stood up, walked slowly back to his table and was wondering what he should do next.

The sequence of events, which then occurred in the following seconds were made of the stuff Hollywood action film directors like to accompany with the sounds of dramatic music. But in the Jerusalem reality, everything happened without exciting sounds.

Roberts noticed the young man who had just entered the cafe and immediately realized that it was Aaron Levi. "Shit, that's our target, Levi," he muttered.

Levi, dressed in khaki slacks and white shirt – "the unofficial uniform of the Zionists in the Land of Israel, sometimes worn with a very funny hat called *Kova Tembel*[87]", as determined by the official guidelines of the British Criminal Investigation Department – was confidently striding along Jaffa Road, but stopped abruptly, perhaps because of the hustle and bustle on the terrace of the Cafe "Vienna".

Levi, who, at this point had not yet recognized Tamar among the guests of the cafe – most of whom were jammed together like in a rugby scrum on the raised area – didn't like the sight that greeted him. He noticed Alisa, Tamar's girlfriend, who was alternately kneeling down and standing

---

[87]Literally: dunce cap

up, bellowing orders that sounded like medical instructions. Even the people who were huddling excitedly in a circle looking down on the floor did not bother him. His eyes focused on the silhouettes of two men who were wearing summer coats.

During the past few weeks, as he was becoming more and more involved with the leadership of the organization, Levi felt increasingly that he was under surveillance, so much so, that the recognition of tails became his obsession. He practiced constantly identifying suspicious characters, stopped occasionally at shop windows and looked back, went into shops to watch the passersby on the street, trying to determine whether he recognized people he had seen a few streets earlier.

The real surveillance expert in the organization was the command post's radio operator, Bahar, who personally taught Levi the basics of this specialty. "The CID tries to sit on our tail, so that without realizing it, we would lead them to meeting venues in secret apartments and residential addresses, thus enabling them to gather information about our activities," said Bahar.

"The safest method to detect being followed is to plan a route, which begins in a quiet street, where it is easy to identify and mark suspicious characters and then go into a lively area – but if necessary, return to peaceful surroundings."

Bahar said the route must contain logical points, so the tail does not suspect that their target has something to hide. "Don't be conspicuously inconspicuous like 'tiptoeing through the tulips'. Throughout the entire attempt of detecting tails you need to behave like a normal citizen."

So, for example, he demonstrated how to stop and tie one's shoelaces to exploit the opportunity of discreetly scouring the environment. "However, the trick with the shoe-laces should not be repeated more than twice. The third time an experienced tail will immediately recognize that you are looking for a shadow; and one who looks for shadows, has something to hide, which instantly drops you in it. It increases the motivation to nab you."

Another way of spotting the tail is to stop in front of a shop window. "This is also a natural action, but again, provided it is not repeated too often." Bahar's favorite recipe for recognizing shadows was what he defined as "the trick of turning the granny."

"After you have walked the route of detecting the tail for about half an hour and you've marked suspicious characters, the easiest way to identify and confuse you pursuers, is to turn around and double back. Why? The tail followed you at a distance, which is just large enough to avoid being discovered by you, but as close as possible to you so as not to lose you at the next corner," he said, explaining how " to turn the granny" without arousing suspicion. "You walk at a normal pace; at the intersection you turn the corner and stop the first person who comes towards you – preferably an old busybody, and ask her for directions to a point that is behind you. While she explains, you naturally look to the corner and wait for the arrival of those following you. Then they come running, one after the other, pouring into the street, confused when they discover that you're facing them and that they have been identified. Then they'll try to turn back, pretending to have forgotten something. In short, they are exposed. The directions given by the granny must be followed by hand movements, so that the tail understands that you are getting directions. So, that's it. If you discover a tail, you have to try shaking it off by the usual methods such as boarding a bus at the last minute or mingling with the crowd. Most importantly, if you've discovered a tail, don't, under any circumstances, come to the meeting! Because even if you're sure that you have shaken off your pursuers, the very fact that you were shadowed requires automatic cancelation of the meeting and shifting to an alternative venue."

From the moment of leaving the conversation about his future in the offices of the History Department at the University on Mount Scopus until his arrival at the Cafe "Vienna", Levi had applied all the tricks he knew to make sure that he wasn't dragging a tail of detectives behind him. The evasive maneuver of "turning the granny" he had executed twice to ensure that he was free from pursuers.

"What a nice life you have built for yourself," he reflected philosophically. "You are on your way to a date with your girlfriend, but instead of a smile in your heart and a bouquet of flowers in your hand, you are 'turning the granny' and looking for British detectives..." Now, at the entrance to their meeting place, at the foot of the steps to the terrace of the Cafe "Vienna", Levi's internal alarm sounded and set off loud bells ringing in his head.

Despite their efforts, to behave freely and naturally, Levi immediately recognized two suspects – elegantly dressed men who were communicating with each other almost imperceptibly. "Damn it, CID" the thought flashed through his head. "Who else looks like that and sits in a cafe in broad daylight. Only Morton the Murderer's detectives."

While maintaining a calm countenance, which betrayed nothing of the waves of panic that threatened to burst from every cell in his body, Levi avoided a sudden suspicious change in direction and stepped quite naturally over the threshold of the cafe. "Go in, as if you intend to sit inside, maybe at the bar," he instructed himself. "Act naturally, ask someone where the toilets are, even though you know that they are in the backyard; then you jump over the low wall to the neighboring backyard and disappear."

But reality dictated a different approach with unpredictable consequences. As he was walking through the entrance with tense nonchalance, he noticed the young woman lying on the ground, her head supported in Alisa's hands. Tamar. There was no doubt. That was Tamar.

"Step aside, let me through," he ordered – shouted at the gawkers, broke into the circle and fondled Tamar's head.

"Aaron, where have you been? She suddenly fainted, just like that. Wham!!!" Alisa, who was surprised by Aaron's appearance, but also relieved that she was now able to share the responsibility with someone, told him in short sentences what had happened.

That is, basically nothing had happened, because her friend Tamar fainted in mid-sentence for no obvious reason. The thought even crossed Alisas's mind, that Tamar's sudden fainting had something to do with the fact that she was pregnant. But even she, the gossip, knew that this was the wrong time to raise this issue and decided to postpone it to a more convenient opportunity.

The cold water that had been sprayed on her face and the professional slaps that Alisa had administered achieved their purpose. The veil clouding Tamar's brain, like thick mushroom soup, began to lift. Familiar faces filled her field of vision. A small smile emerged and the line of a slight laugh became visible at the sight of Aaron's worried face, which was looking at her from so close. He was saying something. She noticed his lips moving, but the voices she was hearing were distorted – as if they were channeled through a device which slowed their speed and compressed their sound.

"She is recovering, she is coming to, the ambulance is no longer needed," someone in the crowd of the gawkers shouted joyfully.

Paul Roberts gently, authoritatively, pushed the two women aside who were separating him from the middle of the circle, surveyed the situation and immediately thought of the romantic scene in the movie ***Gone With the Wind***. His "protagonist", in a squatting position, gently holds the young woman's head, whose file he had just read a few hours earlier in the office. But the woman was not Vivien Leigh and the man, despite some superficial similarity, was not called Clark Gable. His full name was Aaron Levi, history student, suspected of being a *Stern Gang* terrorist.

"God, that's Victor Levi, the young history fan from the ship. What was she called? 'London Star'. Yes, the ship on which I arrived in Palestine in 1937. No wonder that he looked familiar to me on the photo."

Just then, Aaron Levi lifted his head. He recognized in the fraction of a second the man, who was scrutinizing him from above, as the friendly Englishman, with whom he had spent interesting hours in instructive conversations during the trip five years ago. But since then much water has flown even down the small *Yarkon*[88]; their paths had diverged and they had gone their separate ways until that moment on the terrace of Cafe "Vienna".

Paul Roberts' trained eye caught the strap of the ankle holster on Levi's right leg, who was now a wanted terrorist, as far as he was concerned. He even recognized the muzzle of the gun and instantly determined that this was probably a Smith & Wesson with five rounds. The sight of the gun totally erased from his mind the explicit instruction he had received during that morning's briefing – observation and surveillance only. Instinctively, he pushed aside the front of his jacket while his hand reached for the shoulder holster holding his pistol.

❄ ❄ ❄

During the police reconstruction of the bloody incident on the terrace of the Cafe "Vienna", eyewitnesses provided different versions about the course of events. Elisheva Finkelstein,

---

[88]Small river in the centre of Israel, flowing into the Mediterranean Sea.

the wife of an attorney who specialized in conveyancing the sales of large plots of land by Arab Effendis to the Jewish authorities, while slicing off a fat cut for the welfare of the Finkelstein family, told of a loud shout, "Stop, police!" also in Hebrew, which emanated from the direction of one of the cafe's guests – a corpulent man, elegantly dressed, who pulled a gun.

"Also, the man who earlier was sitting with him at the table next to ours, pulled out a gun, broke into the circle, and threw me to the ground. I was scared, grabbed the first thing that came to hand, which was his jacket and then we both fell to the ground. But he fell on top of me; I broke my hand and will make sure that my husband submits a hefty compensation claim."

Heinz, Cafe "Vienna's" experienced waiter, was emphasizing to the investigating police officer his past credentials as an experienced journalist – meant to lend his description greater credibility, since he could indeed distinguish between trivia and interesting facts – supported, on the whole, Mrs. Finkelstein's statement.

"It was actually the plump chap who caused the explosion in the chaos. He tried to arrest the young man helping the unconscious woman and made the first move. But the fellow, preempted him, drew first and was also the first to shoot," Heinz testified. "He shot in the air. He would have had no problem in hitting the detective who had identified himself by shouting 'police'. No problem at all. But he shot into the air. He aimed at no one."

"Levi's shot surprised me," Detective Jim Lennon reported in his version. "I was trying to get closer, but collided with one of the women and we both fell down. A serious panic ensued; people were screaming and running in all directions. I saw Levi shoot in the air and at once pistol-whip Detective Roberts in the face. However, I have to say in Levi's favor that he would have had no problem shooting Roberts, as he had been the first to draw. However, for some reason, after he had fired into the air, Levi jumped up and gave Roberts a terrible uppercut. Roberts doubled up and fell to the ground like a boxer after a knockout blow, but he did not lose consciousness. Levi took advantage of the confusion, jumped over the low fence at the front of the terrace and fled, running toward Sollel Street."

Roberts had recovered quickly. Pressing a handkerchief to the ugly wound on his cheek, which he had received as a result of contact with the hammer of Levis gun, the experienced detective gave chase on foot.

"Stop, police!" He yelled out loud again, rummaged around in his jacket pocket, pulled out a police whistle with which he blew shrill tones in all directions. Despite his injury and the turmoil, he noted that Tamar or Henrietta or whatever her name was had passed out again, immediately following Levi's shot. His young colleague, Lennon, joined the chase. Seconds later, a jeep with two military policemen came roaring up and braked sharply. "*Stern Gang* terrorist," Roberts briefed the driver quickly.

The second MP was already holding the microphone of a bulky radio in his hand and reported factually "Gunfight in Jaffa Road. Request assistance of all available forces in the area, who hear this announcement." With a quick dart and screeching wheels, caused by releasing the clutch too quickly, which almost ejected Roberts and Lennon, who had jumped into the back seat, their legs dangling out, the Jeep crossed the dozens of meters between Jaffa Road and the corner of Sollel Street. A group of Australian soldiers, who were walking along the road, some staggering due to excessive beer consumption, also joined the chase. They were not armed, except for two sergeants, who had clumsily drawn their service revolvers under the influence of alcohol.

Bat-Yam, Autumn 1995

A blue seascape of an almost wintry sea, but with a strong sun that easily penetrated the fabric of clouds at sunset in the west, was the view from the window of Alisa's small room on the fifth floor of her retirement home. "Eat, eat. Take another piece of this wonderful cheesecake," she urged her guest Jonathan.

Her calm demeanor disguised her inner turmoil. She had no idea about Jonathan's level of knowledge concerning his intricate family saga. "Why did I initiate the contact with him? Why should I reveal all the facts to him, provided of course that he doesn't know them already? I am actually closing a circle here, out of my own need to shake off a yoke. So stop seeking extenuating circumstances for yourself."

Jonathan was sitting on the red couch in the middle of the room. He politely drank the fresh coffee Alisa had brewed and consumed small bites of cheesecake. "What do you do? What's your occupation?" Alisa asked. "And forgive the personal questions, but are you married? Do you have children?"

In short, measured sentences, he told her about the small business venture for renewable energy he had founded in collaboration with scientists from the Weizmann Institute and experts from Germany, "confessed" to being married and the father of twins. Since she did not pursue the matter, he felt no particular need to share with her the difficult process of in-vitro fertilization Dalit and he had gone through to bring the twins into the world.

"At the funeral I noticed a few men of your father's generation, some of whom are known to me as members of the intelligence services, especially '*Shabak*' and '*Mossad*'[89]," she said. "It's nice that they still maintain contact with the family."

"Yes, they have tribal loyalties from another era. I was a baby, of course, when my father was killed."

"Nearly 30 years have passed since then. I know a number of families who have lost their dear ones in the war and from most of them I unfortunately hear comments deploring the fact that the number of those who attend memorial services is shrinking from year to year" she remarked dryly.

"Not with this gang, the security guys. By the way, one of them made it to the rank of deputy chief of the Mossad and others have also achieved senior ranks over the years. They make a point of appearing at every funeral. Some representatives appeared at my bar mitzvah as well as at my wedding. I admit that sometimes, when I need to pull strings, I just pick up the phone. And that helps. 'Your father, Ronen, was the Benjamin of our group', they'd continually emphasize, stressing how much they liked him, and had predicted a great future ahead of him. They said that he was an 'operator', had a creative mind, that he was indeed the salt of the earth. This was not just an empty phrase, because his outer appearance suited their assignments well at that time. They told me how their unit was hunting the Nazi scientists who were helping Egypt's then Dictator, Gamal Abdel Nasser, to build his rockets."

---

[89]Shabak is Israel's homeland security service; Mossad is its intelligence agency

"Sure, I remember it very well," she interrupted. "Nasser even bragged that he had missiles capable of hitting anything 'south of Beirut'. Back then it was Nasser, now it's Iraq's Saddam Hussein and this chain never ends."

"Yes and dad back then looked like an advertising poster of the Third Reich's Office for Racial Purity – tall, blond and blue-eyed. He also spoke German quite well from home. One of the operations against a rocket scientist called Kleinwächter failed because the gun didn't go off or something and they managed to escape from the area only thanks to my father, or so they told it anyway. Ironically, my German partners' plant is located in a small town in southern Germany. When I visited there, and after the Germans and I had already developed a relationship of trust, they mentioned that the town elders are still talking about a kind of James Bond affair that had happened in the mid-sixties there, when unidentified armed men tried to murder a respected citizen, a scientist named Kleinwächter."

Alisa laughed.

Jonathan smiled and stretched out his legs.

"The security guys, as I call them, also told me that during the waiting period before the Six-Day War, dad made it clear to his commanders that he could not sit idly around in Europe with folded hands. He returned to Israel, enlisted in his reserve regiment, and fell in the battle for the Golan Heights. But you are probably familiar with these details."

"Yes," Alisa lied, waiting for this phase of the "small talk" to end.

"I'm glad you came, but you should know that it isn't easy for me. Your grandmother stopped talking to me decades ago and declined all reconciliation attempts on my part since then."

"Was it you or her? Which one of you was responsible for the break-up?" Jonathan was interested in knowing.

She ignored the direct question and chose her words as she began to describe their first meeting in the kibbutz during the late summer of 1938 and from there developed chronologically the story of her special friendship with Tamar. After the third or fourth sentence, she sank deeper into her armchair and delved into the description of the details. Viewed from the side, it looked as if the two wings of the old-fashioned piece of furniture were embracing her. Hardly aware of Jonathan's presence, Alisa spoke in an unstoppable torrent of words. But she noticed his eyes widen as she described in glowing terms and extensive use of expressions like "crazy love birds", his grandmother's affair with Wolfgang, the handsome young man from the German colony, in all its manifestations.

"Oh, how beautiful and sweet they were together, but it was an impossible love affair," she sighed. "You have to understand the atmosphere which prevailed in the land at the time. The Nazis had occupied Austria and Czechoslovakia and the land was full of refugees, *Yekkes* who had been expelled from their homeland. But, here, in Palestine, in the German neighborhoods and colonies, the Templers hoisted swastika flags, greeted each other with raised arms, and celebrated the Fuehrer's birthday on April 20 with parades! In his community, they put him under pressure to get rid of ' his Jewess' and from her side she was urged to sever her relationship with that 'Nazi from *Emek Refaim*'. But it was actually the Jewish side, which was violent and hurt her physically. In the end it all fell apart."

"Who was the initiator? Which one of them broke off the relationship?"

"It was your grandmother who practically initiated the separation."

"When did this happen? How long were they together?"

"Their meeting was a twist of fate. You know, it was the kind of encounter that usually occurs only in films. On the street, while waiting for a bus or something like that. As I recall, it was in October '38. It was a winter love, short, stormy and it ended or was broken off sometime in the spring of 1939."

"That's it, and they never met again?"

"No. That was the end. Your grandmother was crying all night, but she was determined and maybe even a little scared. To this day, I don't understand how she could still work and study. For weeks, she could not sleep. And the desperate Wolfgang went to Germany to study. Then she discovered that she was pregnant."

Jonathan muttered a few words.

"Oh, did you say something?" she asked.

"From him, I suppose. Pregnant by him," he said, without knowing whether he wanted to hear a positive or negative answer.

Alisa, with her background of working in the psychiatric ward for many years, did not find it hard to notice the feeling of turmoil that enveloped the short question. "Your question reminds me of a joke, and I beg your pardon, if I digress," she improvised, trying to cheer him up. "In a literature seminar at the university, the professor gave the students a particular task: write the shortest possible essay, which should combine three elements – religion, sex and a mysterious phenomenon.

A gifted student was declared the winner, having submitted the following essay:

"God!

I'm pregnant!

But, by whom?"

A smile spread across Jonathan's face. He tried to cover up the confusion still flaring within him by running his right hand through his hair in a back-combing motion.

"We are talking about small-town Jerusalem of the late thirties, aren't we?" He interposed a question. "She was a student at the School of Nursing, whose strict discipline I have heard stories about since my early youth. What did she do? How did she manage to abort the fetus?" He asked and by way of response received a scrutinizing glance from head to toe.

After a few seconds Alisa sighed, wondering to what extent this question was motivated by instinctive self-preservation or perhaps an emotional barrier.

"That's just it; she did not have an abortion. She decided to keep the baby," she said softly, almost whispering the words and kept going before a heavy silence could fill the room. "The term 'persistence' in the dictionary could have been replaced with her name. When Tamar dug her heels in, even a bulldozer would not have been able to make her budge."

A slight blush was spreading across the front of his neck, but Jonathan did not say anything. He held on to the empty coffee cup and waited for more.

"I was privy to her secret from the first moment when she discovered that she was pregnant," Alisa said. "Tamar tried to delay the inevitable and because she was tall and her pregnancy was characterized by a small belly, her pregnancy was not noticeable during the first few months. At the end of the summer vacation, when it had become difficult, she turned to Matron Landsmann. Landsmann was tough, with the mentality of a Prussian drill sergeant. By today's standards, she was a latent lesbian and Tamar had realized that Landsmann had a soft spot for her, a kind of hidden, unconsummated love."

In well-ordered sentences, as if more than fifty years had not passed since then, she explained the practical strategy that Landsmann had formulated. "Landsmann suggested the idea to Tamar that she report the pregnancy as a result of her rape last spring. The clinic was already holding notes about the serious injuries she had suffered a few months earlier."

"So was she raped or not?" Jonathan butted in.

"What rape," Alisa said impatiently. "She had copped a severe beating from Jewish thugs who opposed her affair with Wolfgang. But after it had happened, she did not report to any official authority, what the origin of her bruises was and only told of 'strangers' who had attacked her. Now that she could no longer hide her pregnancy, she invented, with Landsmann's help, a story that the attack had actually been a rape; a drunken British soldier had raped her and because of her shame, she refrained from telling anybody anything about the incident. If you have connections, you don't need to pull strings and because Landsmann held a senior position in the school, this version got the official seal of approval. They even enabled Tamar to continue studying until shortly before the birth and to resume her studies shortly after the birth."

For a moment Alisa had forgotten that she was speaking of Ronen, Jonathan's father. Only when he put his head in his hands, closed his eyes, and uttered a few deep breaths she stopped her gush of words.

"Would you like some more coffee or maybe something cold to drink?"

"No, no, please continue," he said in a weak voice, accompanied by an exhalation of air from the nose, indicating a certain restlessness and irritability.

"Now there isn't much more to continue. In the meantime, the war had broken out. Tamar was left alone in the country, without family, almost without friends. Later she found out that her parents had managed to escape at the last minute from Nazi Europe, but the British turfed them out to Mauritius where they remained until the end of the war. She had to hide the fact that she was an unmarried mother from those around her. Landsmann also ensured that the baby was circumcised and found him a place in a special orphanage in *Talpiot*, belonging to a dear Jew called Zimmerman. His wife was a distant relative of Landsmann's."

"So did she not see her baby, my father? Did she not raise him? Who paid for the orphanage?"

"My goodness," a silent sigh escaped Alisa's lips. "So many questions. Your grandmother had some money. Her father had hidden a few Maria Theresa Thaler, antique gold coins, in the covers of some books she had brought from Vienna. These financed the first two years. After that, she already earned a few quid as a nurse. In those days, nurses actually earned quite good salaries. So she economized a bit and paid Zimmerman, regular as clockwork. To his credit, it must be said that he was very good to her and Ronen. Ronen was not only looked after well, but also received good care, a lot of love, hugs, and attention. Your grandmother used to sneak into the home at night, caress the baby and hug it. Once she asked me to accompany her. What can I say? Even as a baby you could see, that he was a copy of Wolfgang and you have inherited this amazing similarity."

"This phrase about the amazing similarity brought me here," Jonathan thought, but did not say a word.

Alisa sighed again. "After each visit to *Talpiot* Tamar would return crying to the dormitory for single nurses. I served as her Wailing Wall, and believe me, she was suffering."

"And where does Grandpa Asher come into the picture?"

"An angel. Asher was an angel that God had sent her. How was your relationship with him? After all, he raised you."

"Between me and Grandpa Asher? So-so," he said. "He tried. He really tried to be a surrogate father, but it was not genuine and he was also older than the other fathers in the neighborhood. Don't forget that he also suffered from movement restrictions so that playing football with him was somewhat out of the question. I knew from an early age, that my father was killed, although I didn't quite understand that for a long time. However, ever since I can remember I called him 'Grandpa', not 'dad'.

"An angel," she repeated. "White as snow was your grandpa as befits someone whose name was *Weiss*[90], although you are aware now that he was not your real grandfather. And to my great regret, that was the issue which caused the split between me and Tamar."

"Can you elaborate?"

"Your grandmother knew Asher already before Wolfgang came into her life. They had already made friends on the ship that had brought them to Tel Aviv in the summer of 1938 and at that time, he was called Arthur. They went their separate ways, although I believe that they moved in the same circles in the early forties, while Asher was studying at the university. When Rommel moved into Egypt and approached Palestine, Arthur, who had changed his name to Asher, enlisted voluntarily in the German Section of the *Palmach*. Have you heard of them?"

Jonathan nodded in agreement.

"After Rommel was defeated in the fall of 1942 at El Alamein and had retreated westward, the German Section was disbanded and Asher voluntarily joined a British commando unit which operated behind the German lines."

"Sterling's ghost army?" asked Jonathan.

"Yes, yes, the ghost army, as they were called. They later became known as the SAS. They would roam through the desert to German airports and command posts. Asher was a true hero. During one of the last battles in May 1943 in Tunisia, just before the *Afrika Korps* surrendered, he was

---

[90]German: white

severely wounded by a mine. That's why it was hard for him to play football. "

Jonathan smiled sheepishly.

"Asher spent several months in a hospital in Alexandria, then he was transferred to the Augusta Victoria Hospital in Jerusalem. There, in the classic situation – so beloved by writers and film directors – of the wounded soldier and the compassionate nurse they met again."

This time it was her face on which a smile appeared.

Jonathan was silent, waiting for her to raise some more memories from the 1940s.

"To tell you the truth, it was because of Asher that Tamar and I stopped talking to one another."

Jonathan moved on the couch, but said nothing.

"I fell in love with him first," she said, and it seemed to Jonathan, as if he perceived a blush on her face.

"During his first week in the hospital in Jerusalem, I was stationed on his ward. We nurses worked alternately in the Hadassah and Augusta Victoria, which had been confiscated at the beginning of the war, it being a German property, and was turned into a military hospital. When Tamar arrived at the Augusta Victoria in the second week of his hospitalization, I was already in love with him. But as soon as she arrived, Asher fell in love with her. You know the expression 'hit by lightning?' That was what had happened to him. But Asher was a gentleman. He took me aside, told me that they had known each other for a long time, apologized and said 'it's my fault, not yours; you know how it is'. At that time, he knew nothing of Wolfgang and certainly nothing of the small Ronen in the *Talpiot* orphanage."

She paused and poured herself a glass of water.

"To be honest, I was mean. I acted like a witch in the Brothers Grimm Fairy Tales. I don't want to go there now, but I had not yet gotten over my previous love affair with an Arab boy, who was murdered. So the whole thing is therefore more complicated, because we were at that time a foursome – Wolfgang, your grandmother, my Arab Nabil and I. I was jealous, angry. I thought she had pinched Asher from me. Once, when I changed his dressing, I blurted out the name Wolfgang as if by chance."

Alisa looked down, embarrassed, as if not even 50 years had passed. "And when his round face became one big question mark, I said casually, 'oh, you don't know that Tamar had a complicated love affair with a German Templer?'"

Jonathan did not move.

"How stupid of me. What was I thinking? Like, when Asher heard that Tamar had slept with a Templer he would drop her and come back to me? What an idiot I was," she said, tapping her forehead with her index finger. "But exactly the opposite happened. Instead of breaking up, they became even closer. He did not flinch, asked her who Wolfgang was and she told him everything. Absolutely everything, including all the details about Ronen and the Zimmerman's orphanage."

"So, you say that Asher did not leave, but on the contrary?"

"Well, he was an angel, like I said." A touch of bitterness now accompanied her words. "But with me she stopped talking. She came up to me, and I remember it to this day, in the long corridor with the high ceiling in the German hospital, looked at me with flashing eyes and just said: 'you've disappointed me. I had expected more of you. I'm through with you '. In fact, she broke off all contact with me and ignored me as if I was air. Our strong friendship had just evaporated, gone, melted away. That was Tamar. You knew her. A woman of contrasts."

Alisa stood up from her chair, visibly upset. With quick steps, she went to the dresser, opened a drawer and pulled out a blue cigarette pack.

"I gave up smoking a year ago. For decades, I used to smoke three cigarettes a day, Gitanes, French, acrid. Those that leave behind nicotine stains, not in the lungs but directly in the panties."

She lit a cigarette, which was followed by some more till the end of the meeting. "Anyway, it took months until Asher had recovered from his injuries and infections. Keep in mind that we did not know about antibiotics and everything took longer. During that time, they were together a lot. Asher's father was a senior manager in one of the banks in Tel Aviv and money was no object. Then they got married and Asher petitioned the court to adopt Ronen as his son and to register him as Ronen Weiss." She emptied the glass of water with a quick sip and flicked the ash from her cigarette. "That's it," she concluded. "That's the whole story. Your real grandfather was a German Templer, who might even have served in the Nazi army and disappeared during the war. Asher is your adoptive grandfather."

Alisa was expecting a visibly violent reaction, but Jonathan did not move. In his mind the image of the famous Israeli sculptor Yigal Tumarkin emerged, who had described in a weekend supplement, how he dealt with the news that he had close relatives on his father's side, who had been active Nazis. Jonathan remembered an interview that he had heard with Tumarkin, in which the sculptor described how his attitude to the Holocaust had changed after he had heard of this kinship.

But Jonathan had so far not completely digested the fact, that his biological grandfather had been a Nazi soldier.

"Do you know, perhaps, what happened to Wolfgang's family, especially his parents? And no, I won't go looking for them," he added immediately, when he noticed that her eyes widened in amazement. "I'm not going to enquire with a search organization for lost relatives or anything like that. It's pure curiosity."

"A sad end awaited the Schwartes. Though they were anti-Nazis, the British put them in with a group of Templers, who were expelled through the mediation of the Red Cross to Germany in exchange for a group of Jewish citizens of Palestine. You know, tourists who were stranded in Europe at the outbreak of war and European Jews who were in possession of immigration certificates to Palestine, mainly Dutch Jews, who had been incarcerated in the Bergen-Belsen Concentration Camp. I can imagine that the Schwartes were not very excited about being sent back to Germany and that they would have preferred to join the other Templers who were exiled to Australia. Only much later did I hear from a Templer nurse, one of the last Templers to have been expelled by the British after the war, that the Schwartes arrived in Stuttgart, were housed in some official reception centre and all of them died that night in a heavy RAF bombing raid."

An awkward silence descended on the small room. The powerful landing lights of an airplane on the way to Ben Gurion Airport pierced the evening sky.

"An interesting story, like a movie," concluded Jonathan dryly as if the recent revelations did not touch him.

"Strange, but I still don't understand why grandma and Asher – he was aware that he called him by name and not Grandpa – concealed this story so deeply in a box."

"Maybe because it was a different generation. They thought differently. The conventions were different," she said with a sense of relief similar to slight tipsiness after a glass of champagne, followed by the emptiness of a deflated party-balloon that had lost its rubber band.

"I hope that I haven't turned your life upside down with the story of Wolfgang."

"You have turned me inside out and how. But you have also helped me to understand some things in my life. As a child I did not understand what was going on around me and your story has scattered the fog of silence, with which I grew up. Only now do I understand why the genealogy project I was doing at school, had triggered such a loud argument between them. Also, there are several other question marks that have suddenly gotten different shapes. I am truly grateful for the initiative and hope you are prepared to meet with me again to enlarge the picture, "he said, and parted from her with a warm embrace.

"I believe that Grandma Tamar would actually have liked this gesture and your decision to talk to me," he concluded while he was already standing on the other side of the threshold. "Let's stay in touch, because I'll probably have a lot more questions. And again, thank you very much."

Jonathan hugged Alisa again, who barely managed to stop the flow of tears that threatened to pour out of her eyes and waved her goodbye before he was swallowed up by the elevator.

In the spacious lobby of the old people's home, on the way to the main exit, he heard a report from the television on the reception desk, that "due to the imminent end of the peace rally, all the roads around the *Kikar Malchei Yisrael*[91] are closed and the police recommend that drivers not travel to Tel Aviv," and opened the car door.

"Just don't let me get stuck in a traffic jam caused by the end of the rally," he thought as he was listening with half an ear to the impromptu chorus of Peres and Rabin led by Miri Aloni singing the *shir lashalom*[92] off key.

"What the hell am I supposed to do with Alisa's story? Should I tell the family or preserve tradition and hide the facts? Dalit's parents are Auschwitz survivors. She herself is a classic example of the second generation of Holocaust

---

[91]Literally: Kings of Israel Square. After the murder of the Prime Minister, it was renamed Yitzhak Rabin Square.

[92]Literally: A Song to Peace. Minutes later, Prime Minister Yitzhak Rabin was assassinated by a Jewish fanatic.

survivors. The twins are still small, but later they are certain to participate in the 'March of the Living' in Poland. How can they suddenly be confronted with the fact that my grandfather was a German and had possibly even served in the Nazi army? Wow, I really can't cope with a traffic jam right now, certainly not after what I've been through tonight."

Jerusalem, Summer 1942

After three years of absence, Wolfgang Schwarte, now a German paratrooper on the run, felt almost like a tourist in his hometown. At night, he kept moving through *Wadi Kelt*, getting away from the battlefield and trying to ignore the worsening nagging pain in his injured leg. After drinking massive amounts of water, like a camel, from a small spring at the entrance to the Wadi, he was delighted with the disappearance of the painful headache, which had plagued him during the first hours of his escape. The route was very familiar to him from his trips with the Scouts; he knew what awaited him at every turn, and therefore did not bother to open the map in his escape kit. When the morning star shone in the sky, he reached the Jerusalem-Ramallah road. During the slow climb from the Judean Desert to the mountain top, he passed a small house whose inhabitants were still asleep. With quick movements, he removed from the clothesline a civilian shirt and a *keffiye* that had hung there to dry.

"God will forgive me for this theft. It is, after all, his duty to forgive," he muttered to himself, amused that he retained not only his operational capability, but also his sense of humor despite the bind he was in.

The windbreaker, the military shirt, and leather belt – all products from the Wehrmacht provisions store – he threw into a deep cistern. He pulled the stolen shirt over the military singlet that looked like a civilian item. He pulled the trouser cuffs out of the paratrooper boots to hide their military appearance. Satisfied with the improvement of his external appearance, Wolfgang discovered a neglected small building, near the road, which was built of bricks, but without plaster. The metal door opened easily, accompanied by an annoying creak. He entered cautiously and examined the concrete floored room, which was probably used as storeroom. Now the room was empty. Hungry, but above all, physically tired and mentally exhausted, Wolfgang picked a corner that looked relatively clean, lay down on the ground, made an impromptu pillow from the *keffiye*, and fell asleep after a few slow breaths.

The voices of playing children awakened him. To his surprise, he realized that he was welcoming the new day with a big smile. Only after a few seconds, when he remembered where he was and how he had come here, his smile disappeared and he was again the hungry and tense commando soldier behind enemy lines. It was already three o'clock in the afternoon.

"You slept well," he praised himself, cautiously opening the door and looking out. The sound of children playing was gone, and after he had convinced himself that the coast was clear, he left the building and limped to the bus stop on the main road. Behaving quite naturally, acting like a day laborer – "I stink of sweat, have a dirty face, the *keffiye* is hiding my short blond hair. In a nutshell, I'm fine," – and mingled with the others waiting for the bus: workers, craftsmen, farmers with bags of products and officials who had apparently already finished their work.

He had no idea how much a bus ticket cost, so he looked over the shoulder of the passenger in front of him and gave the driver as a matter of course the appropriate sum in Palestinian money, which he had previously removed from his escape kit. One of the passengers, with a friendly face, turned to him with a brief question in Arabic. Wolfgang smiled with the stupidest expression he could muster and indicated by gestures that he was deaf and dumb. This guaranteed him a smooth ride without any further disturbing questions.

On the way to Jerusalem, the bus stopped at a military checkpoint. A British soldier climbed through the front door, looked at the passengers with a bored look, got out, and ordered the driver to be on his way. Until the central bus station of the Arab bus companies near the Damascus Gate, Wolfgang sat sunk in his seat, pretending to be dozing, as befits a worker at the end of a heavy work day. But despite this posture, he was looking through the narrow slits in his eyes and noticed with amazement and excitement the remarkable changes that had occurred in his hometown. The open expanses that had previously characterized the north side of the city were now built up with new buildings, some of them magnificent, three and four stories high. The Hebrew University Campus on Mount Scopus had grown and expanded in all directions. On the road there was heavy traffic, particularly lorries, vans, and military vehicles in both short and long convoys.

His heart was beating when he saw the various towers of Jerusalem. The ornate, oh so English Anglican Church buildings just beyond *Sheikh Jarrah*. The square turret of the Italian Hospital. The Notre Dame building with the Madonna statue on the roof, white and prominent. The golden dome of the Omar Mosque. The dome on the Church of the Holy Sepulchre. The white tower of the German Church and the spires of Gethsemane – he devoured all of it with his eyes, always carefully keeping up the pretense of dozing, despite the excitement that these sights aroused in him.

The first place he visited in his hometown of Jerusalem after an absence of three years was the *falafel*[93] stand in the compound of the central bus station. "Chew slowly, drink slowly, and don't gulp. Otherwise you only draw attention to yourself," he told himself. "Wow, this is the best tasting meal I've ever eaten. Oh, how I have longed for a dose of *falafel*."

Wolfgang was amazed at the wide variety of food and drinks that were offered at the buffet "as if there is no war".

Satiated and happy about the experience of his return to Jerusalem, he walked slowly – and not just because of the painful leg – away from the Arab bus station to the city center, while pondering what to do next. After he had moved away from the bus station and was approaching the new Jewish city, he folded his *keffiyeh* into a small bundle, which he stuck in one of his pockets.

A quick analysis made it clear to him how desperate his situation was. Alone, in enemy territory, without communication means, without an exit plan.

"I need to find someone who can help me. Nabil Nashashibi? Assuming I can find him, what do I know about what he's been through in the last three years? Maybe he's working with the British? The most logical thing is to find someone from the community," he mused, whilst turning into Jaffa Road, next to the branch of Barclays bank, near the western corner of the old-city walls.

The so familiar chant of the *muezzin* from one of the nearby mosques mingling with the ringing bells of the Franciscan Church near the New Gate almost brought him to tears. He remembered details that had come up in conversation with his comrades only three days ago on the base near Athens.

---

[93]Middle Eastern specialty made from chickpeas.

"True, Dinninger did remark that most Germans had been arrested by the British, but that some Templers allegedly continue to live in the colonies. Perhaps there are also some Templers in Jerusalem."

He decided to find out what had happened to Schultz's butcher shop in Sollel Street. After all, he had known Schultz since childhood. The butcher's small house was located at the end of his street in the German colony. He remembered Schultz as a funny, chubby guy, who obviously enjoyed eating his own excellent sausages, which he produced in a closed back room of his shop. He refused to disclose the manufacturing process, as if it were a state secret.

"There are two things, the creation of which should never be shown to any person – laws and sausages," he used to joke.

Although he lived in the *Emek Refaim* Colony, Schultz was not a Templer. He was the son of a Protestant clergyman from Hamburg who had arrived in Jerusalem at the time of the Turks and was connected to the staff of the German church, which was built opposite the Church of the Holy Sepulchre. "Perhaps because he is not a Templer and, if I remember correctly, married to a Christian Arab from Bethlehem, the Brits might not have deported him. What do I have to lose?"

Wolfgang merged with the crowd. It was the usual mix of Jerusalem's secular and orthodox Jews, Arabs from the city and the villages. Sometimes a small group of nuns passed by or a few priests appeared and a lot of soldiers. A group of cheerful Australian soldiers, all proudly wearing the wide-rimmed slouch hats of the Australian regiments – some of them holding large half-empty beer bottles despite the relatively early hour – came towards him on the narrow sidewalk. Wolfgang leaned against the wall, waited until they passed and went into Sollel Street.

Schulz's butcher shop was at the upper end of the almost deserted street. Two orthodox Jews dressed in long black coats walked toward him. They were walking swiftly downhill, talking fast in idiomatic fluent Yiddish. Their hands were waving in the air like Dutch windmills. On the other sidewalk an elderly Arab peasant woman was walking slowly, balancing on her head a large metal tray with rolled up bundles of different spices.

He sighed with relief when he saw the colorful sign that was hanging above the door of the butcher shop – a drawing of a happy, smiling cow that clearly did not know what was awaiting her and her various parts in the back room of Schultz's business. Due to the distance between him and the shop, Wolfgang did not notice that the name "Schultz" had been removed from the old familiar sign.

Suddenly the sound of a gunshot was heard.

Wolfgang was startled. He estimated that the sound of gunfire had come from the main street, from Jaffa Road. To his trained ear, it sounded like a pistol or some other small firearm.

The two Jews had slowed down, stopped their conversation, and were looking around in search of an explanation for the sound of the shooting.

The peasant woman had also stopped, unsure what to do.

Instinctively Wolfgang pressed himself against the wall next to the entrance of a clock shop. He reached for the Luger in his belt to make sure that the gun was still there.

A young man, dressed in a white shirt and khaki pants, came running around the corner, a black object in his right hand. The man looked back, as if he was searching for pursuers. He did not notice the peasant woman, collided with her violently and both crashed onto the sidewalk. Bunches of green leaves flew in all directions while the metal tray rolled slowly, rattling down the street. At the same time the shrill tones of a police whistle, the howl of a strained engine and the pounding of boots were heard. A military vehicle came screeching around the corner in a wide arc from Jaffa Road. Some soldiers came running and within seconds the sounds of shots and bursts of gunfire terrified the center of Jerusalem.

❄ ❄ ❄

Levi managed to fire three rounds at the jeep. One of them hit the shoulder of the young detective, Lennon. "You are lucky that you caught it from a small short-range pistol. By the time it got to you it was already exhausted, scratched some skin, but did not penetrate deeply," explained the friendly duty doctor in the ward of the military hospital, to which he had been rushed.

Roberts had emptied the entire magazine of his pistol toward Levi and hit him twice, in the abdomen and the head. Levi was seriously injured. He doubled over, his body collapsing on the sidewalk, his arm outstretched with his hand reaching the roadway.

The Arab peasant woman was killed on the spot by one of the bullets from Roberts' pistol. But that was not what the public heard, because this fact was concealed by instruction from a higher authority, so that the press reported that she was killed by shots from Levi, the "*Stern Gang* terrorist."

The military policeman who was sitting next to the driver, fired a long burst from his submachine gun, Sten Mark II. However, he had not aimed at Levi, but at the man who was leaning against the wall next to the clock shop.

"The detective who had jumped into the jeep, told us to pursue a dangerous terrorist who had escaped into the next street," the policeman explained to his commander, why he had shot at someone who, at first glance, looked like an innocent civilian, instead of aiming at the suspect, who was fleeing from the detectives Roberts and Lennon. "We raced into Sollel Street and as we came around the corner someone was shooting at us. Instinctively I ducked, looked up and saw from my side of the jeep a man at a distance of some twenty meters away from me with a large pistol in his hand. In such a situation, you react instantly. Besides, I had no precise description of the suspect, only an oral statement from Detective Roberts that some terrorist had fled into Sollel Street. I was absolutely convinced, even a hundred percent sure, that this was the terrorist, so I shot him."

The Sten submachine gun is notorious for being a very imprecise weapon. But, as it turned out, it was this military policeman, of all people, who, on that day had been assigned for duty in the center of Jerusalem and was an excellent shot. His salvo riddled the man with bullets from top to bottom.

"When the shooting was over, Roberts screamed at me that I was stupid and had taken down an innocent civilian. I was sure that he was killed on the spot and became very depressed. I was also sure that you would throw me in jail. You know what happens to a military police officer who goes to jail! You know, how the other inmates abuse such a policeman! It's a disaster! I thought calamity had befallen me. But then, a few minutes later, it turned out, that the civilian, whom I had hit, was not so innocent after all and I even got a day off as a reward."

❄ ❄ ❄

The ambulance that was originally called for Tamar when she had fainted at the sight of her beloved German, walking through central Jerusalem, reached Sollel Street only minutes after the shooting. Until the arrival of the medical team and having ascertained that his colleague Lennon would easily survive his injury, Roberts skillfully undertook an initial crime scene investigation. His mind quickly processed the facts and he had already started to put everything in logical order so that his report would shift responsibility for the carnage in downtown Jerusalem away from him.

"It's fortunate that the shops are closed, otherwise there would have been more deaths," the thought flashed through his mind. He cautiously approached Levi, who was lying on the sidewalk, aiming his cocked weapon at the seriously injured man, who was barely moving. Roberts kicked Levi's right hand and flung the little gun into the middle of the road. The wanted terrorist sighed. Blood was oozing from his mouth, an ugly wound on his ear and another in his stomach. His lips moved slowly, trying to utter a sound. Roberts knelt next to Levi in an effort to understand what the injured man was muttering. "Tamar...Tamar ..." whispered Levi, trying to lift his head. He turned his head painfully looking down Sollel Street towards Jaffa Road, froze, and did not move again.

Roberts felt his pulse, to ensure that Levi was dead. With practiced movements, he searched his pockets. From his back pocket he pulled out a wallet, containing papers with the correct name of the deceased, Aaron Levi, and 20 pounds – a very respectable sum – in notes and coins, but no document or object which could have advanced the investigation. Then there was also a small bunch of keys, but without any tag or address of the hardware store, which had perhaps produced the key, nor was there any other clue an experienced detective could have used to crack the case.

Roberts looked fleetingly at the dead peasant woman. "It is important to ensure that the official announcement will state that she was killed by the terrorist," he noted to himself again, but did not even bother to bend down and examine her more closely.

"Block the exits and take the two Jews in for questioning," he ordered the Australian sergeant who arrived puffing on the scene with six somewhat drunken soldiers.

"I want you to record eyewitness statements from the Jews. Actually, that should be done by the military policeman. You just block the exits until reinforcements of military police get here. After than you are dismissed."

Roberts crossed the street signaling the police officer, who had shot the civilian on the opposite sidewalk, to join him. "Looks like you've got yourself into a real pickle," he remarked sarcastically to the police officer, who looked utterly stunned. "But do me a favor, secure the Sten. It still has the safety off and I can somehow remember that this weapon emits deadly volleys without any particular reason."

"But he had a gun. I shot at him because he was holding a large gun in his hand," the policeman was wailing in protest, while he secured the Sten. As an additional precaution, he took out the magazine, which still contained some rounds.

"Gun? I saw no weapon. But let's see what we have here," Roberts tormented the police officer with hidden sadism. He looked at the body of the stranger, admitting to himself that he was behaving like a "bastard" to the poor MP whom he was torturing for no good reason.

The stranger was lying on his stomach, his shirt soaked in blood, his right hand under the body, the other at an odd angle as if broken. "He's still alive," Roberts shouted. "Stretcher, quickly, here."

The injured man muttered something unintelligible.

"Hammer, he says 'Hammer'", the policeman decided.

"Not 'Hammer'. Actually sounds to me like 'Tamar' and I can't understand for the life of me what is going on here," Roberts said, while watching the doctor who came running from the ambulance and had begun to examine the injured man.

"Hopeless," the doctor determined, shaking his head. "He's finished."

"Doctor, try to perform a miracle," Roberts said sarcastically. But before he could finish the sentence, the doctor indicated that his diagnosis had just been confirmed. The stranger had breathed his last breath.

"Well, that changes things. Let's see what we have here," Roberts said in an authoritative voice with which he intended to impress the doctor, the MP and the soldiers who took part in the chase. "European, probably a Jew. Hit by five or six shots, not bad for a volley from the Sten."

The policeman who had shot the civilian, snorted in desperation.

Cautiously, but skillfully, Roberts searched the deep pockets of the deceased. From the wide, right-hand pocket, he took out a folded *keffiye*. "Strange. What does he have to do with a *keffiye*?" From the other pockets came a small sum of money in notes and coins, as well as a strange wallet – more like a small jewelry box. "Fucking shit, what the hell is this?" Roberts hissed. He carefully opened the box and found some gold coins, a tiny compass, and a small map of Palestine printed on smooth paper, almost like silk, which he had never seen in his life.

"Sir, I'm no expert, but have you noticed his strange boots," said the policeman, who recognized that the recent finds presented for him a glimmer of hope that he might not have to go to jail for the unjustified shooting of civilians.

"Military boots. No doubt. But not British Army issue. Maybe he is a deserter from one of the foreign units that are stationed here," the policeman continued with another exculpatory contribution.

However, Roberts was already soaring in higher regions. It was clear to him that what had begun as surveillance of a potential suspect in a terrorist organization, had now assumed wider proportions. In his mind echoed the remark by the officer at this morning's briefing about a German spy unit that had allegedly been observed in the area of Jericho. He knelt down and with the Sergeant's help turned the body over. The deceased was still holding a loaded and cocked Luger pistol in his right hand, which had been hidden until now.

As an experienced detective who was accustomed to take in unusual details, he noticed that the deceased had an elegant pilots' watch strapped to his right wrist; furthermore he also noticed that the stranger was wearing a military singlet under his civilian shirt. "Just as I thought, a German pistol. This connects him with the group that had landed in *Wadi Kelt*," Roberts determined, but did not say it out loud. He decided to have the body undergo a detailed examination, including autopsy and fingerprints.

"I'm sorry," he patted the friendly military policeman on the shoulder. "I regret what I said earlier. You were right. He was armed. Everything indicates that this is a deserter from one of the foreign armies stationed here or perhaps a prominent trader on the black market. But anyhow, I understand why you did shoot. You acted absolutely correctly. I'll make sure that your commander is informed and I hope that he will reward you appropriately."

Meanwhile, several senior police officers had arrived on the scene and requisitioned the civilian ambulances for reasons of "national security".

The three bodies were taken on stretchers into the ambulance, which left the street with blue lights flashing. The ambulance drove past the open space of the Cafe "Vienna". For a moment it drew the attention of the gawkers, who, only a few moments earlier, had encircled the young woman who passed out on the terrace for no reason at all.

"I have to find out what has happened in Sollel Street" Heinz, the Cafe "Vienna" head waiter said.

But the call to order by Mr. Moses, the owner, brought him back to his place. "Heinz, there are guests here. You're not a journalist anymore," Moses said gently.

A few hundred meters away, on King George Street, Asher and his companions of the Palmach's German unit were wondering about the origin of the shots and volleys they had heard to their east. They were taking a short break for a cold ice cream in the Cafe "Allenby" to celebrate the successful completion of their mission.

"Probably an Arab wedding of someone with connections, who received permission to shoot in the air. You know, Oriental fantasy," remarked Lotz.

"Wedding. Why, if I hear the word wedding, do I think of Tamar," he mused while he was greedily licking his ice cream. "Wow, four years ago we reached Palestine and a new beginning. Interesting, where she might be now. Probably in the Hadassah after graduating from nursing school. It seems as if my friendship with Bracha is leading nowhere, so maybe time has come to find new relationships? Perhaps Tamar is open to suggestions? Maybe we can revive our youthful love affair aboard the Adria. It's worth a try." This thought caused in him a welling up of an inexplicable wave of bliss. He licked with pleasure the last remnants of the ice cream. Still smiling, he responded to the urgent calls of his comrades and climbed up on the back of the lorry.

In the Cafe "Vienna", Tamar came to, sat back in her chair, and tried to reconstruct what had happened and why she had fainted. A civilian ambulance with a soldier in the passenger seat, erupted from Sollel Street, passed the Cafe "Vienna", drove up Jaffa Road, overtook a military lorry laden with soldiers, and, with sirens blaring, raced the bodies of two men and an elderly woman to the hospital.

"Wolfgang? In Jerusalem? Impossible. I simply must have been dreaming," Tamar mused. "When Aaron comes I'll tell him the truth. No, not this thing about an image of Wolfgang suddenly appearing, but the truth about us, me and him – that our relationship has actually no future and that it is better if we split up."

Completely unaware that she had woken up from a blackout into a criminal scene and still dazed, Tamar held out her hand to the cup of coffee that had cooled in the meantime, but was still spreading its former fragrance. Only when she put the cup to her lips, did she notice Alisa's tormented face, the overturned tables, scattered chairs and a pair of police officers, who came rushing into the cafe, notebooks and pencils drawn; they began looking for witnesses of an as yet unexplained incident, which had begun with the sudden fainting of a young woman and ended in a bloodbath

Epilogue: Fact or Fiction

In writing this novel, free use was made of real or invented events and characters as well as some people and occurrences partially based on fact.

German paratroopers in *Wadi Kelt*

In a secret operation, the Nazi Wehrmacht dispatched a German-Palestinian espionage and sabotage unit to Palestine. Three of this unit's soldiers were members of the Templer colonies and two of them were Palestinian Arabs, followers of the Mufti. The five were dropped in the area of *Wadi Kelt*. The Germans were Kurt Wieland from Jaffa, Werner Frank from Jerusalem and Friedrich Dinninger from Waldheim.

One of the Arabs was Ali Hassan Salameh, who, a few years later, became a leading commander of the Arab forces during the 1948 war. He was killed in a battle with the Israelis not far from Tel Aviv. His son of the same name, was the commander of "Black September", planned the massacre of the Israeli Olympic athletes at the Munich Olympics, and was killed by Israeli Mossad special agents in 1979 in central Beirut.

The British, who were forewarned about that operation thanks to the cracking of the German Code succeeded in capturing the members of the unit – except for Dinninger who escaped and hid until the war ended, and Salameh, who probably separated from the unit immediately after their landing.

The British prevented publication of the report about the unit's landing. Even after the war, details of the incident were kept a secret for decades. In the late 1990s, a rumor of unknown origin began to spread that the unit was sent to Palestine to poison the water sources of Tel Aviv. It seems that this rumor had arisen because of a mysterious white powder found in the paratroopers' equipment, described as a powder "to confuse the sniffer dogs."

The squad members were equipped with a large quantity of gold coins to finance their activities, but these were not found in their possession when the British took them captive. Rumors of the "paratroopers' treasure" are still circulating today, and occasionally one hears of Bedouins or adventurers who search the caves of *Wadi Kelt* for the lost treasure. In fact, the unit landed in October 1944 – about six months before the end of the war and not in the summer of 1942, as described in the book.

The Templer Colonies

In a process that began in the late 60s of the 19th century, several hundred German Templers from the south of Germany settled in Palestine. Over the years, they grew and expanded into seven thriving colonies – Jerusalem, Haifa, Tel Aviv (*Sarona*), Jaffa, Wilhelma (*Bnei Atarot*), Waldheim (*Alonei Aba*) and Bethlehem in the Galilee. Individual families of the community also settled down in places like Nazareth, Tiberias, and Ramallah. On the eve of World War II, their numbers had grown to about 2,500 Templers, including children.

Until the 1930s, the Templers kept up good relations with the Jewish community. But relations deteriorated after Hitler came to power, as many Templers, about 800 of them, had joined the Nazi Party. Immediately after the outbreak of war, the British arrested the Templers because they were German nationals and held them in detention camps in *Atlit* or under house arrest in their homes. During the war, most of them were exiled to Australia while others were repatriated to Germany as part of an exchange agreement for civilians signed through mediation by the Red Cross. The last 200 remaining Templers in Palestine lived in Waldheim, Bethlehem of the Galilee, and Wilhelma. They were expelled by the British Mandate authorities in April 1948 one month before the establishment of the State of Israel. The restitution agreement that was signed in the early 1950s between Israel and the Federal Republic of Germany contains a specific section on compensation payments in the tens of millions of dollars to the descendants of the Templers.

The Schwartes are my invention and are representative of many Templers who were not Nazi sympathizers and some who even vociferously expressed their opposition to the Nazi ideology.

The story of the Wennagels, including the anecdote about hiding a pile of gold coins in the basement walls of their *Sarona* home, is true. Their real name was Wennagel. The first names of the couple were Hugo and Christina. Their son Peter, who had been deported as an infant, perished at the age of 26, while serving in the Royal Australian Air Force. The Wennagels small coin treasure was found after 60 years by Dr. Daniel Goldman, in one of the old *Sarona* buildings in the Kirya, today a compound of the Defense Ministry in Tel Aviv, and returned by the Israeli Embassy to family members living in Australia. Joseph Wennagel was indeed the partner of the Jewish engineer Josef Treidel and, together, they built many projects in Palestine and other parts of the Turkish Empire. In addition, they built the house on the shores of the Sea of Galilee, which, according to some traditions is featured in the song "*al sfat yam kineret*" by Jakob Fischman and Hanina Karchevsky.

Luftwaffe Squadron 200

The Nazi Air Force, the *Luftwaffe*, actually operated a secret squadron – Squadron 200 – which specialized in the use of captured airplanes. It was an American aircraft of the type B-17 that transported the paratroopers to their jump-zone over *Wadi Kelt*. Werner Frank – one of the paratroopers, whose figure I replaced with the invented character of Wolfgang Schwarte – described in an article he published in the 1990s in the Templer journal in Germany, the sequence of events related to the parachute jump near Jericho. His testimony was the basis for the description of this event in my book.

The German secret agent "Milton"

Milton was the alias of an agent who worked in the service of the German military intelligence, the *Abwehr*, in Tel Aviv. I got an insight into parts of his operational file during my posting in the 1990s as a reporter for the Israeli daily, **Ma'ariv**, in Germany. The file contained basic, almost amateurish reports, but did not reveal Milton's true identity. Speculation about his identity ranges from a German Jew whose family was imprisoned in a German concentration camp, through a Greek Nazi-sympathizer to a South African citizen.Milton operated in Tel Aviv until the end of 1942 and left Palestine without the British Security Service discovering him.

U-372

The German submarine 372 was sunk in August 1942 off the coast of Haifa. Its real job is unknown. Six days later, the Italian submarine "Scirè" was also sunk in Haifa Bay while trying to infiltrate underwater commandos into the military port.

The German section of the *Palmach*

Such a unit was established in the summer of 1942 under the command of Simon Koch, who had Hebraized his name into Shimon Avidan. During the War of Independence, 1948-1949, he commanded the Givati Brigade, which stopped the Egyptian army 30 kilometers south of Tel Aviv. Among the soldiers who served there was Avri Seidenberg, who later in 1954 became known as the commander of an Israeli sabotage cell in Egypt. He was accused of having betrayed its members to the Egyptian authorities.

Another one of the unit's soldiers was Wolfgang Lotz, later known as the "Champagne Spy" – an intelligence officer of the IDF[94], who was sent in the 1960s on a spy mission to Egypt and who was detained by the Egyptian security service.

Einsatzgruppe Aegypten

On the orders of the SS High Command, an officer named Walter Rauff founded a special squad to be attached to Rommel's forces, whose job it was to exterminate the Jews of Egypt and Palestine. *Einsatzgruppe Aegypten* was created under Rauff's command similar to the other Einsatzgruppen, i.e. special squads that wreaked havoc by

[94]Israel Defense Forces

murdering hundreds of thousands of Jews in Poland and on the Eastern Front. Rauff did reach Rommel's headquarters in *Tobruk*, but Rommel refused him permission to join his forces. Rauff returned to Athens, where he waited with his men for the German breakthrough to the east, which never came.

In November 1942, after the decisive British victory at *El-Alamein* and the retreat of the *Afrika Korps*, the unit was disbanded. Rauff fled to Syria after the war and served as a military adviser there.

The irony of history is that he was recruited at the same time by the Israeli secret service and gave accurate information about Syria. It is not clear to this day whether his Israeli handlers knew his past as a serial killer of Jews. Rauff immigrated to Argentina and then moved to Chile. The application by the German Federal Republic to have him extradited and put on trial was rejected by the Chilean government. He died of lung cancer in 1984 in Chile.

Henrietta Tamar Landwehr

Part of the history of this main character is based on my mother's life story. She was born in Vienna, was a member of a Zionist youth movement, immigrated to Palestine in August 1938, and studied at the Hadassah School of Nursing. Her parents, my grandparents, were among approximately 900 European Jews who were exiled by the British Mandate authorities to Mauritius. Here begins and here ends the similarity with Henrietta-Tamar.

In fact, my mother did have a boyfriend named Naftali or Tolek, as his friends called him, a young graduate of the Hebrew High School in Vienna, who reached Palestine a few months after her. He volunteered for the British Army and served in Egypt, including in the campaigns of El Alamein, Libya and Italy. During his long service they got married secretly, because Hadassah students were not allowed to marry before completing their education. This is my father.

Aaron Levi, one of the *Lechi* leaders

My creation.

Arthur Asher Weiss

Ditto

Herbert Weiss

This, too, is a fictional character, but it is based on a combination of several people I knew in the past. The German Jews enlisted massively in the German Imperial Army during World War I, and hundreds of them were awarded the "Iron Cross" for bravery in the field. These decorations protected neither them nor their families from persecution by the Nazis and those who did not or could not flee in time from Germany, were murdered in the extermination camps.

The father of one of my friends served as a combat officer in the First World War, was awarded the Iron Cross, and in "recognition" for his services to the German Fatherland, he was taken away by the Nazis to the concentration camp *Theresienstadt* in the last transport out of his city. He died in the camp. His wife was murdered in Auschwitz. His son, who had immigrated to Palestine as a young man, served in the "*Mossad*", took part in the kidnapping of Eichmann and the elimination of the "Hangman of Riga" – Herbert Cukurs.

Haviv Canaan

Lubor Krummholz had emigrated, in 1935, from Poland to Palestine. He joined the British police and served in the *Emek Refaim* district, which he later commanded. In September 1939, he headed the unit that arrested Imberger, the leader of the Nazi Party in Jerusalem. He later changed his name to Haviv Canaan and wrote many years for the **Ha'aretz newspaper**.

Ida Pfeiffer

Ida Pfeiffer was the first backpacker in the Middle East and a book of her travels has been published in a large number of editions since the mid-19th century.

Frank Foley

He served in the 1930s as a visa officer at the British Consulate in Berlin. In fact, he was an agent of British Intelligence in Nazi Germany and helped hundreds of Jews to leave the Third Reich.

Other figures in the book are the fruit of my imagination and any connection to reality is purely coincidental.

Printed in Great Britain
by Amazon.co.uk, Ltd.,
Marston Gate.